SHY

BY JOE ELLIOTT

DORTCH LANE PRESS

Dortch Lane Press
306 Dortch Lane
South Hill, VA 23970

Website of the Author: www.thescribblingsage.com
Twitter: @scribblingsage1

Shy

Chapter 1

Sunday June 6th, 1993

Mark, doing his best to imitate a British aristocrat, says, "Pot? Why yes, I say…. let's grow us some fucking pot."

"And why the fuck not? Sure…shit yeah, let's grow us some goddamn pot," I reply, with my best attempt at a haughty British accent.

"And then, we'll smoke us some fucking pot. Why not?"

"But then, most importantly, we'll sell us some fucking pot. By God"

"By God, let's grow us some fucking pot. Why the shit not?"

"Seriously man, let's do it, let's grow us some fucking pot," I say, laughing.

"Listen, man, I just happened to run across that book the other day. I was going through my brother's shit. I didn't really have anything in mind. Just some stupid book he had."

Mark's older brother, Mike, died a few years back from complications associated with his alcoholism. He was only thirty-two. Mixed in with his stuff was a book about growing pot for fun and profit.

"I think we should do it though," I say, as I look up with a sly little grin on my face.

"Have you ever even tried the shit?"

"Never really had the opportunity. I mean, you never offered me any."

"Well, you never have been the type to party all that much. Just didn't think you were all that interested."

"No, I wasn't really. I guess I just value my brain cells a little too much. Thinking clearly just seems so much more attractive than getting high."

"Yeah, that's great…..thinking, but sometimes….well you just want to feel good for a while."

"Well, I feel good when I'm thinking."

"Yeah….not quite the same," says Mark, rolling his eyes.

There is some truth to that. I do in fact greatly value my brain cells. But the real reason I've never been a partier is because I never quite fit in all through my high school years. I never had the opportunity to go to keg parties and the like. It was somewhere around the sixth or seventh grade that I was stricken with what turned out to be debilitating and life altering shyness. Because of this, I had an absolute total lack of any sort of social life all through high school. In fact, the lack of social life continues to this day. Mark's the only one from the old neighborhood or school that I remain friends with. He's really my only close friend.

"I have been drunk a few times," I say, raising my finger to emphasize the point.

"Yeah, I remember that one time you just showed up here with that bottle of Wild Turkey. We got loaded that night."

"Yeah, but it just doesn't appeal to me all that much. The after effects outweigh whatever good feeling you get….at least to me."

"So, why the fuck are you so into this? You see a book and all of a sudden you're ready to grow the shit?"

"I don't want to smoke it…………..I want to fucking sell it."

I may smoke a little, too, actually. I kind of want to escape reality a little now.

"So, you were serious about that?" asks Mark. "You actually want to sell the shit?"

"Well….that is what the book's about."

"Yeah…but to actually grow the shit and sell it?"

"I don't know, man, I just want a different life than what I've got now," I say. "I just can't stand the thought of a normal life, whatever normal means anyway. I have to do something different."

"Well….I agree with you there. I can't see myself ever conforming to the standard bullshit way of life. I don't want to be like my fucking parents."

"You know…. with my dad having to sell my grandmother's farm, all of the dreams I had about that place are over. I had it all laid out," I lament.

I had such elaborate plans for how that would work. I had all these different schemes for how I could make money. I wanted to make my own furniture from wood on the property. I wanted to build ponds to raise fish. The lone bad part of this is that I envisioned myself doing all of this alone. I'm already alone, so why not make it official and move to the boondocks? I didn't envision a woman being a part of this. The idea
of a woman in my life just seems so far off and unattainable. I'm just

absolutely unable to get close to women. It's the shyness. I guess when I contemplate my life I don't picture a woman in it. I imagined myselfgetting old on that farm. But I never pictured myself with anyone. But, that's all gone now anyway.

I never had any claim to the farm. There are cousins who may have been interested in it, too. It's possible that my grandmother would have let me move up there with some sort of agreement on how I could buy the place from her. But she came down with Alzheimer's disease and everything had to be sold to pay for her care. It really broke my heart, both what happened to my grandmother and the fact that the farm is lost forever. Because of that, I've been somewhat at loose ends lately.

"You wanted to move up there and kind of live off the land" says Mark. "That was a nice place. I remember that one time we went up there and attempted to hunt deer, but you couldn't bring yourself to shoot Bambi."

"I know…I don't have the heart to hunt."

"But that would be a neat way to live. Just find ways to survive. Live off the land the best way possible."

"I just don't want to be tied to a job, where I've got to be there every day, at the same time, year after year, until I get to retirement age," I say. "Then I just sit on a fucking porch waiting to die? No! One way or the other, that just ain't gonna fucking happen."

I know many people have similar sentiments. But with me it's a deeply ingrained need. I really have a deep aversion to living the so-called conventional life. One way or the other, that has to change.

"So what's selling a little pot going to do?" asks Mark, laughing. "I mean, really?"

"No," I say, shaking my head. "Not just a little. I'm thinking bigger."

"So…..let me get this straight. You come in here and see a book….. and all of a sudden you're ready to be a full-fledged drug dealer?"

"No… no, the idea's come to me before. It's just….you know… well….how do you just bring something like that up? I saw the book…..and well…. here we are. Icebreaker."

"Is it really worth the almost certainty that we'll do time at some point?" asks Mark. "Is it really worth prison? Cause I can tell you, it ain't fucking worth it to me."

"Listen, we don't have to be like the rest of the dumb asses. Most of the fools who get caught are careless. But we can be smarter than that. We can set this up so that we're almost totally immune from being found out."

"Shit, you are serious, aren't you?"

"Yeah, I've actually been giving this idea some serious thought."

"And you think you have it figured out," says Mark, skeptically.

I can't really blame him for that. I'm one of the last people one would figure to be proposing to start a narcotics business.

"The real key to this is to do business with as few people as necessary," I explain. "The less people who know we're doing this, the better. But that's obvious."

"But how do we make that happen? How do we arrange it so that we only deal with a few people?"

"Think of this as just another business. We'll be the manufacturers. We'll supply distributors and they'll supply the dealers. Hell, we could get by with doing business with one guy, if we're lucky. But that would be the perfect scenario."

"Okay…..but we probably won't get the perfect scenario. We'll have to deal with several people at least, if we hope to make any real money."

"Our goal will be to deal with as few people as possible."

"And what are the other keys to setting up a successful narcotics empire?" asks Mark, smiling. "If I may ask."

"You don't think I'm serious," I say, shaking my head.

"No….I'm listening. I'm intrigued actually."

"Well, if we're gonna do this….another key is to not get too greedy. If a particular deal or situation feels wrong, we have to just walk away, even if we miss out on a good deal in the process. We have to be very cautious that we aren't walking into a trap."

"So, we have to be patient…and just let the deals come to us."

"I don't know about them coming to us," I say. "But we have to be patient. We can't be so anxious to make a deal that we do something stupid."

"We have to be super cautious if we have any hope of staying out of prison."

"Right. Now, third on the list are our spending habits."

"Spending habits?"

"Yeah, how we spend the money is one of the most important elements to avoiding being caught."

"I'm not sure I follow."

"It's simple," I say. "We can't spend extravagantly. Excess spending without an obvious source of income does nothing but draw the attention of the cops. That's a common mistake so many idiots in the business make. They have all of this shit, but no job. That just puts out a big red flag for everyone to see."

"Well, if we can't really spend the money, what's the fucking point?"

"This is what we do. We have normal jobs as a cover. Of course, I already have a job. But we only spend what could reasonably be justified with the jobs we have. We can spend a little more when it comes to small things. We just can't be driving expensive cars and shit like that."

"Okay, and like houses and boats and shit?"

"Yeah, that's right, the big ticket items are the problem. Nothing that draws attention. We just stash most of the money we make, then when we have enough, we quit the business, move to Mexico or somewhere and live like fucking kings."

"Why Mexico?"

"It doesn't matter," I say. "Live wherever you want to live. I just like the idea of some Mexican beach somewhere."

"And living in Mexico, a little money would go a long way."

"That's right. And just think how far a whole lot of fucking money would go."

"I don't know though. Like I said, I don't want to go to no fucking prison. None of this is worth that."

"That's part of the fun though. At least for me it is."

"What's fun?"

"The challenge of avoiding being caught," I explain. "A little cat and mouse with the police or DEA or who the fuck ever. Prove that we're smart enough to get away with it."

"Yeah, but no matter how good you plan though, some ass that we deal with, at some point, will be stupid enough to get caught, then they cut a deal and give us up. That's how this shit always works. You see it all the time."

"Even if that happens, we still have a way out."

"How?"

"We run."

"Run?"

"Well....yeah. We're already going to have money stashed. We bail out.... and if it looks like we're going to prison, we take the money and get the hell outta here."

I would hope that it would work that way.

"Well, that wouldn't be a boring life at all, now would it?" says Mark, smiling.

"You see, that's the way I see it. This'll be the ultimate kick. To see if we're smart enough to pull this off. I think we are."

At least I am. I'm not so sure about Mark. It's not so much being smart enough. I'm just not so sure he has the self-control to do this. But I need a partner. And he's the only real option for something like this.

"But how do we get started?" asks Mark. "All of this is well and fine.... but we have to start somewhere."

"Well, I think we need to talk to Ronnie White, you know, the guy who runs the pool hall. He can at least get us the seeds. And he may know some people we can sell to. You know, some of these guys don't want to deal with growing the shit themselves. They just want to sell it."

If I didn't know Ronnie from when he worked at the plant, I wouldn't have a clue as to where to go to get seeds. I just don't travel in those circles. And as far as selling the shit is concerned, Ronnie may be my only hope. I know no one else who does that sort of thing. I really am out of my element here. But in some ways, that could work to my advantage.

"Okay, here's a good question, where do we grow it?" asks Mark.

"Well, we don't really have any place of our own. So there's only one solution. We grow it on other people's land. We can plant the first ones right out here in the woods."

"But they monitor that shit from the air."

"I know that," I say. "After we get more established, we scout more distant places. We set them up where they can only be accessed by an ATV or a boat."

"A boat?"

"Yeah, we plant the shit along some river or in some back out of the way cove on the lake. Then we just take a normal canoe ride like anyone else would do. We get off the river, do our business, then continue with our trip."

"What if they're waiting for us?"

"That almost never happens. What are they supposed to do, wait days or weeks for us to show up? No, they won't do that," I say, dismissing the possibility.

"But if they find our shit, and take our shit, there goes all of our hard work, sorry, but…. up in smoke. They'll burn that shit in a bonfire and nobody'll get high from it."

"Okay, but that's why we'll have multiple locations at any given time."

"Okay, you seem to have answers for everything. But how about we just find out whether we can actually grow some plants before we keep going on and on with all of this drug empire shit."

Good point.

"Okay, we'll go talk to Ronnie about the seeds," I say.

"And again….. Why are we planting this shit behind my house? You never really answered that question."

"Because no one ever goes out there."

"But…like I said… I'm sure those planes fly over here like they do everywhere else."

"Sure, but the only way in is from this side. If the cops find it, you're bound to see something. Then we know to be careful, and not go back there for a while. Even if they were to be waiting for us, we could wander by like we were just hunting or something. There's no way they could nail us with the shit back there."

"Well, if it's such a good fucking spot, why not grow it there all the time?" asks Mark.

"We can't afford to get complacent. I like the idea of growing it somewhere more remote than that. It would be easier to connect us with it back there, especially if we kept growing it back there long term."

"Alright, I guess I'm in, let's just get the seeds and see what happens."

"Yeah, if this works out, maybe we can actually get your ass out of this house before you're forty."

"What the fuck? I'm only twenty-five now. I'm a long ways from being forty."

"Yeah, you're only twenty-five, but you live at home with your mother and you've never had a real job, at least as far as a career is concerned."

"For your information, I don't want no fucking career."

"Well, you've got your wish so far."

"Well, you know, my Dad dying when he did, kind of screwed everything up for me."

Mark's dad died pretty young. He was only sixty.

"Yeah, I remember, you were going to move with him back up to Michigan to raise Christmas trees when he retired."

"Yeah, but he died, and his ass of a sister took the land right out from under us. We only got about twenty thousand dollars apiece. I would have rather had the land. That bitch robbed me of my inheritance."

"Bitch," I say. I'm actually tired of him talking about this shit. It's over and done with. But Mark has a hard time letting go of all the little injustices that life throws at us.

"I was really looking forward to working with my Dad. He worked so much when I was a kid that I didn't get to spend all that much time with him."

"Well, don't forget that you were also such a huge ass when you were a kid that you were fighting with him all the time."

"But I was really looking forward to his retiring and moving to the farm so that we could have a real relationship. But, I got fucked out of that."

"Yeah, that's life, I guess. Things hardly ever work out the way you want them to."

Mark's really great at revisionist history. He had no intention of moving to Michigan with his father. That thought only appeared after his father's death. He wanted no real part of his father in life, only in death. It's just a way for him to feel as if he was robbed out of something, this idea that his dad was taken from him before he could have a real relationship with him. Mark had his chance. Mark's greatest flaw is that he loves to be the victim. Someone or something is always at fault if something fails to go the way Mark would prefer.

"But you're right," says Mark. "I do need to get out of this pig sty of a house."

"Why does your mom save all this shit? She's one of those fucking hoarders."

"She's a pack rat."

"No, she's mentally ill," I say. "Hoarding is actually a disorder. She has it, my friend."

"It's because she grew up in the Great Depression, she thinks she's got to save everything."

"I know she had you when she was in her forties, but there ain't no way she could be old enough to have grown up during the Depression. At least she wouldn't remember all that much about it."

"Well, even if she wasn't around in that exact time, it was in the general era."

"Listen, a lot of people grew up in that time and most of them don't do what she does. Don't you remember? We found that box in the attic that had coupons that were over twenty years old."

"Yeah, or that book that came in the mail that she's never even opened."

"Yeah, that's about ten years old itself," I say.

"Fifteen."

"You and your brother are going to need a fleet of tractor trailers to deal with this shit when she's gone."

"We'll just burn this little playhouse down, that's all."

"Now, now, boys, don't talk about my treasures like that," says Diane Sinclair, as she walks in to hear us discussing her treasure chest.

"Yes, Mom, we were talking about your many and varied treasures, and what Matt and I are going to do when you die. We're going to just burn this fucking joint down. What do you think about that?"

Matt is Mark's other brother.

"I don't give a goddamn what you do after I'm gone, but they ain't going nowhere now," she says. "I need everything here."

"Everything?" I say, laughing.

"No one likes a smart ass, Don," replies Diane.

"But what are you going to do with those coupons in the attic?" asks Mark. "They're expired. They expired when I was a kid. They're no fucking good."

"I might need some paper to start a fire someday," replies Diane, sarcastically.

"No, that's the first thing I'll light when I burn it down."

"What about those drink can tabs?" I ask. "We found a box of them in the attic, too."

"I will have you know that there is some sort of charity, I don't know who, but they take them and they get money for them. They're for a good cause."

"But they aren't any good if they're in…..the…..fucking…… attic, Mom."

"I don't have time for this shit. And stay out of my attic. Stop stirring up fucking trouble."

"You gotta get out of here man," I say, as Diane leaves.

"Yeah, I know."

"Listen, I'll get back to you about talking to Ronnie. Maybe we'll go down there this weekend. I'd better get home. Some of us have an actual job to go to."

"Well, I'm glad I fucking don't."

"I'll be glad when I don't."

Most would never figure me for a drug dealer. On the outside I appear as straight-laced and buttoned down as they come. But that's the shyness. The shyness suppresses what I believe to be the true me. Is the true me a criminal? No. I don't think of it that way. Pot should be legal anyway. I just want an exciting life. Do I want it to be the police after me kind of exciting? Maybe not. As I said, the plans I had so carefully laid out in my mind are now useless. Something has to change. I have to get out of the rut I'm in. I'm meant for something greater than what I'm doing now. I'm convinced of that. Maybe I'm just grasping at straws. Maybe this makes no sense at all. But I'm desperate to just do something different. I'm desperate to be someone else. No, not someone else, I'm desperate to discover and uncover the true me. But I simply don't know how to do that. So, I have to try something.

Chapter 2

Monday June 7th, 1993

It's Monday morning and I'm back at work at Raymond Mills. We're a textiles dyeing and finishing plant. This was actually the first of many plants. It all started here. The Raymond family started the company right where the town is now, which is also named after the family. The plant was actually in a field by itself, they say, and the town grew up around it.

I'm going to visit a couple of friends. Roger and Jerry are the plant carpenters. Yes, this plant is so big that we need our own carpenters. But they also paint and unstop toilets, that sort of stuff.

They're both around my age, which is thirty. Jerry's from this area. This is his first inside job. His work history before this was all in construction. But the plant offers better benefits and a better work environment. At first sight, you'd think Jerry to be a typical southern guy, and he is in some ways. But there's something different about Jerry. He's a little odd. But I like that. And he thinks for himself. He isn't conventional in the least.

Roger, on the other hand, does seem to like to be normal. He likes to conform. He's originally from Kentucky. He moved to North Carolina because the job prospects weren't as good where he was from. Roger will probably move on to greater things at some point. I even wonder why he's here sometimes. His background's in retail management more than in building things. But they're a couple of great guys. I always enjoy shooting the shit with them.

"What the hell are you two doing, I thought you're supposed to be painting bathrooms?" I ask, as I stroll into the office of the plant manager.

"Well, when the plant manager's office has a leaky window, all other things must be dropped," responds Roger.

"Yeah, the better question would be, why are you up here?" asks Jerry.

"Yeah, at least we're actually working," says Roger, looking around for effect. "But there isn't any instrumentation up here as far as I can see."

"And what exactly is instrumentation? Do you actually know?" I ask.

"Good question, what exactly do you do all day?" responds Roger.

"Yeah, Roger, instrumentation must mean that you walk around all day with your hands in your pockets," says Jerry. "And worrying about what other people are doing."

"Well, for your information and education, instrumentation has to do with controlling a process," I explain. "And heating and cooling is a process. To make it simple, for you two, I'm just up here checking that Max's thermostat is working alright."

"Yeah, we want the plant manager to feel all nice and comfy, don't we?" says Jerry.

"It takes some pretty big balls to risk being seen hanging around up here when you're supposed to be on the floor somewhere, probably supposed to be working on some machine right about now," says Roger.

"That's the beauty of this radio on my side here," I say, touching the radio clipped to my belt. "They never come looking for me. They just call."

"And then you lie about where you are," responds Roger.

"Not exactly, no….now….if they ask for my location, and I don't want them to know, I just say that I'm on my way to the shop. Then I start towards the shop. See? No lie. Tell the truth. Avoid trouble."

I actually came up with that on the spur of the moment to get a guy out of a jam one time. We were all in the conference room trying to watch a football game. Our supervisor called one of our electricians, wanting to know his location. He froze for a few seconds. He didn't know what to say. I told him to say that he was on his way to the shop. We had to wait awhile to leave though. A production supervisor happened to be engaged in a conversation just below the only way in or out of that conference room. We get away with murder in this place.

"What if they do just walk up on you though?" asks Jerry. "I mean when you're somewhere you aren't supposed to be."

"Which is most of the time," cracks Roger.

"Listen, that's when you have to know what kind of power you have."

"Power?" asks Roger, laughing. "You think you have power?"

"With as much as I do for them and as much as I know, there's not much chance they'd fire me. I would have to practically set fire to the plant."

"And you're so modest, too," adds Jerry, rolling his eyes.

"You just have to know how much you bring to the table, then you know how far you can push it. Besides.....well, I happen to know that Max and Bob are both away from the plant for the day. I can handle just about anyone else."

"Bond, Max Bond. Plant manager of this little podunk cotton mill in the mighty town of Raymond," says Roger, trying to sound like James Bond.

"Well, he is a little like a secret agent," I say.

"What do you mean?" replies Roger, laughing.

"Well, most people don't know who this guy is."

"And you do?" asks Jerry, skeptically.

"Yeah, well, I happen to know that this guy has a reputation for either straightening a plant out, or.....well...he shuts it down. This guy's actually a VP. He's here to fix it, or to close it."

"Are things that bad?" asks Jerry.

"Well, we're not really making money," I say. "Those damn Chinese imports are so cheap. Textiles is a dying industry in this country."

"Well, I don't know about all that. Aren't they ordering some new machines?" asks Roger.

"Yeah, I'm not saying it'll be tomorrow. Maybe he'll find a way to keep it going. I'm just saying that when this guy comes, it's your last chance."

"That fucker doesn't miss anything, either," says Jerry.

"That's what I'm saying. This guy is really like James Bond. He knows everything. He's hiding in corners just watching. Not too much is getting past him." I say.

"He sure inspects our shit. Sometimes he'll take the brush and touch up a few spots himself," adds Jerry.

"He's like Hitler with his beautification campaign," jokes Roger. "Wants the whole plant spit-shined and polished."

"Well, fuck'em both today," I say. "No plant manager and no maintenance manager. Sounds like a perfect day to me."

"Who do you fear more, Don....Bob or Max?" asks Roger.

Bob is our boss, the maintenance manager.

"I fear no man," I say. "You should know that by now."

"Alright then, who would you rather not be caught by, while in the act of fucking off?"

"Which is constantly," cracks Jerry.

"I would have to say Bob."

"Why?" asks Roger.

"Well, Max is almost impossible to bullshit. But on the other hand, he actually appreciates good workers. Bob doesn't know all that much. I can bullshit him a lot of the time. But the problem with Bob is that he values the wrong people. He values the ass kissers. But seems to have something against those of us who actually know what we're doing. Max sees the bigger picture. He knows what I do for this place. Bob is just an ass. All he wants is to squeeze as much labor out of us as he can."

"Man, you instrument guys just think you do everything, don't you?" asks Roger.

"Well, we seem to. A mechanic can't figure it out, they call am instrument guy. An electrician gets stuck, they call us."

"Well, we're not having any trouble doing our job, so.... what are you doing here?" asks Roger.

"Well, its Monday, I'm just taking it easy today. Need time to get back into work mode."

"Taking it easy today? How's this different than any other day?" asks Roger.

"And when are you ever in work mode?" asks Jerry. "Whatever the fuck that is anyway."

"Funny," I say. "You two are a couple of funny guys."

"I'd like to think so," says Jerry.

"But we're accurate, too," adds Roger.

"Well, since I'm not appreciated here, I think I'll just leave you two to whatever it is you do and take a little walk on the roof."

"Yeah, you do that. We'll manage in here," says Roger.

Just as I get to the roof through the little hatch at the end of the hall, my radio crackles with a message from the dispatcher saying that I'm needed at Tenter Frame 1 to look at a problem production is having with a burner. I make my way to a ladder on the west side of the plant which will drop me right in front of a door beside Frame 1.

"Oh.....," utters the startled Karen, as I near the ground.

I know who Karen is. I've actually been somewhat obsessed with the girl for some time now. But I've never had the ability to have any real conversation with her.

"I'm sorry...didn't scare you, did I?" I ask.

"Yeah.....a little, I guess," she says sheepishly.

"I'm sorry, I'm just on my way to Frame 1. You run the curing range, don't you?"

Of course, I know which machine she runs.

"Yeah, that's right, I'm just getting a little air. It's real hot in that little hole they got me working in," she says.

"Yeah, it's bad around any of those dryers."

"Yeah…it's hot."

"Well, speaking of dryers, I guess I better go and look at that frame. Heat problem"

"So you're going to go in there and heat it up even more?" she asks, only half in jest.

"Heh, heh, yeah, I guess that's right. Well, sorry I scared you," I say, as I quickly move towards the door into the plant.

"Bye.".

I've wanted to speak to Karen for weeks now. But I just haven't been able to bring myself to do it. It seems fate has intervened. The ice has been broken, even if I took little advantage of it. This may seem insignificant to a normal person. But to me, this is huge. I have a way in now.

I don't think anyone really knows how deep my dysfunction with women runs. I'll be blunt. I've never even kissed a girl. When I say I have debilitating and life altering shyness, I mean just that. I'm shy in other situations, but with women it rises to a whole other level. I have no idea why I'm this way. And I see no way out. I probably won't be able to do anything about it, even though the ice has been broken now.

When it comes to meeting people, it's important that the ice be broken in some way before I can really talk to them. I need the other person to make the first move, or I need circumstances to make that happen. But I cannot simply come up to a person and just start a conversation like most normal people can. And this is especially true with women. There have been a few instances where I've been able to actually speak to women, but it never seems to get beyond superficial chit chat. I never seem to be able to venture into that territory of letting them know that I'm interested in them sexually or romantically or whatever. Maybe it'll be different this time.

Chapter 3

Friday June 11ᵗʰ, 1993

Ronnie's place is your typical southern, good ole boys type of joint. Confederate battle flags adorn the walls. There's no need for a sign saying "No Coloreds Allowed". The point is not so subtly implied and very clearly understood.

I don't normally hang out in places like this, or bars in general. For one, the shyness causes me to hate crowds. I just feel overwhelmed in crowded places. And secondly, I really don't have the desire to drink. I have a certain distaste for even being around people who are drinking. I don't like it when people are out of control. And maybe I don't like to be out of control myself. Is that because of the shyness? I'm not sure.

"Just let me do the talking when we get in there, okay?" I say, as Mark and I walk through the door of "Ronnie White's Grill and Billiards".

"Yeah, no problem, you do the talking," replies Mark. "What's the big damn deal?"

"The big deal is that these types of guys don't take no shit, especially when it comes to their illegal activities."

"Hey, handle it. You're the one who knows the guy."

Ronnie, the owner, used to work at the plant. He was fired because he was caught smoking pot on the roof. Ronnie's your typical biker dude. He has his long hair pulled back in a ponytail. And he has that kind of weathered and rough face that one can get from riding motorcycles. Ronnie is kind of rough around the edges, but would do anything to help you that's within his power. But he's also the type of guy you don't want to fuck with. Ronnie is probably around forty or so. He's been running this joint for the last five years.

"Well, god fucking damn, is that Don Higgins?" booms Ronnie. "Never seen your ass in here before, man. Haven't really seen you since they canned my ass at the mill."

"You miss the place?"

"Shit no! My old man keeping you guys in line over there?"

"Yeah, I guess. Hey…uh….Ronnie, this is Mark, a buddy of mine."

"Well, how the fuck are ya, Mark?"

"Hey, man, how's it going?"

"You know, I've seen this cocksucker in here before," says Ronnie, looking at me. Now, turning to Mark, "I believe I had to throw your ass outta here, didn't I?"

"Yeah, well, you know....I guess I just had a little too much that night, maybe," responds Mark, somewhat nervously.

"Fuck, it ain't no problem, man. Fuck it and forget it. That's what I say. Well, what can I get for you ladies?"

"Actually, Ronnie, we have something to ask you," I say, looking around to make sure no one's listening.

"Yeah man, what is it?" asks Ronnie. He seems amused at my attempt at secrecy.

"Well, Ronnie, it's no secret why you got fired from the mill."

"Yeah, I was smoking weed on the roof. So, what?"

"Well, that's what I, well, what we wanted to talk about."

"What, man...you want to score some weed? I thought you were too fucking white bread to do that shit."

"No, man, not to smoke," I reply.

"Well.....actually..... I'd like a little to smoke," interjects Mark. "If you're holding."

"What we want are seeds," I continue, ignoring Mark's comment.

"Seeds? What the fuck? You wanna grow some?" asks Ronnie.

"We want to grow a fucking lot," says Mark.

"Mark, shut up," I say, out of the side of my mouth.

"What the fuck are you guys talking about?" asks Ronnie.

"We just want to experiment with a few plants....and...well....if that works out.....we want to go into business," I say.

That does sound kind of foolish when I say it out loud.

"Go into business? Do you guys have any fucking idea what you're talking about?"

"Yeah, actually...I think we do," I reply, trying to appear calm and in control.

"So, what are you gonna do with this shit after you grow it?"

"Well, we were hoping you may have some connections to help us in that area as well," says Mark.

"Listen, fucker, I hardly know you. You come to me wanting me to set you up in some sort of drug business?" says Ronnie, directed at Mark.

"Listen, Ronnie, I'm sorry....I told him to let me do the talking.

Listen, we really have a good plan. We just need the seeds and connections. We don't want to sell this shit directly. Our idea is to supply some sort of distributor or whatever you would call it. We aren't interested in selling to individuals. We want to grow it, then sell it in bulk. Preferably sell the whole lot to one person."

"Well, it sounds like you have put some thought into this," says Ronnie, as he ponders the situation. "And Don, I know you're pretty sharp. I don't know this fucker you want to go into business with. But I do trust you."

"We don't want to step on anyone's toes or anything. We don't want anyone shooting at us, okay?" I say.

"No, no....I think we can do some business here. We'll take it slow at first. I might be able to be...the... how'd you put it....the distributor. I kind of already do a little of that," says Ronnie.

He shifts gears a little.

"But I will tell you fuckers, and you better believe I'm serious. You too, Don. You better not talk about this shit to no one. If they catch you, you better not give me up. If you do....and this is a promise...I will fuck you up so bad, that you would have rather gone to prison and gotten ass fucked by fifty niggers in the shower. Do not cross me. Do not send me to prison and we just may be able to have a happy and mutually profitable business arrangement."

"We really appreciate this Ronnie. How about the seeds? How much? I mean.....do you have them here?" I ask, sounding far too eager.

"Yeah, I've got the shit here. Actually, if you want, I can sell you a couple of plants. It might be a little late to get some plants started from seed."

"Yeah, sure," I say. I hadn't thought about that.

"I can give you enough to get started with for...well...let's say...two hundred."

"Deal."

"Hold on here a second, I'll go fetch 'em for you."

"Right out here in the open?" asks Mark.

"They ain't huge fucking plants. They're seedlings. I'll put them in a fucking box, you pussy."

"Alright, man, just asking."

"We're in business now," I say, excitedly.

"Why does he have to be such an ass?" asks Mark, agitated.

"We're coming in here asking him about going into business for something that could send us all to prison. I'd be touchy, too. I'm just amazed he agreed to it."

"He doesn't think we'll follow through. He makes an easy $200 on the plants and thinks he'll never hear from us again."

"Well, you may be right. But we'll prove him wrong."

I'm kind of surprised that Ronnie has plants here. He must have some sort of secure bunker in the basement. This building he's in is an old three story building like you see in many small towns. It used to house a general store with living quarters on the floors above. Now, it houses his establishment on the ground floor and who knows what on the other levels.

"Here you go ladies. Enough seeds and plants to get you started in the wonderful world of weed."

"And here's your money."

"You fuckers know anything about growing this shit?"

"We've got a book," I say.

"Oh....you've got a book....well...let me know how it works out," say Ronnie, laughing.

"Alright man, appreciate it." I say, as we leave.

Chapter 4

Saturday June 12ᵗʰ, 1993

"Okay, we've got the little pots, potting soil. What else do we need?" asks Mark, as Mark and I roam the aisles of the gardening section of Dickens hardware.

"We have to see if they have a PH meter, then we need some lime, in case we have to adjust the soil," I respond.

"Adjust the soil?"

"Yeah, we need to make sure the soil we plant in is the perfect PH."

"We're getting a little technical here, aren't we?"

"I'm just trying to look at this like a business, not just a couple of fools throwing some plants in the ground. I'm going by the book. And the book says PH is critical."

"Okay, let's see if they have a PH meter…..oh, well….here's one," says Mark.

"And we need lime…uh…I forget….you use lime to correct the PH one way…but there's something else to get it to go in the other direction. I don't know. Just forget it. We've got time for that. We'll just test the soil first. Then we'll know what to get."

"Doing a little gardening?" asks Jim Perry, a co-worker of mine, seemingly appearing out of nowhere.

Jim is in his late thirties. He came to work here after a stint in the Navy. Jim is like me, he doesn't belong in this town. He doesn't belong at the plant. I'm not sure why he's there really. He's too intellectual for this place, too civilized. The women say that Jim looks like he should be on soap operas or something. I can see that. He does kind of have those classic good looks.

"Oh hey, Jim, how you doing?" I ask.

"Doing alright….uh….just saw you over here, thought I'd see what you're up to."

"Up to? We're not up to nothing," responds Mark, somewhat nervously.

"Just going to do a little gardening," I respond.

"Tomatoes! My mom just loves tomatoes," adds Marks, rather unbelievably.

And why in the hell would he mention that his mother loves tomatoes? I guess that's what you'd expect from a guy who still lives at home with his mother.

"Yeah, Jim, this is Mark, a buddy of mine from when we were kids. Mark, this is Jim, he works with me at the plant."

"Hey, man, how's it going?" asks Mark.

"You're getting pretty carried away here, aren't you....I mean...a PH meter?" says Jim, with a bemused tone, and a shit-eating grin.

"Well, we read this book, and PH is really important when it comes to tomatoes," says Mark.

"Okay....if you say so...see you at work, Don," says Jim as he continues on his way, smiling as if he's sure what we're up to.

"Do you think he suspects anything?" asks Mark.

"Even if he does, he's cool, he won't care."

"Alright, do we have everything?" asks Mark.

"Yeah, we're alright for now, I guess."

"Well, let's go home and plant us some tomato plants."

"Hey, that can be our code. When we talk about the plants over the phone or around other people they're just tomato plants."

"Smart."

"Yeah, I hope we're as smart as we think we are," I say, as we move towards the checkout.

"So, we'll just leave the pots in my garage by the window until they get big enough to plant in the woods. My mom never goes in there anyway," says Mark.

"I feel like we're a couple of teenagers instead of grown men," I say. "But that's probably because you live at home with mommy."

"Well, speaking for myself, I prefer to remain somewhat childish."

"So, are you just going to tell your mom that they're tomato plants, if she does happen to see them."

"She'd never believe it. Even if she knew, she ain't gonna turn in her own son. I mean, would she?"

"I think she just might," I say. "The way you two go at it sometimes."

"Oh, that's just the way we are. My family's always been pretty fucking dysfunctional"

"Just make sure she doesn't see them," I say, smiling.

"Yeah, she'd wonder where all the tomatoes are anyway."

"Yeah, all this shit and no crop."

"Yeah, can't let her see it."

"Keep the bitch in the dark."

"Watch it, the bitch is my mom….. my mom is the bitch," says Mark, smiling.

"And that makes you the son of a bitch."

"And you're simply….an ass."

"I try…son…I really do."

Chapter 5

Monday June 14ᵗʰ, 1993

"Good morning, gentlemen….uh… you too, Roger," I say, as I enter the Instrumentation Shop for the morning meeting of the electrical and instrumentation group.

"Don, take a look at our boy Jim. Do you notice anything different about him this morning?" Roger asks, so that the whole room can hear.

"Yeah, now that you mention it, there is something different," I say, even though I really don't know what he's talking about.

"I believe our old buddy has used a little Nice & Easy Formula 103 on that thinning and graying head of his."

"Hehehehe, yeah, it does look a little darker than it did when I saw him Saturday," I say. "At which salon did you have this done, Madam?"

"So I colored my hair a little, what's wrong with that? A lot of men do it these days," responds Jim.

"Well, what do you expect?" adds Roger. "We've got a little playboy ladies' man on our hands here."

"Yeah, I guess you can expect this from a single man, with no children, who gets a vasectomy at the ripe old age of 25," I add.

"It wasn't 25, it was 35."

"Oh, oh, well excuse me. That does make a difference," I say, rolling my eyes.

"Yep, nothing but a playboy on the hunt for all of our little innocent girls," adds Roger. "Pervert."

"Okay, time for all of you little non-technical people to get out. It's time for the intelligent ones, the ones who really run this plant, to have their meeting now. Roger, you just run along and do what you little carpenters do. I'm sure there's a door to paint somewhere that has your name on it," Jim says, as our fearless supervisor, Butch Hilliard, comes into our humble domain.

Butch is an ex-marine, although, I know they say you never stop being a marine. Butch can be kind of gruff at times, but he does care about the job and he cares about us. Butch is just doing his time until he can retire.

"Morning, boys and girls," booms Butch.

On the way out, Roger just can't resist getting one last jab in at Jim. "Butch, if you don't mind, can I just bring one thing to your attention? You'll appreciate this, I'm sure."

"Just spit it out, I've got a crew to run here."

"It's just, do you notice anything different about your boy Jim here?"

"Well, nothing really...except the fact that his hair is about three shades darker than it was Friday, and it....well..... may be a little orange, too."

"Nice & Easy Formula 103," I add.

"Oooo laaa laaa," says Roger.

"Okay, enough of this shit, get the fuck outta my shop, Roger," booms Butch.

"Sure boss, don't hit me."

"Alright, let's get to it," says Butch. "We've got Frame 8 for P.M. today. Don, you know the problems we've been having with the burner controls recently. Let's see if maybe we can't get a little resolution. Okay? Now if you can't handle it, then maybe I'll just have to put Nice & Easy on it."

"I think I can handle it, boss. Just keep Jim in the dye house, where he belongs, you know, with all that dye," I say. I couldn't resist that one.

"Yeah, maybe he just dipped his head into one of the mixing tanks, instead of the Nice & Easy," says David Johnson, an electrician.

"David, you got the frame today, too," says Butch. "Don't have any special complaints concerning the electrical. Guess you electricians are doing a better job than these instrument guys."

"Sure we are, boss, sure we are," says David.

David's a good guy. He has a little bit of a chip on his shoulder. That's understandable considering that he's a young black guy working in a trade that was denied to blacks for decades. He thinks he has something to prove. He doesn't to me. He knows his shit as well as any other electrician in the plant.

"Jim, the dye house is yours as usual, just stay out of the goddamn dye, will ya?" says Butch.

"Raeford, you know what to do, keep the polywrap running, and...let's see... I've got a few lights that need your attention," says Butch, as he hands Raeford Crowder, another electrician, a stack of work orders.

Raeford is one of the old timers. The story is that Raeford can't read. He's been working in the plant since he was fifteen or sixteen. I guess they allowed that sort of thing back then. He never finished school. He's an electrician only in the sense that he does work on some electrical shit. But he can only work on things that he's seen before. He can't read blueprints, therefore he's lost if the machine or the problem on the machine is one that he hasn't seen before. He's a decent guy though. But he's one of those who still holds onto those old ways of the South.

"Israel, take a look at the counterflow on Bleach range 3. They've had problems with it overnight," says Butch, to Israel George, an instrumentation technician.

Israel's from Nigeria. He's been in the country for fifteen years or so. He's the one who trained me when I first started at the plant. I have a lot of respect for what he has had to put up with. Being a black man from another country must be tough around here. He's another one that's too smart for this place. I'm not sure how he wound up here, but I know he has plans to get out one day.

"Lisa, you'll be on general breakdown today," says Butch, to Lisa Delaney, the only female electrician at Raymond Mills. She's a rare breed in the male dominated field of industrial maintenance. "Okay, any questions, ladies? Good, get to it."

Talk about having something to prove. Lisa really has it tough. She is literally the only woman in the entire maintenance department, if you exclude secretaries and the dispatchers. She actually started as a dispatcher. But she wanted to train to be an electrician. And the truth is that she's pretty good. Lisa is not what you would call a beauty. She's kind of ordinary looking, but at the same time interesting. Yeah, I bet she would just love to hear that she looks interesting. Lisa is around my age. I really don't know much about her. Like many women, I've had a hard time connecting with her on a personal level. We talk about the job plenty, but not any further than that.

"Hey, Don, get those tomatoes planted?" asks Jim, as everyone else leaves the room.

"Yeah, actually, we did."

"Funny thing is, I didn't see any tomato plants."

"We got them later."

"Oh really?" he says, in mock contemplation. "Well, the funny thing is, I saw you leave not two minutes after I left you and you didn't have time to get plants."

"We got them somewhere else"

"Now, why would you do that? You have to know that Dickens

has the best plants around. "

"Well, we don't happen to agree."

"The real kicker is that it's actually a little late to be starting tomato plants. Don't you think? You seem to know so much about it. I mean, a PH meter and all. But you don't even know that you plant the things in the fucking spring."

"These are late season varieties."

"Bullshit! Since when do two young single men such as Mark and yourself spend your Saturday nights shopping for gardening supplies?"

"We just do."

"Don, I know what you're up to, or I have a pretty good idea."

"And what's that?"

"You two are growing weed."

"You get all of that from our shopping for gardening supplies?"

"I don't know…I just have a knack for it," says Jim, smiling.

"I don't guess you'll say anything?"

"No…of course not….maybe I'll even buy some off of you."

"Yeah, we'll work something out. We're just growing a little really. Just want to have a little fun."

"It's cool, man, just let me know how it turns out."

I do trust Jim. But I don't want anyone to know what we're really planning. I'll just let Jim think we're just dabbling for our own personal use. The trouble is that I doubt Mark will have the same discretion when it comes to telling people.

Chapter 6

Later that morning.

"How long are we gonna run it?" I ask, referring to Frame 8.

"Well, have you seen what you need to see?" responds David.

P.M. stands for preventative maintenance. When we P.M. a machine, we usually run it first so that we can identify any problems that need our attention that we do not already know about. I already know about the issues with the heat. Speaking of the heat, a Tenter Frame is simply a big dryer. Cloth that has been dyed is run through the Frames to dry and cure it. Don't ask me what curing the cloth is all about. To me, it's either dry or it's not.

"Yeah, I'm done," I respond. Just as I say this, Butch calls me on the radio.

"Come in, Don, come in, Mr. Higgins," says Butch.

"Go ahead, Butch."

"Before you get started on the frame, how about checking out the curing range, they're reporting that something isn't right with one of the controllers."

"10-4, boss," I respond, as I immediately move in the direction of the curing range. I've been waiting for a chance just like this.

There she is. The one I've thought so much about. It's been a week since we met. I still needed an opportunity like this. I needed a reason to go over to her machine. Karen is one hot black girl. She just has the perfect body. Those breasts are just so nice and round and big. That ass is just amazing. And she has this long curly hair that frames her face just right. I have spoken to her before. But at that time I wasn't as infatuated and motivated to talk to her as I am now. She used to run the Alea dryer. I had to ask her about the heat controls and problems she was having a couple times back there, but didn't talk about much else. I guess that was the beginning of my obsession with her. My first contact.

"Hey, man, how you doing?" asks Karen, as I approach the curing range.

"Oh, well, I'm doing alright," I respond.

Predictably, I'm nervous as hell.

"At least you didn't scare me this time."

"Oh yeah, right, didn't drop down from the sky on you like I did…well….I guess it was a week ago."

"Still hot, you're not working on any heat today, are you?" she asks.

"Well, actually, that's why I'm here. They called saying y'all had a problem with a controller or something?"

"Oh, I don't know, the guy on the entry end never tells me anything. All I know is that the cloth is still coming out good."

"You like running this thing?" I ask.

"It's a change."

"You used to run the Alea, didn't you?"

"Yeah, but I kinda like that this thing is brand new, not like that old thing."

"You know that this is the first machine of its type in the world. Made in Switzerland. Dries and cures the cloth all in one pass."

"I just know it puts out the heat."

"Yeah, I guess you're pretty much stuck in this oven that we call tubular finishing most of the time. I can go to the shop or outside and get cool. But I guess you don't get too many chances to get outta the heat, do you?"

"That's right, thanks for reminding me."

"Sorry for rubbing it in. But you know that those of us in maintenance are the privileged ones," I say, kidding, at least in part.

"You're in maintenance. Why don't you do something about the heat?"

"Hey, even I'm not good enough to fix nature."

"Ha, ha, real funny, I mean can't you do anything about these fans or something? Not all of them are working. At least get the hot air moving around a little more."

"Sorry, but that's not my department."

"Then what good are you?"

"Guess not too much."

"Hey, aren't you the one who used to have the really long curly hair?" she asks. "Like a rock star or something?"

"Yeah, that was me. That was all kinda stupid. I had delusions of being a rock star back then. My sister gave me a perm. That's where the curls came from."

"Do you sing?"

"No, I play the guitar. Well.... I should say.... that I was attempting to play the guitar. If I would have actually learned to play, then maybe I would be somewhere else now. I did actually write a few songs though."

"What happened? I mean, why did you stop?"

"Well, I guess I just didn't want it as bad as I thought I did. Just didn't practice all that much. Then after a while I just lost interest, I guess."

I didn't really lose interest. Because of the fucking shyness, I just couldn't meet the people that I needed to meet to actually have a band. I had this big dream. I had all these plans. But I somehow always knew that it could never come true. It was just a stupid dream that was never rooted in my reality. My reality is the shyness. The shyness rules my life in ways that most people around me wouldn't even know about.

The whole rock star fantasy thing was probably more about escaping the shyness than anything else. Being a rock star, the women would have just come to me. The shyness wouldn't have mattered any more. The funny thing is, I think I could perform on stage. That isn't the problem. I just have a feeling I could do that, despite the shyness. It's the meeting people and opening myself up to them to actually be able to form a band that's hard for me to do. To be in a band you have to really expose yourself to others. You have to share ideas with other people. It's something that's almost impossible for me to do with me being the way I am.

"If this was such a burning desire of yours, then why didn't you keep going?" she asks.

"Well, I think I was in love with the idea of being rich or famous or whatever, more than I actually wanted to play music. I just moved too fast. Like I said, the whole thing was just stupid."

"I think you just wanted all the women running after you. Big rock star and all of that."

"Well, sure, that was part of it. But I realize now that there has to be more driving you than fame and fortune or women."

"Like what?" she asks.

"I see now that you have to love the music first, if you ever want to be successful. I just want so bad to be doing something different than working in this place that I just latched on to that rock star fantasy stuff."

"I think most of us would rather be doing something other than working here," she says. "But we gotta do what we gotta do."

I don't think I'm like most people though. I do think I'm

different. Most people can get pretty comfortable as long as they have a decent job, a family, a hobby and whatever else people want. Would many of us like to be rich? Would we like to have a better job? Sure. But the drive with me is different. I'm meant to do something greater than this. I really feel as if I'm meant for big things. I simply could not tolerate doing this work for the rest of my life. I couldn't handle being stuck in this life. I want more. No, I need more.

"What do you do when you're not here?" I ask.

"Mostly things for the Lord."

"Oh, really? That's nice," I say.

I wonder if she caught the disappointment in my voice.

"Yeah, I was saved about four years ago. That changed everything for me."

"What type of church do you go to?"

"Well…Pentecostal Holiness. I don't know if you're familiar with that or not."

"Oh, aren't you the ones who're real strict? I had a friend in high school who went to a Pentecostal church."

"Yeah, that's right," she says, somewhat defensively. "We are strict….strict when it comes to living according to the word of God."

"But what are some of the things that you can't do?"

"Well, if you have to put it that way, I don't wear pants, as maybe you've noticed around here. I only wear a dress or a skirt. We believe women should dress like women and men dress like men."

"But why?

"It's simple. Because the bible says that women shouldn't dress like men and men shouldn't dress like women."

"But are you sure that means that you've gotta wear dresses and skirts all the time? Does it say that women can't wear pants?"

"No, it doesn't specifically say anything about pants. But it seems pretty clear to me that for there to be a difference, women should wear skirts or dresses. It's really not that big of a deal."

"So, I guess you don't believe in what's going on today with all of these guys wearing earrings and stuff? I mean, isn't that stuff reserved for girls?"

"If they're not Christians, it doesn't matter what they do or what they wear. They need to be saved first. Then we'll worry about the other stuff."

"Oh, okay, so this only applies to you, I mean those of you in the church."

"Yeah, I don't care what you do if you're not a Christian."

"You don't care what I do?"

"Yeah, if you're not a Christian, then that's the only problem I'm concerned about. Nothing else matters but that."

"So, if I were in your church, you would not have approved of me having that long hair that I had back then, because that would make me look like a woman?"

"Well.....yeah," she says.

"So, what else is against the rules?"

"Well, we don't believe in listening to worldly music and we don't go to movies. Stuff like that. We try to avoid worldly stuff."

"But what's wrong with music and movies?"

"They have all of the cussing and sex and stuff."

"That's what makes it all so much fun."

"You know, I don't even know your name," she says.

I think she wants to change the subject. I do, too.

"It's Don."

"Mine is Karen."

"Imagine us working here so long and never even knowing each other's names."

I'm not sure if she already knew my name, but I knew hers. She's discussed quite a bit by the guys in the shop. I've never joined in. I've just overheard the comments from the guys.

"Hey, it's not my fault," she says. "You're the one who doesn't talk to anyone."

"Yeah, I know. I'm just kinda shy."

"Well, don't be a stranger anymore, okay?"

"I won't. I guess I better be getting to work. I'll go up there and see what the problem is."

"Yeah, get my machine running right, man."

"Yeah, I'd better do at least a little work before break time."

"You guys in the shop have got it made. Walk around all day talking, hardly doing nothing."

"We earn that privilege though."

"How?"

"Some of us are just so good that they don't care what we do most of the time. As long as we're available when they need us."

"Oh, so it's like that?"

"Something like that."

"Okay, get to work now. Earn your privilege."

"Yeah, see you later. Don't go to any movies tonight."

"Bye, and uh...do something about the heat."

Well, that went alright, as far as my having a normal conversation goes. But I never expected her to be a Christian, and to be a heavy duty one at that. I don't think the guys are aware of that little detail, either. I guess my fantasy of talking her into bed is out the window now.

Chapter 7

Just a few minutes later.

"Nice little hiding spot you two have here," I say, as I sneak into the women's restroom located in the dye house.

"What are you talking about? We've already done more work than you'll even think of doing all day." says Roger. "And we're not even to first break yet."

"Yeah, I'm sure. But this is perfect. The women aren't going to come in because you have the "Out of Order" sign up. Men won't come in because they don't want to look like perverts."

"You came in," says Jerry, without looking up.

"I just need to advise you two on any instrumentation issues you may face in here today."

"I'm sure we'll run into a lot," Rogers responds, dryly.

"Have you actually done anything today, Don?" asks Jerry.

"Well, it's early, but yeah, I'm just coming back from the curing range."

"Man, that's one hot black girl working on the exit end of that thing," says Jerry.

"Yeah, she's pretty hot alright," I agree.

"I mean everything's just perfect. Round, fat ass. Big tits. Damn, I'd like to nail that thing," continues Jerry.

"Good luck with that, she's a Christian," I say.

"So, Christians fuck, don't they?"

"She's one of those holy roller types," I say. "Pentecostal Holiness."

"How do you know?" asks Roger.

"I talked to her a little," I say. "Her name's Karen."

"Well, so were you hoping for a little taste of brown sugar, too?" asks Roger.

"Well, she is something. I just talked to her a little."

"But your hopes of pussy were dashed by her religion. Ain't that a shame," cracks Roger.

"A damn shame," adds Jerry.

"A dirty damn shame," says Roger.

"Hey, Jerry, I'm sure Roger told you about our boy Jim, didn't he?" I ask.

"You mean Nice & Easy 103," says Jerry, as he runs his hand through his long hair, much like a woman would.

As if on cue, Jim creeps in, acting as if he is intruding into forbidden territory.

"Well, speak of the devil, and he appears," says Roger. "What was that you were saying, Don, that men wouldn't come in here because they wouldn't want to look like perverts. Well, I guess we got ourselves a couple of perverts here, don't we?"

"I'm not really surprised at Jim, he seems like the type to hang around girls' bathrooms anyway," says Jerry.

"You two are the perverts. You're the ones living in bathrooms the last couple of weeks," says Jim.

"Well, when the plant manager says that he wants the bathrooms painted, you paint the fucking bathrooms," says Roger.

"Hey, did you guys hear about what happened this weekend?" asks Jim.

"Yeah, we already know that you dyed your hair," responds Roger.

"I mean about what happened between Israel and Tommy Cash," says Jim.

"No, no, what happened?" asks Roger.

"It seems that there was, what is being called by Israel, a racial incident," begins Jim. "I heard that Israel's going up front to try to get Tommy fired."

"Well, from what I know, it's Israel who should be fired, if anyone is," says Jerry.

"Oh, so you know something about this, too?" I ask.

"I saw it," responds Jerry.

"Saw what?" I ask.

"I saw Israel grab Tommy around the throat and try to choke him," responds Jerry.

"That's right. Most everybody was around when it happened," adds Jim.

"Why did Israel try to choke Tommy?" asks Roger.

"Well, that's the part that's in a little dispute. I'll just give you the story as I know it," says Jim. "From what I hear, there's this calendar in the dispatch office that has a picture of a monkey on it. Apparently, someone wrote Israel's name over top of the monkey. Israel thinks it was Tommy. Tommy says he didn't do it."

"Why is that racial anyway?" asks Jerry. "Maybe he was just making fun of Israel without having anything to do with the fact that he's black. These blacks are just too damn sensitive about this race shit anyway."

"You might be a little sensitive, too, if you would have gone through the shit that blacks went through in this country, and in particular in the South," says Jim.

"Israel didn't even grow up here, he's from Nigeria. He's only been in this country about ten years or so," Jerry says.

"Fifteen," I say.

"Same difference," says Jerry.

"I've got to agree with Jerry on this one," says Roger. "This political correctness garbage from those pinkos that run things is screwing everything up."

"It's all political," Jerry says, with a dismissive wave of his hand.

"But did he really try to choke him?" I ask.

"Yeah, he was about to lift him off the fucking ground," responds Jerry.

"Well, I must say that I am severely disappointed in you, Roger," I say.

"Why's that?" responds Roger, with a faint laugh.

"I want to know why you, the one who knows all, didn't know about this?"

"This was one of the few weekends I didn't work," says Roger. "But you would have thought that my partner would have said something this morning while we've been toiling away in here."

"I just didn't see it as all that big of a deal," says Jerry.

"I was here this weekend but somehow missed it," says Jim.

"It was right before we left Sunday," explains Jerry. "But you'd already slipped out."

"Wait a minute. Let's get back to this, Jerry," says Roger. "It's not a big deal when Israel tries to strangle Tommy in the middle of the shop floor?"

"I just saw it as a dispute between two guys that was over and done with. I didn't know it was going to turn into an international incident. We're liable to see Jesse Jackson down here before it's over," says Jerry.

"Well, we need a little action every now and then," I say.

Actually, with a plant this size, there's always some sort of drama going on.

"It's all political," says Jerry.

"Time for break," I point out.

"Yeah, like you really need one," says Roger.

"Company policy says that I get a break," I respond.

"Does company policy also say that you hide out in bathrooms during your normal work hours?" asks Roger.

"Not exactly."

"You and Jim have it made," says Roger.

"You see, what you have to understand is that we are paid for our minds, what we know, not for how much labor can be squeezed out of us," says Jim.

"Oh, well la-de-da,. Jerry, stand aside so that these two important intellectuals can go to break before us lowly peasants," says Roger.

"Well, thank you, you lowly and common laborers," I say, as we proceed to break.

Chapter 8

A few minutes later.

"Well, well, Tommy Cash, of all people," I say, as I enter the Instrumentation Shop.

"Of all people? What the fuck does that mean?"

"Well, you seem to be the hot topic, from what I hear."

"Hot topic?"

"Yeah, I hear Israel tried to choke you this weekend."

"Yeah, that bastard wanted to kill me. Grabbed me by the throat and damn near lifted me off the fucking floor. He just better be glad I don't carry my piece in the plant."

"What are you gonna do?"

"I'd like to shoot his ass," says Tommy. "But I did go up front on him."

"Are they gonna do anything?"

"Hope they fire his ass, but all he'll probably get is a write up. Who knows?"

"Why did he get so mad anyway?" I ask. I already know the answer. I just want to see what he says.

"He said I wrote his name over a picture of a monkey on a calendar in the dispatch office."

"Did you?"

"No, I don't know who did and I don't wanna talk about this shit. I better leave before that motherfucker comes in here. I'm not sure what I'd do," says Tommy, as he gets up and leaves.

Tommy is the type of guy who would pull something like that. He's one of those good ole boys. He's young, like me, but he was indoctrinated in the old southern ways, which is distinctly unlike me. After a while, you kind of get an idea about who believes what in the South. There seems to be very few truly enlightened ones here. But there are so many shades and layers to the whole race thing that it's hard to know what's what and who's who most of the time. Who knows what this whole monkey thing meant. Was it a serious stroke of racism? Or was it just some stupid prank?

"Did he say anything?" asks Roger, as he and Jerry come in. "He looked pretty hot as we passed him."

"Say anything about what?"

"You know about what, getting choked."

"Said he went up front," I say. "But he said he'd like to shoot his ass."

"What does he want them to do?" asks Jerry.

"Well, he wants them to fire Israel. But he talks like they might just write him up, if even that."

"Did he admit to writing Israel's name on the calendar?" asks Jerry.

"Do you really think he would, even if he did do it?" I respond.

"Goddamn it, Jerry, you can be such a dumbass sometimes," says Roger.

"Yeah, you're right, he'd just be asking to get canned. No one can take a joke anymore," says Jerry.

"As much as I like Israel, I've got to admit that I think they should fire him," says Roger. "It doesn't matter what Tommy did. What Israel did was uncalled for."

At this point Jim walks in.

"They'll never fire him. They're afraid the NAACP will sue them or something. They're just going to sweep it all under the rug like everything else. It's all political," says Jerry, with a dismissive wave of his hand.

"I'll bet it would be different if it were the other way around. If a white guy were trying to choke a black guy, you know he would be out the door in a heartbeat," says Roger.

"And probably in jail," adds Jerry.

"Well, I'm not so sure about the jail part, Jerry," I say. "I'm not so sure the sheriff in Franklin County is exactly enlightened when it comes to race."

"Yeah, this whole thing would have been different if it would have happened in some trailer park somewhere," adds Roger. "Israel would be in jail now, that's if he wasn't shot dead."

"With the way blacks have been treated so badly for so long in the South, maybe there's nothing wrong with having it the other way for a change," says Jim. "Maybe Israel should get away with it."

"But Israel physically attacked Tommy," says Roger. "How can that be tolerated?"

"Tolerated?" asks Jim. "It used to be that a black person couldn't look at a white person the wrong way without getting slapped, beaten, or worse. I don't have a problem with them getting a little preferential treatment for a change. The tables should be turned on these yahoos we got running around in here."

"He's right," I say. "In the old days, if Israel would have done that, he would have gotten an ass beaten right out there on the floor. Then they would have called the sheriff and had his ass thrown in jail."

"What are you guys talking about?" asks David, already knowing the answer.

"About Israel and Tommy," I respond.

"What do you think should happen?" asks Roger.

"They ought to fire Tommy. No question," says David.

"Well, that was predictable," says Roger, with a roll of his eyes.

"Predictable?" responds David.

"Yeah, I wouldn't expect any black person to see this any other way. Any hint of racism and the witch hunt begins," says Roger.

"Witch hunt? You know Tommy did that shit. You've had to have heard the word nigger come out of his mouth plenty of times," says David.

"Yeah, but he didn't write nigger over Israel's name," I point out. "He wrote Israel's name over a picture of a monkey. Is that automatically racist? Is the mere mention of a monkey in connection with a black person now considered racist?"

"Yeah, from him it is," says David. "His family is known for this type of shit, man. No, he did it. And he meant it to be racist. Even if he didn't do this, he's done plenty in the past. Fuck him."

"I don't get the logic here. Why should they fire Tommy? There's no proof that he did anything. And like Don said, no proof that it was even racist to begin with. Everybody saw Israel try to choke Tommy. Israel should be gone," says Jerry. "End of argument. The evidence is clear."

"Well, thank you, counselor," says David. "But you aren't the judge and jury here. Max will decide this one."

"I've got a feeling it'll go beyond Max," I say. "This will end up at corporate. That is, if they want to fire him. If they decide to do nothing then that's that."

"Not if they get calls to corporate," says David. "Some people are really pissed about this."

"Black people," says Roger.

"But there isn't any evidence that Tommy did anything," says Jerry. "What are you gonna demand that corporate do?"

"We're gonna demand that Israel not be fucking fired," says David.

"He physically assaulted someone right out there in front of everyone. It doesn't matter what Tommy did or didn't do. He assaulted someone who may just be innocent," adds Roger. "How can this possibly be let go? I just don't see it."

"Yeah, is it open season on whites now?" asks Jerry.

"Don't be stupid," says Jim.

"No, it's a valid question, if they fail to act," says Roger.

"Listen, yeah, he flew off the handle a little," says Jim. "But there was a valid reason for it."

"Yeah, you have to understand where we're coming from. We have a different perspective on this than you. We've been beat down by y'all for so long that we have this…you know…rage built up. We took this shit for a long time. Now you expect us to hold all of this in no matter what anyone may do. Sorry…but it ain't gonna work like that," says David.

"What's this y'all shit? What have I ever done to you?" I ask.

"It's what your people have done," answers David.

"My people? Exactly who are my people?"

"Come on…man…don't be stupid…white people."

"So you're holding me accountable for what any white person may have done in the past?"

"Not any person……but what white people as a whole did in this country."

"Why should I be held accountable for any of that? Do you know for sure that any of my ancestors actually owned slaves or did anything to blacks at all?"

"No…but…"

"No, that's it, there are no buts," I say, cutting him off. "You're being just as much of a racist if you hold all white people accountable for something that some white people did."

"And that's a pretty broad category, too," says Roger. "There are many different types of white people. Many different countries."

"Do you know that my ancestors actually came to this country after the Civil War?" I ask. "They had nothing to do with slavery. I wasn't raised to be a racist, either."

"That's right!" says Jerry. "You're lumping all whites into one category. Isn't that exactly what you say we do about blacks. Aren't you saying that we look down on all of you because of what some of your people do? Most white people aren't racists. And there are actually plenty of black racists, if you really want the truth."

"And all this great knowledge is coming from someone who

defends the South's role in the Civil War," responds David. "Thank you, professor."

"The Civil War was not really about slavery, it was about states' rights," says Jerry.

"Yeah, the state's right to own slaves," says David, getting increasingly angry.

"Jerry, I have to admit that it does seem as if the South was fighting to preserve slavery," says Roger. "And I'm as southern as they come."

"I think that's true to a certain extent, but the issue of states' rights isn't something that most people really understand," I say. "It does have implications that are valid today."

"It was all about slavery," says David, as Israel and Lisa enter the room.

"What you guys talking about?" asks Israel.

"Well, we're talking about the incident that you were involved in this weekend," I say.

"What? What incident?" asks Lisa. Lisa and Israel recently started seeing each other.

"Israel hasn't told you?" I ask.

"Israel tried to choke Tommy Cash this weekend, right out there in the middle of the shop," explains Roger.

"I saw it," adds Jerry.

"I wish I'd seen it," says Roger.

"What happened, Israel?" asks Lisa.

"That bastard wrote my name on top of picture of monkey on calendar in dispatch office," says Israel, with his halting accented English.

"Did you see him do it?" asks Jerry.

"No, but he in there right before I saw it. Sarah, the dispatcher, didn't see it until then, either. She was out of office."

"You see, the fucker did do it," says David.

"He still shouldn't have choked him," says Jerry.

"Listen, I know it not right. I just lose it. I tired of that shit."

"Couldn't it have just been a joke?" asks Roger. "Do we know that it was racist?"

"Sure, there's no question it's a joke, but it's a joke rooted in racism," says Jim. "At the very least there's a hint of it."

"Yeah, if race has nothing to do with it then why not write Jerry's name over the monkey?" asks David. "It's always a black person that's the target of this sort of shit."

"Like that time in high school where someone drew a picture of a buck in a wheat field in Mr. Washington's class," I say.

Some kid in my class actually drew a picture of a deer standing in a field of wheat. I'm not sure why, really. Mr. Washington looked nothing like Buckwheat.

"Exactly," says Jim. "It was no doubt a joke. But there's no denying that it was racially motivated."

"It not just this one thing," says Israel. "This just last straw. I just get it from all sides. It because I not born in this country. I black. I talk funny. I just want to work hard and fit in. But these people won't let me. Just piss me fucking off."

"That's what you guys just don't get. Yeah, things are changing. But that makes it almost worse. At least in the old days down here you knew where you stood. Now, you don't know who's wearing the hood and who isn't," says David.

"Exactly," adds Jim.

"Listen, we know most of you guys are alright. But the trouble is that we never know for sure. We don't know what you're saying when we're not around," says David.

"Yeah, you guys have to understand that it wasn't all that long ago that blacks were still getting beaten, thrown in jail, or lynched," says Jim.

"And a lot of those people who were involved are still living," adds David.

"Some may be right here in this plant," says Jim.

"Yeah, and I know a few that probably were involved," I say.

"Listen, I know I overreact. I sorry. But I can't help it. If they want to fire me, they fire me. I be alright," says Israel.

"Hey, we better get back to work," says Roger. "Bob might not appreciate this little town meeting."

"Fuck a Bob," I say. "But I guess we'd better get back out to that frame, David."

"You sound like you want me back in those cotton fields there massa," says David, joking.

"No, not the cotton fields, but we better get back out to Frame 8 and at least look like we're doing some work. We've done overshot break by fifteen minutes."

"Okay, massa, whatever you say, massa," says David, laughing.

I actually like the debates we have involving David. He has

some inane viewpoints sometimes, but at least he isn't afraid to express them. And he seems to be able to keep his sense of humor. That's a skill I don't always seem to master.

Chapter 9

Still later, the same day.

"Hard at work, I see," I say, as Jim leans against a hand rail behind one of the dyeing machines, gazing at nothing in particular.

"Yeah, just like you."

"Well, I'll get around to the frame in a little while," I say, joining him in holding up the hand rail.

"Think anything'll come of the Israel thing?"

"Doubt it."

"I mean, I see where you guys are coming from," says Jim. "He shouldn't have choked him."

"Yeah but….I don't know….I think he realizes he flew off the handle. I kind of think Jerry was right when he said earlier that it was just a thing between two guys that was over and done with. Why does everything have to turn into such a big fucking stink?"

"But you know that there's a good chance that Tommy is the one who did it," says Jim. "I mean writing the name over the monkey, that's something he'd do. What he meant by it, well, that's another question."

"Well, you were here, can you think of anyone else who…you know…kind of thinks along those lines that was here this weekend? Is there someone else who could have done it?"

"There are plenty of fools who could have done it."

"I mean one of those good ole boy types."

"Not really…except for Tommy….but ….you know, it might not have been someone who meant all that much by it. People know that Israel's a little hot-headed. Maybe someone did this just to get him to blow his top."

"Or go ape shit," I say.

"Yeah…..good one," says Jim, laughing.

"That's the problem though. Israel and David and most of the black folks here just assume that this was some sort of nasty racial slur, when it was probably just some fool trying to provoke the guy."

"And they sure as hell succeeded."

"Even if it was one of these idiot diehard bigots, what does that mean? Do they have any real power to do anything now? This isn't the forties, fifties or sixties anymore. Most of this is nothing more than words now. Too many blacks act like this means that the nooses and white sheets are about ready to come out again."

"True, things are much different than what they used to be," says Jim. "It's probably true that they overreact to some of this tamer shit now."

"No, you're right. I understand....well....I can only begin to understand what it's like to live in the South, with the history that exists, as a black person. I'd probably be sensitive, too."

"Yeah, it's definitely understandable."

"The ones who seem to be the most sensitive are actually the younger ones," I say. "But they didn't live through the same shit that the older ones did."

"But the younger ones have at least heard the stories of what happened in the good old days. We can't expect them to just wave off all this type of shit as harmless. We may see it as harmless, but they have a different viewpoint. There's just too much of this shit that's recent history. Really recent."

"Yeah, believe me, I know."

"You know some of the clowns we have running around here," says Jim. "They probably still have their old white sheets stored away in the closet somewhere."

"Yeah, you know what always gets me is when these idiots just assume that you think the way they do just because you're white."

"Yeah, I know, some of them will be 'nigger this' and 'nigger that' as long as it's just whites in the room, but then be all smiles and kind words when blacks are anywhere near."

"Yeah, and I'm sure many of our black brothers and sisters are aware of that fact, too."

"Yeah, how do they know who believes what?"

"We should start telling them," I say, with a sly grin.

"Maybe we should."

"I do feel like I should say something sometimes but....I don't know.....it's hard," I say. "I mean say something to the Tommy's of the world."

"It's easier to just find a way to make a quick exit when that shit starts."

"I just wish I had more courage sometimes though."

"It's easier to just walk away. You aren't going to change their minds anyway."

"I always wondered how many people were actual racists and

how many were just cowed into keeping their mouths shut," I say. "I mean in the old days, our parents, our grandparents. Because I know my parents don't think that way. But I also know that they weren't exactly civil rights activists, either. Where did they stand exactly? I'm not really sure."

"I would imagine that many simply never really had the courage to speak against what they assumed was the majority opinion. They didn't participate, but they also did nothing to stop it."

"That's the thing though, was it the majority? Or even if it was the majority, was the majority as overwhelming as it seemed?"

"I think it depended on the particular town or county. Some were better, some were worse. Even today."

"Yeah, probably so."

"There are still some small towns around here that a black person wouldn't necessarily want to be in after dark."

"My grandmother always called black people colored," I say. "As a kid I didn't think anything of it. But now, I know, of course, that it's regarded as a somewhat bigoted term."

"Yeah, but did she really mean anything by that? Or was it just what they called them back then? You know what I mean? We can read something into things that aren't really there."

"Like the monkey?"

"Perhaps."

"I never really heard her say anything bad about black people," I say. "It's just that one word. Makes me wonder."

"I think the problem many people had back then is that they just looked at black people as alien beings or something. You know what I mean? It wasn't necessarily a hatred or bigotry but they looked at them as exotic beings that they didn't know how to deal with."

"That actually makes sense."

"Think about it. How many of these people do you think actually ever went anywhere outside of the South?"

"Probably not many," I say. "My family never really did. The farthest we would go would be to Myrtle Beach on vacation."

"Many of them were never exposed to other cultures or other people. It's really easy to keep your narrow little views if you never venture out of your comfort zone. That's why big cities tend to be more liberal. All kinds of people and cultures are thrown together."

"How the fuck did you become so enlightened?" I ask. "You're from the around here, too."

"Yeah, I actually grew up in one of those really racist towns.

Down near the border with South Carolina, Spring Hope. But my parents, for whatever reason, just weren't that way. My dad was in the Navy for years. He met my mom in San Diego."

"Was she from California?"

"Yeah."

"See....she's a west coast liberal," I joke. "That's where you got it."

"That probably helped. No question. But we moved around some, got to live in different places, exposing me to different types of people. And then, of course, I spent some time in the Navy, too. But Spring Hope was always home."

"But spending time in the service doesn't have that same effect on everyone."

"For many it does though. They're forced to serve with minorities. They travel the world. They see other cultures. It has an effect."

"I think it still matters what your background was though."

"That's true. My family were never hard core southerners. My grandparents on my dad's side moved down here from New Jersey. So, we were never true southerners, I guess."

"Carpetbagging yankees," I say.

"Guess so."

"But your parents still live down here, don't they? Spring Hope, you said?"

"Yeah, they love it there. Despite some of the bullshit, there's something about the people in that town, and in the South as a whole."

"That's part of the charm of the South. Nicest people on earth, if you can see past some of the baggage."

"Speaking of baggage, do you seriously believe that anyone who works in this joint is going to actually have the ability to grasp the concept of states' rights, except for the mistaken idea that these yahoos hold on to, that it was the real cause of the Civil War?"

"Yeah....I know....I hear you," I say. "But there was more to all of that than just racism and slavery."

"But not much more."

"I know that slavery was probably the root cause. I'm not claiming to be a scholar or anything, but the whole thing wasn't quite as black and white as it's made out to be now. No pun intended."

"But when you support this states' rights shit, you just support those who want to use it as some way of hanging on to the old ways or the old days, or whatever."

"Well, in some ways I'm just playing the devil's advocate. I think you know that," I say. "I'm not one of those good ole boys out waving a Confederate flag in everyone's face."

"Yeah, I know."

"I just believe there are two sides to every issue. Actually, there are usually many sides to any issue. I just think the whole thing was more complicated than we think it was."

"But what's the point? Why worry about that shit now?"

"I don't know....I just have a hard time letting falsehoods or half-truths or whatever go. I just believe in the truth."

"I'm just not sure that a full airing of the truth is all that useful when it comes to this shit."

"Truth isn't useful?"

"You know what I mean," says Jim. "Why stir this shit up? Why is it that some whites just can't let this shit go? All this southern pride bullshit? What exactly are they proud of anyway? Is it slavery....or segregation? Or is it the lynchings....or the beatings? Cross burnings? What?"

"Jim, I don't know," I say. "I wonder myself what all this damn rebel flag waving southern pride bullshit is all about."

"But there's no doubt that it still has something to do with race."

"To some, sure, I think it does. But I don't think that means that all of them want to return to the old days, or old ways, as you put it."

"Then what the hell do they want?"

"They just want the rest of the country to stop imposing their way of life on them."

"But by continuing to wave that fucking flag around, they just look like they're holding onto all that shit from the past," says Jim. "It makes them look like a bunch of fucking racist bigoted idiots."

"I know. It really makes you think they want the Confederacy back or something."

"Whether they mean that or not, yeah, that's the impression you get."

"And how does that make black folks feel? The Confederacy represents nothing but slavery to them."

"Exactly, how comfortable could they possibly be, having to see that flag displayed all over the damn place?"

"But I don't think most of those people really know what they want," I say. "They just seem to have this vague notion of southern pride without really knowing what that means."

"I know. I know that most of the people who talk about the southern shit don't have bad intentions. But they align themselves with those who do."

"It's that natural inclination to pick one side or the other. You're either southern or you're not, so the ones who mean no harm end up being associated with those who do. It's like I said. There are many sides to most issues. I think we have to resist the urge to lump people into neatly defined categories."

"But isn't that exactly what they do with blacks?" asks Jim. "Isn't that the very nature of bigotry? They condemn all blacks as worthless for what a few do."

"No doubt there are still some hard core racists in the South. But for that matter, there are racists everywhere. But then you have others that aren't true bigots and racists. They just have varying shades of prejudice."

"I'll admit that I have my thoughts sometimes."

"Yeah, I do, too," I say. "I think it's hard to not at least have some level of prejudice. It's hard to not have some negative thoughts about people who are different than you."

"There are some to whom it's actually some sort of ideology, while most people just have certain degrees of prejudice from upbringing or whatever bad experiences they may have had."

"Hell, there are plenty of blacks who have racist attitudes, too," I say.

"I've even run into a few who're convinced that they should be second class citizens or something."

"Remember that black lady, Pearl, that used to work here?" I ask. "She would actually say it as a matter of fact that white people were smarter than blacks."

"She was older though. She had her mind filled full of that shit by whites."

"I know. But the point is that it's complicated. Not everyone believes the same things. There are so many shades and levels to this thing that it isn't funny."

"Part of it is this paternalistic attitude that you see. This idea that blacks are somehow inferior and need to be taken care of by the white man."

"White man's burden," I say.

"Exactly, it's not hatred, just a feeling that they need to know their proper place and all of that sort of shit."

"And you can tell that many older blacks seem to buy into that."

"Yeah, you've seen how some of the older ones try to quiet the younger ones down when shit gets all stirred up. But I doubt they all actually buy into that shit. I just think some are afraid to rock the boat. The status quo is more comfortable to them than any sort of change."

"The whole thing is really strange though," I say. "They called slavery that peculiar institution. But this whole damn thing is peculiar to me. It's like you really don't know who really thinks what. And that applies to blacks and whites."

"I know. It's really easy to think that you have it figured out. Someone like Homer White and all of his bullshit. Yet Ray seems to be one of his best friends. How do you have views like that while having black friends?"

"That's another thing though. Homer's racial shit comes from the bible. How do you argue with someone who believes God has ordained this shit or something?"

"Yeah, they believe that the blacks are supposed to be beneath the white race or something like that," says Jim.

"Yeah, they don't look at it as being bigotry, they're just trying to live what they believe to be the truth."

"You would think that with things changing so much in the last couple of decades that there wouldn't be the tension that still exists."

"That's part of what I'm saying," I say. "It's like you still have to walk on eggshells or something."

"Not just for whites, but for blacks, too. How do they know who believes what?"

"You can even say something that happens to be true about a minority, but if it doesn't paint them in a positive light, then you're looked at as having racial motives."

"Like what?"

"How about the obvious? All the crime. And so much of it committed by blacks. Try mentioning that and see what it gets you. It's like they don't want to accept the truth, if the truth isn't convenient."

"I don't know. Some of the guys around here will be very clear that you better not come to certain parts of town. I think that's a pretty strong admission of the truth."

"But take this monkey thing," I say. "Trying to get someone fired over something that could be totally innocent? They're just so damn sensitive that they're turning over rocks looking for the least little speck of racism. That's just bullshit. You can't expect absolutely perfect behavior out of everyone all the time."

"But if that's how they feel.....well...what are we gonna do? Are we gonna say those feelings aren't valid?"

"But we don't have to give into their demands all the time."

"And I don't think we do actually."

"And we should never when it comes to someone's job."

"I doubt Tommy will get fired."

"Only because there's no proof he actually did anything," I say. "If there were proof, he'd be gone."

"I'm not sure about that."

"My point is why can't we get credit for what has changed? Instead, all they do is keep trying to ferret out the last little shreds of racism."

"Yeah, good point."

"Look at us," I say. "A couple of white southern guys trying to solve complicated racial problems."

"And while standing around in a shitty textile factory."

"You ever get the feeling that we're too smart for this place?"

"The plant or the town?"

"Both."

"All the time."

"Me, too."

"Hey, here comes Bob, we better break this up," says Jim, as he starts to walk off.

"Don!" shouts Bob, before I can get away.

"Oh...hey, Bob," I say, pretending as if I didn't see him coming.

"Butch says that he told you to look at the heat controls on Frame 8."

"Yeah...he did."

"We really need this problem fixed...it's a quality issue. The cloth is not getting cured consistently."

"Yeah, I know."

"When are you planning on working on it? I've been by that frame several times and haven't seen you once."

"I can't really do what I need to do on the heat until the frame is running."

"There's nothing that can be checked while it's down?" asks Bob, skeptically.

"Maybe a few things. I'll get to it."

"You need to be at that machine doing something, not standing around talking."

    "Okay…sure," I say, as I walk off.

Chapter 10

Still the same day, after work.

"Hey, Don, Bob didn't ream you out too bad, did he?" Jim asks, as we leave the plant.

"No, not really, but I don't think he totally bought my line of bullshit, either."

"Yeah, he might be a little smarter than we think."

"Yeah, but not by much, I'm sure."

"Wanna grab something to eat at the diner?" asks Jim.

"Yeah, I guess, why not? You gonna walk?"

"Yeah, I'll come back later and get my car."

"Nice day anyway."

"You two ain't going drinking, are you?" asks Jerry, as he and Roger catch up from behind.

"Why'd you ask that?" I respond.

"You're leaving your cars at the plant. Only drinkers do that."

"No, some normal people do as well," responds Jim.

"You know we don't hang out in places like that," I add.

"In places like what?" asks Roger.

"In places where the peasants fry their brains," I say.

"Who says were gonna get loaded?" asks Jerry.

"What's your name again?" I joke. "And besides, you just said that only drinkers leave their cars at the plant, dumbass."

"Not to mention all the second hand smoke that's coating your lungs with black shit," adds Jim.

"We prefer to preserve our brain cells and avoid the inevitable fate of lung cancer that awaits you both," I say, trying to sound pompous.

"Well, I know how impressed you both are with your...how do you say...smarts," says Roger, intentionally emphasizing his Kentucky twang for effect.

"Yeah, we wouldn't want them to burn any of those little gray cells that keep our plant running, would we, Roger?" adds Jerry.

"It's just that we thought we could interest you two in a little continuation of our conversation about the Tommy and Israel episode," says Roger. "You know Ronnie has something to say, and ole Raeford's always there. You know he'll be entertaining."

"What do you say, Jim?" I ask. "Wanna spend some time debating these ole rednecks?"

"What were y'all doing? You were probably getting something to eat anyway," says Roger.

"Yeah, we were going to the diner," I respond.

"Well, Ronnie does serve burgers and shit like that, you know, besides the beer and booze," says Roger.

"Burgers, beer and booze. How can we pass that up, Jim, really?" I ask.

"Why not, at least we ought to get a good laugh out of it," says Jim.

"Well, I'll be goddamned, Don Higgins in here twice in one fucking week," booms Ronnie, as they walk in.

"Twice in one week?" asks Roger, looking at me. "I've never seen Don in here once. You been slumming or something?"

"He just had a little business with me, about my old man," says Ronnie, lying. "But to what do I owe this visit. Not just Don, but Jim, too. Thought you fuckers were too good for this joint."

"We promised them some stimulating conversation," replies Roger.

"Yeah, we just thought we'd come in here to the capital of the Confederacy and discuss the latest racial controversy with you good ole boys," I say.

"Yeah, Ronnie, I don't know if you heard what that goddamn African spear chucker did down at the plant this weekend?" asks Raeford, already half-way through his first beer.

"Yeah, my pop told me all about it," replies Ronnie. "Personally, I don't give a shit one fucking way or the other. If Tommy's too big of a pussy to put that boy in his place, then, fuck it and forget it. That's what I say."

"You're right, with these jackass, nigger-loving liberals running things there ain't no use expecting them to do the right thing and kick his black ass outta that place," says Raeford.

"The only one who has a place to do anything is Tommy. Personally, if the nigger lifted me up by my neck, he'd have a fucking blade stuck in him," replies Ronnie.

"And that ain't nothing but fucking personal protection," adds

Raeford.

"Well, I'm not so sure the courts would see it that way, at least not in this day and age," says Roger.

"Yeah, a knife is not necessarily a measured response to someone putting his hands around your throat," says Jim.

"Well, man, I don't know nothing about no measured fucking response," replies Ronnie. "I just know I'll do what I have to do. No black ass fucker, for that matter no white ass fucker is ever going to put his rotten hands around my throat. Remember, I could blow his ass away with my forty four. If I cut him, I'm actually using restraint."

"Listen, I don't have nothing against blacks, but I don't like their music, I don't like their big mouths. Why can't they just keep to themselves?" asks Jerry.

"What does that mean, Jerry, as it relates to this?" I ask. "Israel wasn't provoking anyone. Some jackass had to write his name on that calendar. It's one thing to not want them to creep into every part of your life, but why provoke them?"

"I didn't, and I wouldn't," replies Jerry.

"But someone did, and plenty of people probably know who. Plenty of people get a kick out of it," I say.

"Listen, guys, before we go any further, don't let me forget my wallet," says Ronnie.

"What do you mean?" asks Roger, with a faint laugh.

"I mean, are you bitches going to order anything?"

"Yeah..... give me one of your famous bacon cheeseburgers and fries.... with a beer," says Jim.

"Ah....I don't know....just gimme some of those hot wings, fries and a coke," I say.

"Beer," says Roger.

"Jack," says Jerry. "And how about pouring the drinks first? Their food will wait."

"Alright, you just sit tight, I've got a little more I want to say. Be back in a moment with your orders, ladies," Ronnie says, as he heads towards the back.

"Sonny, how about getting those bitches their drinks while I go to the back," Ronnie says to his bartender.

"Guys, I don't wanna give y'all the wrong impression," says Raeford. "I get riled up from time to time. But I don't mean no one no harm. I just want to be left alone. I don't want nothing forced down my throat."

"Yeah, and I'm tired of being made to feel guilty for the least little problem that blacks have," says Jerry. "I'm not responsible for any of it. I ain't doing nothing to hold anyone back. I just get so tired of blacks being so sensitive to the least little thing."

"Hell, they call themselves niggas, why can't I do the same?" asks Raeford

"Where the hell did that comes from?" asks Roger.

"Just popped into my head," says Raeford. "Something that's bothered me for a while now."

"Well, I think that's up to them, isn't it," responds Jim.

"No, I don't know, I have a problem with that one myself," I say.

"Sends mixed signals," says Jerry, with a dismissive wave of his hand.

"Bullshit!" says Jim. "You know damn well that you mean something totally different than they do when you use that word."

"It's just a goddamned word," says Raeford. "If they can use it, I can use it."

"But it's a word that has sinister origins," says Jim.

"Sinister origins…whew….well, if it's so fucking sinister then why do they use it?" ask Jerry.

"Because they're being smarter than you," explains Jim. "By taking the word for their own, they take the power out of it."

"Well, if they take the fucking power out of it, why can't I use it?" asks Jerry.

"Jerry, what are you talking about anyway? I never hear you say that," says Roger.

"It just pisses me off that they make such a big deal out of a word they use themselves. They want equal rights? Then why can't we use that word without being called racist?"

"Damn right! I want my civil right to say nigger whenever I want," says Raeford.

"You do pretty well as it stands now," I say.

"Your shit will be out shortly, ladies," says Ronnie, as he comes back from the kitchen.

"What do you think, Ronnie? Shouldn't we be able to say nigger whenever we want?" asks Raeford. "I mean anywhere and everywhere."

"Well, man, I don't know about that, I mean fuck….shit, I ain't trying to go outta my way to start no fucking trouble," responds Ronnie. "We can cut loose in here, but fuck, no, we can't be doing that just anywhere."

"Didn't see that coming," I say.

"Why's that, Don? Don't judge me, man. I just don't want anyone to fuck with me, black or white. I ain't looking to start nothing. Let's just live our lives, separately," says Ronnie. "Or as separately as possible."

"Listen, I ain't saying I want to go around saying nigger, I just get sick of all this political correctness and double standards," says Jerry.

"Fuck, I do wanna say nigger…" says Raeford, trailing off.

"Ronnie, you say you want to live separately from blacks? How far does that go?" I ask.

"You fuckers think that just because my old man is so fucking religious and has all these beliefs about race that that's what I believe," says Ronnie. "Fuck, don't you already see how different I am from him? I got fired from the job he got me at the mill for smoking pot. I run a fucking bar. I ain't like him."

"Okay, can't argue with that," I say.

"All I'm saying is that what's wrong with whites having places like this for ourselves? Fuck, blacks have their own places. I just don't get why there's this big push to integrate everything," says Ronnie. "We have this place. We can cut loose. Talk like we want. But then they have their places where they can cut loose and say what they want about us. I don't see the fucking harm."

"Actually, I happen to agree with you," I say. "I mean about it being alright to have our own places."

"Fuck, I ain't got no problem with the schools and all that shit. Why is it that they can have something like the NAACP and that's fine, but when whites want something similar, we're called racists?" asks Ronnie.

"But there's a difference between the NAACP and some white equivalent," says Jim.

"Why? Why is there a fucking difference?" asks Ronnie.

"Because of what went on it the past," says Jim, wearily.

"It doesn't matter what went on in the past. It's called principle," I say. "We shouldn't be going from one extreme to the next. Equal should mean equal."

"Right, if they want equal, then let's be equal," adds Jerry.

"But things aren't equal yet," says Jim.

"But they're a lot more equal than they were. Fuck, let's move on already," says Ronnie.

"Easier said than done," I say. "I'll have to admit that much."

"Fuck it, life goes on no matter what. We all seem to manage. Things are changing. But we all seem to manage," says Ronnie.

"Yeah, we seem to somehow keep moving forward," I say.

"I did it," says Jerry, out of the blue.

"Did what?" asks Roger.

"I wrote the fucking name on the calendar."

"You ass," says Roger. "You motherfucking ass."

"Why?" I ask. "I mean, I think I know."

"I just wanted to see what would happen."

"Well, a whole lot fucking happened," says Roger.

"Weren't we saying that some fool probably just did this to piss Israel off?" I ask.

"Yeah, and we found us our fool," responds Jim.

"I didn't expect him to get violent. I just wanted to piss him off. He's funny when he's mad. With the accent and all."

"Do you realize that you could have gotten two guys fired over this, Jerry?" asks Roger. "They could have really gone off on each other."

"Tommy could have fucking killed Israel," I add.

"All this fucking shit, and it was just this cocksucker," says Ronnie.

"Good job, Jerry," says Raeford, with a wink. "Keep things stirred up."

"Hey….you guys won't say anything, will you?" asks Jerry.

"Don't say anything? You have to say something," I respond.

"They might fire me though."

"No, I think Don's right on this one," says Roger. "You can't let this just hang there."

"Tommy may just kick your ass," says Ronnie.

"Israel, too," adds Roger.

"Everyone took it far too seriously," says Jerry. "I just thought it was a funny thing to do. But when Israel reacted the way he did, well, I got scared. I thought they'd fire me for racial harassment or something."

"Inciting a riot is more like it," says Jim.

"Seriously though, you have to say something," I say. "Tommy may do something to Israel if you don't."

"Will it change anything though?" asks Jerry. "Israel still attacked Tommy. Tommy ain't gonna forget that."

"But he may back off if he realizes that you started the whole fucking thing," says Roger.

"It's just the right thing to do," I say.

"What do you think, Ronnie?" asks Jerry.

"Yeah, man, you gotta fucking come clean," says Ronnie. "I ain't fucking digging you outta this shit."

"Fuck 'em, don't say a word," says Raeford. "Keep the shit stirred up."

"No, don't keep the shit stirred up," says Jim.

"Alright, I guess I'll have to do it," says Jerry.

"Well, you did give us plenty to talk about," I say. "That's for sure."

"I just thought it was a funny little prank," says Jerry.

"And that's all it really should have been," says Roger. "All this uproar over a damn monkey?"

"I understand that people have compared black people to monkeys," says Jerry. "But that ain't what I meant at all."

"Gotta watch what you say, man," says Ronnie. "Just the way things are now."

"I guess," says Jerry. "But why should we have to walk on eggshells all the time? I don't know what's gonna be offensive and what isn't."

"But there is some history with that word," says Jim. "You knew something would happen or you wouldn't have done it."

"I know, but it's still bullshit that it turned into this," says Jerry.

"Political correctness run fucking amuck," says Raeford.

"That's the point I was trying to make," I say, to Jim. "We shouldn't have to be worried about offending someone with the least little comment. They need to get over some of this shit."

"They wanna call all the shots now," says Raeford. "But that shit ain't right."

"They ain't looking to call all the shots," says Jim. "They just want to be treated with respect and to not be harassed."

"But that was just a dumb joke," I say.

"It's all political," says Jerry, with his trademark dismissive wave of the hand.

"Well, that may be," says Ronnie. "But it's what we got to live with. Just apologize to both of them boys and get it over with."

"Fuck, I guess so," says Jerry.

"No, my partner, you will do it," says Roger. "We don't need a murder on our hands, now do we?"

"I guess not," responds Jerry.

"That would be a great day for the safety manager," I say. "Murder in open width finishing."

"Yeah, can you imagine?" asks Roger.

"What a fucking day," I say.

"That, it was," concludes Jim.

Chapter 11

Friday June 25th, 1993

"Hey...how you doin'?" I ask, as I walk up to Karen at the curing range.

"Hey...uh...sorry, I forgot your name," she says. "It's been a couple of weeks, hasn't it?"

I could never forget her name. But I guess I left a great impression on her.

"It's Don."

"Oh..okay...yeah...Don, how you doin'?"

"Pretty good...I guess."

"We don't have a problem with the machine, do we?"

"No...I'm going to try to get through today without working on too much of anything," I say. "Just thought I'd come by and say hi, if that's alright?"

"Sure, it's alright. I should have known you weren't doing any work. You shop guys hardly do anything at all, most of the time."

"Know what the really good part is?" I ask. "We instrument guys do even less than anybody else in the shop."

"Why's that?"

"We're just so good that our stuff doesn't break down like the other stuff does."

"Oh...you're that good...huh?"

"That good."

"If you say so," she says, as she rolls her eyes and laughs.

"Remember, I get paid for what I know, not for what I do."

"Where can I sign up for a job like that?"

"They're all taken at the moment."

"Let me know when something opens up."

"You'll be the first to know."

"I'll be holding my breath."

"Did you go to church Sunday?" I ask.

I guess I'm hoping that she didn't.

"Yeah, always. Did you?"

"No, I don't really go to church."

"Why not?"

"I don't know. Just don't. I don't see the point. I used to go when I was a kid, but I just stopped going after my parents stopped making me."

"Guess I'm kinda opposite from you," she says. "I didn't really go to church when I was a kid. I just started going about four years ago, after I was saved."

"Saved?"

"Yeah, you know, after Christ came into my life and I became a Christian."

"What happened to cause you to be a Christian, if you weren't raised in it?"

"Really, it was because of my father. He was saved first. I saw what the Lord did in his life and I started to believe partly because of that."

"But what happened in your dad's life that was so dramatic?"

"You would have had to have known him back then, but my dad drank a whole lot and went around with a bunch of different women. But for some reason, he went to a revival one night. After coming home and going to bed, God spoke to him and he was saved."

"So…he had a dream….and because of that, all of a sudden he believes in God?" I ask.

I know that I'm being very obvious with my skepticism.

"It was more than a dream," she says, seeming defensive. "The Lord woke him up and spoke to him."

"Okay….so what happened after that?"

"He changed. He stopped drinking and running after women. The Lord did a real work in his life."

"So, he changed? I mean, he really changed?"

"Yeah, he really changed," she says, seeming slightly annoyed now.

"No, I'm sorry for being so cynical. It's just that I've seen so many people claim that they're all religious, but they keep on messing around and doing stuff they shouldn't do. You know, like some of those television preachers who've been caught with prostitutes and stuff like that. I just don't know how much anyone ever really changes."

"Not all Christians are like that," she says. "Some really are changed by the power of God."

"The church I grew up in even had something like that happen. We kicked a preacher out for messing around with one of the women in the congregation."

"Is that why you don't go to church now.....the hypocrites?"

"Not really. I just don't see the point. It's just a bunch of stories that are told over and over. At least that's the way it was at my church."

"It's really so much more than that, man. Christ has made a real change in my life. I've seen his power work. I mean, really."

"How have you seen his power work?"

"I've seen people healed. I've seen people delivered from demons. I've seen people set free from all kinds of things."

"You mean miracles?" I ask.

"If you want to call it that. To me....it's just the power of God. But yes, God has the power to do all things."

"I mean....yeah, I see that stuff on TV, the supposed healings and that stuff. But I have to say that it all looks like a put on to me."

That's actually putting it mildly. I'm trying to have some respect for her. But most of these TV preachers are clearly con-men just out to make money.

"Well, I can only say what I've seen with my own eyes," she says. "I've been in the room and seen some great works of God."

"But what do you think of those TV ministers?"

"Some are alright. Nobody's perfect. But I know that some of those men have the anointing."

"The anointing? What's that?"

"The anointing is just God's power."

"So, you believe that these men have God's power?"

"Some of them....sure."

"I don't know...just hard for me to believe in all of that, especially from some of those clowns."

"Clowns? Be careful how you talk about God's anointed."

"Why?" I ask.

I can't contain a little bit of a laugh as I say this. But she's dead serious.

"A curse can come on those who speak bad about the anointed men of God."

"A curse?" I ask, not believing my ears. "You mean that an actual curse can come on those who speak ill of these clowns?"

"Yes, an actual curse."

I don't know why I persist in challenging her. I guess I know that I'm not getting any pussy from her, so why worry about pissing her off?

"Well, that's just the way I see them," I say. "I'll have to just risk the curse then. Just doesn't seem real to me."

"Well, you can't believe unless God allows you to see it."

"Allows me to see it?"

"Yeah…you can only see the truth of God if he allows you to."

"He has to allow me to see it? That's odd."

"It's not odd. It's just the way it is."

"What's the point, anyway?" I ask. "What are they trying to prove with all of that stuff?"

"The miracles aren't really important. They just show us the power of God."

"But why do we need to see the power of God?"

"So that we can believe in God and be saved."

"Saved from what?"

"Saved from hell."

"I'm not sure I really believe in hell. I have a hard time believing in the idea that God would subject us to torment for eternity, just because we didn't believe in him."

"Well, you don't have to….. but…..it's real."

"And you know this?"

"Yeah…I think so."

"I don't know….like I said, I grew up in church, but they didn't really talk about hell and stuff like that. It was just the same old bible stories over and over. I know they wanted us to go down in front and join the church and then be baptized, but I never understood what was so important about all of that. I just felt like I was joining some club."

"So, you've been baptized?"

"Yeah, when I was around twelve or thirteen they put me in this special class with the pastor of the church. Actually, it was the pastor that we ended up kicking out. But the basic idea is that when you got to a certain age they would put you in this class and try to convince you to go down front and join the church."

"So, do you think you're saved?"

"You see, I'm not really familiar with that term. They never talked like that. I joined the church and was baptized, but beyond that nothing changed."

"Nothing changed?"

"Not really. The only thing I remember was that I had a strong desire to read through the entire bible after I was baptized. But that didn't last for long. I don't think I ever really started."

"I read my bible all the time."

"The only time I really read a bible was in Sunday school when

I was a kid. Never read it on my own."

"You don't think there's anything in it for you?"

"It just seems like a bunch of old stories to me, fables…whatever."

"Really….it's so much more than that. The bible can speak to every part of your life."

"Well, I don't know. I don't see much use."

"Hey, man, not to change the subject, but what was all of this about the calendar and Israel?"

"I would think you'd know the whole story by now," I say. "As fast as word travels in this place. It's been a couple weeks now."

"I heard most of it, I guess, but wasn't it that guy that you talk to all the time? The one who's been painting all the bathrooms. The guy with the long hair."

"Jerry."

"Yeah, I didn't know his name."

"Yeah, he just meant it as a joke. But it got blown all out of proportion. He apologized to both Israel and Tommy. I guess it's alright now."

"When I first heard it, I couldn't believe that Tommy would do that anyway."

"Do you know him?"

"Yeah, he's a good guy."

"I thought he and his family were kinda known to be racists."

"Nah, man, Tommy's a good guy. He's been to cookouts that my family's had."

"Okay, I just got the impression that he was kinda stuck in the old ways."

"Not Tommy."

"Well, turns out that it was that idiot Jerry anyway."

"Israel shouldn't have done what he did though," she says. "It was just a stupid joke."

"That's not how a lot of black people saw it."

"Listen, man, stuff like that just doesn't matter that much."

"That's what some of us were thinking about it."

"It won't no big deal to me."

"Well, it's over now, however any of us saw it. It turns out that we all got worked up over some stupid prank."

"Hey, here comes my supervisor," she says as she nods towards the entry end of her machine. "You'd better scoot."

"Okay, I'll talk to you later. Don't want to get you in trouble."

"Yeah…you know how he is."
"Talk to you later, Karen."
"Okay, man."

That's an example of what I'm talking about when I say it's hard to figure this race shit out. I've heard Tommy say nigger this and nigger that numerous times over the years. But Karen says he's a good guy. He apparently socializes with her family. How can both of these be true? How does one reconcile this? But you see this sort of thing all of the time in the South. Someone who appears to have these racist views will have genuine friendships with black people. It just isn't as black and white as many people make it out to be.

Chapter 12

Saturday July 3rd, 1993

"So, how are our tomato plants doing?" I ask, as I let Mark into my den.

"Well, I went ahead and planted them back in the woods," replies Mark, as he takes a seat.

"They were big enough?"

"Yeah, I think so."

"You think so? You should have consulted me."

"Consulted you?"

"Yeah, we're trying to start something here. This is a fucking business."

"This ain't no goddamn business yet. We're just a couple fools trying to grow some fucking weed."

"Where'd you put them?"

"In the spot we found," says Mark, sounding exasperated. "There's no problem. I'm keeping them watered. They're doing alright."

"Okay, good."

"Man, what's this here?" asks Mark, grabbing a book from my coffee table.

"It's a bible," I say.

"A bible?"

"Yeah."

"What the fuck are you doing with a bible?" asks Mark. "I thought your Sunday school days were long since passed."

"Actually, I've been reading it."

"Why?"

"I don't know, there's this girl at work that I've been talking to some."

"A girl, huh?"

"Yeah, just some things she said......well....they got me interested. Just had the urge to get one."

"Interested in what?"

"I don't know, it doesn't mean anything. Just some things she's said. Not sure what it was really.....I'm just reading."

"You're not going to get all religious on me, are you?"

"I don't know. I've just always had a fascination with prophecy and shit like that."

"What? You mean end of the world type of shit?"

"Yeah."

"So, she's one of these nuts who thinks the world's getting ready to end?"

"No....we really didn't talk about that."

"So, you're just into that shit on your own?"

"Yeah, I remember back when I was a kid, I found this book that my mother was reading that talked about all that stuff. One part that always stuck with me was that the end of the world would be connected with some sort of war in the Middle East. You know we just had the Gulf War a couple years back. I was kind of looking for something then."

"So, that's all this is?"

"I guess...I don't know. Talking about religion with her just got me interested. She just seems to...I don't know...well....really believe. And some of what I read just rings true to me somehow."

"So, what's this girl like?"

"Well, she's black for one thing."

"So, you want a little brown sugar...huh?"

"Well....yeah...she is hot."

"I didn't know you liked black girls."

"Yeah, it's happened kind of gradually really, after high school. I never really cared for the black girls in school. It's just something that developed."

"Do you still like the white meat though?"

"Well, yeah, but even then I tend to prefer the darker white girls if you know what I mean. Dark, exotic."

"I've never really had a thing for black girls," says Mark. "I prefer blonds, because I'm a gentleman. Gentlemen prefer blonds."

"You sir, are very far from a gentleman."

"Takes one to know one."

"It's funny. The black thing isn't just about how they look."

"Then what the fuck is it about?"

"I don't know," I say. "I just like their attitude better or something."

"Well, many black chicks definitely have plenty of attitude."

I don't know how to explain it really. This feeling came on me over the years since high school. But white girls just seem to have this snotty bitchy attitude or something. I feel bad saying it really. I see this bitchy attitude or whatever even when I'm just looking at pictures. I don't even have to hear them talk. Logically, it doesn't make sense. I know that it isn't true. It's just some stupid perception I have. What deep dark psychological reason is behind that?

"Yeah, I don't know why I feel that way," I say. "Just forget it."

"So, you've been talking to this black chick at work," says Mark. "You gonna hit that ass, or what?"

"Well, the thought had crossed my mind, originally. But, like I said, we've been talking about the bible. I'm afraid that she's one of those serious Pentecostal types of Christian."

"So, in other words, you're shit outta luck."

"Seems so."

"Okay, so getting back to your little bible study," says Mark. "Can you now predict the end of the world, my prophet?"

"You know, a lot of that prophecy stuff is actually really interesting. We never got into that stuff when I went to church."

"Church for me was just a bunch of boring shit."

"Same for me, except for all the horsing around we did," I say. "We boys raised so much hell in Sunday school one time, that none of the girls would come anymore. We just harassed them so much that they just didn't want to be there. They had to keep trying different men to teach the class in an attempt to rein us in."

"I didn't have too many kids to play with at my damn church. Bunch of fucking old people."

"Well, that's about all I got out of church. Fun with friends and good food when we had covered dish suppers."

"I mean, I believe in God, but I just don't see the point in going to church."

"Yeah, I don't understand how anybody cannot at least believe in some sort of God, or supreme being, or whatever, considering how complex and beautiful this world is," I say. "It's just too complicated and organized to have just happened by accident."

"Yeah, there's just too much to it to believe that it all just happened by accident or something."

"You know, the thing that's always blown my mind, when we're talking about where this all came from, is the thought of absolute nothingness," I say. "At least that's what I call it."

"Absolute nothingness?"

"Yeah, you know, there had to have been a time, at least I think so, when there was absolutely nothing. A time before all matter existed. A time when this space right here around us had nothing in it. No particles or matter of any kind. Just nothing."

"So…no planets…no stars…no matter…nothing at all."

"Nothing. Absolutely nothing at all."

"Hence, the term absolute nothingness."

"Yeah, wouldn't there have to have been a point where there was nothing?" I ask. "Isn't there a beginning to everything?...even if we say that matter has always existed in one form or the other. What does that really mean? It still seems like there would have to have been some beginning point.

"I guess….you would think so," says Mark. "You would think there would have to be a beginning somewhere. But who knows?"

"But let's just say that matter hasn't always existed. That God created everything at some point. The question then becomes, has God always existed?

"I do remember that much from church. Yes…God has always existed."

"But, how? Where did God come from? How did it all begin? I mean, how? Really, it can blow your mind if you just sit here and ponder it for a while. How could all of this just come out of nothing? Not even thoughts would exist….nothing would have existed. Nothing to create all of this. How?"

"Yeah, I think I know what you mean. How? Because nothing is nothing. So, how could there have ever been just nothing?

"Doesn't everything have to have a beginning? You see, that's the part science can't explain. They say that all matter was compressed to the size of a pin head. Then there was the big bang. But where did that matter come from originally? What was the source of that energy? They can't answer those questions."

"I don't know if religion can even answer those questions."

"That's just it. How could there be a satisfactory answer?" I ask. "Nothing that I can imagine could explain how all of this, all of this matter just came into being."

"It's probably just outside of our ability to understand."

"But doesn't it seem like religion should be more concerned with bigger questions like that rather than being so worried about some of the stupid shit they get hung up on?"

"Definitely."

"I just never heard anyone at the church I grew up in ever talking about questions like this."

"Well, they don't have the answers."

"No one does. We think we're so smart, but we can't answer everything," I say. "Not Einstein, not Freud, not Sagan. No one can answer the deepest questions."

"So….is that what you're looking for….I mean in reading the bible?"

"I don't know…I guess. I'm not sure why I'm interested really. Never been a fan of organized religion."

"Yeah….me either. I prefer organized chaos."

"The Chaos theory!" I say, raising my index finger.

"We can get off on some tangents sometimes. Can't we?"

"I know…but that's the cool thing about us," I say. "We talk about anything and everything, whether it's the origin of all matter, or the size of the tits on Pamela Anderson. Some of what we talk about I could never talk to those jackasses at work about."

"Yeah…I guess people would be surprised at how deep we can get sometimes."

"Now let's talk about Pamela Anderson's tits."

"Let's"

Mark is the person that I can confide in the most. He's really my only friend outside of the plant. I can talk about certain subjects with certain people at work. But I can talk about anything with Mark. He may seem like a typical crude and uncultured man sometimes, but he is capable of thinking about some of the bigger questions of our existence. And of course, sometimes we just talk about Pamela Anderson's tits.

Chapter 13

Sunday July 4ᵗʰ, 1993

"Hey, Pop, how's it going?" I ask, as I enter the home of my parents, Joan and Jack.

"Hey, Donald, how you doin, boy?" asks Dad.

"Pretty good, I guess."

"How are things at the Mill? Your sister says things aren't so good."

"Yeah, things are kind of slow. Imports are killing us."

"Hey, Don, ready to eat, I bet?" says Momma, as she peeks in.

"I'm always ready to eat, Momma."

"It won't be long," she says. "You're the first one here…as usual."

"Yeah, I hate to be late."

The hating to be late comes from the shyness. My goal is to be the first one to an event. I hate to walk into a crowded room. And this is true even if the room is full of no one but family. There are so many little neurotic quirks that come out of this shyness that it isn't funny.

"Why don't you two go out to the porch while I finish things up," says Momma.

"We eating out there?" I ask.

"Good day for it," says Dad. "Not that hot considering it's the Fourth of July."

"Are Dan and Mel both coming?" I ask.

"Yeah, and Hugh and Marie, too," responds Dad.

"Speak of the devil. And I do mean devil," I say, as Hugh and Grandma come around the side of the house to the porch.

Hugh is Grandma's second husband. I never knew my grandfather. He died the year before I was born. I guess Hugh is good for Grandma, but he sure is a hard one to handle.

"I thought you'd be out here," says Grandma.

"How you doing, Grandma?" I ask.

"Just fine. My daughter in the kitchen?"

"Yeah."

"I'll go and see if I can give her a hand."

"And how are you two gentlemen doing?" asks Hugh.

"How you doing, Hugh?" I ask.

"Have a seat," offers Dad.

"How's it going down at the plant, Don?" asks Hugh.

"Well, like I was just telling Pop, it's slow."

"All those damn imports from those slant-eyed chinks, I bet."

"Yeah, we're getting slowly but surely put out of business by that cheap Chinese labor," I say. "We have a new plant manager. And this guy has a reputation for either straightening out a plant or shutting it down."

"Is it getting that bad?" asks Dad.

"It won't necessarily be soon, but yeah, it'll probably come to that, unless they can pull off some sort of miracle. But there are some things in the works that may help out. Automating what we can. That sort of thing. Anything to reduce the labor cost."

"Textiles is a dying industry, Don," says Hugh. "You need to get into something else."

"I know….but it's hard to leave. I've got first shift. I'm lead man. It's hard to just give all of that up."

"But with your talent, son, you'd quickly rise through the ranks of any place you went."

"Thanks, Hugh. You're probably right."

"There's no probably about it. I know some of the guys down there. They're really impressed with you."

"I guess I just have a knack for it or something."

"You're young. You don't have a wife. You should do what I did. Do power plant shutdown work. Do some travelling."

"One of the older guys at the plant is always saying I should get out of there and get into pharmaceuticals," I offer.

That's funny since I'm trying to get into the narcotics business.

"There you go. That's a good idea, too," says Hugh. "There are several good drug plants around here."

"I don't know, Hugh. I'm not sure I want to keep doing this type of work."

I am sure. I know I don't want to be doing this type of work.

"What do you want to do then?" asks Hugh.

"I'm not sure."

"Don't squander your abilities, son. You've got the mind for this work. Don't waste it."

"I'm just not sure I can keep doing this the rest of my life."

I absolutely must do something else. I will simply not be able to survive if I have to do this the rest of my working life.

"Hey, how's everyone doing?" asks Melody, as she comes in

through the front of the house to the porch.

"Hey, Sis, how's it going?" I ask.

"Hey, Sweetie," says Dad, as he gets up to hug her.

"I didn't know y'all were coming, Hugh," says Melody.

"You know me. I wouldn't pass up a chance at your mother's cooking," says Hugh. "Now your Grandmother's…well….that's another story."

He's always got to make those derogatory cracks about her.

"Are Momma and Grandma in the kitchen?" asks Mel.

"Yeah," responds Dad.

"I'll just leave you men to yourselves and see if they need any help."

"No offense intended," says Hugh, under his breath so that the departing Mel cannot hear. "But, Don, don't be like you sister. Don't squander your talents and opportunities."

"What do you mean?" I respond. "How is she squandering her opportunities?"

"Well, your sister started college but never finished. And what's she doing now?"

"She's the office manager at the plant. So?"

"She had the opportunity to reach for more and squandered it. She's working at a plant that'll eventually close. Just like you. Damn it! You kids today just don't appreciate the opportunities you have."

"We don't know that it'll close. There are options that could keep the company alive. New product lines. And like I just said, automation to reduce labor. There are ways."

In the long run, I don't believe any of that will work.

"If you don't know what the future holds for that place…well….you're in a fucking dream world."

"If it does close…we'll figure it out then," I say. "In the meantime, we are paid pretty well. At least for the industry we're in."

"I'm just saying to not squander the opportunities you have."

"But we have to be happy in whatever choices we make," I say. "Mel just decided that college wasn't for her."

"But it would have given her a shot at such a better future."

"What? She's just supposed to do it because it's supposed to guarantee some sort of a future? And I'm supposed to keep doing this work even if it doesn't make me happy?"

"Just make yourself be happy, for God's sake."

Why is he so fucking worried about this?

"I don't know how to do that," I say. "I'm either happy or I'm not."

"Your brother is the only one of you three that has any ambition and drive to succeed."

"Yeah, that's true. Dan is the only one who's been able to really keep any momentum going when it comes to school and stuff like that," I admit.

"He's made the most of his opportunities."

"But are Mel and I just supposed to stick with what we chose no matter what? What if we made the wrong choice? What if instrumentation isn't for me?"

"You got your Associates. You could have gone two more years and gotten your engineering degree. Just like your father here."

"I just wanted to get out of school and get a job. This isn't a calling or anything like that."

I really just kind of fell into this anyway. I had done a year at some junior college. I announced that I wasn't going back for the next year. I had no idea what I was going to do. Bruce, a guy at church, was involved in starting the instrumentation program at the community college. That's how I got into this. I just thought that it sounded kind of neat. So I did it. But it's not like I have this great drive to do this. I needed to do something, so I did this. This is a default career.

"But you're good at it," says Hugh. "So what if it's not a calling."

"I just have a knack for it. But it's not really what I want. I'm just getting numb working in that place."

"That's why you need to get into another industry. Better technology would keep your interest up."

"I'm not convinced of that."

"Hey, how's everyone doing?" asks Dan, as he makes his entrance from the yard.

"Take a lesson from your brother here. He got his degree in accounting and now he's got his own firm."

"That's great for him. But I don't know what I want to do yet."

"What's happening?" asks Dan.

"Hugh thinks I should be more like you."

"How so?"

"In being more motivated."

"Oh."

"And Mel, too," I say. "You're supposed to be the model for us."

"Well, I don't know about that," says Dan. "We all have

different motivations and desires. This isn't one size fits all."

"I was trying to tell him that. But he'll probably accept it from you…. since you have your degree. And you're successful to boot."

"All my kids are successful," says Dad.

"If you say so," says Hugh, rolling his eyes.

"Time to eat," says Momma.

"Thank God," I say.

As we fix our plates, Hugh asks about the incident. I knew that was coming.

"Don, tell me about this incident down at the plant. My buddy was telling me that some damn African nigger tried to choke some white guy down there."

"Yeah, it happened," I say.

"They're not gonna can his black ass, are they?"

"Probably not."

"Bastards. I would have taken care of it differently of course. That Cash boy is a pussy for not putting that nigger in his place."

"Hugh!" exclaims Grandma. "Please?"

"What?"

"Please watch your language."

"We're all adults here, aren't we?"

"Please?"

"Fine baby, I made my point."

"I just think it was an incident that should be over and done with," I say.

"Didn't it end up being caused by some idiot just trying to pull a prank?" asks Mel.

"Yeah, Jerry, one of the carpenters," I say. "He was just trying to have a little fun with Israel."

"Israel? Is that his damn name?" asks Hugh. "Is he a Jew or a nigger?"

"He's black," I say, glaring at Hugh. "Actually, he's the guy who trained me when I first started at the plant. Smart guy, actually."

"Why'd he fly off the goddamn handle for?" asks Hugh. "Over a prank?"

"Yeah, what exactly did this Jerry do anyway?" asks Dan.

"He wrote Israel's name over a picture of a monkey that happened to be on the calendar that's in the dispatch office," I explain.

"Is that all?" says Hugh. "Damn, these blacks are just too damn sensitive."

"Well, I can't believe I'm saying this, but I happen to agree with you," I say. "It was just a stupid prank. Who's to say what it meant anyway? Many of the blacks at the plant just took it as this huge racial slur that it wasn't."

"It was an unprovoked attack, yet that boy gets to keep his job," says Hugh, shaking his head.

"Well, Jerry apologized to both of them," I say. "I think it's over now."

"There's a little unfinished business there if you ask me," says Hugh. "Cash has some work to do."

"Well, whatever," I say. "Does everything have to be this huge deal?"

"If we don't do something, those damn niggers are going to take over. They think they can do anything now. Damn that Martin King."

"Hugh, you know, I never thought I'd agree with you on this subject, but lately something's changed my mind," says Momma.

"What happened?"

"Well, there are two black girls that work in the office with me."

"Having problems with them?"

"Yeah, well, they want to palm all their work off on me."

"Typical lazy ass niggers."

"Joyce is the office manager and I'm doing most of her work. She makes me do far more than Angela, the other girl. They just sit around talking all the time."

"That's the problem with niggers. They either don't want to do the work, or they don't know how, so they get the white man to help them. And this black bitch is in power now, so she can make you."

"And some of the stuff they talk about...their sexual encounters and stuff like that. Stuff that shouldn't be talked about in a proper office. And playing that music of theirs."

"Jungle bunny boogie music," says Hugh. "That's what I call it."

"Jungle bunny boogie music?" I ask. "Actually sounds kind of cool."

"I was thinking the same thing," says Dan, winking at me.

"You kids today just don't understand," says Hugh, shaking his head. "These jungle bunnys are corrupting our culture."

"Then I'm happily corrupted," I say.

"I'm just being made to feel very unwelcome by them

dominating the office," says Momma.

"Yeah, but blacks have to be in plenty of environments where it's dominated by whites," I say.

"You don't understand, son," says Momma. "It's hostile."

"Well, it is for them in many places."

"You work in the shrink's office at the army post, don't you?" asks Hugh.

"Yeah, the base hospital."

"What about the doctor? Would he be any help?"

"There are two, Dr. Jones and Dr. Hayes."

"Think either of them would change the situation? Maybe boot that black bitch out of there and give you the job? I mean you're doing the work anyway."

"Well, Hayes is black....."

"Forget that. They always stick together. What about this Jones fella?"

"Well...he may help. Just didn't want to stir anything up."

"Give him a shot. But the fact that he's a head shrinker....I don't know....most of those fellas are liberals."

"I don't know. I can say something."

"Do that. See if Jones will stand up for one of his own."

"I've just had enough," I say, as I leave the table.

Normally I can somewhat tolerate Hugh's bullshit. But not now.

"Can you believe Momma agreeing with Hugh like that?" says Mel, as she follows me into the den.

"We've tolerated that dick for years, and now all of a sudden she's on his side? And what the fuck got him so wound up today anyway? He's always bad, but it's like he's in high gear today."

"We only tolerate him because he's married to Grandma."

"What in the world does she see in him? There's all that racist shit. Then he bosses her around all the time."

"I don't know, but there must be something there."

"Don't get me wrong," I say. "The guy's smart. He has many interests that interest me. But that racist bullshit.....especially now."

"Why now?"

"Well....I've just been talking to this black girl at work."

"Really? Is it serious?"

What is it really? I don't know.

"No...not really. I don't know though. There is something

about her."

"Where does she work at the plant?" asks Mel.

"She runs the curing range. Exit end. That new dryer."

"Okay…yeah….I know who you're talking about."

"Yeah, I'm talking to her. Maybe starting to hit it off. Then this shit."

I'm not even sure why I said we were hitting it off. Am I so desperate that I would cling to the least little hope of a relationship with a woman?

"Listen…you know Momma….she's just frustrated at what's going on at work," says Mel. "She doesn't mean it."

"Uh…are you two going to join us?" asks Dad, as he comes in. "I said something to Hugh. I think he'll behave now."

"Sure, Pop, we'll come back. I just had to step away for a minute," I say.

"Your mother will be fine. She's just been catching it from those two at work…that's all."

"That's what I told him," says Mel.

"Come on…we'll try to steer things away from that stuff."

"Okay, Pop."

"Everything alright?" asks Hugh, as we all three come back to the table. "I didn't mean to offend anyone."

"Sure…everything's fine," I respond.

"You know….changing the subject…..when are you boys going to bring a girl home?" asks Hugh. "Mel here has had her share of boyfriends, but you two have never brought anyone around. At least that I've seen. Did I miss something?"

"No, you're right, Hugh. Neither of them has ever brought anyone home," responds Momma. "I've been waiting."

"You two aren't fags, are you?" asks Hugh.

"Hugh!" says Grandma.

"Just asking," says Hugh, holding up his hands.

"Ass!" I say, as I get up to leave. "I've got to go. He just won't stop."

"Son…I'm just asking a question."

"Hugh…it's our business. It has nothing to do with you. And you may not be happy with who I may or may not be seeing anyway," I say.

"Yeah….the same goes for me. You won't be happy at all," says Dan, getting up to leave as well.

"What the hell did I say? You two are leaving because of that? It was just a little joke."

"Hugh, I asked you to stop," says Dad.

"I did stop talking about the race shit," says Hugh. "Since some people seem to be so sensitive to that."

"Hugh….you're just so thoroughly full of shit," I say. "More so than usual."

"Don!" says Momma. "You shouldn't be talking to Hugh that way."

"Momma, I just can't take this right now. I'm not sitting here listening to this racist crap, and then this homophobic crap, too?" I say. "And then you join in."

"Maybe I hit paydirt with my little joke," says Hugh. "Did that hit just a little too close to home?"

"Maybe I'll hit you…or rather… beat the shit out of you. How 'bout that?" I say, moving towards Hugh.

I shouldn't let him get to me like this.

"Okay….leave!" says Momma, pointing to the door. "You're the one out of line now."

"Any time, son….any time," says Hugh, standing now. "Take a swing…..I beg you."

"You fucking bitch," I say, enraged now. Does he actually think I won't kick his ass?

"Such language," says Hugh, smiling, enjoying every minute of it.

"Donald! Leave…now!" says Dad, standing now as well. "And you, too, Hugh. Get your ass outta my house."

My Dad must be pissed. You hardly hear profanity from him.

"Fine," I say, as both Dan and I leave. "I can't take this fucker anymore."

I normally don't use words like that around my parents.

"Wait outside for me, son," says Hugh. "I'll show you something."

"Don, just leave," says Dad.

"Don't worry," I say. "We're gone."

"I thought you were going to kick the old man's ass," says Dan, as we make our way to our cars.

"I've just had it with that shit."

"I know…why do you think I live in Raleigh. It's still a southern city, but it's better."

"I know. Some of that's just that small town bullshit. These old people who can't get with the program. Can't accept change."

"Don't let him get to you like that though."

"I know. He gets off on it anyway."

"That's right. Don't give him the satisfaction."

"It's just hard for me to keep letting that shit go. Slant eyes, niggers, chinks, fags....it never ends."

"He'll never change though."

"I know. Most people never change," I say. "We are what we are."

"Ain't that the truth," says Dan. "We are what we are."

"You know I have friends down at the plant?" says Hugh, walking up to us.

"So what?" I ask.

"I know that you've got a thing for some nigger girl," says Hugh. "You'd better watch yourself with that shit."

"Hugh, the world's changing all around you," says Dan, standing between Hugh and me. "It's leaving you behind."

"Well, I ain't changing for nobody."

"Well, we ain't either," says Dan.

"Just for the record," says Hugh. "I know you're a little sweet."

"And you're a sour old fool," says Dan. "Let's get outta here before we have to kick his ass."

"I've got your numbers," says Hugh. "I did hit paydirt. Queer bait and nigger lover."

"Using the words of Axl Rose," I say. "Why don't you just.....fuck off."

Where the fuck does he get his information? I've got a thing for Karen? I don't even know if I have a thing for her yet. How could word get out about something that isn't even true yet? We've only spoken a few times? Is that why I took Hugh's shit so personally this time? I've never flown into a rage at Hugh like that before. I'm sure my family was a little surprised at it, too.

Chapter 14

Monday July 5th, 1993

"Hey, Don......uh......the new curing range having problems already?" asks Jim, with his trademark bemused smirk. "Haven't really heard about all that much going wrong over there."

"No, not really. Why do you ask?" I respond. I am, in fact, on my way to the curing range.

"Well, it just seems like you're spending quite some time over there. I just wonder why?"

"Just keeping an eye on things."

"I bet you are," says Jim, as he walks off, with a shit-eating grin painted across his face.

"Hey there, man. How you doing?" asks Karen, as I stroll up to the curing range.

"I'm doing alright. Have a good fourth?"

"Yeah, we had a cookout, then went to see the fireworks."

"Yeah, that's about what I did, too."

Except that my fireworks were with my family.

"So, what've you been up to?" she asks.

"Actually......you may be interested in what I've been doing."

"Really? What?"

"Well....I went and bought a bible."

"Hmm....okay. But why?"

"I don't know really. Just some of these talks we've been having got me interested."

"But what did I say that was so special?"

"It's just that you seem so different from what I usually think of when I think of Christians."

"How?"

"I don't know....it's just that you seem to believe in something that's actually real. Maybe that's the wrong way to put it. You're just different."

"Well....I hope that I'm different. That's the point. Christ makes a difference."

"It shows."

"So....what have you been reading?"

"Well…I actually started in Revelation," I say.

"Revelation? Why there?"

"I've just always been interested in prophecy. That end of the world stuff has always fascinated me."

"I don't really get into that stuff all that much."

"Well…besides that, I've actually read through the entire New Testament, too."

"Wow….that much already?"

"It's just so interesting somehow. I'm not even sure why, really."

"What do you mean that you're not sure why?" she asks.

"I don't know…..in some places….well….tears have come to my eyes. Like when they were talking about what Jesus went through."

I wasn't expecting that. I never dreamed that the bible could get to me like that.

"That's just the spirit of God. That's the way He works," she explains. "He gets to us through his word. Those tears are just Him touching your heart."

"I don't know…it's just that so much of what I read I've never seen before."

"Yeah, there's a lot of good stuff in there."

"It's just that I never knew that it was any more than all those same old bible stories that they used to teach us in Sunday school. We seemed to just go over the same ones time and time again."

"I can't believe you read that much so fast. It takes me much longer," she says. "But I'm not a real good reader though."

"I love to read. It was just hard to put it down."

"Well, I'm glad you've been reading. So….when are you getting saved?"

"Saved?"

"I'm just kidding…well…sort of."

"I'm not saying that I believe everything I read."

"I know…but God is working on you."

"Well…I'm not sure about all of that."

"Just keep reading. You may not realize it, but God's working on you."

"Oh, I plan to keep reading."

"And keep coming by my machine…."

"Huh?"

"And we'll get you saved."

"We'll see…," I say, laughing.

"Well, besides the stuff from Revelation, did anything else stand out to you?"

"Actually, yeah, something really interesting."

"What?"

"I see where women should remain silent in church. I like that one," I say, laughing.

"Yeah, it does say that, but you have to realize why."

"Okay…why? Why did Paul say that women should keep their traps shut."

"He doesn't say anything about keeping their traps shut."

"He might as well have put it that way."

"You have to understand that in that area, at that time, women weren't permitted to do the things we can do now."

"So…because things have changed in society, we're not to go by this scripture anymore?"

"We still go by scripture, but we have to realize when things were only meant for that time. And this was one of those things. He was only saying this because these particular people already had certain views of women."

"But that's not the way it was presented," I say. "It seems like he was laying down the law to me. He was saying that women should not only not speak in church, but not be in authority over men, either."

"Well, I believe that part's true. Men are supposed to lead."

"So, there should never be a female President, or even supervisor here at the plant? Women should never lead men?"

"Not if there are men to do those jobs."

"Wow, you really believe that? I was just kind of joking when I brought this up."

"We all have our jobs to do. Women are meant for certain things and men are meant for others."

"Most Christians don't believe this sort of stuff."

"Well, it's right there in scripture."

"But for that matter there are plenty of things in scripture that no Christian seems to be doing."

"Like what?"

"What about the scripture where it says it's better to cut off a hand or foot than to sin?"

"You're just trying to be funny."

Yeah, I am trying to be funny.

"No…I'm just wondering about a few things," I say.

"Ok…what about it then?"

"Well….why aren't there people running around with missing hands and feet?"

"What?"

"Uh…well…excuse me…it would be hard for someone to run around with missing feet"

"See…you're just messing around."

"No…seriously. Is anybody obeying this passage?"

"You can't take it literally."

"But, why? Where does it say to not take it literally?"

"It's just common sense."

"But what's the standard? If it's too hard to go by, we just decide that it's not to be taken literally?"

"I don't know. We just know."

"I mean, I can see what you're saying about that passage. It's just saying that sin should be taken seriously. I don't really expect people to be cutting off hands and feet."

"Well, good. At least you see that."

"But I don't understand why we don't take the passages about women seriously."

"We do take them seriously. We just have to understand who it applies to and all of that."

"If the bible is meant for all of us, then why was that one passage about women keeping quiet, only meant for that one particular time, when they thought less of women? Why would God just give in to the way they believed? Why wouldn't he make them do the right thing?"

"I don't know."

"Or maybe it is meant for today. If that's supposed to be the word of God, then maybe it is meant for us today."

"Why are you trying to stir things up?"

"How?"

"All you're talking about is these controversial verses."

"It's fun to stir things up. I just have a questioning mind. I want answers and I want them now, woman," I say, laughing.

"Yeah…okay," she says, rolling her eyes.

"I saw in there about speaking in tongues. Do you do that?"

"I have."

"I know that you're a Pentecostal…….so I figured you did"

"The power of God works on different people in different ways though. Not everyone speaks in tongues."

"So, it's the power of God doing it?"

"Yeah, during a service, when we praise the Lord, if the Spirit gets high enough, He'll fall on everyone."

"And he makes you speak in tongues?"

"Yeah, sometimes."

"What other things happen when the spirit falls?"

"All kinds of things.

"Like what?"

"Nothing as important as the change that the Lord has brought to my life."

"What sort of change has he brought to your life?"

"I don't love the things of the world anymore. I only concern myself with things of the Lord."

"So, like the movies and music and stuff like that?"

"Yeah, but more than that."

"Like what?"

"Well, like ministering to others, serving at my church, just doing things for the Lord."

"What about a boyfriend?"

"Well…what about a boyfriend?"

"Is there anyone?"

"Why do you want to know?"

"No reason. Just wondering. You said that you do things for the Lord now. Just wondered if there was room for a boyfriend."

"No, there isn't anyone. But there's a reason for that."

"Okay. What's the reason?"

"I'm not sure I should tell you."

"Your secret's safe with me."

"No, it's not a secret really. Just don't need everyone in my business."

"Come on, tell me."

"Well, I haven't had sex since I was saved. And since most guys want sex…well….no boyfriend."

"Really? So you don't believe in sex before marriage?"

"That's what the bible says."

"Yeah….I guess that's what it says."

"I was seeing this guy at the time I was saved. But the Lord led me to give him up. I'm just waiting on Him now. The Lord will send me someone if that's what He wants for me."

"Was it hard? I mean giving up sex and your boyfriend?"

"I loved him. But after I was saved, we were just going in two different directions. He was still in the world. I was with God."

"Since we're telling secrets.....can I tell you something?"

"Sure. I guess."

"But please don't tell anyone. I really can't believe I'm telling you. No one knows. I mean no one. But I feel like I can trust you."

"Okay."

"I've never had sex."

"Wow! Really? Man, that's such a blessing."

"A blessing?"

"Yeah, just think of the gift that you can give to your future wife. She'll be the only one."

"Doesn't seem like much of a blessing to me."

"It is though."

"It wasn't on purpose. I can assure you of that."

"Then, why?"

"I've always been really shy. Painfully shy. Never had a girlfriend. Never kissed a girl. Nothing."

"Yeah, like I've said before, people do wonder about you. You keep to yourself so much, at least around some people. Then we see you laughing and joking with other people, mainly the guys in the shop. But some people you never talk to."

"I know. I've just always had a hard time connecting with people. Just can't seem to find a way to break the ice, especially with women. I'm just a mess with women. Not sure why really. But once the ice is broken, I can talk your ear off. It's just that until now, I've never really connected with a woman like I have with you."

"Yeah...I see. I mean, I hear," she says, laughing. "You're definitely talking up a storm with me."

"I don't know where it came from, the shyness or whatever. I've just been like this for a long time now. I'm pretty dysfunctional, actually."

"But you're a nice guy. A lot of girls would like you."

"I guess I know that. But the shyness just takes over. Believe me, this isn't a choice."

"Well...as far as the sex is concerned...I hope you can see it as a blessing."

"No, it's embarrassing. I feel like a freak."

"Well...I promise I won't tell."

"Thanks. The guys would never let me live that down if they were to find out."

"Hey, not to cut this short or anything, but you've been over here for a while."

"Yeah, I guess I'd better get to work. Or at least find somewhere else to not work. This spot is just a little too out in the open."

"Yeah, you better get going. You know that the supervisor from open width, Ed Harris, is always looking to see what everyone's doing."

"I know."

"He worries more about other departments than he does about his own people," she says. "For some reason he seems to have his eye on me lately."

"I don't think he likes that fact that we're talking."

"But why? We're just talking."

"Yeah, I know. But he may think it's more than that."

"But it's not."

"I know. But some of these white guys get uptight when they think something may be happening....you know....mixing the races and all that stuff."

"You think that's what Ed's problem is?"

"Wouldn't surprise me."

"I don't know. Never got that from him."

"Anyway, I guess I'd better get back and at least appear to be working. Don't need to give him any ammunition."

"Yeah, go do something."

"Talk to you later."

I cannot believe I told her that. No one knows for sure that I'm a virgin. Plenty of people suspect that's the case, I'm sure. But no one knows it. I'm sure some people may even think I'm gay. I know she won't tell. She's just that kind of a person. There's something really special about this girl. I must feel some sort of connection with her to reveal something like that. It's probably the biggest embarrassment of my life.

Chapter 15

Wednesday July 7th, 1993

"Don, can I speak to you a second?" asks Butch.

"Sure, boss," I respond.

"Let's step over here into this office," he says, as he ushers me into a vacant office just outside of the maintenance shop.

"What is it?" I ask. "This seems serious."

"Well, it kind of is."

"Okay."

"I really hate having to say this," says Butch. "It really isn't coming from me."

"Then from who?"

"This is from Bob."

"Oh, great."

"Well, he does have a shred of a point," says Butch. "But I know what the real motivation is here."

"Are you going to tell me?"

"He says he's getting complaints about you hanging around at the curing range so much."

"And I can guess where those complaints came from."

"That I don't know."

"That ass Ed Harris."

"Well, I had to mention it."

"I'm assuming the shred of a point you mentioned is the fact that I'm fucking off?"

"Yeah."

"Are you having this talk with all of your people who are fucking off?" I ask. "And what about other crews in the shop? Is Bob just having a general crackdown on fucking off? Or, is this directed at me?"

"I'll be honest with you. You were the only one mentioned."

"Because I'm the only one that's violating the race mixing bullshit that these assholes hate so much."

"I can't argue with that assessment."

"The thing is…right now…all we're doing is talking."

"I'm just relaying what Bob said."

"I know. What about Lisa and Israel?"

"Well, they actually work together, so there isn't anything that Bob can do about that."

"I see."

"I'm sorry, Don. I hate what these bastards have me do sometimes."

"I guess I just have to decide if I'm going to listen."

"Just try to watch the time a little," says Butch. "And also realize that Bob is holding me responsible for this. Don't make me lose my job over this shit."

"I just hate this shit where they single someone out and don't deal with everyone the same."

"I know. You're right about that."

"Okay, boss. I'll try to adjust myself some. But they aren't putting me in a prison that others aren't in."

"I hear you. Just stay outta the way of that Ed Harris asshole."

"I'll try, boss."

"I would appreciate it."

"Butch, can ask you something?"

"Sure."

"Do you personally have a problem with it?"

"I'm not sure my opinion matters."

"I just want to know."

"No, it don't make no fucking difference to me."

"Okay, nice to know."

I thought something like this was coming. Ed Harris just loves to get people into trouble. And Bob doesn't like me anyway. And they both seem to have that old way of looking at race. I pushed it too far. I've spent far too much time at Karen's machine. But I just can't seem to stay away. I guess I'll have to find a way now, though. I'll at least cut it down a little. Butch is a good guy. I don't want to risk getting him in trouble.

Chapter 16

Thursday July 8ᵗʰ, 1993

"Hey there, man. Hard at work I see," cracks Karen, as I come to visit her at the curing range, yet again, despite the warning.

I know that people have to be talking. It's definitely unusual for me to be talking to a girl, and so often at that. I just can't seem to stay away now. Maybe Ed Harris is just jealous.

"You always make some crack about how little I do," I say.

"If the shoe fits, wear it."

"Well, it does seem to fit."

"Whatcha been up to?"

"Not much."

"Still reading?"

"Yeah, still reading."

"Good."

"What's going on with you?"

"Nothing special," she says. "Just working, and doing things for the Lord."

"Anything particular that you're doing for the Lord?"

"Well, my mother and I are going to start going into the jail to minister to the women in there."

"Wow…okay," I say, I'm sure, visibly taken aback.

"What? You're surprised by that?"

"Just never met anyone who wanted to go to jail."

"The Lord says that we are to minister to those who are the most messed up."

"The most messed up?" I ask. "I haven't seen that phrase in my reading the bible."

"You know what I mean."

"I guess when you're in jail you do feel pretty well abandoned."

"But God's there for the worst of sinners. I know you've seen that in scripture."

"Yeah, I have."

"We're just preparing ourselves now," she says. "Praying and fasting for strength and wisdom to do this."

"Fasting? What's that? You mean going without eating?"

"Haven't you read anything about fasting? How important it is?"

"I guess I've seen it mentioned, at least in a few places."

"When you want to go to God with something in prayer, it helps to fast."

"What? If I become a Christian I'm not going to be able to eat sometimes? That just may be a deal breaker," I say, laughing. "I love my food."

"Oh, come on man, it's not that bad."

"I'm not sure I understand what it's all about."

"It's just about denying the flesh, so that you can approach God in the Spirit."

"I remember seeing things about fasting in scripture, but it didn't seem as if it was emphasized all that much."

"Fasting is very important. Might want to read again."

"Okay.....but I have read through the New Testament three times already."

"So..... He is getting to you."

"Who?"

"The Lord, silly."

"I don't know," I say. "The bible's just fascinating to me for some reason."

"I keep telling you, that's the Lord working on you."

"Well....maybe."

"He is."

"You know, I'm still fascinated by the verses about women."

"I'm sure you are," she says, rolling her eyes.

"I am, really."

"Okay, if you say so. Which ones?"

"Well, like the one that says that the head of woman is man. I like that," I say, with a smile.

"Oh, you do, huh?"

"And where it says that wives should submit to husbands. That's a good one, too."

"You see everything that talks about women, but you miss the stuff about fasting?"

"I'm just kidding."

"Well, you know that the rest of that passage about wives submitting to husbands says that husbands should love their wives.

Make sure you get it right."

"I know, wives submit and husbands love."

"I have no problem submitting to a man who loves me," she says. "Because if he loves me, really loves me, he'll only do what's best for me anyway. That's why you have to take the whole thing together."

"So, do you believe that the head of woman is man?"

"Yeah, the man is the head of the household. That's what God has ordained."

"Okay, as long as you can handle it."

"God does everything for our own good. He has an order for everything."

"I'm just not sure I could submit to someone else like that."

"But we all must submit to God."

"That's different though," I say. "I'm talking about people."

"Yeah...but when I submit to a future husband, I won't be submitting to him really. I'm only submitting to him because he'll be in God's will. So really, I am submitting to God."

"If you say so."

"But that's the way it is. When you submit to any authority, you're submitting to God, because he ordains everything. He's set everything according to his will."

"Yeah...I see the passages about that. That we should submit to the government, because they're only in power because God has put them there."

"That's right."

"But does that include any government?" I ask. "What about governments that are clearly wrong....or just plain evil? Do we still submit to them?"

"Scripture says that no man is in authority without God putting him there."

"That's a hard one to swallow. Hitler was put there by God? All those people he killed?"

"Well, sometimes God's truth is hard to swallow. But we just have to trust that He knows best."

"I'll have to think on that one a little. I'm not sure there's not some other way of looking at that one."

"We have to make ourselves fit God's word, not the other way around."

"But we have to make sure we know what His word is actually saying, don't we?" I ask.

"Yeah….that's true."

"Hey, changing the subject. The reason I came over here today….uh….I was wondering……uh.."

Suddenly, I'm nervous. I should be. This is the first time I've ever done this.

"Come on man…spit it out."

"It's just hard for me..uh..I was just wondering if maybe you weren't doing anything…..that you may consider going to Kings Dominion with me this Saturday? I know you said you like going there."

"Oh…Don…I don't think so…I…"

"No…uh…I'm sorry…that's okay..," I say, cutting her off.

"Don…it's just…"

"No…my mistake.," I say, trying not to show how crushed I am. I quickly walk away.

"Sorry…."

I'm not even sure why I asked her out really. What am I doing here? We aren't compatible at all. She's this devout Christian. I'm far from that. Almost every dream and desire I have are solidly against the life she leads. I'm trying to get into the drug business, for God's sake. There's just something drawing me to her, though. I'm kind of starting to believe that this is all meant to be somehow. That's probably stupid to think. I don't know. But, well, she's rejected me now. I can't blame her for that.

Chapter 17

Saturday July 10th, 1993

"Hey, man, what's up?" asks Mark, as he lets me into his den.

"I just wondered if you'd be interested in some turkey?"

"Turkey?"

"Yeah, some Wild Turkey!" I say, pulling a bottle of the bourbon from behind my back.

"Damn, is that the only shit you ever want to drink?"

"Gets you there fast."

"Okay, man, let me get some Coke or something to mix it with."

"Alright, hurry up. I have some troubles I need to drink away."

"Alright, here we go," says Mark, setting down some glasses and a bottle of Coke.

"Listen, you didn't have any plans, did you? I don't want to impose on you."

"Fuck no. I wasn't doing anything. Just going to watch TV and drink a few beers."

"Okay."

"So, what are these troubles you need to drink away?" asks Mark, as he pours the first round.

"It's just this girl, Karen."

"Karen?"

"Yeah, the black girl at work that got me reading the bible and all that shit."

"Yeah, I remember. So, what's going on with her?"

"I asked her to go to Kings Dominion today and she said no."

"So?"

"So, I wanted her to go with me."

"Are you getting wrapped up in this chick or something?"

"Well, there is something special about her."

"Okay, but there are plenty of girls out there. So, what if she turned you down? You're not a teenager, dude."

"You don't understand," I say, shaking my head.

"I guess I fucking don't."

"Haven't you ever noticed that I've never had a girlfriend?"

"Well, yeah, but I thought maybe you were just gay or

something."

"Funny. No, I'm not gay," I say. "I'm just shy. Severely fucking shy. Socially retarded kind of shy."

"Shy? Well, I little I guess. But you're pretty much a loud fucker around here."

"It's really mainly with girls. I just can't seem to approach girls at all. I just freeze up and end up looking like a fool."

"Oh…okay. Didn't know."

"And I'm finally talking to a girl, and like her, and feel like she likes me, and she fucking rejects me."

"So…you're how old? And never had a girlfriend? Sorry, just trying to get my mind around this one."

"Yeah, that's right, I'm a thirty year old virgin. Never even kissed a girl. Nothing."

"Damn."

"Listen, man, you won't tell anyone, will you?" I ask.

"Who the fuck would I tell?"

"It's not like she'd have sex with me anyway, with all that religious shit."

"So, you were hoping that she liked you and that this could be some sort of relationship?"

"Yeah, I just want to be fucking normal. Why do I have to be so goddamn dysfunctional when it comes to women?"

No one really knows the torture I've went through all of these years. I've wanted a girl so much. But no matter what I try, I simply cannot get past this shyness. Believe it or not, but Karen is the closest I've come. I've talked to her more than I have any girl. Maybe that's why I'm so hung up on her. Maybe I'm just that desperate.

"I can't believe I didn't know this," says Mark. "You did a damn good job of hiding it. But you should have told me about this a long time ago."

"What the fuck for?"

"Listen, man, it ain't hard getting pussy. Shit, if you want to, we can go down to Ronnie's and get us both a little something right now."

"Sure, that's no problem.….for you. But what about me?"

"What about you, what?"

"I won't be able to talk to anyone. I'll just freeze up like I always do."

I tried going to a bar in Raleigh one time. I couldn't even bring myself to walk in the door. I just knew that I was going to be awkward and make a fool out of myself. I have no problem going to Ronnie's to talk about Israel and Tommy or to buy pot plants, but to go with the intention of meeting women…..well….I just don't see the point. I know what the result will be.

"This shit we're drinking now is just the thing you need for that. Believe me, you get a little liquored up and you'll be fine," says Mark. "Especially if we can manage to find us a couple of skanks, which shouldn't be too hard at Ronnie's."

"I don't know. Maybe, I don't do all that well in crowds. I feel like everyone's watching me or something."

"You'll be fine. Especially fueled by the Turkey," he says, holding up the bottle.

"I guess….if you say so."

"I just had no idea that you were having such a hard time with this shit. Like I said, I just thought you were gay or something," says Mark as we drive the short distance to Ronnie's.

"I don't know. Whatever caused it happened around the 6th or 7th grade. I just went into a shell and never fucking came out."

"Like I said, I never saw it."

"It wasn't with you guys in the neighborhood. It was more at school and more with girls."

"I just figured you had no game. I didn't know that there was something deeper going on."

"Whatever it was, it started after the fifth grade I think. I was so loud and disruptive in fifth grade that Mr. Tomlin had to put me way in back of the class, at a table all by myself. So, it happened after that, I guess."

"Tomlin….isn't he the guy who ate that sandwich that had been covered with ants?"

"Yeah, that's him. He did that in front of us in my class."

"So, you don't know why you're this way?" asks Mark.

"No, I don't know. It may have been the fact that I had to get glasses around the 6th or 7th grade. You know, I used to have those really nerdy horned rim things."

"Yeah."

"But I remember liking them back then."

"You must have, because you kept wearing them all through high school."

"But I didn't want to keep wearing them."

"Then why did you?"

"It's the fucking shyness. I don't like making changes about myself. I feel like people are noticing me too much."

"Even if it's a positive change?"

"I know it makes no sense, but that's the way it is. There are so many choices that I would have made differently, if it weren't for this fucking shyness."

"I know that you never seemed to want to go out when I said something," says Mark. "I just thought you weren't interested."

"No, I was. It was just that I knew it wasn't going to do any good. I'd just be stiff and frozen like I always am."

"I would have tried harder if I'd known."

"That's alright. I'm not sure anyone could have changed what was going on."

"Well….I don't know."

"Speaking of things I couldn't change," I say. "You have to remember my bowl haircut?"

"Yeah, but we all had one when we were younger."

"But I kept my bowl until I was finished with the 11th grade. I knew it made me look like a fucking nerdy geek, but I just couldn't bring myself to change it, until then. Even then, it was so hard to do. I almost couldn't tell Cary, you know, the barber, what I wanted. And even after I did it, I was so self-conscious for a while. I even hated it when people complimented me on it."

No one knows the shit I've gone through. There are so many little ways that my condition has affected me through the years. There are so many ways that I've had to alter my life to compensate for my shyness. I don't even think shyness is the right word for it. Shyness seems to minimize the impact somehow. It is a condition. It's a life altering condition. There are so many things that I could have done or would have done if it weren't for this shit. I actually think my life would be profoundly different if it weren't for this.

"I just had no idea, man," says Mark. "I had no idea you were going through this shit."

"I'm not sure if anyone really knows how I struggle with this," I say. "My parents of course notice things, I'm sure. But I doubt they know just how fucked up my life is."

"Man, your life is far from fucked up."

"You know, I'm somewhat comfortable being different now. I accept some of it. But I want a woman. I need a woman."

"And you'll get one tonight. And least some pussy. At least that'll make you realize that women find you fuckable."

"Fuck! I won't even know what to do."

"It'll come naturally," says Mark. "Besides, whoever the slut is, she'll be wasted herself, so what'll she know? Just stick your dick in and pump. And that's true whether it's her mouth or her pussy or any other orifice you may be interested in."

"Well, here we are," I say, as we pull up to Ronnie's place.

"Shit, ain't hardly anyone here. Where are all the sluts?" I say, as we come in.

"Hey, man, cool it. Just give it time. Someone will come along."

"I want some pussy," I say, the Wild Turkey now taking full effect.

"What the fuck? Don in here again? I need to give you a fucking prize," says Ronnie.

"Pussy. I'll take pussy."

"You'll have to handle that part on your own. What can I get you ladies?"

"A bottle of Jack and two glasses," responds Mark.

"Where's the best place to sit to get some pussy?" I ask.

"Damn, man, slow down. Uh...how about that table over there?" says Mark, pointing to a booth.

"Yeah...by the window, so we can see the skanks when they come in."

"Yeah....hey....try to tone that down a little. Most skanks don't want to be called skanks, or sluts."

"Fuck, there ain't no skanks in here yet anyway."

"I know...but maybe you need to get in the habit of not saying pussy and skank every two seconds."

"Oh...skanks don't like hearing us say we want some pussy?" I ask.

"No, it takes maybe a little more finesse than that. At least with most women it does."

"Finesse....okay."

Like I know the first thing about finesse, considering the state I'm in.

"What would Karen think if she saw you now?"

"Fuck Karen! I don't give a shit."

"So, you've never had any sort of girlfriend? Nothing?"

"I can count the times on one hand where girls even showed the slightest interest in me," I say. "But I was probably imagining all of that."

"Tell me about them."

"I think the one I remember the most was this time our church youth group went to a hockey game. Coming back, this girl, Beth, asked if she could lay her head on my shoulder."

"And you didn't let her."

"No, I let her. But with my fucked up self-esteem I never did anything about it. I just assumed she wanted somewhere to lay her head. I didn't think it meant anything."

"Well, it's not like you could've done anything in the back of the church bus," says Mark.

"No, I know that. I mean I never asked her if she was interested or anything like that."

"How old were you when this happened?"

"It was somewhere around the seventh grade, I think."

"Yeah, it most definitely meant something," says Mark. "That was a definite sign. She liked you."

"I know. I know that now. Too late.....but I know it."

I've always wondered if that would have made a difference. Would I have conquered the shyness if something happened with Beth back then? Would I have felt worthy of the attention of girls? I kind of believe that this was like a vicious cycle. The longer it went on, the deeper it got. The more time went by without me having a girlfriend or anything the weirder I thought I seemed to people. I just got deeper and deeper into my shell.

"Any other girls that have thrown themselves at you?" asks Mark.

"Yeah, there was this girl a few years later. It was down at the pool at the community center. I was probably a junior or a senior at the time. But she kept following me around the pool. Talking to me. I knew she was interested."

"And you didn't do anything?"

"No, I figured that once she saw me out of the pool with those fucking glasses on, that she wouldn't be interested anymore."

"Did you know who she was?"

"Didn't recognize her," I say. "I'm not sure who she was. I hoped to see her again, but never did. I don't think she was from Raymond."

In my typical fashion, once I thought about it a little I realized that I should have handled that differently. I should have talked to her. I should have gotten her phone number. I knew she was interested. And maybe the glasses wouldn't have mattered to her. Maybe she wore glasses. But once the moment passed, it was lost.

"Any others?" asks Mark.

"Not really. My senior year this girl Ann asked me to go to the prom with her. But I had no interest in going to that damn prom. I think she just wanted someone to go with."

"But she may have been interested."

"Fuck….look there….there's a couple hot ones right there," I say, leering out the window.

"Shit, that's Cheryl and Gina. Cheryl and I used to see each other."

"Did I ever meet her?"

"Don't think so," says Mark. "Hey, Cheryl, how you been doing?"

"Hey, Mark. Doing fine, I guess," says Cheryl, sounding not exactly thrilled to see Mark.

"What are you two up to?" asks Mark.

"Just looking to have a little fun," responds Cheryl, looking around.

She obviously wants to have fun with someone other than Mark.

"You know, baby, I've really missed you," says Mark.

"Well…you know…I just need someone with a little ambition. Someone who actually wants to get out of their mother's house."

"Hehehehehehe, shit…hehehehe….she's got you pegged, man," I say, laughing.

"I do, don't I?" responds Cheryl. "I'm Cheryl."

"Don."

"And this is Gina."

"Hey, Don, how you doin?" asks Gina. "What's up, Mark?"

"Gina….that's a fucking pretty name," I say.

"Well….hehehehe….thank you. I'm glad I have a fucking pretty name."

"Yes….fucking pretty…..fucking pretty you are," I say. "Why don't you girls sit down?"

"Don't mind if I do," says Gina, sitting close to me.

Damn. Is it really this easy? Gina's a hot little thing. I can't believe I actually invited her to sit down. Liquor is the magical elixir for all that ails me, apparently.

"This isn't exactly the night I had in mind," says Cheryl.

"Listen, why don't we all go to my place?" proposes Mark.

"We can take the bottle. We've also got beer and some Wild Turkey there. Let's have our own little party."

"What the fuck do you have in mind?" asks Cheryl.

"We'll...who knows....maybe that," responds Mark, with a grin.

"What?"

"Fuck....or fucking, of course..," says Mark. "Just for old time's sake."

"In your fucking dreams," says Cheryl. "Gina, let's get the fuck outta here, okay?"

"No, why don't we go," says Gina. "I'd like to get to know Don better. He seems nice. This place is dead anyway."

"Yeah, come on," says Mark. "I was just kidding about that. Let's just go and catch up on things. I've thought about you a lot, sugar."

"Yeah....sure you have."

"Let's just go to my place and have a good time. Let's just see what happens."

"What do you say, Gina?" asks Cheryl.

"Sure...let's go," responds Gina. "You're the one who needs convincing."

"Fuck.....why not, I guess," says Cheryl.

She still doesn't sound all that thrilled.

"Okay, it's settled," says Mark. "Let's roll on outta here."

"Where the fuck are we going?" I ask. "We just got here."

"We're taking the girls back to my place" says Mark, whispering.

"Both of them?"

"Of course, both of them."

"Gina's kind of hot," I say.

"I know, and she said she wants to get to know you better."

"So...we getting some pussy?" I ask.

"I wouldn't be surprised. But play it cool, please. I'm on thin ice with Cheryl."

"Okay....coooool."

Gina wants to get to know me better? Why? Is it really this easy? Am I actually going to get my first taste of pussy tonight?

"So...here we are," says Mark, as we all make our way into the den.

"Yep...just as it's always been," responds Cheryl. "But maybe even more shit."

"His mom is one of those fucking hoarders," I offer.

"You've got to be shitting me, Don," says Cheryl, sarcastically. "I wasn't aware of that."

"No...I shit you not.....she's mentally ill."

"Why does she save all of this shit?" asks Gina.

"Don's right, she is mentally ill," says Mark. "Let me go get two more glasses."

"So, Don...what do you do?" asks Gina.

"I'm an instrumentation tech...uh....down at the mill."

"So, at least one of you is making something of yourself," says Cheryl.

"Well....yeah....but we're working on a business together, but, uh, I can't tell you what it is," I say, holding my finger up to my lips."

"I'll bet you can't," says Cheryl.

"No...I really can't."

"Okay....here you go, ladies," says Mark, as he gives the ladies each a glass. "And there's beer in that fridge right there. Everyone help themselves."

"Don was telling me some cock and bull story about you two starting some business or something. What's that shit all about?" asks Cheryl.

"Uh....he what? No....he's just drunk...maybe he's talking about that time we were cutting grass....I don't know."

Yeah, I was talking about grass alright.

"Well....didn't sound like that...but anyway...I figured it was just bullshit," says Cheryl. "He's just trying to make you look good."

"Listen, baby...can't you just forget that shit and let's just have a good time?"

"Well, the evidence of your success is everywhere in here," says Cheryl. "Big businessman, you are."

"Let's just go to my room. Talk a little," says Mark. "Those two will be alright out here."

"No...I can't leave her alone with him," says Cheryl. "I don't know him. She doesn't know him."

"He won't hurt her or anything. He's a nice guy. Besides...we'll be right in there. The very next room."

"Yeah...I remember where the bedroom is."

"I know you do."

"Bedrooms are good for talking."

"And other things."

"So, you want to take a nap with me?" asks Cheryl.

"You're funny."

"Gina...do you mind if we go to Mark's room for a while?" asks Cheryl. "I hate to leave you out here with Don....but..."

"No problem," says Gina. "I can handle this character just fine."

"Yeah....handle me baby," I say. "Handle me good."

Where is this shit coming from?

"You're feeling pretty good there buddy, aren't you?" asks Mark.

"I'll take care of him," says Gina. "You two go do whatever it is you're gonna do."

"Okay....you two have fun," says Mark as he grabs the bottle of Jack. "After you, baby."

"So...Don...it's just you and me now..." says Gina. "What am I gonna do with you?"

"Anything you want."

"Anything, huh?"

"Am I gonna get some pussy?" I ask, getting right to the point.

I really cannot believe I just asked her that.

"Damn, man....not shy, are we?"

"No....God...I'm sorry....fuck...I didn't mean it."

"No...it's cool, man," says Gina. "No problem in coming right out and saying what you want. Whether you get it or not is another story."

"I'm all talk though.....that's it. And the talk's only because I'm drunk."

"What do you mean that you're all talk?"

"Damn it....I've never had pussy....never fucked...never been fucked....never kissed...never nothing....and I'm fucking thirty years old....pretty pathetic..."

"No....not really," she says, none too convincingly. "If you don't mind me asking, what's the problem?"

"I'm just fucking shy with girls. Can't talk to them. Just a big fucking mess around them."

"Shy? You don't seem so shy to me," she says, laughing.

"It's just the liquor. I told Mark tonight and he said he'd fix it. He said we'd find us a couple of skanky sluts and fuck the shit out of them. Well, I may have added the part about fucking the shit out of them."

"And we're the skanky sluts?"

"No…no….of course not….no…"

"You know, Don…..I'm not a skank….or a slut….but…I do love to fuck," she says, as she climbs onto my lap.

"Well, that's nice."

"Shouldn't I have the right to go out and just get me a little dick from time to time?"

"A little dick?"

"Some dick….how about that? I should have the right to go get me some dick every now and then. Cause you know I want a big dick if I can get it."

"Mine's probably about average."

"Average is better than small."

"Of course, I've never gotten another opinion on it."

"That's right. No girl has ever seen it."

"No….no one."

"Let me have a peek."

"Help yourself."

"I can tell you right now…..from what I feel…..just sitting on top of you…..that you feel pretty big to me."

"Does size matter?"

"I know you guys get all hung up on that. So, you wanna know the truth?"

"Yeah."

"Size does matter. You have to at least be able to fill my pussy. Know what I mean?"

"Well…."

"And I don't think you'd have any problem in that category."

"I guess not."

"Don, I'm fucking horny as hell. Can you tell?"

"Yeah….I can."

"And I think you're as cute as hell, with that shyness and all, so innocent."

"I guess you can tell that you turn me on."

"So…..the million dollar question…….wanna fuck?"

"Yeah….I wanna fuck really bad."

"I want you to fuck me, Don. Like you said….fuck the shit outta me."

"But I don't know how to fuck the shit outta you."

"That's alright….I've always wanted to teach someone," she says, as she unzips my pants. She gazes down at my rock hard dick. "Ummm…..yeah……that'll fill me up just fine."

"Are you gonna suck my dick?"

"Is that what you want?"

"I want it all."

"You want it all, huh?"

"Yes."

"Does that include tickling my clit with your tongue?" she asks. "I really need that."

"If you tell me what a clit is."

"Yeah, I'll show you where everything's at."

"I can't wait to have my face buried between those beautiful thighs of yours."

"Am I gonna be able to handle you, man?" she asks. "You must have a whole lot of pent up shit just waiting to explode."

"Well, if you can't handle the job.....I may have to find someone else."

"Damn, man....you're coming out of you shell tonight. That's funny. No, I'm the one who's gonna be your first."

"I am so ready."

"Well, let's get to fucking and sucking and anything else our little hearts desire."

"Yes.....please."

I cannot believe it was this easy. I should have told Mark about this years ago. I could never have done this on my own. And of course, the Wild Turkey was the biggest help of all. I cannot believe that I'm fucking a girl as hot as Gina. Why would she want me? Is it just the alcohol? Does she just fuck anyone she comes across? Well, the important thing is that I'm fucking a girl, a hot girl. The ice is broken. The ice is fucking shattered.

Chapter 18

Tuesday July 20ᵗʰ, 1993

"Come in, Don Higgins...come in, Mr. Higgins," says Butch, over the radio.

"Go ahead, boss," I reply.

"Don, could you please look at Frame 1, they say they can't get it to purge."

"10-4," I say.

I reluctantly head towards Frame 1, which happens to be beside the curing range. I've been trying my best to avoid Karen since that day she turned me down. And besides that, I haven't felt much like discussing the bible, considering my little encounter with Gina. And that seems like all Karen and I usually talk about.

"Hey, man....uh...you gonna say hi or what?" asks Karen, as I try to slip by unnoticed.

"Hey, Karen....what's going on?" I reply.

"Nothing new. Haven't seen you in a while though."

It has been quite the feat to avoid her. I've been avoiding the breakroom when I know she may be in there. I've been trying to avoid this part of the plant as much as possible. It hasn't been easy.

"Just busy, I guess," I say.

"You....busy?"

"Well....."

"Listen....did I hurt your feelings or something when I said I wouldn't go to Kings Dominion with you?" she asks. "It's pretty obvious that you've been avoiding me."

"Well....I was a little disappointed, I guess. But that's okay."

"Don, you didn't let me explain. I just don't know you well enough to go that far away. But...if you were to ask me to go out somewhere around here.....then...."

"So....are you saying that we could go out? It would just have to be closer?"

"Yeah...it could be possible," she says, smiling.

"Okay....uh...how about pizza and putt putt.... or I don't know.....whatever?"

Putt putt....where did that come from?

"Okay...when?" she asks.

"This Saturday?"

"Okay."

"Great. Say seven?"

"Okay…I'll meet you in front of the diner," she says. "Is that alright?"

"Sure….it's a date."

"Don…I don't really go out with guys. You're the first since I broke up with my boyfriend after I was saved."

"Why me, then? Why am I the first?"

"I don't know…there's just something different about you. I just think the Lord's doing something in your life. I just like you."

"Well….I don't know," I say, trying my best not to betray the truth. "I'm not sure how much the Lord's doing in my life."

If she only knew that I just lost my virginity in a drunken tryst with some girl I had just met.

"No, I can see it," she says.

"I am still reading."

That sounded kind of feeble. But I do have a fascination with scripture. I am still reading the bible. I'm not sure why really.

"That's good. Have you run across any other scriptures that you have a problem with?" she asks. "Wanna stir up any trouble?"

"Listen, I wasn't trying to be difficult when I raised those issues before. I just question what I'm told, or what I read. That's just me."

That's one positive quality that I attribute to the life I've been forced to lead because of the shyness. I'm seriously independently minded. I absolutely cannot stand to just go with the crowd. I am very far from being a sheep being led by the nose to slaughter.

"Okay….so is there anything that's giving you a problem?" she asks.

"There is one thing."

"What?"

"Well….this one may just be a dealbreaker."

"Another dealbreaker," she says, rolling her eyes. "What is it now?"

"Well, the bible says that everyone who serves the Lord will be persecuted."

"Yeah…that's right."

"So, why would I want to knowingly do something that'll get me persecuted?" I ask, with a laugh.

"Being persecuted means that you're sharing in the suffering of

Christ. You're a part of Him. And those who suffer in this world are not a part of this world anymore. We are a part of Christ. He suffered, we must suffer."

"But is that really happening to anyone? I know many Christians....and I can tell you that many of them...no... most of them, are not getting persecuted at all."

"Well...many Christians are going to dead churches. And if they're going to dead churches, they won't be persecuted."

"Dead churches?"

"Churches where the Spirit isn't present."

"So...they won't be persecuted because they aren't really a part of Christ, they're still a part of the world?"

"The world won't persecute one of its own."

"Okay...."

"The bible says that not everyone who calls on the name of the Lord will be saved," she says. "There are many false believers and dead churches out there."

"But who decides which churches are dead and which aren't?"

"You can just feel it. The Spirit is either there or it isn't."

"I would say that the church I grew up in was probably what you're talking about. I think that's why I sense such a difference in you, as opposed to what I was used to there."

"I hope my life does show a difference. I hope people can tell that I'm full of the Spirit of God."

"So.....we're persecuted because Christ was persecuted," I say. "And we're supposed to be like Christ?"

"Yes...having the Spirit of God means that we can be like Christ in every way."

"But most Christians aren't getting persecuted like Christ did?"

"Here we go again."

"No, really, who's getting beaten or killed or thrown in prison?" I ask. "Are they all part of a dead church? Are they all false believers? Are you getting beaten or thrown into prison?"

"But there are other forms of persecution. Some are getting persecuted in a way that you may not be able to see."

"But you would think that someone would be getting the worst of it."

"But some do. Especially in countries that aren't Christian."

"But it says that everyone will be persecuted," I say. "No exceptions."

"But for some of us the time may not have come yet."

"But for most it never comes."

"Then God has blessed them."

"How would it be a blessing to avoid persecution if persecution is supposed to be some sort of honor?" I ask.

"I don't know....I'm really not concerned with it actually," she says, getting obviously annoyed.

"Okay. But it just seems like another way where things aren't happening the way scripture says they would."

"Everything can't happen all at once though. There are seasons for this and seasons for that."

"Sorry for getting you upset."

"No, it's alright."

"I just question what I'm told."

"And there's nothing wrong with that."

"Well...I guess I better get to the Frame," I say. "They're actually down over there. I shouldn't be talking like this when I actually have something to do."

"Alright man, get to work then."

"Alright, talk to you later."

"And I'll see you Saturday."

"Yeah, that's right. I can't wait."

"Bye, Don."

So, she does want to go out. Why do I even want to now? I feel more normal after the night with Gina. I feel as if I finally belong, at least in some small way. I still have my doubts. Was it just the alcohol? What does Gina think of me now? Could I do the same thing now, except without drinking? Could I get a woman without being under the influence? I don't know. My condition is deep and complicated.

And then there's Karen. Would she still want to go out with me if she knew what I did? She's only going because she thinks the Lord is doing some sort of work in my life. Is that even true? It is true that I'm being drawn to her for some reason. I'm just not sure why. Is that the same as being drawn to the Lord? Because that seems to be happening, too. I shouldn't even be considering going out with her. She's so far from the type of girl that suits me. As odd as this sounds, I think Gina is actually more my speed. I just can't seem to leave Karen alone though.

Chapter 19

Saturday August 7ᵗʰ, 1993

"See what I'm saying?" asks Mark, as we stand in the woods beside our tomato plants.

"Shit, what are they doing?" I ask. "Clearing to make a road or something?"

"Looks like it. You know that Barber's wanted to develop this land for years."

"Yeah, I remember when the plans were in the newspaper."

"Well…that must be what this is."

"Damn, and that place they're clearing isn't but maybe a hundred or so feet from the plants."

"I know."

"Just our fucking luck…we plant some weed, and Barber all of a sudden decides he's ready to start building something back here," I say.

"What should we do?"

"Fuck…they aren't doing all that well anyway. You been keeping up with the watering?"

"Yeah…I think so."

"You think so?"

"Yeah, when it hasn't been raining I've been watering them."

"We might as well destroy them," I say. "These ain't worth getting in trouble over anyway."

"We can try some more. Use another spot?"

"I don't know, man…maybe this is a sign or something."

"So, you don't want to do it now?" asks Mark, annoyed. "Just like that?"

"I don't know…it's just stupid. I got carried away."

"You sure did. You were the one acting like we were starting some drug empire or something. Now you don't want to do it."

"Yeah…I know…I guess I'm just so desperate to do something exciting or different that the risk was worth it."

"We can still do it."

"No…I'm looking at things differently now, I guess," I say.

"At least as far as this is concerned."

"It's that girl at work isn't it? You're getting religious on me."

"I don't know…maybe…who knows."

"What would she think of you getting drunk and fucking Gina? I mean, you lost your virginity in a drunken fuck with a bar hopping slut of a woman. I bet she'd love to know that."

"Well, there's no reason she should know that."

I should tell her. I know I have to at some point. I just don't want to screw this up.

"Are you actually a couple now?" asks Mark.

"Well….we've been out a couple times."

"But no brown sugar?"

"That ain't gonna happen," I say. "I already know that."

"Good thing Gina busted your cherry for you then."

"Gina is hot. I'll have to admit that was one great night," I say. "We fucked like three times. If you count the time she let me fuck her in her mouth."

"Sounds like you wouldn't mind taking another ride on her."

"I never dreamed my first time would be so good. It really did come naturally to me."

"Well, most of us experience our first fuck with some equally inexperienced teenage girl. You were lucky enough to fuck a pro for your first."

"You didn't pay her, did you?" I ask.

"I don't mean pro in that sense. I just mean that Gina has been around the block a whole lot of times. She really knows what she's doing."

"She does that. Boy, the things she did with her mouth."

"So, why are you messing around with this religious chick?"

"I don't know….I just like her."

There really is something there. We're really hitting it off. It's really starting to feel as if it's meant to be or something.

"Gina is more your kinda girl, believe me," says Mark.

"No, I don't think so. There's more to this than you think."

"If you say so."

"I do."

"Why don't you take Karen to Ronnie's," suggests Mark. "Maybe you'd run into Gina. That'd be good."

"Sure….yeah…..she'd love that. Redneck bar…and then some woman saying she fucked me….after I already told Karen I'm a virgin."

"I would pay to watch that show."

"You sir…are a sadistic bastard."

"I just enjoy being entertained by the pain and embarrassment of others," says Mark.

"Yeah…I know."

"Alright…let's rip these bastards out of the ground so we can get out of this fucking heat."

"And so ends the narcotics empire," I say.

"Yeah, in your mind, maybe."

"What are you two up to…strolling around in the woods?" asks Diane, as Mark and I come into Mark's den.

"We were just seeing what they're doing back there," responds Mark.

"Yeah…it looks like Barber's finally starting on his little project," I say.

"Hate to see it. Enjoy having the woods behind the house. But I guess he has the right to use his own land," says Diane.

"But those aren't going to be houses. He's going to build townhouses and some high rise condo down there at the marina," says Mark.

"Yeah, I know that's what the original plan was for. Your father was active in trying to prevent that when it was first proposed," says Diane.

"But the town council approved it anyway," I say.

"It's all about the money. More taxes for the town," says Mark.

"Well, too, Barber's pretty powerful in this town. They're going to take care of one of their own," I say.

"Yep….nothing we can do now," says Diane.

"Changing the subject….but you know, Mark…there's an opening down at the plant. It's an instrumentation job," I say.

"But you know I don't have any experience."

"Listen…with my position down there, I believe I can get them to take you on as an apprentice."

"He needs to do something," says Diane.

"I don't know."

"What don't you fucking know? You're going to have to get out of this house at some point. Don's offering you a great opportunity. Spots don't open up down there all that often," says Diane, as she leaves.

"And it is instrumentation," I say. "We're the guys who do less work than anyone else."

"Yeah…you have mentioned how easy you have it down there."

"It's a cake job…most of the time.

"Well…okay…what do I have to do?"

"I'll set it up. I'll talk to Butch…my boss…and see if he'll talk to you."

"Alright man…appreciate it."

"That'll be cool, if we could work together."

"Would you be training me?"

"Yeah…for the most part."

"Cool."

Chapter 20

Later the same day.

"Well, that was pretty good," I say, as Karen and I make our way into my house.

"Yeah, I would say that's the best seafood I've ever had," says Karen.

"Cheap, too. Don't know how they do it."

"I know...really."

"Wanna watch a little TV?"

"Yeah, see if there are any good movies on."

"Okay....well.....what about a western?" I suggest. "This one's pretty good."

"John Wayne?"

"Who else?"

"John Wayne was the man!"

"This is the one with the boys in it, where he trains them to be cowboys."

"Yeah...I love this one."

"Actually....before it starts...there is something I'd like to tell you," I say.

"What?"

"Well...I went ahead and accepted the Lord."

"Praise Jesus.....thank you Lord! I knew you would. He's been calling you."

"I just realized that everything I read just rings true somehow. I just know that this is the right thing."

"I'm so happy. Thank you Lord!" she says, clasping her hands together, looking up.

"I struggled for a while. I was reading all this time. And like I said, tears came to my eyes at some points," I say. "But it wasn't until last Sunday. I was over at my parents. I picked up this church magazine. I started looking through it. It just felt so comfortable somehow. I just knew that this is the path I want to be on."

I guess that was just the confirmation of everything that's been happening. This whole thing just seems so pre-ordained somehow. It wasn't a miraculous event like some people experience, but nevertheless, I know that this is the path for me.

"Well, praise Jesus," she says. "God works in all kinds of ways."

"I mean it wasn't like it was with your father, where God spoke to me or anything. I just all of a sudden got this feeling like this was the way I wanted to go."

"Well, it's like I've been telling you, the Lord's been working on you for a while now."

"There's actually another thing I'd like to say, too."

"What?"

"Well, one test that I used to see if I really believed, was if I was going to still be a Christian if things didn't work out with you."

"Work out with me?"

"Yeah, if this didn't turn into something permanent, would I still keep seeking the Lord."

"We've just been going out and having fun."

"But I think I'm falling in love with you."

"What?"

"I'm just thinking of you all the time. I'm so happy when we're together."

"Oh, Don.....I can't believe this."

"I know it might not be what you want to hear."

"I'm not looking for a man. I was waiting on the Lord to send me someone."

"Well, maybe he has," I say. "Remember how we first met?"

"Yeah, you dropped down from that ladder."

"An angel sent from above?"

"So, you're an angel now," she says, laughing.

"You know what I mean. Maybe God was sending me into your life."

"You are the only guy I've even gone out with since I was saved."

"And you said that was because you knew that God was doing something in my life."

"And he has."

"Are you feeling anything at all for me?"

"Yeah...I have to admit it. There's something special about you. I just wasn't ready for this."

"I love you. And I love the Lord. What more could there be?"

"I love you too, Don. I wasn't ready for this right now. But I can't deny the truth."

"You've made me so happy."

"I'm happy, too."

We share our first kiss.

"Everything's just falling into place," I say.

"Okay...now that you're saved, it's time for you to start going to church."

"Yeah...I guess it is."

"And...because of the other thing, I think it's time you met my father."

"The other thing?"

"That you love me. I mean that we love each other."

"That's right. Get it right," I say.

"I just have to warn you though."

"Warn me of what?"

"You'd better read up on your New Testament before you see my father. He might give you a quiz."

"That's funny."

"You think I'm joking? No, my father's tough. A true man of God. You'd better be prepared."

"I can't wait," I say, rolling my eyes.

"It'll be fine. Just be ready."

"It's time for the movie to start."

"John Wayne is the man!"

"I like John Wayne, but I really prefer Clint Eastwood."

"Is this gonna be our first fight," she says, smiling. "Because I'll go to the mat for my man, John Wayne."

"Clint just has a darker side to him in his movies," I say. "That's why I like him."

"Clint's alright, but John Wayne is...."

"I know.....John Wayne is the man."

"That's right. You admitted it. Now let's watch the movie."

It's hard to explain how this all happened really. I just believe. And I know that I'll continue to believe. It wasn't miraculous. There was nothing special that happened. I just reached a point where I just knew that I want to start following the Lord. It just feels as if all the pieces were laid out for me. How Gina fits into that I do not know. Maybe that was just so I knew how much I need a good godly woman? Maybe just another sign to show me that the road I'm going down is wrong? I don't necessarily buy into this whole wicked sinner in need of being saved. I just know that the path I was going down wasn't a productive one. And this path just feels right somehow.

Chapter 21

Monday August 9th, 1993

"What the hell is this?" I ask, as Jim and I walk up on Roger and Jerry.

"Uh…it's called working. May want to try it some time," responds Roger.

"No, thanks," I say.

"We're just uncrating a new machine," says Jerry.

"What? Is this that prototype bleach range I've been hearing about?" I ask.

"Yeah, is this the wonder machine that's gonna save the plant?" adds Jim.

"I don't know what the hell it is. Just know that we were told to get it uncrated," says Roger.

"Maybe the plant's alright after all," says Jerry. "If they're buying machines."

"Machines don't mean anything. They can always ship them to another plant. Or sell them," responds Jim, dismissively.

"Hey, look out there in the parking lot," I say.

"Boonie has his head buried in that trash can," says Roger.

"Always scrounging for aluminum cans," I say.

"He's always on the side of the road, too," says Jerry. "Like some homeless dude."

"Anything for a buck," I say.

"Look…hehe….what's happening?" asks Jerry, laughing.

"What the hell is he doing?" I ask.

"It's like he's struggling with something," adds Jim.

"Oh my fucking God….look! It's a goddamn possum," exclaims Roger.

"It's got him!" I say.

"Nope, he's getting the upper hand," says Jim, as we observe the unbelievable spectacle of Boonie furiously beating the possum against the side of the building.

"This is so fucking funny," I say.

"Thing is…wonder how many times that's happened to him?" asks Roger.

"As much as he goes into trash cans, it has to have happened before…..crazy ass," I say. "Racoon, skunk, something."

"He doesn't know anyone saw him," says Roger.

"Here comes Ray to investigate," says Jerry.

"Ray's saying, 'What seems to be the problem here?'" I say.

"Now…why the hell is Boonie giving that thing to Ray?" asks Roger.

"And why the hell is Ray putting it in his truck?" I ask.

"A little possum stew perhaps?" asks Jerry.

"And get ready for the possum cap," I add.

"Yeah, Ray is to roadkill, what Boonie is to aluminum cans," adds Jim.

"Damn…what a place we live in," I say, shaking my head.

"Never a dull moment," says Jim.

"So, Don…you and Karen?" asks Roger.

"What?" I respond. I guess the questions were bound to come at some point.

"The whole plant knows that you're seeing each other," says Roger.

"Well…okay…yeah," I say.

"Why haven't you said anything?" asks Jerry.

"I don't know. I mean, you know how things are. Some people aren't all that fond of the whole interracial dating deal," I say. "Just wasn't any point in advertising it. It's our business."

"I've heard more shit from some of the black guys than from whites. Actually, I haven't heard a thing from any whites," says Roger.

"I'm just curious…but who are the black guys that have a problem with it?" I ask.

"Israel and David."

"They're just jealous because you have her and they don't," says Jerry. "Fuck em."

"But David's married and Israel's seeing Lisa. What the fuck is their damn problem?" I ask.

I really have a problem with things like this. Why would they have a problem with my seeing Karen when they already have women?

"I don't think it's about them wanting to get with her or anything like that. It's just that you're intruding into their territory," explains Jim

"See? Blacks are sometimes the worst racists there are," says

Jerry. "Israel wants to fuck white women but he doesn't want you with a black girl."

"Do you understand how fucking stupid that sounds?" asks Jim. "Israel is fucking Lisa, but he's racist?"

"Well, I think he is," says Jerry.

"I think part of it's that you're not exactly known as a ladies' man. They just wonder what you have that they don't," says Roger. "More jealousy than racism."

"It just amazes them that she would have the audacity to prefer you over them," says Jim.

"I'm surprised that there hasn't been more shit from whites than there has been," I say. "Because you know that this is that one line that many whites still don't want crossed. They've somewhat accepted everything else, but the mixing of the races is not permitted."

"Who's given you shit about it?" asks Roger.

"Butch said something to me some time back," I say.

"Butch?" asks Roger.

"No, he was just relaying a message from Bob. Said I was spending too much time at her machine. It was really because of that ass Ed Harris."

"Figures," says Roger.

"If anyone's going to catch hell, it's Israel and Lisa," says Jim. "Because that's the least tolerated thing of all. A black man corrupting our little innocent virginal pure white girls?"

"Yeah...he's right. A white man with a black girl is just poor judgment, but a black guy with a white girl is cause to break out the sheets and a rope," says Roger.

"Well....hopefully not quite that extreme today. But yeah....you're right. They do look at it differently," I say.

"But if you think about it, that kind of fucks up their whole argument," says Jim.

"What do you mean?" I ask.

"Well...you hear Homer and some of these other biblical scholars saying that race mixing is prohibited by God. Okay...if that's really the truth, then they should have the same problem with a white guy with a black girl as they do with a black guy with a white girl. But they don't, which just makes it plain old unadulterated bigotry. They just don't want those nasty black guys fucking their daughters."

"Yeah...you got it," I say.

"But....they can't stop it now. Change is inevitable. It's here," concludes Jim.

"Yes it is. Right in their fucking faces," I say.

I do kind of like the fact that we're sticking this in the faces of the bigots. But with my condition the way it is, I'm really self-conscious when Karen and I are out. I feel like everyone is looking at us. I've always feel this to a certain extent. But it's worse when we're out together. On our first date she even thought I was ashamed to be out with her because I was so nervous and jumpy. I just feel like all eyes are on me when I enter a crowded room. I know logically that this isn't the case but logic doesn't play a role when it comes to my condition.

Chapter 22

After work, the same day.

"I don't guess we have any Rays back there cooking. Do you think?" I joke, as Jim and I sit down to get a little to eat at the diner.

"That was just unbelievable, wasn't it?" asks Jim.

"Some of these older backwoods types will eat anything though."

"I just always assumed possum stew was some sort of joke. Maybe not."

"Yeah…maybe not."

"So, is this thing with you and Karen serious?" asks Jim.

"Actually, yeah, I think it is," I say. "We've said the magic words to each other."

"Not the dreaded 'L' word?"

"Yep."

"Whirlwind romance…huh?"

"Yeah, it has been kinda quick," I say. "But it just seems meant to be somehow."

"Well, what does this all mean? Are you gonna be one of those holy rollers? Or is she gonna convert over to your side?"

"Convert over to my side?"

"Well, it would seem that many of your interests do not mesh with her interests."

"How would you know what her interests are?" I ask.

"I just know that some of the things you like to do couldn't possibly agree with how she lives."

"Like what?"

"Well, hanging out in bars, growing pot….shit like that. Not to mention fucking one of the town skanks."

"Damn, did word of that get around?"

"You know that everything gets around in this town."

"All that was just an aberration or something," I say. "That wasn't the real me. I'm actually quite boring. Hardly go out. Hardly do anything at all."

"So, if that was just an aberration, who is the real you?"

"That answer's different now than what it would've been a few weeks ago."

"How's that?"

"Because I did convert to her side, as you put it."

"So, she finally got to you."

"Well, I started reading the bible because of her," I say. "But no, I believe what I read. I just decided this is the way I want to go."

"I was raised in church myself. But, I don't know, it just seems kinda outdated to me now. Maybe that's not the right way to put it. It just doesn't seem valid in today's world."

"Well, many churches probably are outdated or stuck in the past," I say. "But I'm not talking about a church. I haven't even been yet. I'm just talking about what I've been reading."

"But it's still all basically the same shit."

"I don't know…many things in the bible just kind of ring true to me somehow. I was raised in a church, too…but kind of drifted away after my parents stopped making me go. But this is different. This just seems right. Hard to explain, actually."

"Just seems like such a radical jump to make so quickly."

"Do you believe in fate?" I ask.

"I'm not sure, really. I think we tend to make our own fate somehow."

"Well, I just believe that this was all meant to be. I met Karen and found the Lord all in one shot. It was just preordained or something. It just fits somehow."

"Just seems kind of fast to me," says Jim. "And I don't mean to be questioning it. I don't know. I just have a hard time seeing you speaking in tongues and all of that shit."

"We'll see. But yeah, I'm probably too reserved for that. I'm going to start going to church with Karen this Sunday. We'll see what happens."

"It should be an experience. I hear those churches can be sort of wild."

"There's just something different about Karen. Hard to describe really," I say. "It's just that she really believes. She's just so happy all of the time, too. It just seems so real with her. That's what really got me looking into this and reading the bible and all of that."

"But she could be just really convinced of something that isn't real. It's easy to fool ourselves into believing shit that isn't true."

"I'm not basing what I believe on her though. The way she is just convinced me that there was something to all of this. But I do believe for myself."

"I'm not knocking anyone's faith. I don't know. I just see so much hypocrisy that it's hard for me to participate in organized religion."

"That's the thing though. I'm not participating in organized religion. They're a tiny little independent church. Only a few families go there. I'm actually meeting her father Saturday. He's the pastor of their church."

"Meeting the parents, huh? You two are serious. And her dad's a damn preacher?"

"Yeah…a preacher."

"Set a date yet?"

"No, we haven't gotten that far."

"But you expect to?"

"Yeah, probably so. Karen isn't the type of girl you just have a little fun with and move on. And that's not what I want anyway."

"No, that's what the Gina's of the world are for."

"Gina isn't the slut that people say she is," I say.

"If you say so."

"She was sweet."

"I'll bet she was."

"But anyway….I'm going in a different direction now."

"I just hope you know what you're getting yourself into. Interracial marriage and then on top of that this religious shit."

"Yeah, I know. But I just think it's meant to be. It's like God just sent this girl in my life to get me straight or something. I was trying to set up a business growing pot. You have no idea how far I was planning that. Then right in the middle of that I meet Karen. It's like God saw my life getting ready to go out of control and he sent her to get me straight."

"So, you look at this as one big package deal?" asks Jim. "You get a woman and religion all in one fell swoop?"

"Yeah, that's why I say it's all just meant to be somehow."

"I just hope you're not mixing up the two in some way."

"No, Jim, I'm not mixing anything up."

"What ended up happening to those plants anyway?"

"Well, they weren't doing too well. Then they started doing some clearing right near where they were, so we just destroyed them."

"So, it wasn't going to happen anyway," says Jim. "The Lord didn't deliver you from that, the plants just didn't grow."

"That's true. But I'd lost my motivation for that shit after I started reading the bible anyway. We could have tried again but I'm done with that shit now."

"What about this Gina thing? Didn't that happen after you'd been talking to Karen?"

"Yeah, it did actually."

"So, what happened there?"

"That was just a bad episode. There's a whole lot involved with what happened that night."

"You got drunk and picked up some girl and fucked her. It's not actually all that complicated."

"I don't normally drink. I was just feeling down that night. I went and bought some liquor and well, the rest just happened."

"Yeah, anything's apt to happen once the drinking begins."

"It's really embarrassing, actually."

"Why?" asks Jim. "Many of us have had episodes like that in our past, if not our present."

"It's more about what caused it to happen."

"Okay."

"I guess I don't feel as bad admitting this now. Especially since it's kinda been taken care of....... by Gina. And I know you aren't like the other guys."

"What? What is it?"

"I was a virgin before Gina. Gina was my first. My one and only."

"Wow! I don't know what to say to that."

"Yeah, I know. I was just feeling bad that night because Karen did what I thought was reject me for a date. I thought I finally had a chance at having a girlfriend. But then she said no. I bought a bottle of Wild Turkey and went over to Mark's house. I told him what I just told you. He said we could find us a couple of bar skanks to fuck........and we did."

"Damn."

"And this was after I had already confided in Karen about my problem."

"So, she thinks you're still a virgin?"

"Sure. She wouldn't have anything to do with me if she knew what I did," I say. "I told her because she told me that she hasn't had sex since she became a Christian."

"Why were you a virgin anyway? I mean, I can't imagine being your age and never ever having gotten some pussy. You're a decent looking guy. What the hell was the issue?"

"I just have this problem with women. I just can't seem to go up to women and talk to them. I call it a condition, extreme shyness. But it's been different with Karen. It's like God opened the door. It makes it seem even more meant to be. It was just so easy with her."

"But, you didn't have any problem getting Gina into bed."

"We actually didn't do it on a bed. We did it on Mark's couch in his den. And the only reason that happened was because I was drunk. Turns out, the cure for my fucking shyness was in a liquor bottle all along."

"Well, it's not really the cure," says Jim. "Just a way to overcome it."

"Yeah, I know. I don't really like to drink anyway."

"Do you know why you're this way?"

"No idea."

"I have to say that I've noticed, and others have, too, that you don't seem to really talk to any of the women at the plant," says Jim. "Most of us are hitting on the good looking ones all the time, but not you."

"It's like I need the ice broken or something. I almost need a written invitation, which usually never comes," I say. "No, actually, it never comes."

"I think Mark had the right idea. You've just needed to be dragged out to the right places. Not the part about getting all liquored up, just to get out."

"I've had opportunities. I always turn down the guys when they want me to go out somewhere. I just don't think I would function well in clubs or bars or whatever."

"I've tried to get you to go to Raleigh with me a few times. But you never seemed interested."

"Actually, I did want to go," I say. "I just knew it would be a disaster. I didn't want anyone to know that I had absolutely no game at all."

"Well, we'd already figured that out."

"Yeah, I guess so."

"Getting back to Karen and this thing with Gina," says Jim. "Do you really think this is the way to start a relationship, especially with a girl like Karen?"

"I've learned my lesson. God is all about forgiveness. He

would have never brought us together if he didn't intend us to stay together."

"I just hope that you aren't trying to force this to work because Karen's your first girlfriend."

"No, this is meant to be, Jim. My whole life's changing. This is a whole new direction for me."

"You aren't going to turn into one of these crazy right-wingers, are you?"

"Nah...I doubt it. I tend to think for myself too much to just jump in with that crowd."

"Good. I don't think I could handle it if you were to turn into a Jerry Falwell or Pat Robertson."

"I won't. I tend to believe that God is much bigger than some of the petty things that religion gets hung up on."

"I couldn't agree with you more."

"There's just so many bigger questions about our existence on this planet to get all hung up on stupid shit."

"Well....I hope that everything works out for you, if this is what you want."

"Yeah, it is what I want."

Chapter 23

Saturday August 14th, 1993

"I hope you're ready for my Daddy," says Karen, as she and I approach her house.

"I guess so," I say.

I'm actually nervous as hell.

"Daddy?"

"Hey, how's my baby doin?" asks Claude.

"Daddy, this is Don, the guy I told you about. Don, this is my daddy, Claude."

"Nice to meet you, son," says Claude, shaking my hand.

"Nice to meet you," I say.

I'm sure he can sense how apprehensive I am.

"Well, come on over and take a load off. I've got a few questions for you," says Claude.

"Take it easy, Daddy. Please?"

"I've got to see what this young man's intentions are, don't I?" says Claude, with a sly grin.

"Fire away," I say.

I sound more confident than I am.

"Karen says that you've accepted the Lord, son."

"Yeah, I have."

"Well, praise God. The Lord's doing some mighty things these days. Do you have a church home yet, son?"

"No, but my intention is to go with Karen to your church."

"You wanna see how the black folks praise the Lord?"

"Yeah, I guess."

"It's very important that you have a good church home. You need to be up under the teaching of a true man of God. Doesn't have to be our church. But you need a church."

"Karen tells me that you're just starting this church," I say.

"Yeah, the Lord's leading us away from the church that we

were saved in."

"Why is that?"

"Pastor Allison is not in the Lord's will, too legalistic, trying to control the people of God too much."

"Is that why Karen's wearing pants now?"

"Sure, that's one thing. God isn't concerned with stuff like that. Doesn't matter in the bigger picture of salvation."

"Okay."

"Now recite me a bible verse," says Claude. "And don't give me no Jesus wept crap."

"Jesus wept crap?"

"Yeah, Jesus wept. It's the shortest verse in the bible. It's what some lazy people use when they haven't bothered to learn a bible verse."

"Uh...I don't know if I know one."

"Didn't Karen tell you to study, son?" asks Claude, with no visible sense of humor.

"Well....yeah..

"We got him, sugar," says Claude to Karen, laughing.

"What? You were just messing with me?" I ask.

"Gotcha!" responds Karen.

"Seriously, son, memorizing verses is well and fine, but what's important is that you actually learn what the Lord is trying to get through to you in his Word," explains Claude.

"I think I am learning a lot. There are things in there that I never knew were in there. I was raised in a church, but I don't remember us covering most of this."

"Yeah, I was raised in church, too, but drifted away, chasing tail and getting drunk. But once the Lord saved me, I left that all behind. Haven't touched a drop of alcohol or a piece of tail since then. That's what the Lord does, son. He purifies us. He delivers us from all those sinful desires. People talk about miracles. But the real miracle is salvation. The real miracle is how he transforms our lives."

"My Daddy can really start to preach if you let him," says Karen.

"I just love the Lord so much," says Claude. "It's just hard to contain myself."

"Karen told me about how you were saved," I say. "The Lord speaking to you and all of that."

"I was one of the worst sinners, son, but the Lord had other plans for me."

"We believe that before it's over, God will save our whole family," says Karen.

"That's right, sugar, God's gonna do a mighty work in this family."

"I can't say that I had an experience like you," I say. "Mine was nowhere near as dramatic."

"How did the Lord save you, son?" asks Claude.

"I just knew that it was the way I wanted to go."

"You knew it in your heart, didn't you?"

"Yeah, I just knew."

"The Lord works on our hearts," says Claude. "Don't let anyone fool you. You don't need no dramatic thing to happen like what happened to me. Some folks might say you ain't really saved. I say bull crap, you are."

"I know that I want to be a Christian."

"Have you been baptized yet?" asks Claude.

"Actually, I was when I was about twelve or thirteen. Do I need to again? I went down front and accepted the Lord then."

"No, see…. if your heart was right, back then, you were already saved. You were just backsliding all these years," says Claude. "God is just calling you back to the fold."

"Backsliding?"

"Just means that you weren't living the life of a Christian," says Claude.

"I'm not sure I was really saved back then though."

"Was there any change?" asks Claude.

"Just a desire that didn't last all that long to read the whole bible. I just felt kind of religious for a while."

"Well…maybe you should be baptized again, but this time in the water and in the Holy Spirit. Maybe that was the problem before. Maybe it was a dead church where the Spirit of God wasn't present. You got shortchanged, son. You didn't get the Spirit when you were saved."

"You can be saved and not receive the Spirit?"

"Sure you can. That's the problem with Christianity today. Too many supposed Christians don't have the Holy Spirit."

"That's the whole point of salvation, isn't it?"

"You have been studying scripture."

"Yeah, I have."

"It is very important to have the Spirit of God dwelling inside of you," explains Claude. "But don't get hung up on some of the wild stuff that some folks do. You don't have to do that to have the Spirit."

"Good, because I don't know if I can see myself doing but so much. I'm kind of reserved."

"But the Lord don't care about that. Who knows, you may be the wildest one in the house once the Spirit falls."

"Well, I don't know. We'll see, I guess."

"Besides the baptism issue, I also want you to know how important it is to fast. The Lord says that some things only come but through prayer and fasting."

Again with the fasting. Why do they emphasize that so much?

"Yeah, Karen did make that point," I say.

"And it's very important to pay your tithes faithfully. We have to give to God what is rightfully his, so that he may bless us."

"I have seen the tithe mentioned, too."

"It's very important. We must not cut off our blessings, by robbing God."

"Okay."

"Okay, daddy, we have to go," says Karen. "He'll talk your ear off about the Lord if you let him."

"Oh…okay. I'm sorry, sugar. Look forward to seeing you at church, son."

"I look forward to it, too."

"Hope you know what you're getting into," says Claude. "We can get buck wild in that place when the Spirit falls."

"It will be something new for me, I'm sure."

"Okay, daddy, see you later."

"Okay, baby girl…love you. It was nice to meet you, son."

"Nice to meet you, too, Claude."

Overall, my impression of Claude is good. I can tell he's very sure of himself and opinionated. He knows what he believes and isn't afraid to preach it. Some of the things he says don't quite ring true according to the things I've read. But I am new to all of this. Maybe I just don't understand it all yet. He does seem somewhat unconventional for a pastor. I do like that. Talking about being self-conscious, church will be really hard for me. I'll be the only white guy in a church full of wild black folks. It's the perfect place for a shy guy like me.

Chapter 24

Monday August 16ᵗʰ, 1993

"And what are you two geniuses up to today?" I ask.

"We're building a couple of offices here for the tubular finishing manager and supervisors," responds Roger.

"So, the plant carpenters actually get to build something?" I ask.

"Yeah, we finally get to do more than paint," says Jerry.

"I see you're training Mark right," observes Roger. "Teaching him to fuck off like a true instrument guy."

"Of course. And he's catching on so well, too."

"You see, we get paid for what we know, not for what we do," adds Mark, holding up his index finger to emphasize the point.

"Oh my God. You do have him brainwashed already," says Roger.

"Just telling him the truth," I say. "The Instrumentation group is an elite team of high level troubleshooters."

"Please, stop," says Roger, holding up his hands in surrender.

"I don't think they can handle the truth," says Mark.

"They're mere peasants," I say. "Pay no attention to them, my protégé."

"I won't. I already know they are far below me," says Mark, laughing.

"Well, I had an experience Sunday," I say.

"And what might that be, my elite one?" asks Roger.

"I went to church with Karen."

"How was that?" asks Roger.

"Long, for one thing."

"How long?" asks Mark.

"Well, we got there a little before ten, for Sunday school. And didn't leave until probably two thirty or so."

"Damn."

"The sermon itself was probably longer than the entire service was at the church I grew up in," I say.

"Our services at First Presbyterian were always one hour," says

Mark.

"That's what I'm saying," I respond. "It was a long haul."

"Well, besides lasting so damn long, how was it?" asks Roger.

"It was good. It was actually kinda interesting."

"How?" asks Roger.

"Well…I don't know…it was just so unlike the church I grew up in. They just have so much fire for the Lord. They're just so into the whole thing. At my church it just always seemed like we were going through the motions or something. But it's not like that with these people."

"Roger probably knows about all that shit," says Jerry. "Being from Kentucky, he probably went to one of those snake handling churches."

"I did not. But I did pretty much grow up in a Pentecostal church. My grandmother's a Pentecostal. My parents made me go with her, even though they hardly went. But they didn't handle no goddamn snakes."

"When they were having what they call the praise service, that place was jumping," I say. "They have a band and everything. I mean, it was loud and a little much, but I enjoyed it."

"Did you speak in tongues?" asks Jerry.

"No, but there were a few who did."

"What was it like?" asks Mark.

"Kind of hard to explain," I say.

"But did it sound like actual languages?" asks Mark.

"No, it just sounded like jibberish or something. Didn't make sense at all."

"You could have joined in." says Mark. "If it was just bullshit mumbo jumbo then what would they have known."

"Sure, my first time in church in years and I'm gonna fake something."

"Did you think it was real?" asks Jerry.

"I don't have any reason to think that it's not."

"I've heard it before," says Roger. "It could be faked. But most people aren't doing that."

"If you can't understand what's being fucking said, then what's the point?" asks Mark.

"It's supposed to be the Spirit talking directly the person, so that no one else knows what's being said," explains Roger.

"Mr. Pentecostal over here," says Jerry, gesturing towards Roger.

"Well, I grew up going to those churches," says Roger. "I do know what's going on."

"All kinds of stuff was happening," I say. "All at the same time."

"What kind of stuff?" asks Mark.

"Well...some people were just shouting out, praising God and stuff like that. Some people fell on the floor."

"You see that all the time with these TV ministers when they lay hands on someone," says Jerry. "They almost always hit the floor."

"They call it being slain in the Spirit," explains Roger.

"And it's like some of these women are praising the Lord so hard.....getting so carried away, that there are other women who kind of guide them to keep them from banging into pews and other people," I say. "It really seems like they're losing control. Like something's coming in and taking over."

"So, you believe that it's real?" asks Mark.

"I'm not saying it's all real. I'm not saying I even understand what's happening really. I just don't see how everything I saw could be faked, or really, why they would fake it. This wasn't TV. This is just a small little church."

"No, it isn't faked," says Roger. "But I just think they get themselves all worked up into a frenzy or something."

"They do get that beat going on the drums," I say. "It's almost like they're working things up to a fever pitch and then it all breaks loose."

"That's when they say the Spirit falls on the church," says Roger.

"What about you, Roger? Did you ever fall out in the Spirit or do any of that shit?" asks Jerry.

"I went when I was a damn kid," says Roger. "You know how you are when you're a kid in church? We were always just playing around wishing it would end."

"There was this really odd thing," I say. "This one woman was bending at the waist....kind of far...with her head almost to the floor. It just looked odd, like she wasn't doing it on her own. Like her body was being contorted by something."

"Then what the hell was doing it?" asks Mark. "Was it like the exorcist or something?"

"It just had an odd quality about it," I say. "It just seemed unnatural somehow."

"Yeah, why would God want someone to bend at the waist?"

asks Jerry. "What would be the purpose?"

"I know. That's what's kind of odd about it," I say. "But then again, most of it was odd to me. But that one, more so."

"Do you know what you're getting into?" asks Roger, with a faint laugh. "You think that's odd? You just wait."

"Hey, it's a little loud and confusing, and there are some things that I just don't get, but these people are on to something. They seem to have a fire that I want."

"Well...they have something. That's for sure," responds Roger. "I'm just not sure what."

"How they pray is one thing I don't quite understand," I say.

"What do they do?" asks Mark.

"Well, when they pray, everyone prays at once...and I mean out loud. And some of them are really loud. It's really confusing, so many people speaking at once."

"Yeah, my grandma's church did it the same way. I think they believe that it just has more power if they all pray at once," explains Roger.

"Well...yeah....I get that," I say. "But does everyone have to pray out loud at once? Can't God read our thoughts? Why does it have to be so confusing?"

"I don't know what their reasoning is on that one," says Roger.

"Well...overall...I did enjoy it," I say. "Well, enjoy may be the wrong word. I was intrigued by the whole thing."

"Oh shit!" says Jerry. "We've got ourselves a holy roller on our hands."

"I don't know...I'm probably too shy and reserved to ever do what they do."

"Well, isn't the Spirit supposed to carry you away or something?" asks Roger. "Never know what you may end up doing if you let the Spirit take control."

"Yeah...I guess that's how it's supposed to work. That's what Karen tells me. Just let go and the Spirit will take over."

"I would love to see you speaking in tongues," says Mark. "It would be quite amusing."

"I don't know...I have a long way to go before that happens, I think."

"You never know....if the Spirit gets high enough in there, you may do anything," says Roger.

"Yeah...we'll see," I say.

"Holy Roller Don," says Mark.

"White Shadow…holy roller," adds Jerry.

"Yeah…I was the only white face in the place. But they made me feel welcome."

"How did it feel to be the minority?" asks Jerry.

"Alright, I guess…a little weird, especially for me. I'm not good in new situations where I don't know what to expect. And I felt like everyone was looking at me, like who is this white boy in our church. Not in a bad way…just that I felt like the attention was on me to a certain extent."

"They just wanted to know who this white guy is who's taking their black girl from them," says Mark.

"It really wasn't that. There really wasn't any younger guys there. It's really a small church. It's basically just a few families. They started this church because they had some problem with the church they used to go to. You should see this building that they use. It's some sort of old schoolhouse. The building has a noticeable lean to it. You're going uphill as you approach the pulpit area. You can even see the wall leaning forward at the front of the church on the outside."

"One day that place is going to come crashing down on them with all that stuff going on," says Jerry.

"It kind of added to the charm of the whole thing if you know what I mean."

"Yeah…the possibility of disaster is always good," jokes Roger.

Going to church was both overwhelming and intriguing. Overwhelming because this is so far from what I'm used to. I could never imagine myself letting go like that. I'm so far out of my element there. But it was intriguing because they seem so genuine. I went in really without any preconceived notions about what to expect. I have had zero exposure to these types of churches. But they have something that I've never seen before. They have a real and active faith. They have a living faith. That place was alive. They were alive. I see now what they mean when they call other churches dead. Compared to them, other churches are dead.

Chapter 25

Saturday September 11th, 1993

"Now it's my turn. You're on the hot seat now," I say, as Karen and I approach my parent's front door.

"I'm nervous."

"No need to be. You're just the first girl I've ever brought home," I say. "And also, you're black, and I'm white, and we live in the South. No pressure."

"But you said your parents aren't prejudiced."

"Oh…they're not. It'll be fine. I'm just kidding you."

"Come on in, you two," says Dad, opening the door before I could ring the bell.

"Expecting us, I see," I say.

"Hello, I'm Karen."

"I'm Jack. It's nice to meet you."

"Hey, Momma, this is Karen."

"So glad to meet you. Don's told us so much about you," says Momma, as she hugs Karen.

"Glad to meet you, too, Mrs. Higgins."

"It's Joan."

"And here comes little sis. Karen, this is my sister, Melody."

"Nice to meet you," says Karen.

"Nice to meet you," replies Melody. "But I have seen you around at the plant."

"Yeah, you work in the office, don't you?" asks Karen.

"Yeah, that's right."

That just goes to show how big the plant really is that Karen and Mel have never really met before. But Mel's job really doesn't involve coming in contact with any of us on the production floor. The people in the offices have their own little world going on up there.

"Okay, now that all the intros are out of the way, can we have a seat?" I ask.

"To the den, then," says Dad, like he's leading a charge.

"To the den," I say.

"So, Karen, Don says he's going to church with you," says Momma, as we make our way through the house.

"Yeah, the Lord's doing something in his life," replies Karen.

"He's just coming back home. He just drifted away for a while," says Momma.

"I don't know, Momma, I'm seeing stuff in scripture that we never covered at First Christian," I say.

"Well, you only went to church when you were a kid. It does get a little deeper in the adult classes," says Momma. "And I'm sure you hardly paid attention to the sermons most of the time."

"Yeah, I know. But it's not just the classes or the sermons. It's the service itself. It's just different."

"Well....all churches are different," says Momma, stiffly. "There are different ways to praise the Lord."

"You have a beautiful home, Joan," says Karen.

"Well, let me show you around," offers Momma.

"And while you're doing that, I'll get the grill going," adds Dad.

"I was wondering when you would bring a girl home," says Melody, after everyone else leaves.

"I couldn't bring one home until I had one," I reply.

"I was beginning to think I had two gay brothers," she says.

"So, you know Dan's gay."

"Well, don't you?"

"Yeah."

"I think the only ones who don't know are Momma and Daddy," she says.

"They're just in denial though."

"It's just a matter of time until he brings someone home."

"How do you think they'll react?"

"Well, neither one of them has ever shown any real prejudice against homosexuality," she says. "But of course they were raised in a different time than we were."

"Thing is, I'm not sure how I feel now."

"What do you mean?"

"Well...it is spoken of in scripture," I say. "And not in a positive way."

"But he's our brother."

"I know that, Mel. I don't have anything against it in any

philosophical way. I'm not a homophobic bigot or anything. But I see where it's prohibited in scripture. I don't know…"

"Well…you'd better decide because I have a feeling that it won't be long before he comes out."

"Just have to cross that bridge when I come to it."

"Please don't get all crazy religious on me, brother."

"Listen, Mel, one thing is sure. I'll never believe something just because some other person believes it. I'll have to see it for myself. I'm not a mindless sheep being led to slaughter."

"It's just that you know that Dan will need our love and support when he does finally come out. I just never figured it would be a problem with you."

"And it probably won't be. I'm not going to shun him or anything. But I can't really see myself giving him my ringing endorsement, either."

"But you know it's not a choice, right?" asks Mel.

"Yes, absolutely. I'll never believe that homosexuals have normal heterosexual desires, but then they just decide to be gay. That's total bullshit."

"I just hope the irony of the situation isn't lost on you."

"Irony? What are you talking about?"

"Well, you were all upset about Momma and Hugh and all that shit, because you were talking to Karen. And now you don't know if you can support your brother."

"Well, they aren't quite the same thing. There isn't anything in the bible that speaks about being black as being a sin. But with homosexuality it's another matter."

"How can it be a sin if it's natural?"

"I'm not saying it's natural," I say. "I just don't believe it's a choice, either."

"How can both be true?"

"I don't know. That's where I'm at though."

"What are you two talking about so seriously in here?" asks Dad, sticking his head through the door.

"Nothing, Daddy," responds Mel. "Need me to get you anything?"

"Yeah, how about handing me that tray with the hot dogs on it. It's on the kitchen counter."

"Need me to do anything?" I ask.

"No…I've got it under control, son," says Dad, closing the door.

I know that Mel's right. I know that I should be able to support Dan. But I just cannot get away from what I see to be the truth. I haven't thought this out fully yet, but I do know that there is nothing in scripture that even comes close to suggesting that homosexuality is accepted by God. But there also isn't anything in there that suggests that it should be the primary issue that Christians focus on. I have my feelings on this. But you can't always trust your feelings. Scripture has to be my guide now.

Momma comes walking up to me.

"All done with the tour?" I ask. "Where's Karen?"

"She needed to use the bathroom," responds Momma, starting to tear up.

"Momma, what's wrong?"

"Don...I just feel so awful."

"Why?"

"Karen's so nice."

"And that's bad?"

"No....it's the way I've been acting recently....about the girls in my office."

"You mean agreeing with Hugh and all that stuff?"

"Were you seeing her at that point?"

"We had just started talking. It did kind of make that spectacle sting that much more."

"I'm sorry. You know that isn't what's really in my heart."

"I know, Momma."

"I think she's great."

"I do, too."

"You do too, what?" ask Karen, as she rejoins us.

"I think you're great," I say.

"Awww....you're so sweet."

"Come on....let's join your Daddy outside. I'm ready to eat," says Momma.

"Need me to help with anything?" asks Karen.

"Yeah...come give me a hand. I have a few things to bring out from the kitchen."

"Umm...smells good," I say, stepping out onto the patio.

"Momma and Karen still touring the house?" asks Mel.

"No...they're just getting a few things from the kitchen."

"I must have just missed them."

"She seems like a nice girl, son."

"Seems so happy. Smiling all the time. I even notice that at work. The few times I've seen her she's always smiling," says Mel.

"I know. Most people aren't that way when they're slaving away in that place. But she sure is," I say. "I think it's her faith. She just has this peace about her."

"Here comes the food," says Karen, as she and Momma come out.

"Let's eat," says Momma. "Karen, would you do us the honor of blessing the food?"

"I would love to, Joan. Everyone bow their heads, please."

It was a good day. My family really seems to like her. And of course there isn't anyone that Karen can't get along with. We chatted. We made small talk. We of course shared how we met that day outside of the plant. But I'm not so sure how much better anyone knows one another after all of that.

Do they really know her? Does she really know them? But that's pretty much par for the course for any family events we have. There is never but so much real conversation going on. It's really nothing more than idle chit-chat. I'm not sure how well any of us really knows one another in my family. But I'm sure many other families are the same. We've spent all this time together but somehow fail to really understand one another. Maybe I just expect too much. I'm not blaming the others. I'm as much to blame as they are, maybe more so, with my condition and all. But the reality is that I know so little about my parents, and my brother and sister. And I know for a fact that they know very little about me.

Chapter 26

Later that day.

"Well, do you think your family likes me?" asks Karen, as we drive back to her house.

"They love you," I say. "They think you're great."

"Did they say that?"

"Yes, they actually did. But I can also tell by the way they got along with you."

"I love your family, too."

"Well....we've now met each other's families," I say. "And that went well."

"Yes....I would say that it did."

"I'm saved now.....and going to church."

"Praise God."

"And I love you."

"And I love you, too."

"It seems as if all the pieces are falling into place now," I say.

"For what?"

"For our getting married."

"Okay."

"That's it....okay?"

"Yeah....okay....let's get married."

"I was just expecting some sort of argument or resistance."

"No....it's like you said.....all the pieces have fallen into place. But there is one problem."

"What's that?"

"Where's my ring?" she asks, smiling.

"I just didn't plan on asking you now. But with you getting along with my parents so well. I don't know...it just seemed like the right time."

"Okay."

"You just have no idea how you've changed my life. How much you've turned me around from the direction I was going. I was going down the wrong road...and then you came along."

"It wasn't me...it was the Lord."

"I know...but the Lord worked through you. I love you, Karen. I want to spend the rest of my life with you."

"Don...you may not know it or believe it, but the Lord has great things in store for you."

"I believe that. I've always felt that I wasn't cut out for a normal life. This is what I've been waiting for. I'm going to do great things for the Lord."

"It's there waiting for you. All you have to do is claim it as your own."

"I claim it."

"So...when do I get my ring?"

"Well....we can go shopping for it tomorrow if you want. We can go after church."

"You can pick it out if you want."

"No...you'd better do it. The engagement ring's a very important thing for a woman. It should be what you want...exactly."

"It will be.... just because it'll be from you."

"Still...why don't you come along anyway."

"Okay."

"So...as far as the wedding's concerned..... any particular time frame that you'd have in mind?" I ask.

"Whenever you want."

"Well, how about next summer....June? Gives us time to plan things."

"Sounds great."

"I know that there's this thing about being a June bride."

"It doesn't matter. I'll be married to you. Don....I'm so blessed. I cannot believe that I will be the one and only woman that you will ever be with. That is such a blessing. I know that this is what God wants."

"Yeah...it is a blessing," I say.

"I knew if I just had faith, that the Lord would bless me with a man. Praise God!"

I know I should tell Karen about the thing with Gina. I know she'll understand. At least I believe she would. I just don't want to mess this up. This has to be the Lord doing all of this. This all just fits so perfectly. I was lost. I was heading down a bad road. I had no direction. Now the Lord has changed all of that. The Lord forgives us of all sin. It's like the sin never happened. Maybe that's the way I should look at the Gina thing. The Lord looks at it as having never happened. Maybe I should just look at it the same way. It never happened.

Chapter 27

Saturday September 18th, 1993

"Hey, Jim...what's going on?" I ask, as I come up on a gathering crowd in front of the service station, which happens to be across the street from the police station.

"That's Harold Goins in the back of that cruiser," responds Jim.

Harold Goins. What a character he is. He's what you find in the dictionary when you look up backwoods, redneck or hillbilly. Harold is all three combined. His wife is actually a Pentecostal minister. She and Harold are white, therefore she preaches in white churches, considering that for some unknown reason most churches remain segregated. I'm not sure what Harold does for a living. He worked at the plant but was gone long before I started over there. I get the sneaking suspicion that not all of the sources of his income are legal.

"Harold got raided last night," says Roger.

"For what?" I ask.

"Oh, he's just making some of that peach brandy," says Homer White, as the police escort Harold into the station.

"Peach moonshine," corrects Jerry.

"I think it's more than just a little this time," says Roger. "They've been up at his place for quite some time."

"Why?" I ask.

"I heard he's got quite the operation going. I think he may be in real trouble. Moving the stuff over state lines and all that shit," adds Roger.

"He ain't hurting no one," says Homer. "Government just wants their money."

"You don't have a problem with this?" I ask. "Seeing that you're a bible believing Christian and all of that."

"Don...there ain't nothing wrong with a little sip every now and then," responds Homer.

"Or a guzzle," says Roger, glancing at Jerry.

"I've never even tried his shit," says Jerry.

"I don't think he meant Harold's stuff in particular," clarifies Jim.

"He meant guzzle booze in general," I explain.

"As opposed to sip," concludes Jim.

"Fuck you guys," says Jerry.

"Well….show's over, I guess," says Homer, walking off.

Homer White is Ronnie White's father. Homer is a mechanic at the plant. He comes across as the perfect southern gentleman. He's polite, courteous and soft spoken. But Homer also has certain views on race. And those views are shaped by the bible. So far, he hasn't said anything to me about Karen, but I'm sure it's coming. I know for a fact that the whole thing with Lisa and Israel gets to him. He has made some comments about them. And I can see the disapproval in him when they're around together.

"What are you up to?" asks Jim, as everyone starts to go their separate ways.

"I was just going to get a little lunch at the diner," I respond.

"I'll join you."

"Isn't this just typical of this little hayseed town we live in?" I ask, as we take a seat in the diner. "I mean seriously….people are still getting busted for moonshine?"

"It ought to be legal if you ask me. The whole thing of regulating alcohol is from a bygone era," says Jim. "The state having their own stores to sell it? Come on."

"Oh, I agree. I'm just saying that it's just funny that someone's getting busted for moonshine. It's just one of those redneck type of things. You never hear of someone getting busted in New York for something like this."

"I know…that's life in a small southern town, I guess."

"There are many things that should be legal if you ask me," I say. "Pot, for one."

"Like I didn't know you felt that way already."

I guess he's referring to my failed pot venture.

"Actually, there would be less money in it if it were legal," I say. "People could just grow their own."

"Pot actually does less damage than what alcohol does, if you ask me," says Jim.

"Exactly. But the older generation that's still in power has this irrational fear when it comes to drugs. Reefer madness and all of that shit."

"It's just about what's socially acceptable."

"Alcohol's fine because it's a drink," I say. "But drugs are just a way to get high. That's what they think."

"Like that's not why most people drink."

"Yeah, how many would drink what they drink if there wasn't a buzz to be had?" I ask.

"Yeah, it's all bullshit. But what are you gonna do?"

"Hey guys, how you doing?" asks Lisa, coming up to us.

"Getting a little something to go?" I ask.

"Yeah...my son has a football game down at the park in a few minutes. Thought I'd grab a little something for us to eat. Hey...why don't you two come?"

"What do you think, Jim?"

"Yeah, why not."

"What's this I hear about Harold getting arrested?" asks Lisa.

"Yeah, we just watched them haul him into the police station," I say.

"What the hell did he do?"

"Harold's known for making this peach liquor," I say. "Apparently he got a little too ambitious."

"Oh...okay," says Lisa. "Just another day in the town of Raymond."

"Well, see you down at the park after we eat," I say.

"Alright, see you then."

"Okay, continuing with our discussion," says Jim. "I'm curious, would you stop at pot....or would you legalize other stuff, too?"

"I'd legalize it all. Legalize, tax and regulate."

"Okay....Mr. Libertarian."

"That's actually what I am," I say. "If other people aren't being hurt then why should it be illegal?"

"So, people should be free to totally fuck their lives up if they want?"

"Well, yeah. Because people are going to find a way to fuck their lives up no matter what, anyway."

"But you want to make it easier."

"As long as there's demand, there'll be supply," I say. "We aren't going to change that."

"Yeah, it seems we have the universal need to escape reality."

"So, why not legalize it? Collect taxes on it. Regulate the quality and all that shit. And then spend the money we spend now on treatment."

"So, you would just legalize heroin, cocaine, meth....all of that shit?"

"All of it."

"I don't see you getting elected to office any time soon with that platform."

"No, I suppose not," I say, laughing. "I don't think it would ever happen really. It's just how I'd do it. Just an idea."

"But some of that shit really destroys people's lives."

"But shouldn't I have the right to destroy my life if I want to?"

"Yeah, but society's affected, too."

"But society's affected by alcohol," I say. "How many people die at the hands of drunk drivers? But they continually just get their fucking wrists slapped."

"And some of these yahoos still complain about sobriety checks and all that shit."

"I've heard so many stories at the plant where one of these fools has driven home stone cold drunk," I say. "They think nothing of it. It's like they think they should have the right to drive drunk."

"Unfortunately, some judges seem to think they do, too."

"Everything should be legal. But if you do anything that even comes close to hurting another person, it's automatic prison time along with mandatory rehab."

"Wait a minute," says Jim. "How does this pro-drug stance jibe with your new found faith?"

"I'm sure many Christians wouldn't even come close to agreeing with me."

"Yeah, I'm sure they wouldn't."

"It's not up to Christians to try to make laws that make people live the way they think they should live."

"That's my main issue with religion," says Jim. "Don't try to regulate my life."

"I'm just saying that this is a better way to deal with the drug problem."

"Yeah, but it ain't happening."

"I know. Let me get off of my soapbox now. I get carried away with some of this shit. I know it ain't gonna happen."

"Well, you aren't alone," says Jim. "There are others who believe what you believe. I agree when it comes to pot. I'm just not so sure that we should legalize meth and all that shit."

"Speaking of my new found faith....I have some news."

"What?"

"Karen and I are getting married....next June."

"Wow…that was fast."

"Yeah…it has been. I just know she's the one for me. I have such a purpose in life now."

"Forgive me, and I know I said all this before….but how do you go from growing pot plants one moment….then drunk fucking Gina….to becoming a Christian and getting married to a girl like Karen so quickly?"

"What do you mean….a girl like Karen?"

"I just mean that she's one of those heavy duty Christians. Are you sure that's the life you really want? It just doesn't seem like you."

"Jim….it's hard to explain. But she's made such a difference in my life. And reading scripture….I just see that I was on the wrong track. But it's alright now."

"I don't know, man….I just wonder if you shouldn't take a step back or something."

"No, I don't see any reason for that."

"I wasn't going to say anything about this…but…the reason that the Gina story is going around is because she kinda got off on being the first one to fuck you."

"So, that's part of the story, too," I say. "Everyone knows that was my first time."

"I don't think that matters all that much now. You fucked Gina. She may be a little loose….but she is hot. You've got some street cred now."

"Well….I'm not really proud of it. My first time was a drunken romp on Mark's sofa with someone I hardly knew."

"Are you sure this all isn't just an extreme reaction to all of that?" asks Jim.

"What do you mean?"

"Well….it's almost as if you look at this as if Karen is saving you from your debauched life. Your life of growing pot and drunkenly fucking sluts."

My debauched life? That does sound funny. There were really only those two things. Besides that, I'm as white bread as they come. But I do feel as if I was starting to slip off of a cliff or something. I really had some far-fetched ideas about the whole pot thing. I was even going to buy a gun.

"No, it's not that," I finally say. "I really believe the things I'm reading in scripture. I'm looking at things in a whole different way now."

"Okay….still wish you'd step back a little and think about what you are getting into."

"No need….it's all good."

"But you may want to talk to Gina," says Jim. "You wouldn't want this getting to Karen, I would guess."

"I'm not sure what I would say, though."

"Just tell her you're getting married and to shut her fucking mouth."

"Yeah, right. She'd respond to that," I say, rolling my eyes.

"I'd try something, though."

"Yeah, I know," I say. "But hopefully this won't get to Karen anyway. She doesn't exactly fly in the same circles as Gina does."

"Believe that if you want, but I think you have a problem. The part about taking your virginity is going to make it really believable."

"That's true. Karen thinks she's the only one who knows that," I say. "And she would be if it weren't for that night with Gina."

"What are you gonna do?"

"Shit, I don't know. I don't like confrontation. Probably just hope for the best."

I really do hate confrontation. I avoid potentially emotional scenes like the plague. I tend to repress things, hide things. I know that I should deal with this issue but I just can't bring myself to. I know it's most definitely true that Karen will eventually find out about Gina. I know I'll have to deal with it eventually. I just want to avoid it for now. I want to avoid it as long as I can.

Chapter 28

Just a little while later.

"Oh shit....look! Tommy and Israel are both here," I say, as Jim and I make our way to the bleachers at the football field.

"Ronnie, Raeford, Jerry and Roger..ummm...this could be fun," says Jim, with his trademark bemused smirk.

"We get such amusement out of these clowns."

"Redneck party with a Nigerian in the middle," jokes Jim.

"The only reason Israel's here is because he's seeing Lisa."

"I know. Interracial couple in the middle of the redneck party," says Jim. "Even better."

"Hey, watch it," I say. "I'm part of an interracial couple now."

"Oh....that's right. Sorry."

"Hey, glad you two could come," says Lisa, as Jim and I take a seat beside her.

"Should be fun," I say. "How are things between Tommy and Israel now?"

"I think that whole thing's just ancient history now," says Jim.

"Yeah, it seems that way," I say. "I was just wondering if that was really the case."

"You want the inside scoop from the girl who shares his bed," says Jim.

"Exactly. I know how Tommy can be. I was just wondering if he's fucking with Israel."

"Well, I don't think Tommy's completely over it," says Lisa. "After all, Israel attacked him for what turned out to be no reason. I don't think Tommy has too much to do with Israel and vice versa. But no, he's not fucking with Israel."

"So, did Jerry apologizing help at all?" I ask.

"It helped Israel," she says. "But I'm not sure it did much for Tommy."

"Karen claims that Tommy isn't a racist," I say. "She says he's come over to cookouts that her family's had. Said he's a good guy."

"I don't know one way or the other," says Lisa. "I know I've heard things about the Cash family. But I can't say I know what Tommy thinks."

"Which one is your boy?" asks Jim, as Israel joins them.

"Brett's number twelve," she says. "They're warming up now. They'll start in a few minutes."

"Is he a quarterback?" I ask.

"He sure is."

"He got a really good arm," says Israel. "He a fucking little Joe Montana."

"Football's a totally different thing in Nigeria, isn't it?" I ask.

"Yes, football is soccer in my country."

"Soccer's having a hard time catching on here," I say.

"I like this sort of football, too....lots of action," responds Israel. "And I like seeing people knocked on their ass."

"Except for Brett," says Lisa.

"She worry too much about him," says Israel. "He tough. He can take it."

"Seems we have quite a crew here today," I observe, looking around.

"Yeah, Roger's boy Nick and Jerry's boy Billy play with Brett. Tommy and Ronnie both have boys playing on the other team," explains Lisa. "And of course Homer is here to see his grandson play."

"Who's Raeford here to see?" asks Jim.

"I think he just likes watching them play," says Lisa.

"Well, this is nice and cozy....everyone sitting on the same side," I say.

"I bring a chair so I can sit behind Brett's bench if they happen to get the side without the bleachers. But don't need it today."

"Small town....can only afford one set of bleachers, I guess," adds Jim.

"Jim, you don't have any kids, do you?" asks Lisa.

"Kids? He's had a vasectomy," I say.

"Pretty much made up your mind, huh?" she asks.

"I was married....but we didn't have kids. And after that...well...I just realized that the life I want to have doesn't involve children," explains Jim. "It's as simple as that."

"What about you, Don? When are you going to settle down and have a family?" asks Lisa.

"He is," says Jim.

"What?" asks Lisa.

"Well...yeah...I'm getting married. But I don't see children coming any time soon."

"I'm assuming we're talking about Karen?" asks Lisa.

"Well.....it could be Gina," jokes Jim.

"Who's Gina?" asks Lisa.

"You're maybe the only one who doesn't know who Gina is," says Jim.

"I know," says Israel.

"Yeah, I'll bet you know who she is, Israel," says Jim.

Lisa glances at Israel, who just shrugs and stares at the field.

"No, it's not Gina," I say. "He's just trying to be funny. It's Karen."

"Yeah...I knew that you two were seeing each other," says Lisa. "But I didn't know it was serious."

"Well...I guess it did happen kind of fast," I say.

"Kids will come fast, too," says Jim.

"No...maybe one day...but no plans now."

"Is that what Karen wants?" asks Lisa.

"I don't know really," I say. "We really haven't talked about that yet. But she does love kids. I know that."

We haven't talked about that at all. I'm like Jim in that I've never pictured myself with children. And now I'm getting married to a woman that most certainly will want them. That never occurred to me.

"Might want to discuss that," says Lisa. "That's a pretty important issue when it comes to marriage. My ex never really wanted kids. He just gave into me. See what that got me?"

"I just feel like children are such an important step," I say. "I don't want to have them unless they can be my number one priority."

"I agree," says Lisa. "There are far too many people who have kids but then totally neglect them. Just go off and keep doing their own thing. My jackass ex-husband for one."

"That's what I don't want to be," I say. "I want to be able to commit to my kids one hundred percent. I can't do that yet. I'm too selfish and too unsure of where my life's going at this point."

"I can tell you that if you're waiting for that perfect time to have kids....well....it'll never come," she says. "But they will change your life....mostly for the better."

"It's just when I picture my life....imagine what it'll be like....I just never picture kids there."

I can't believe I actually admitted that to her. Why am I telling things to other people that I don't tell my future wife? It should be the other way around.

"What do you picture then?" asks Lisa.

"I don't know really," I say. "I just want to be different. I want to make my mark on the world somehow. I simply cannot stand the thought of leading a conventional type of life. I just can't do it."

"What's a conventional life though?"

"Working at some job, having a family, retiring and then dying," I say. "I just want to do something different. But I'm not quite sure what though. I just can't stand the thought of being chained down in any way."

I do know what I want to do. My dreams seem so outlandish for someone like me that I can't bear to reveal them to anyone. But my priorities are different now anyway. Those ideas are in the past.

"But now you're getting married," she says. "You're giving in to the conventional."

"Yeah…but there's just something special about Karen," I say. "Her faith has such an impact on her life. And that's made an impact on me. I still don't envision myself with a conventional life. I believe I'll have a spiritual purpose now."

Do I envision myself as a minister? Probably not. How could I speak in front of a group like that? But I do know that I want to do some great things for the Lord. What exactly that means, I don't know yet.

"What sort of church does Karen go to?" asks Lisa.

"It's Pentecostal. I'm not sure they would call it that, but it's that sort of thing."

"Hey, Brett's dropping back to pass! Come on baby….," says Lisa.

"Completion!" I say. "That was one hell of a throw."

"That's my baby," says Lisa.

"Told you he good passer," adds Israel.

"Billy's got the ball," says Lisa.

"Not sure Jerry even knows," observes Jim. "He seems pretty toasted right now."

"Hey Jerry! The field's over there," I say. "Your boy has the ball."

"I know where the goddamn field's at," responds Jerry.

"You don't act like it. Your fucking kid just ran for ten yards," I say.

"Uhhh……ohhh….good job Billy….way to run it," says Jerry.

"He's got it again," I say.

"Damn!" says Jim. "See that kid yank his little head around?"

"Goddamn it, ref! He grabbed him by the fucking facemask," yells Jerry. "You blind bitch! Where's the fucking penalty?"

"Why don't you just pipe the hell down there, chief? That was a good fucking tackle," booms Ronnie.

"Why? Just because it was your goddamn boy?" responds Jerry.

"No....it was just a good fucking tackle."

"You saying he didn't get the fucking mask?"

"So fucking what? It was goddamn incidental. It won't fucking intentional."

"Ref's an ass!"

"No...you're a drunk ass," says Ronnie. "Who comes to a fucking kids goddamn football game all tore up?"

"What's it to ya....," asks Raeford.

"Why you chiming in on this one?" asks Ronnie. "Stay out of it."

"Because's he's lit, too?" I offer.

"No, you stay out of this shit," says Raeford. "This is between Ronnie and me."

"Oh....you want it to be something?" says Ronnie, standing. "Then let's go."

"Son....sit down," says Homer. "Like you said...this is a childrens's game. This ain't no place for it."

"Okay, pop, you're right."

"Are these games usually this much fun?" I ask Lisa.

"Sometimes," she says. "Some of these people forget that this is just some kids playing a game. And these guys hate that one ref anyway. They're convinced that he makes calls just to piss them off. Or...in this case fail to make calls."

"That kind of explains Jerry's little outburst," says Jim.

"I tend to think that too many parents are trying to live out their failed dreams through their kids," I say. "They get far more emotionally involved in the games than the kids do."

"Well....and then the alcohol doesn't help either," adds Jim.

"No, but most of these idiots aren't drinking," I say.

"The operative word there is idiot," says Jim.

"So, Don, have you gone to Karen's church yet?" asks Lisa.

"Yeah, and I must say that it's interesting."

"I'll bet. I've heard how wild those black churches can be."

"Of course, Israel doesn't take Lisa to church," says Jim. "It's voodoo for them."

"I am a Christian," says Israel. "I don't do no voodoo."

"The thing is, even though they're wild, as you say, I want what they have," I say. "There's just so much fire and energy around them."

"You just don't seem like the type to do all of that," says Lisa. "You're kind of reserved."

"That's true. I haven't done anything wild yet. But they're onto something good."

"Onto what?"

"Real belief. Real faith. A real God. I don't know. It's just so different from the kind of church I'm used to."

"That's Tommy's boy, Mike at receiver," says Lisa.

"Come on, son....concentrate on running your route," says Tommy. "Keep your eyes on the ball."

"Tommy's son's struggling a little catching the ball," says Lisa.

"But he damn fast runner though when he catches the ball," adds Israel.

"Who gives a shit what you think about my boy?"

"I say he good. What the fuck wrong with that?"

"Goddamn it, Tommy, just because you were too big of a pussy to put this boy in his place when he choked your ass, don't start no shit over nothing now," says Ronnie. "That goddamn shit's in the past."

"Who the fuck you calling a pussy? Dick!"

"Ohhh.....look at that," says Lisa. "That kid took Mike down hard."

"What the fuck, ref? He can't fucking clothesline him like that," says Tommy.

"Yeah....that was fucking bullshit there hoss," adds Ronnie.

"Fuck it....I'm going down there," says Tommy, as he takes off towards the field. "That fucking ref ain't letting that shit happen to my boy like that."

"Oh shit!" says Ronnie, as he and many other parents follow Tommy.

"We got ourselves a brawl," says Jim, beaming.

"Not again," says Lisa, as she takes off towards the field.

"What the fuck is Raeford out there for?" I ask. "He don't have no kid in this game."

"Raeford just likes a good fight," explains Homer.

"Well, Ronnie just cold-cocked him," I say. "So, I guess he got what he wanted."

"Why the fuck did he do that?" asks Jim.

"That's why you don't go down there," I say. "Once the fists start to fly it don't matter who's on what side. They just all beat the shit outta each other."

"Somebody need to call police," says Israel.

"No…just let the rednecks beat the shit out of each other. It's fun!" says Jim. "And by the way, good move on not going down there, Israel."

"I not stupid. They'd beat shit outta me."

"I see Lisa got Brett," I say.

"Yeah, pretty sure the game's over now," says Jim.

"Sure you don't want to go down there and choke the shit out of Tommy again?" I ask.

"You got jokes," replies Israel.

"Shouldn't be joking about that, son," says Homer.

"Why not?" I ask.

"That boy's already messing around with a white woman. Then he had the nerve to attack a man for no good reason. It ain't funny to me," says Homer. "Not funny at all. It ain't been forgotten."

"What the fuck you say, old man?" says Israel.

"Well, if you must know, Homer," I say. "I'm getting married to a Karen. What do you think of them apples?"

"Yeah….I know all about you seeing her. I ain't got nothing to say about that."

"Old man…suck my dick!" says Israel, as he leaves to join Lisa and Brett.

"Don't argue with me. This is God's word I'm talking about."

"Well, Homer, I've been reading quite a bit of the bible lately and I don't see what you're saying," I say. "You, sir, all full of shit."

"Just read a little closer, son," says Homer, as he gets up to leave. "And you might want to read up on those vulgarities you're using, too. You've got quite the vocabulary for someone who claims to be a Christian."

"What am I doing in this hick town anyway?" I ask. "Unfuckingbelievable."

"It's hard for these old timers to let go of the old ways," says Jim. "And then you add the fucking bible into the middle of it?"

"Don't they know that things are changing, whether they want them to or not?"

"Listen….you're dealing with people who get in a drunken brawl at a kids football game. What the fuck do you expect?"

"Look at them go, too."

"Yeah…don't worry about it. Just look at it as entertainment."

"Ronnie's one tough bastard," I say. "He's beating the shit out of all of them."

"Yeah…ain't it fun?"

"Look at us. The intellectuals being entertained by the lowly peasants beating the shit out of each other."

"Isn't that just the way of the world though?"

"Seems so."

I really feel like I'm a person living in another country sometimes. Don't get me wrong. I have a good time with many of these guys. But it's like I'm being entertained by watching this freak show unfold before my eyes. I don't know where I belong but it sure isn't here. There are a few exceptions. There are a few bright spots. Jim is one. Lisa is another.

I just wish I could connect more with Lisa. I wish I could connect more with women in general. I feel as if I have more in common with women then most of the men around here. I hate to use this word, but I'm just more sensitive than many men. I'm more thoughtful. I guess I'm more in touch with my feminine side than many men. It's so ironic that I would rather be around women, but have this condition that makes it almost impossible to really connect with them.

Chapter 29

Sunday October 10ᵗʰ, 1993

"So, who the fuck are your beloved Steelers playing today?" I ask, as Mark and I prepare for a day of football in Mark's den.

"They're gonna stomp the Chargers today," responds Mark. "And who, pray tell, are the Cowgirls gonna get ridden by today."

"Very funny," I say. "My Cowboys are gonna break them Colts. Because that's what cowboys do."

"How is it that you're free today?" asks Mark. "Why no church?"

"Well, Karen's out of town at some church conference for women, so, I just decided to lay out today."

"You must miss quite a few games having to be in church now?"

"Yeah, well, that's true. It is too bad that it goes on so long."

"Are you getting into the flow yet?"

"No, not really," I say. "It's kind of overwhelming actually."

"Uh, I hope you don't mind, but I happened to be talking to Cheryl last night. I mentioned that you were coming over today. She said that Gina wanted to talk to you."

"What? No."

"She should be here any minute."

"What does she want?"

"I don't know what she wants."

"Thanks for putting me on the fucking spot," I say.

"Listen, this is your chance to put the bitch in her place and to tell her to shut her dick hole."

"Dick hole?"

"You don't get it? Her mouth? People call a mouth a pie hole. But she has more dick in her mouth than pie, I'm sure."

There's a knock at the door.

"Damn it," I say.

"Hey there, Gina," says Mark, letting her in. "I'll just give you two some privacy."

This is typical Mark. He just loves to put people in awkward situations.

"Thanks, Mark," says Gina, sitting down on the sofa beside me. "How are you doing, Don?"

"Well, fine….except for the fact that Mark only bothered to tell me you were coming not two minutes before you got here."

"Are you afraid to talk to me or something?"

"I'm afraid of what you might say."

"You think I'm pregnant or something?"

"Well, you don't look to be."

"No, Don, I was using birth control. Still am."

"Okay…good."

"You seem so nervous."

"Well, I've never spoken to you except for that one night, when I was drunk," I say. "I don't necessarily relate to women all that well. Remember? I was a virgin."

"So, you think we only hit it off so well because you were drunk?" she asks. "And now you're sober, so you don't know what to say."

"Exactly. I was a totally different person that night…..because of the alcohol. It loosened me up. It made me say witty things. But that wasn't the real me. The real me is totally and completely awkward and dysfunctional in the company of women."

"How can you be that way with me after what we did that night?" she asks. "You've had your dick inside of me. You fucked the living shit outta me that night. We know each other in the most intimate way."

"We did it three times, didn't we?"

"We sucked. We fucked. God, you made me come several times," she says. "Damn, you know how to use your tongue."

"So, I was good?"

"Good? You were fucking great. You were a natural."

"Well….I guess that's good to know."

"So, why is it so hard to talk to me?"

"It just is," I say. "It's just awkward. I'm glad you enjoyed it. I'm sure I did. But it was a mistake. My life's just taking a turn in a different direction now."

"Yeah, I hear you're getting married."

"That's right."

"Listen, the reason I wanted to talk to you was to say that I'm sorry about running my big mouth," she says. "I hope this hasn't gotten to your fiancé."

"So far, it hasn't, but in this town it would surprise me greatly if it didn't."

"I didn't mean anything by it really. How was I to know that you needed to keep it a secret? You said you were a virgin. I thought you'd be proud that everyone would know what we did that night."

"No, of course you wouldn't have known."

"Well, I won't say anything more."

"I would appreciate it."

"I was kind of disappointed that you didn't try to contact me after that night we had," she says. "But I guess you were already talking to this other girl."

"We weren't actually dating yet. Actually, she had just turned me down for a date when we hooked up."

"But if you weren't actually seeing her yet, what would it matter that you fucked me?"

"It's because she's a Christian. Actually, I am now , too."

"Oh...okay, but she would look at you differently or something?"

"Yeah, she thought it was such a blessing that I was a virgin. I told her that before we met. I just don't think she could handle the idea that I got drunk and lost my virginity."

"Yeah, and right here on this sofa."

"Yeah, I'll never look at this sofa the same way."

"Don, it may have been a drunken little fuck fest, but I did enjoy it."

"I did , too," I say. "What I can remember of it."

"I was just hoping for something more. You're a sweet guy. And you're even sweeter when you're sober."

"You're a sweet girl. I'll never forget that night," I say. "But this is more about what the Lord's doing in my life now. My whole life's changing."

"By not calling me or trying to get in contact with me you made me feel like some cheap piece of ass."

"Well, it was pretty easy to get into your pants."

"I can't believe you just said that."

"I can't either, actually," I say. "I'm sorry."

"No, it's funny. You say you don't have any game but you can say some things sometimes....."

"Well, you were kind of easy."

"Well, I can't really deny that now, can I? But I would have still liked to have heard from you. I fucked you because I liked you."

"Sorry. That was new territory for me," I say. "I didn't know what to say to you. I'm not exactly a ladies' man. That night only happened because I was drunk."

"I would have fucked you anyway."

"If we would have even met. I wouldn't have even been in Ronnie's that night if I wasn't already liquored up."

"If things don't happen to work out with this new life of yours, just give me a call sometime."

"I think it'll work out."

"I definitely won't save myself for you," she says. "I can tell you that for sure. But I would love to hear from you. You're a sweet guy, Don. Different from a lot of the guys I mess around with."

"Thanks, Gina."

"I do hope you're happy."

"I am."

"Alright, y'all have a good time watching your little football games."

"Bye, Gina."

"Stay sweet, Don."

Why couldn't a girl like Gina have crossed paths with me a few years ago, or even a few months ago? I know people think she's a slut or a skank or whatever, but I don't have a problem with the way she views sex. I think it's great that she views it as casually as she does. I can't remember some of what happened that night, but what I can remember was spectacular. I'm not sure how many guys have that sort of experience for their first time. I guess it was the porn I've watched, but I did perform rather well. Some of that's just instinct though. I never dreamed how easy it would be to have any sort of interaction with a girl on that level. I definitely look at things differently now.

Of course, now, I'm going to another extreme. I'm going to be married to a girl who hasn't had sex since she was saved. And it was by choice. There's no doubt that there are two diametrically opposed voices inside of me. There's the one who would admittedly love to have a relationship with someone like Gina. But then there's the other side that knows that Karen's what's best for me. I guess this is what the bible speaks of when it refers to the sinful nature and the godly nature. They will always be at war with one another.

Chapter 30

Monday November 8th, 1993

"Hey, David, how long before we can throw the power back to the Fab-Con?" I ask, as I walk into the Instrumentation shop.

"Probably be after lunch. I've got to re-wire one of the fan motors," responds David.

"Okay, just let me know. I've got to run it some to check out those valves I replaced."

"And how are you gentlemen doing today?" asks Homer, as he and Ray Jones come strolling in.

"Looks like we're working about as hard as you guys are," I say.

"Shit....we mechanics....you know we done more than you have," says Ray, with his typical slightly annoyed tone. "And we paid less fucking money, too."

"Ray....where's your possum hat?" asks Jim. "Now that it's getting cold we thought we'd have seen it by now."

"Possum hat?"

"Yeah, we saw you get that possum from Boonie that time back in the parking lot," says Jim. "Figured we see a hat."

"Was the possum stew good?" I ask.

"Fuck you guys."

Lisa comes in at this point. She looks a little pissed.

"Homer.....can I have a word with you?" she asks.

"Sure darling.....what's on your mind?"

"Outside if you don't mind? And I ain't your fucking darling."

"There's nothing that you can't say in front of these guys," says Homer. "Fire away."

"Okay....have it your way. Will you please stay the fuck out of my goddamn business?"

"Please....do you have to take the Lord's name in vain?"

"Yeah.....especially if you don't fucking like it," she says. "Goddamn it, goddamn it, goddamn it!"

Yeah, she is pissed.

"Well, I can see you're a little worked up. Maybe we should talk about whatever this is some other time."

"No, we'll talk about this right goddamn now. You said we had nothing to fucking hide."

"Okay, what have I done to piss you off so severely?" asks Homer.

"Well, I was informed that you complained to HR about me and Israel. You're trying to get him fired."

"No, you must be mistaken....or someone's telling you stories."

"Thank God we live in a more enlightened time," she says. "There was a time when that would have worked."

"I didn't say a word to anyone in management. I know better than to think they'd do anything, even if I wanted them to."

"So, you would want something done if it were possible?"

"No, I didn't say that. I have a personal problem with what you're doing, girl, but I ain't trying to get no one fired over it. That ain't grounds for firing anyway," says Homer. "Those are just rumors. Someone's just trying to stir this all up. You know some folks love to do that in this place."

"Listen to me good. If I want to see a black guy then I'm gonna see a black guy. I don't have a problem with it, so why the fuck should you?

"It's against God's plan. It's in scripture."

"Homer....I've told you this before, but you're just so full of shit," I say.

"How so, son?"

"I'm reading the bible. I'm going to church. I don't see this race shit you're talking about anywhere," I say. "Sorry for butting in, Lisa, but this affects me, too. I guess I'm committing the same sin against my race as you are."

"I don't know, man. All I hear Homer talking about is Israel and Lisa," says David. "He don't seem to be saying nothing about you and Karen."

"Probably like we were saying that one time, Jim. They only have a problem with these black guys defiling their poor defenseless women," I say. "Scripture says it's wrong? Bullshit! It's just fucking bigotry."

"I'm supposed to hear about the bible from someone who's spewing vulgarities all over the place," says Homer.

"Does the bible say anything about those words, specifically?" I ask.

"Let's not get off the subject at hand, son, but yes, I can set you straight on that profane language of yours."

"Homer, you have all of these opinions about race, yet you pretend that Ray is some great friend of yours," says David.

"You guys don't know Homer the way I do," says Ray. "He's a good man."

"Are you all done now? May I please speak?" asks Homer, remaining calmer than anyone else in the room. "I'll tell you why I'm opposed to Lisa and Israel, if you really want to hear."

"This ought to be good," says Lisa.

"This is scriptural. The reason I'm opposed to Lisa and Israel being together is absolutely because scripture says that the races should not be mixed. You can debate that all you want, but it's totally clear to me that that's the truth. Don....the reason I don't oppose you and Karen being together is because both of you are saved. There's unity in Christ. The races can be together in Christ, but not apart from Christ. It's not bigotry....it's scripture."

"Okay, Homer....let's say that what you're saying is the truth. You say that you're opposed to Lisa and Israel because they aren't saved...." I say, before being cut off.

"How do you know we aren't saved?" asks Lisa. "Not you, Don. I'm asking Homer how the fuck he can judge us like that."

"The way you two are carrying on? This is a small town, girl. You can't have any secrets. Everyone knows you spend the night over his house and he over at yours....and you ain't married," says Homer.

"Do you know for a fact that we're fucking?" asks Lisa. "Maybe we sleep in different fucking beds."

"Such crass language from a lady" says Homer, shaking his head.

"But if you say they aren't saved, doesn't that mean that you think they're going to hell anyway....no matter what else they may do?" I ask.

"Yeah, well, if you aren't saved....yeah...you are going to hell," says Homer.

"I do know that much from the bible," I say. "Why are you concerned about the actions of two sinners? Sorry, Lisa, just making an argument."

"No problem....I'm sure I am a sinner."

"I'm not sure what you're getting at there, son."

"If they're going to hell anyway, what does it matter if they're involved with each other? What more damage could they do?"

"Son...it matters in how society functions. Without Christ, the races cannot get along. I'm just trying to save them and society some pain and heartbreak. They're entering into something that's destined to fail. What if they have kids? The kids will have to live in this atmosphere of conflict."

"Like there isn't plenty of conflict in marriages between members of the same race," adds Jim.

"He just doesn't want any of those half-breed mongrel kids running around," says David.

"It's just an excuse for racism," I say, waving a dismissive hand. "He's just using the bible to try to back up some jackass opinions he has because he grew up in the great enlightened South."

"I'm tired of this shit," says Ray. "I don't know all that much about the bible, but I will say that Homer's right. We shouldn't be stirring things like this up. White belongs with white and black belong with black. We were born this way for a reason. Homer's a good friend. But there's a line that shouldn't be crossed when it comes to black and white."

"Uncle Tom has spoken," says David.

"Who you calling an Uncle Tom? You son of a bitch," says Ray.

"You....you old coot. Just cause you scared to stand up to the white man don't mean I am."

"Fuck you....I ain't scared of no man."

"Fuck, Ray, look....Don....shit, even Lisa has more balls than you do," says David. "Willing to go against all of these KKK types and do what they want to do. You're just a scared old man."

"Let me just tell you one thing, son.....this is a fine man," says Homer. "I'm proud to say that he's my friend. You younger people just get so full of yourselves that you think you know everything. I ain't never been in the KKK. I ain't like that. But I have no choice but to live according to scripture. If you can't understand that, then I'm truly sorry."

Ray and Homer leave the room

"Some people are just never going to be able to change," says Lisa.

"Listen...my grandmother....she's the same way. She doesn't believe in mixing the races either," says David.

"Yeah....but that's probably because of what they lived through as blacks in that toxic atmosphere," I say. "They don't want to rock the boat. They don't want to push things too far."

"I just can't believe he's trying to use the bible to justify it," says Jim.

"If you look hard enough you can find something in the bible to justify almost any opinion you want to have," says Lisa.

"Yeah...I don't know though....it wasn't as convoluted as I thought it would be," I say.

"What the fuck does that mean?" asks Lisa.

"I don't know," I say. "Homer seemed like the typical bigot that time at the ballfield when he told Israel that the thing with Tommy hadn't been forgotten, but this is different."

"How is it fucking different?" asks Lisa.

"He just seems less sinister now.....or something."

"Bullshit!"

"I just don't know how you argue with someone who believes what they're saying is in the bible. And I have to say that the part about Christ bringing unity made some sense," I say.

"Don't let him fool you, man....he's racist alright....with his little Uncle Tom tagging along," says David.

"I don't know....I just happen to believe people are more complicated than that. These issues aren't always as clear cut as we think," I say.

"There goes our great philosopher again," says Jim.

"Thinking too much," says Lisa.

"Yeah...I don't know....maybe," I say.

"Fuck, man, you blew his goddamn logic right out of the water," says David.

"I don't think he tried to get Israel fired though," I say.

"I don't understand you, Don," says Lisa. "How the fuck can you defend that shit?"

"I'm not really defending it. I just understand the argument he's using. That one part just made sense. I still think it's bullshit. I just think he's coming from a more reasoned place than I thought before."

"You know.....I just don't get you sometimes," says Lisa. "I guess because he approves of your shit, that it's alright?"

"No, that's not it," I say. "I'm just trying to understand."

"There ain't shit to understand," says David. "He's a fucking bigot."

"I just try to give people the same benefit of the doubt that I may need someday."

I really have a hard time just going with the crowd, even when the crowd seems totally in the right. I know that Homer seems racist. But there are things that contradict that point of view. This whole race thing in the South is indeed hard to understand sometimes. We'll never solve any problems if we cannot at least make an attempt to understand why someone believes what they believe. We have to try to understand where they're coming from. There is a distinct difference to me between a bigot and someone, like Homer, who has principles backing what he believes, even if those principles may be flawed.

Chapter 31

Tuesday May 24th, 1994

"And what are the two lowly peasants doing today?" asks Mark, to Roger and Jerry, as they join Mark, Jim and I in the Instrumentation shop for break.

"Now, that's just too fucking much," responds Roger. "Mark, you have a long way to go before you're any more than a lowly peasant around here. You guys have got to stop filling his head all full of that shit."

"What shit? It's just the truth. He's part of the elite now," I say. "He's been here a while. He has the right to put the peasants in their place."

"Off with their heads!" says Mark.

"Even an entry level Instrumentation Tech is light years above some carpenter," says Jim.

"Well, we're playing your game today," says Jerry. "We ain't done shit."

"Maybe there's hope for you yet," I say. "Half the battle is being smart enough to get away with not doing anything."

"So, how are you feeling now that the big day's approaching?" asks Jerry.

"I don't know. I'm a little nervous about having to get up in front of all those people," I say.

"No second thoughts? You've had several months to think about it," says Roger.

"No, no second thoughts."

That's not really true. There are some thoughts bouncing around in my head. There is a part of me that thinks this is a huge mistake. I'm just not sure we have enough in common. And I'm not sure this life of a good church going man is what I'm cut out for. But there is the other part of me that wants every bit of this. I love Karen. I want to love the Lord. I'm just not sure what that means quite yet. I'm not experiencing what Karen and her church family do. I'm not quite fitting in. Should I just take it on faith that it will all work out? Or should I run the other way?

"I do have one bone to pick with you," says Roger.

"What's that?"

"Where's my invitation?"

"Yeah, mine too," says Jerry.

"Well, come to think of it, you haven't said anything to me, either. Now these yahoos, well, I can understand," says Jim.

"I'm going," offers Mark.

"I don't know…..it just never occurred to me that anyone from the plant would care to go," I respond.

"Mark works here," says Jerry.

"Yeah, but I grew up with Mark."

"There are quite a few production people going. People that Karen works with," says Roger.

"Yeah….I know. You do understand that there won't be any alcohol?" I say, trying to be funny.

"So, it is true," says Roger. "You just think of us as a bunch of yahoos that just want to get drunk and raise hell."

"Well, there was that incident last fall at the ball game…..you know…..the infamous brawl," I say. "At a children's game?"

"Not exactly a strong testimonial," adds Jim. "But how that reflects on me, I do not know."

"But we are capable of cleaning up our act," says Jerry. "When we want to."

"It's just that Karen and her family are so religious. I just don't picture you in that environment."

"But I'm not like these bozos," says Jim. "You know I can behave myself."

"Well, I just didn't think you'd want to come," I say. "Thought you'd have better things to do. It just doesn't seem like a manly type of thing to do…..invite your friends to your wedding."

Honestly, I didn't put any thought into not inviting them. I think I look at my life as being divided into two distinct worlds. And I'm not sure the two would mix all that well. I don't socialize with most of the guys from the plant. Why would they want to come to my wedding? There won't be anyone there but my family, Karen's family and church people. It will be a more civilized crowd there.

"Are you sure that's all it is?" asks Roger.

"Why? What do you mean?" I ask.

"It's not that you think we might not approve or something, is it?" asks Roger.

"No, it's purely the fact that I think you're going to make a spectacle of yourself," I say, still trying to be funny.

"No, seriously," says Roger. "I want an answer to this."

"Well....I don't know....I guess I had my doubts. I mean....so many people in the South do have a problem with it."

"And you just lump us in with them?" asks Jerry.

"You know I don't have a problem with it," says Jim.

"No, not on racial grounds," I say. "But I know you think I'm making a mistake."

"But that's for different reasons," says Jim.

"I didn't really put any thought into it. It just didn't occur to me that you'd want to come to the damn wedding. Fuck, I wish I didn't have to go through the whole thing. I want to marry Karen, but I don't really care about the whole ceremony. I didn't think you would, either."

"We just want the opportunity to bean your ass with bags of rice," says Jerry. "Unopened bags of rice."

"Five pound bags of rice," adds Roger.

"Yeah....didn't think of that. Bounce them right off of that huge melon head of his," says Mark.

"And see what other trouble we yahoos can stir up," adds Roger.

"If you all want to come, then sure, you're totally welcome to," I say.

"Are you going to speak in tongues?" asks Jerry.

"In the wedding?" I ask. "What the fuck do you think we're gonna be doing there?"

"Well....you said they're all religious. I thought maybe they're gonna have church up in there. Drive out demons, speak in tongues, and all of that shit."

"No tongues."

"Have you loosened up any in church? Are you doing any of that stuff yet?" asks Roger.

"No, I don't think I ever will actually. Just too uncomfortable in front of all those people."

"And it's been how long?" asks Jim.

"Almost a year."

"Well....just wait until the wedding night and he'll be speaking in tongues," says Roger.

"Well, I don't know....it isn't like Karen's getting first crack at him," says Jerry.

"Thanks for bringing that up," I say. "Karen's probably heard about Gina by now, too."

"So, most of us have girls we've fucked before we met our wives," says Jerry.

"Some of us even after we've married our wives," says Roger.

"Yeah, but not right after we told them that we were virgins," says Jim.

"Virgin?" asks Jerry.

"Yeah....you didn't get that part of the story? Gina popped Don's cherry," explains Mark. "He fucked the shit outta that girl right there on my couch. Three damn times. Wore her shit out."

"I didn't know," says Jerry. "Where the fuck was I?"

"It's not something I was particularly proud of," I say.

"How the hell didn't you hear?" asks Roger.

"Why the fuck didn't you say anything?" asks Jerry.

"I just figured you already knew," says Roger. "And I knew it was something that Don didn't really want to get around...so, I just kept it to myself, once I heard."

"Thanks, Roger," I say. "At least someone had that thought."

"But why? How?" asks Jerry.

"Why was I a virgin until I was thirty?"

"Yeah."

"I'm just socially retarded when it comes to women."

"But with a little help from me, and some liquor, we took care of that," says Mark.

"I hate to say it again, but do you think that it's the best thing to begin this marriage with a lie?" asks Jim.

"It's not really a lie, it's just the omission of part of the truth," I respond.

Why does Jim think he's the voice of morality around here?

"But I would think that this is pretty important to someone as religious as her," says Jim.

"Yeah...it is," I say. "That's why I can't tell her."

"I don't think he should tell her," says Roger. "It was before they were seeing each other."

"Yeah, I didn't tell Steph about all the pussy I had before I met her," says Jerry.

"But Steph didn't think you were a virgin on your wedding night, did she?" asks Jim.

"She knew I wasn't a virgin because we had fucked plenty of times before then," says Jerry.

"Yeah, my situation is a little different," I say. "The issue isn't that I fucked Gina. The issue is that Karen thinks I'm a virgin. She thinks God's giving her this pure man of God."

"Well, that's far from true anyway," says Mark. "We used to look at those porn flicks all the time that I got from Rackley's when I worked there."

"Yeah, I'm about as corrupted as they come," I say.

"You were sexually active," says Roger. "Just not with a girl."

"With his hand," says Jerry.

"That's why I shouldn't mention it," I say. "I'm very far from pure anyway."

"Not quite the same thing," says Jim.

"You bastards just make sure you don't fuck my wedding up."

"Don't worry…we'll make it a day to remember," says Jerry.

"That's what I'm worried about."

Chapter 32

Saturday June 18th, 1994

"Baby, what are you doing? You know the groom isn't supposed to see the bride before the wedding," I say.

"I know….but there's something I have to ask you," replies Karen, looking quite serious.

"It can't wait until later?"

"No…it can't."

"Okay….what is it?"

"It's just that I heard something through the grapevine….at the plant."

"Let me guess," I interrupt, trying to gain the upper hand on the situation. "You heard a rumor that I got drunk and had sex with some girl?"

"Yeah, it's been awhile since I heard it the first time. I didn't want to believe it. But recently someone else mentioned something about it."

"Yeah, that's an old rumor," I say, trying to sound dismissive. "Someone was just trying to stir things up. You gotta remember, this was right when we first started talking. At least that's when I heard it."

"Yeah, it was around that time. I think we'd been out already."

"You know how some people were," I say. "I wouldn't be surprised if someone like Ed Harris spread that lie just to try to break us up."

"But it's just that it's so specific. Not just that you slept with someone, but her name, too. Gina, I think it was. And there was the part about you being a virgin, too. Does anyone else know about that?"

"I told Mark, I think," I say. "With his big mouth he probably told people at the plant."

"Okay….but I still wonder how it would be so specific."

"That's the best way to spread a rumor. Be specific. It makes it seem more real."

"I guess…"

"I don't even know anyone named Gina. And I told you, I'm shy when it comes to women. Painfully shy. That's why I'm still a virgin at thirty-one. I couldn't hook up with some woman even if I wanted to. And I don't want to….by the way."

Now I've crossed that line into outright lying. Up to this point it was simply omission of the truth. Now I'm denying what I know to be true. I'm affirming something I know to be a lie.

"You know what? The devil is a lie," she says. "Nothing's gonna stop me from marrying my Donnie today."

"Yeah, people would love to stop us from getting married."

"I know. But it ain't gonna work. I'm sorry I doubted you, honey."

"Don't worry about it. I know you had to ask. It must have been a shock to hear."

"It was, but it doesn't matter now."

"Okay, you had better go and get ready now. We don't have much longer."

"Okay...see you in a bit. Love you."

"Love you, too."

"Well, I hope this is as close as I ever get to getting married again," says Jim, walking up, as Karen leaves. "You do know that you're not supposed to see the bride before the wedding?"

"Yeah, yeah....I know. Hey, glad you could make it."

"Wouldn't miss it."

"Man, that was close," I say, looking in the direction of the departing Karen.

"What?"

"Karen asked about Gina."

"What? What the hell did you say?"

"I told her it was probably just someone who doesn't want this to happen and wanted to cause trouble. I even threw out the name of Ed Harris."

"And that idea really isn't that far-fetched, even the part about Ed Harris. That sneaky son of a bitch would do something just like that."

"Yeah....but I did actually fuck Gina," I say. "I just can't believe it took Karen this long to say anything. She said she first heard it way back then, when it happened."

"Women in love don't want to believe that sort of shit."

"And plus, at the time, it wasn't like we were actually together," I say. "So maybe she just didn't think she had the right to say anything."

"Listen, Don, are you sure you want this? You're the one who seems to see all these signs lining up or something. But what about this? Are you sure this isn't a sign that you shouldn't do this? The signs aren't as lined up as you want to believe."

"Even if I wasn't sure, I can't back out now? I couldn't do that to her."

"So, you do have doubts."

"Nothing's perfect, Jim. Things can't always be exactly the way we'd like them. But I still believe that this is meant to be somehow. Even with what I did and the lie."

There is a nagging part of me that says this is a huge mistake. I've broken the ice with women. I had an absolutely great night with Gina. She thought I was hot, even after that night. But, on the other hand, there is this real change happening in my life. I really want to live a life dedicated to the Lord. Karen's as dedicated to the Lord as they come. I'm not saying that I see everything that she sees just yet. I don't have the faith that she has. The Lord still has some work to do on me. But this is the direction that feels best to me. Sometimes we just have to make choices. I've made mine.

"But this is a huge step, man," says Jim.

"It'll all work out. I'm opening up a brand new chapter…with a great Christian woman and a new purpose in life."

"Okay…I've said all I'm gonna say," he says, raising his hands in surrender.

"No problem, man."

"Well, let me go find a seat out there."

"Okay…see you at the reception."

"Good luck."

"Thanks, Jim."

"Well, there's my best man," I say, as Mom and Dad walk up. "You clean up pretty good."

"Donald….you ready for this, son?" asks Dad.

"As ready as I'll ever be."

"We both want you to know that we love Karen so much and love that she's part of the family," says Momma.

"I think everyone got along fine at the rehearsal dinner," I say.

"Claude sure is a character," says Dad.

"But everyone's so nice," says Momma.

"Are there a lot of people out there?" I ask, as I peek through a curtain which shields the area behind the choir loft from the sanctuary.

"Yeah, pretty big turn out," answers Dad.

"I hate standing in front of crowds," I say.

"I know, but you'll be alright," says Momma.

I wonder how much they do know of my condition. They have to have noticed things through the years. But I know that they don't have a true grasp on how deep it is. Many people hate being in front of crowds. But not as many have had their lives altered the way I have. No, Mom, you really don't know.

"That's Homer White out there," I say.

"Who's Homer White?" asks Momma.

"He's this old guy at the plant. He believes that whites and blacks shouldn't marry. Tries to back it up with the bible. I'll bet that jackass is gonna say something when the preacher asks if anyone has any objections. He claims he doesn't have any problem with Karen and me because we're both Christians."

"I doubt he'll say anything, son," says Dad.

"He'd better not."

"Don't worry about it."

"I can't help but see that Hugh's made his feelings clear," I say. "I see Grandma sitting out there by herself."

"He's set in his ways," says Momma. "Nobody's gonna change that."

"Would probably have ended badly if he were to have shown up anyway," I say.

"Okay, it looks like we're ready. I'd better go to the back of the church," says Momma.

"Okay, Momma."

And so the ceremony goes on without a hitch. I wasn't anywhere near as nervous in front of that crowd as I would have thought. Karen is now my wife. I never thought I would get married. I never thought I would find anyone. I never thought anyone could ever break through the shyness, but Karen has. Of course, Gina did, too.

"So, son, you're a part of this family now," says Claude.

"Yes, I am," I say.

"I expect you to take care of my little girl now. It's a man's responsibility to be the head of the household. Do your job. And if she does her job, you'll have a happy marriage."

"I know, Claude. And I intend to take care of your daughter. I intend to be the husband that she's waited for and deserves."

"Good, son. Then the Lord will always bless and watch over you. You always want to stay in the will of the Lord."

"Well, I must say that's very sound advice," says Homer. "You always want to stay in the will of the Lord."

"Claude, this is Homer. I work with him at the plant."

"Claude and I know each other," says Homer.

"Yeah....I used to run the boiler up there quite a few years ago," says Claude. "Glad you could come, Homer. Now if you two will excuse me, let me see what's holding things up. I'm ready to get a little food in this belly. "

"Glad to see you again, Claude."

"Same here, Homer,"

After giving Claude enough time to get out of earshot, I say, "Let me ask you something, Homer?"

"Sure, go ahead."

"You and Claude were just speaking about staying in the will of the Lord. Do you really believe that I stayed in the will of the Lord by marrying Karen?"

"Of course, I do. I wouldn't have come otherwise. I meant what I said, Don. If God's for you, then no one can be against you. In Christ, all things are equal. God has blessed your union. Now you just make sure that you stay in God's will from here on out."

"I was worried that maybe you were going to start something."

"Don, I would never do anything like that. If I didn't approve, I would just not show up. I would never disrupt a special day like this."

"I guess I may have misjudged you."

"You just need to listen sometimes, son. Don't be so quick to jump to conclusions. Sometimes things are more complicated than they may seem on the surface."

"I've often said the same thing myself."

"Well, I can't stay for the reception. I just wanted to say a word to you."

"Alright then. See you at work."

"Congratulations, son, you've got yourself a godly woman there."

"Thanks, I know I do."

"Congratulations, brother," says Dan.

"Thanks, man. But I'll be glad when this thing's all over. Too many people," I respond.

Grandma approaches us.

"Look how nice my two grandsons look today."

"Hi, Grandma, what did you think of the ceremony?" I ask.

"It was beautiful," responds Grandma. "I would apologize for

Hugh not being here, but I know that you'd probably rather have it this way anyway."

"Yeah....I guess that's right," I say. "I do like Hugh though. Some parts about him."

"He's a good man. He's just got these ideas when it comes to certain things," she says.

"I know."

"So, Dan, when are we going to see you tying the ole knot?" asks Grandma.

"Well....I don't know Grandma, but that may be one that Hugh would want to skip as well," responds Dan.

"What? You gonna marry a black girl, too?"

"Never know," Dan says, with a slight grin towards Don.

Maybe a black man? That would be good.

"We have to stir things up a little, Grandma," I add.

"Come on, Grandma, let me help you find your seat," says Dan, as he leads her away.

"I cannot believe that fucking Homer showed up," says Roger, approaching me.

"He was real nice though," I respond.

"Wolf in sheep's clothing."

"No, I don't think so. He's alright."

"I hate to tell you, but Jerry's drinking."

"That ass."

"I think he's got a couple of pints with him. I think Mark's been drinking with him, too."

"I didn't think Mark would pull that shit," I say.

"Well, they both are."

"Keep an eye on them, will ya?"

"If I would have known that this was bring your own bottle, I would have brought something, too," jokes Roger. "But yeah, I'll try to keep Jerry under some sort of control."

"Do you think he has a problem? I mean with the drinking."

"Well, it does seem like he can't go without it. Even when he knows he shouldn't drink."

"And there have been times where you could smell it on him at the plant."

"You think you're telling me something new?" asks Roger. "I work in confined spaces with the guy."

"Should we do something?"

"You mean like an intervention or something."

"I don't know. I guess this isn't the place to talk about it anyway."

"Hey, Lisa, what's that you've got?" asks Roger, as Lisa passes nearby.

"She caught the bouquet," I say. "Lucky girl."

"Yeah, I caught it," she says, sounding less than thrilled. "It just kind of fell into my hands."

"She was fighting me to get it," says Melody, as she stops by to check on me.

"I was not," responds Lisa.

"I'll tell Israel to start planning the wedding," I say.

"Fuck that."

"You don't want to get married again?" I ask.

"I think two losers are enough," responds Lisa.

"Two? You've been married twice?" I ask. "I only knew about the one."

"Yeah....and that's enough. Brett's dad was actually my second husband. My first was when we were both really young. Too young."

"Then why did you fight these women to catch the bouquet?" asks Roger.

"Because she's still hoping that her Prince Charming will swoop in and sweep her off her feet," I say.

"It's funny, all those girls fighting for it, including Melody here, and it just drops into my hands."

"But you were out there to begin with," adds Roger. "You must have wanted it."

"I think you and Don need to just shut the fuck up," says Lisa.

"Such crass language from a lady," I say.

Lisa glances my way with a smile.

"Well...I wanted it. I'll admit it, even if she won't," says Melody.

"Hey, man, the photographer says it's time for you to throw the garter," says Jim.

"Okay," I reply. "Make sure you get out there."

"No....not me," replies Jim.

"If I had to....then you do, too," says Lisa, as she drags Jim to the middle of the floor.

"Don.....Don.....throw it to me.......throw it to me.....I wanna slip that thing up Lisa's thigh," says an obviously drunk Mark.

"Oh God," says Lisa, turning away.

"Goddamn it! Shut your drunk ass up!" shouts Diane, only slightly less inebriated than her son. "Don't you see you're causing a disturbance?"

"Oh God, here we go," I say, embarrassed. "I knew this was going to happen. Is Jerry sharing that bottle with everyone?"

"Just throw it and get it over with," says Roger.

"Okay, we all ready?" I ask.

"Yeah…..throw it!" bellows Mark.

I shoot the garter over my shoulder.

"You dick…….you tripped me," yells Mark, while sprawled across the floor. "What's your damn problem?"

"Who's this drunk fool yelling at?" asks William, Karen's brother, who's standing there holding the garter, as Mark flops around on the floor, trying to get up.

"Son, we ain't gonna have this here. This is a church," says Claude.

"Don…..do something," says Karen.

"Great….now you've done fucked the whole wedding up," says Diane.

"You're cussing more than I fucking am," responds Mark.

"You two just need to go," I say.

"He pushed me," says Mark. "I could have been hurt."

"Are you sure you didn't just stumble?" I ask. "You've obviously had too much to drink."

"No, he fucking pushed me."

"It don't matter anyway," says Israel. "Ain't no one putting that garter on Lisa's leg."

"Come on, man," says William. "It's just a tradition. It don't mean nothing."

"No, no man messing with my woman's leg."

"I wish I wouldn't have caught this bouquet anyway."

"That should have been my garter," says Mark.

"Okay, time to go," I say.

"Fine," says Mark. "Whatever."

"I'll help them out," says Roger.

"We don't need no help," says Diane.

"Somebody ought to drive them home though," suggests Lisa.

"I'll take care of it," says Roger.

Roger, along with several of Karen's relatives escort Diane and Mark out of the church.

Eventually, things settle down and everyone sits down to eat. But before the food is served, Claude offers a toast to the new couple.

"May I have your attention? I would like to offer a toast to the happy couple. Does everyone have their glass of champagne?"

Champagne meaning sparkling apple cider in this situation, considering it is a Christian wedding and all of that.

"First of all, I would just like to thank my Lord and Savior Jesus Christ for this day. Praise be to God! Thank you Jesus for your Salvation. Thank you for your love. Thank you for your guidance. We ask that you please go with Don and Karen as they embark on their new life together. We ask that you always bless them. Keep them in your will. And Father, please bless them with a whole litter of kids. Praise be to God. Now if everyone would please...." says Claude, holding up his glass. "....drink to the happiness of my daughter and my new son in law."

"What the.......this ain't no champagne!" says Jerry, rather loudly.

"Of course not, son....this is a Christian wedding. No alcohol," says Claude.

"You lied then.....you said it was champagne."

"You seem to have had all the alcohol you need."

"Yeah, Jerry, haven't you had enough anyway?" ask Roger.

"I'm not the only one who brought something. Whoever heard of a wedding without champagne?"

"That's it," says Roger. "You have no respect for anything. This is our friend's wedding. How about we just go outside and for a minute? Sound good? That's all it'll take."

"Jerry, could you please just stop?" I ask.

"Sorry, man," says Roger. "I said I would keep him under control and I didn't."

"Control who? Me?"

"Why did you invite these guys anyway?" ask Karen.

"Good question," I respond. "They said they wanted to come."

"Son, you have to start thinking about who you hang out with," offers Claude. "You're a part of Christ now."

"I don't hang out with them really. I work with them."

"That boy has a problem," says Claude.

"I know.....it's becoming obvious."

"Well, your first instinct was right," says Jim.

"What's that?" I ask.

"You shouldn't have let the riff raff in."

"Yeah….but I wasn't expecting this sort of scene."

"I think I'll just leave now before I end up doing something stupid myself."

"Alright, man….thanks for coming."

"Good luck, you two….I really hope it works out," says Jim.

"Thanks," I say, as Jim leaves.

"What did he mean by that?" asks Karen.

"What?"

"That he hopes it works out. That was kind of odd."

"I don't think he meant anything by it. Just joking I guess, because of how things went today."

"It was still a great day though," says Karen. "I'm married to the man I love. What God has put together let not man put asunder."

"I love you too, Karen."

"I can't wait for tonight," she says, with a wink and a smile.

"I know….it's been a long time for both of us."

"But much longer for you. I cannot believe I get the honor of being the one and only woman that you will ever make love to. Praise God. That is such a blessing."

"Yes, it is."

What happened at the wedding kind of illustrates the differences between the world I used to live in and the one I'm entering. I know that choices have to be made if I really expect to be used by the Lord for great works. I shouldn't be associating with certain people if I want this to work. I have to start keeping company with other believers. I'm not supposed to have anything in common with those of the world anymore. At least that's what scripture says should be the case. At some point, I'll have to leave them behind. It's not like I see them outside of the plant all that much anyway, except for Mark. Of course, he was the one who made the biggest ass of himself today. But I can't see leaving him behind. I just can't do that.

Chapter 33

Saturday May 3rd, 1997

"What's up, dude?" I ask, as Mark opens the door to his cave.

Yes, Mark still lives in his mother's house.

"Hey, man, what's up? Come on in."

"Just thought I'd drop by and see what your ass was up to," I say.

"Not much, really."

"I've been meaning to ask, but why the hell are you still living in this pig sty? You've had the job at the plant for almost four years now. Ain't it about time to get out of the nest?"

"Do you have any idea how much money I'm saving by living here? I can take it at least a little while longer, if it means I can save some more cash."

"Yeah….I can see your point," I say. "I just know that as soon as I got the job at the plant I was ready to get my own place."

I'm not even sure why that was. With my being so shy and timid, you would think that I would have wanted to stay at home as long as possible. But no, I was ready to leave as soon as I could. Of course, I wasn't exactly moving away. I was just moving across town.

"I'm getting there," says Mark. "I'm working my way up the ladder at the plant. I keep getting raises. It's starting to pile up a little. I'll be doing something soon."

"Yeah….you're doing a good job at the plant, picking up on things quick. You kind of surprised me, actually. Now, of course you're not on the level that I am, but then again, who really is?"

"Egotistical bastard."

"Hey, we have to deal in reality," I say, smiling.

"You were right though. This job's been good for me. I feel like I'm going in a good direction now."

"I have to admit though that I was apprehensive in recommending you."

"Why?"

"Well, you haven't always been the most reliable person, at least when it comes to employment."

"Well….sure…that's true. But those were little bullshit jobs," says Mark. "This job's interesting. I actually like going to work."

"And it doesn't hurt that we bullshit and fuck off a good amount of the time, I'm sure."

"Yeah, and there's always something going on down there. Always some crazy ass shit from someone."

"Yeah….they're something alright. But they're good people."

"You know, before you came, I was thinking…..it's been almost three years since you and Karen got married, hasn't it? Time sure flies, seems like just yesterday."

"Yeah….that's right. It has been a quick three years," I say. "And might I say, thanks again for getting drunk at my wedding. Ass!"

"Never gonna let me live that shit down, I guess."

"Never, my friend."

"How come we never seem to do anything with Karen involved?" asks Mark. "You never bring her over here. You never invite me over, except when she's busy or something. What's the deal?"

"You got a thing for her or something?"

"Of course not, you dick. It just seems odd."

"I don't know," I say. "I guess I just look at it as two different worlds."

"Two different worlds?"

"Maybe that's not the right way to put it. It's just that she's so into the Lord and church and all of that stuff. She's just not into much else. There's a lot of stuff that just doesn't interest her, but that does interest me."

I really didn't get how little we had in common before we were married. I was so excited about my newfound faith that I guess I just glossed over everything else. Karen's a very simple person. She has simple interests and a simple way of looking at the world. I'm not saying it's bad. It's just the way she is. She's just not interested in what's going on around her unless it involves church or the Lord. And I should throw her family in there, too. She loves spending as much time as possible with her family. And there's a lot of her family in Raymond. The reality is that her interests are very simple and very limited. She has no interest in politics. No interest in any of the great questions of our time. Doesn't want to read any books other than the bible. Doesn't want to listen to any music but gospel. We have one real thing in common and even that's starting to fall apart.

"In other words, she doesn't have that much in common with you or me," says Mark.

"That's about the size of it."

"So, with that being the case, how are things with you two?"

"Well....things are basically alright. But it could be better. Perfect marriages are few and far between."

"So, what's going on?"

"It's just the church thing. It's not getting any better. And it's really the only thing we do have in common. But, it turns out that that wasn't even true."

"What about the church thing isn't getting any better? What's the problem?"

"We're just not getting any closer on things. I'm still not getting what they're doing. It just isn't adding up, even after all of these years."

"All the Pentecostal shit?"

"Yeah, all the shit that goes on in church when they praise the Lord," I say. "The shouting, praising, falling on the floor....all that shit."

"So, you still aren't joining in, I take it?"

"Joining in? No, far from it, actually. The more I study, the more I'm convinced that they're actually doing things that are against scripture."

"Okay, Mr. Biblical Scholar, what are they doing that's so against the bible?"

"Yeah, I know. Sometimes I struggle with that," I say. "I feel like I'm nitpicking them. But they're the ones who claim to be so much in the will of God, accusing other churches of being dead and all of that shit."

"Are you sure this isn't just because you aren't having the same experiences as they are? Maybe you just want to tear them down because you aren't experiencing the same shit."

"Actually, I have had that thought," I say. "And at the beginning that may have been true. I was so convinced that they were really onto something good. I wanted what they had. I wanted the same experiences. So, yeah, maybe I was looking to poke holes in it back then for that reason. But that isn't the case now."

"But is it really so important for everything to line up with scripture absolutely perfectly? What's the big deal?"

"Because these people claim that the spirit of God is speaking directly to them. They claim that all of this is the Spirit. They believe that all of this is supernaturally happening through the Spirit."

"Yeah, that is a pretty bold claim to make."

"It is. That's the point. They want to set themselves up as being different than most other churches. They want to say that they have something that other Christians don't have. They say that God's dwelling inside of them. They've set themselves to a higher standard."

"You mean that they think that God lives inside of them?"

"Well…. scripture does say that. I don't have a problem with the concept. The spirit of God is supposed to dwell in the spirit of a person who accepts Christ. That's what I believe, too."

"It's not like I would know. I'm not exactly a student of the bible."

"I don't even remember that point being made in the church I grew up in," I say. "They never spoke like these people do. They never talked about the spirit of God as being that real in our lives. But that's what I want. I don't want to just be a member of some tired old religion. I want to really partake of the godly nature. I want that supernatural transformation. I want something real."

"No, I don't remember anything like that being taught at First Presbyterian, either."

"The thing is, they actually are different than other Christians I'm used to. There's no doubt about that. Because of that, I can't bring myself to say that they're wrong, just yet. Sure, things don't line up with scripture. But who am I? I'm far from pure. How can I possibly judge them?"

"But who the fuck is pure?" asks Mark. "I sure as shit ain't."

"Yeah, I know that none of us are pure, but there's supposed to be evidence that the Spirit's working in my life."

"And you don't think there is?"

"Well, look at me," I say. "I'm still hiding the truth from Karen about Gina, which makes me a liar. I have the urge to fuck almost every woman I see, at least the young hot ones."

"Which makes you a pervert?"

"Thank you for that."

"You're always welcome, my friend."

"Not that I've acted on any of those urges, except of course, for Gina. But if I could, I probably would. So, it's not like I'm some great saint for not fooling around on Karen."

"What do you mean, if you could?"

"I mean, I'm still a fucking dysfunctional mess when it comes to women. I've never really gotten over it. Gina was just a fucking aberration or something. It was just because I was drunk. For anything to happen the woman would have to practically strip down in front of me and ask me if I wanted to fuck."

I was kind of hoping that the spirit of God would take care of the shyness. I was hoping for a complete transformation. But it hasn't come. I, of course, don't want the shyness gone so that I can pursue other women. I just want it gone so that I can function like a normal human being. I want to be able to be comfortable in my own skin. I just want to be normal.

"If you weren't, as you say, dysfunctional, would you fuck other women?" asks Mark. "Because you made it sound like you want to, but you just can't."

"I don't really want to. I don't have the intention to do that. But, yeah, I hate to admit it, but I probably would. Sometimes the urge is just so powerful. It's just so tangible. I can just picture myself bending some girl over a chair and just pounding the shit out of her ass. You know what I mean? It's like it's so real. I can almost touch it."

"Touch what?"

"Her! The girl. Her ass. Her tits. I can just picture myself doing everything. It's just so real I can't stand it sometimes."

"Whose ass and tits?"

"Whoever," I say. "Sometimes it's someone I've been around or have seen. Other times it's just some imaginary girl I conjure up in my head."

"Good thing you still have that shyness problem, I guess. It's kind of like you have some sort of filter to prevent you from fucking around."

"It doesn't matter though," I say. "I still have those desires. A person who had the spirit of God inside of them wouldn't have all that shit in their head. With all of that, who am I to say that they aren't in the will of God? Where's my authority to challenge them? There's just no evidence that I'm close to God at all."

"So, I take it that you think they're better Christians than you are."

"I've never had the experiences they've had. They all either had dramatic experiences when they were saved or else they have them now in church. I've never had that. And I still have the same dark urges and thoughts that I always did. I can't say that God has transformed me at all."

"Dark urges? What dark urges?"

"Wanting to fuck every single woman that I see? Didn't you hear that?" I ask.

"Yeah....but, isn't that just natural for men to feel that way?" asks Mark. "I'm not sure I would call those dark urges. I think that's just being a healthy man. I thought you were going to say you wanted to torture animals and kill small children or something."

I have that thought sometimes, that this is just natural to feel this way. This urge to fuck every woman I see. I'm sure there are other men who have the same urges. But I have a hard time believing that they all do. I'm starting to believe that part of my problem relating to women is the fact that all I can think about when I'm around them is their different body parts. I seem to only be able to think of women as sex objects. It's like I'm distracted the whole time I'm around a good looking woman. All I can think about is what it would be like to fuck her.

"But it's not just that," I say. "I still love all the things of the world. I still love all my music. Still love my movies with the nudity and sex and bad language. I still cuss quite a bit. I haven't changed a bit, actually, except for acting a little religious sometimes. It's all an act, nothing real is happening in my life to make me believe I really have the spirit of God."

"Is that what that thing about two worlds is about?" asks Mark. "Do I represent your life on the dark side? All these things that you won't let go of? Is that why you don't want Karen around me?"

"That sounds kind of funny when you put it that way. My life on the dark side. But it's true. There's so much I try to hide from Karen."

"The music and stuff like that?"

"Yeah…actually…I threw out all my music. But I've never really stopped listening to it on the radio. But that's only when Karen isn't around."

"Damn, you threw out all of your shit? You really think all that shit's evil or something? You could have just given it to me. I'm a heathen, you know? I would have gladly taken all the music you had."

"If it's evil, I'm not supposed to corrupt someone else with it."

"So, you do think it's evil?"

"No, not evil, just worldly."

"Still could have given it to me."

"I actually kept listening to it for a while after we got married," I say. "I knew what she thought about it. To her credit, she didn't put any pressure on me. I just decided to throw it away one day. I guess I did convince myself that it was evil. And maybe it is. But I still love it."

"So, this is supposed to be proof that you aren't a true Christian or something?" asks Mark. "You're a heathen or something because you still like that good ole rock and roll?"

"I don't know.….I'm really confused by the whole thing, actually. When I look at them as a whole, when I take everything into consideration.….…well.…I have to say that they are better Christians than I am. They don't hold onto all the shit of the world like I do. And I do believe that we should do away with all the things of the world. That's in scripture."

"Well, you think that they aren't holding onto things of the world like you are," says Mark. "But do you really know that?"

"I see pretty much what's in Karen's life. Believe me, it's pretty much the Lord all the time. She really has left the things of the world behind. And I'm around her family, the ones who are saved, and yes, they're committed to the Lord and his work far more than I am."

"Things of the world? You keep saying that. What exactly are things of the world? Isn't everything of this world?"

"Things of this world, as opposed to spiritual things," I say. "It's just the idea that nothing in this world matters, that after we're saved only spiritual things matter. It's not always that a particular thing's evil. It's just that many things just don't matter in the bigger picture of salvation. It's just that nothing else matters but our relationship to God. In other words, our time is precious. Our time on this earth is finite. Why not make the best of it? Why fill it full of frivolous hobbies and meaningless pursuits? There are two different worlds, the spiritual and the worldly. Christians are supposed to focus on the spiritual."

"So, you're saying that they give up these things of the world and you don't?" asks Mark.

"They are far more devoted than I am. That's the thing. They claim to have something real. And they actually show proof of it."

"Well, maybe you are just a heathen like me."

"Even with all of that though, I can't shake this feeling that something just isn't right with all of this stuff that goes on in church. Sometimes, despite all my baggage, I actually feel like the enlightened one."

"Oh, let me bow at your feet, the great enlightened one."

"I only say that because I see this truth that they can't seem to see. Being able to see the truth is the only proof that I'm saved, I guess. That's all I have to hang my hat on."

"What's the big mystery?" asks Mark. "What's to be so confused about? They're just getting all hopped up on emotions. That's why it doesn't line up with scripture. They're just getting carried away.

I see that with these people who go to these TV ministers."

"No, I'm actually there. I know what goes on. I just don't think it's an act. You just have no idea what it's like. Some of this is really crazy stuff. It's just a little too bizarre to be an act. And it just seems like it's deeper than emotions run amuck. And you see little signs of this even when there isn't a church service going on."

"So, what are you saying? Do you think something supernatural is going on? Do you actually think this shit's real?"

"Well, I do believe in the spirit world. I do believe in the supernatural. I know that idea may be falling out of favor today, but yes, I do believe that there's a reality to the spiritual plane."

"Well, from our talks in the past, you know that I do, too."

"Yeah, there are things going on out there that we can't see."

"Yeah, I'm sure that's true," says Mark. "There is most definitely a whole lot of shit going on that we know nothing about."

"And believing in that is crucial to being a Christian," I say. "That's the thing that gets me. How can you be a Christian and not believe in the supernatural? You have to. That's the part that Karen and her church are right about. There is a supernatural component to being a Christian."

"How so?"

"I'm absolutely convinced that we're supposed to be indwelt with the very spirit of God after we're saved. That's what you have to understand. That's why this is all so important to me. This isn't just some religion. This is real. I just need to know where I fall in this whole thing. I'm either a heathen like you say, and that's why this shit isn't happening to me, or they're the ones in error and this is just all some deception."

"Or, maybe you're all just deluding yourselves," says Mark. "Maybe you're all looking for something that doesn't exist. Not the supernatural. Just maybe you're wrong about this being indwelt with the spirit of God shit."

"It's possible. I just feel in my heart that there is something real here. That's what I seek."

"I'm just not sure I believe in the biblical idea of angels and demons and all of that shit."

"I just believe that something real's happening in these services," I say. "And I happen to believe it's supernatural….whatever that means. It isn't fake."

"But, at the same time, you're not sure it's God, either."

"Yeah, not sure at all. That's the problem."

"But if this isn't the spirit of God, what the hell is it?"

"I don't know," I say. "Like I said, I'm really confused about the whole damn thing. But if it isn't faked, and it isn't of God, then there is only one other real possibility. It has to be a deceiving spirit."

"A deceiving spirit?"

"Yeah, they believe in demons and all of that stuff, too."

"Do you?"

"I think I do, actually," I say. "I'm just not so sure many of the things that they attribute to satanic forces are actually that. But if I'm gonna believe in good spirits, why wouldn't I believe there were some bad ones out there, too? The fact that there is good and evil in this world is apparent. Why wouldn't that be true in the spiritual plane as well?"

I know that many people believe that it's a primitive view to have to believe in spirits and all of that shit. But to me it's just common sense. I know there isn't any proof that spirits exist. I just believe it's the case. People who believe what I believe are considered narrow-minded, or even simple-minded and uneducated, but to me it's narrow-minded to just close your mind off to the possibility that something exists just because there isn't tangible scientific proof for it. I want to believe in a world that reaches beyond what we can see. I do believe it.

"I'm not saying I disagree," says Mark. "I was just asking the question."

"There's just too much evidence to deny that spirits exist, including the evil ones, maybe not scientific evidence, but evidence nonetheless."

"But how could these be evil spirits?" asks Mark. "You say that they're better Christians than you are. How could these be evil spirits causing them to do this shit?"

"Wouldn't that just be perfect though? Evil spirits making you think that who you're serving is actually God.....but it isn't."

"Hence, the description of them as deceiving spirits."

"Exactly. How are they deceiving spirits, if you know they're evil? They would have to appear to be something else to actually be causing any deception."

"Shit, you know this is getting a little out there, don't you?"

"Not if you believe in the reality of the spirits," I say. "And I think it's as real as anything else. I know that makes me look like an uneducated fool to many, but that's just what I believe."

"So, are you still going to church with them?"

"Yeah, I'm still going, but I'm little more than an observer."

"It must be at least a little entertaining, I would guess, to watch all this shit going on."

"It's draining more than it's entertaining. But yeah, it is a little fascinating to see what'll happen next. But that's it. I feel like I'm a gawker at some train wreck or something, just waiting for the next outrageous thing to happen."

"Maybe I should come."

"They actually say that they're getting high in the spirit," I say. "And that's the best way to describe it. It's really like they're getting high on something. But it's something that sure makes them feel good. It's like they're experiencing the best sort of ecstasy that you could imagine."

"You can't seem to decide if you want this or not."

"I know. I'm totally confused by the whole thing. Sometimes I think I'm just thinking too much and should just let go and let whatever needs to happen, happen. But then there are other times where I say, wait, why shouldn't I be able to think about this logically. It's like they want you to just throw logic out the door. They say that you shouldn't think too much about it."

We both remain silent for a few moments.

"It's like something's taking over their body or something like that," I say. "And I know that sounds crazy."

"Well.....maybe."

"But you see that sort of thing in other places, too," I say. "Look at some musicians when they play. You can tell that something seems to take over sometimes. That's what attracted me to the guitar. It's like these guys are just a vessel where the music just flows out. I always wanted that."

"Well, I'm not so sure that's happening like that," says Mark. "I think they just get carried away by the music."

"But some of these musicians will say that they play things that they never rehearsed when they get in this zone or whatever. They say that they play things that even they are amazed by. They are just getting carried along for the ride."

"How did we get off on this?"

"I was making the point that other people claim to have experiences where something else takes over their body outside of these Pentecostal churches."

"And you're convinced that something is taking over their bodies?"

"Yeah, I am," I say. "I think I said something to you guys one

time before, when I first went to church with Karen, about this woman I
saw who would bend very sharply at the waist, with her head way
down close to the floor. It just seemed abnormal to me. It's like
something's contorting her body."

"I like contorted female bodies."

"Turns out that that was Crystal, my sister in-law."

"Oh…really? Sorry."

"No, she does have a nice body," I say. "And then when she's
bent over….well….that ass is sticking up in the air…damn."

"Maybe I should come to church with you."

"I know you may not believe it, but I've seen too much of this.
I don't think they have full control over it. Something else is taking
over. They don't have the ability to control it, so they just make
excuses for why it goes against scripture. They're just so convinced
that this is the spirit of God, that nothing else matters."

"Well….I don't know. Do you really think some spirit is taking
over their bodies or something?" asks Mark. "Or are they just getting
all hyped up on emotions where it may look as if they're losing
control."

"I don't know….but I've seen stuff that's really hard to
explain. Karen and I went to my old church last Easter, because my
Mom wanted us to come. Well….you know that my church doesn't do
any of that stuff, none of the pounding music or anything else that gets
things pumped up like they have at Karen's church. But it was like she
was having to fight the urge to shout out and make noise in church. She
knew that it would be out of place there, so she was trying her best to
resist. But it was like it was just welling up inside of her. Her foot
would start tapping real fast and she would let out a few yelps or
whatever. But it was freaky. It wasn't under her control. She was
having to fight to suppress these urges. And you can rule out the
emotional thing, because they definitely weren't doing anything in
there to get her stirred up. It just came out of nowhere."

"Hmmm, that is a little hard to explain."

"Yeah, it would be easy to conclude that they just work
themselves into some sort of frenzy in their church, with the music
pounding and all of that. But what happened that day at my church?
Where did that come from? She would call that church dead. Yet, she
was still feeling the spirit."

"Yeah, I just thought they were whipping this thing up to a
fever pitch and then all hells breaks loose."

"Things do get wild in there, but that isn't the whole story," I say.

"And they think this is the spirit of God doing this?"

"Of course, that's what they think it is. Something real is definitely behind all this stuff. These people seem to be so filled full of fire for the Lord. They're godly people. There's just something so different from them as opposed to the people I grew up around in church. They're onto something. I just can't quite make the pieces fit yet."

"Have you ever tried to say anything to them about all this shit?"

"All they say is that you have to let the spirit have his way. They believe the spirit of God is taking control of the church service. They really believe this. So, nothing else matters. I guess they just trust that the whole thing somehow lines up with scripture, even though it doesn't. It doesn't matter what I say anyway. I haven't praised the Lord in the Spirit like them yet, so they don't consider me to be anointed or anything. And I really can't blame them, I guess."

"Anointed? What does that mean?"

"That pretty much means that you have the spirit of God living inside of you."

"And they don't think you do?"

"Well, I haven't done the things in church that they think are evidence of that. If I haven't experienced this stuff, then how can I know anything? I have no credibility with them, because I don't have the same experiences."

"They think you're a fucking godless heathen. I told you."

"Yeah….funny."

"I know."

"It's confusing. They're supposed to be the ones who're so religious, yet I'm the one who's seeing these very easy to see ways where they're falling far short of what scripture says."

"Well…..who's to say that you aren't right?"

"I don't know….and it's not just the speaking in tongues and all of that stuff. It's like they're getting caught up in all of this stuff that isn't supposed to mean all of that much and they're missing the bigger picture."

"And what, pray tell, is the bigger picture, mine prophet?"

"Haven't you ever heard the phrase that says, 'God is love'?"

"Sure."

"They get so caught up in these supposed gifts of the Spirit that make them feel good and all that. But the bible says that the greatest gift we can get from the Spirit is love. The very nature of God is love. The whole point of the Spirit coming into our lives is that we are supposed to be filled full of love. And this is a supernatural love. A love the rest of the world knows nothing about."

"A supernatural love?"

"A love directly from God. A love that can cause us to love the worst sinners in the world."

"Okay....Mr. Flower Power," says Mark. "Want me to build a campfire so that we can sing Kumbaya."

"Remember that time when your brother gave us shit for having the fire in the trashcan in the backyard?"

"Yeah, he said 'Where do you think you are....New York City?'"

"But we weren't singing Kumbaya."

"So why the fuck did you bring it up?"

"Mentioning the campfire just brought up the memory."

"Hacky was a wacky guy."

"And scary."

"Scary to you cause you broke my goddamn arm."

Hacky was what we called Mark's deceased brother. I think that name came from a hacking cough he had. He was a scary dude to me when I was little. I broke Mark's arm one time and was scared to come out of the house for a while because I was convinced that Hacky was going to do something to me. There was always something not quite right about him. There was something in his eyes.

"But anyway, the whole idea of salvation is that Christians are supposed to be made in the likeness of God," I say. "The point of the being in the Spirit isn't so that we can feel all high or whatever and do crazy stuff. The point is to have the nature of God. And the nature of God is love."

"The nature of God. Wow....that's kinda deep."

"But that's what the whole thing is supposed to be about. It's all right there in the bible. They act like the Spirit is some temporary fix that gets them high for a while. But we're supposed to have the Spirit all of the time. The Spirit should totally transform our lives. How can we claim Christ is the only way unless we demonstrate a real change? This isn't about practicing some damn religion like other people do. What I seek is what the bible says we can have. I want that godly nature."

"Are you saying that they don't have this nature of God that you say Christians should have?"

"No, I can't really say that. On the contrary, they do show love. They do a lot for other people. And as far as the nature of God.....who am I to talk? I know I don't have it. There's a better chance that they do than me. I just know that's what we're supposed to get. Anything short of that is just a manmade religion."

"What are you saying then?" asks Mark. "Who's right?"

"I don't know. It just seems like their emphasis is on the wrong things. I probably am just a godless heathen for saying all of this. I just don't get the whole thing. The pieces just aren't coming together for me. I don't have what I'm supposed to have, but neither do they."

"Sounds like maybe you need to step back a little. You sound like you don't know which way is up."

"I am thinking about stopping going to church. It's just that it'll hurt Karen. But I do need to get away from it all for a while and find out where I am."

"I know it may hurt Karen...but if you aren't really on the same page with them....I mean....is it right to keep going and pretending?"

"Yeah...I know. It isn't. And that's all I'm doing right now, pretending."

Chapter 34

Monday May 19th, 1997

"Hey, brother. How's it going?" asks Melody, strolling up to me by Frame 8.

"Hey, Mel, things are going alright, I guess," I say. "Just got the frame for P.M. today."

"You and Karen gonna be at Momma and Daddy's for Memorial Day?"

"Uh…Mel….actually, I don't think so."

"But, why? You know that Aunt Jill and Uncle Pete are gonna be there. We don't get to see them all that much. And our cousins are gonna be there, too. You can't miss this."

"I don't know, Mel. I just don't see the point sometimes. We hardly have anything to do with them anymore. We live in different places. We live different lives. Then we're thrown together every few years and act like we see each other every day. I'm just tired of it. It's awkward."

"Awkward? We used to go on vacations with them all the time. What's the deal with you?"

"I just look at things differently now. I just want there to be some purpose to things, a spiritual purpose, if possible. I just don't see the point of people who are basically strangers now, just sitting a room for a few hours talking about the old days."

"And is part of this looking at things differently include not going to your brother's wedding?"

"His wedding to a man?" I ask. "Is that what you mean?"

"Of course it's to a man. His name's Steve."

"I know his name. I have met him."

"Dan told us that you wrote him a letter in response to the wedding invitation he sent you."

"Yes, that's right."

"You can't just talk to him?"

"He does live in Raleigh, Mel. I don't really see him all that much. And I thought the idea was that he needed to know who was coming and who wasn't."

"Do you know how hurt he was?"

"Well, I'm sorry about that. But I had to state the truth."

"State the truth? That letter was like some fucking statement to the press or something," she says. "Real nice."

"I thought I owed him a thorough explanation of why I couldn't come."

"It didn't need to be some rant against homosexuality."

"It wasn't a rant. I'm sorry if he took it that way. I was just stating my beliefs."

"Your beliefs? What about his feelings?"

"I'm just supposed to ignore the truth because that truth may hurt someone's feelings?"

"He isn't just someone, he's your fucking brother."

"I know that."

"So, you think you have the market cornered on truth now?" she asks. "You just issue an edict and that's it?"

"I didn't say that, Mel. But it is what I believe."

"I think that's the real issue with you and the family. You're the only one who isn't supporting your brother. You don't want to be around us because of that."

"Well, there may be some truth in that."

"I know there is."

"I just feel like an outsider or something. Everybody seems to be just embracing this whole thing and I just can't."

"We embrace it because we love him."

"I get that. I happen to love him, too."

"Then show it. Get onboard with this."

"I just can't let emotions get in the way of God's truth."

"I was afraid you were going to do this. Why do you have to be such a fucking fanantic? Oh...sorry....I guess I'm a heathen for saying that."

"No, you aren't a heathen."

"Neither is Dan."

"I didn't say he was, actually," I say. "I just can't support the formalizing of something I know to be a sin."

"I never thought we would have two bigots in the family, you and Hugh."

"That's a low blow, Mel."

"I have to call them how I see them."

"It's not bigotry."

"How is it not?"

"Because I don't hate homosexuals. I'm not a homophobe. I

don't have an irrational fear of it. I just cannot get away from the fact, in my mind, that it isn't natural."

"Seems like you're splitting hairs."

"No, I'm actually not. I've never joined in when the guys talk about fags, faggots or queers or whatever words they use. I've never been that way. I just can't see it as being something that's natural."

"Did you feel this way before you got all religious?"

"I never really thought about it much before then."

"So, it is the religious shit that's influencing the way you look at it?"

"Yeah, Mel, it is in the bible."

"You know, Homer White says the same thing about the shit he spews about blacks. It's in the bible."

"Well, he's misusing scripture in that case."

"That's what's so ironic about this," she says. "You're married to a black woman, and now you're being a bigot to your own brother."

"This is different."

"The fuck it is."

"Believe what you want," I say. "But I have to go by what I see in scripture."

"God, will you get your head out of your ass?"

"I don't have my head in my ass. I'm more aware of things than I've ever been."

"Does Karen agree with all of this?"

"She sees the homosexuality thing the same way," I say. "Of course she does."

"Great."

"I'm sorry, Mel. We can't help what we believe. What's funny, is that it may be one of the few things we do agree on when it comes to the bible."

"Glad you could come together on that one," she says, sarcastically.

"Mel, I don't know what to say. I've got a lot going on right now. I'm just trying to figure some things out."

"So, in the process you're going to shun your family?"

"I never said that. I just said I'm not coming Memorial Day."

"And your brother's wedding."

"Yeah, you're right, that, too."

"Yeah…that, too."

"I'm sorry, Mel."

"Yeah, I am, too," says Mel, as she walks off.

Why do I feel the need to separate myself from my family? The answer is that I've tried so many things to get close to the Lord, but nothing has worked so far. I think the reason is because I've never truly separated myself from the world and the things and the people of this world.

How can I ever expect to partake of the divine nature of God if I won't separate myself from those who are not seeking to live in the truth? I am far from pure myself. I am nowhere near where I need to be. But I'm at least seeking to get there. I can't say the same about my family. There are plenty of passages in scripture to back this up. Christians are not to fellowship with so-called believers who choose to deny the truth. That is all that I'm doing. I need the impure things in my life gone if I have any hope of experiencing the transforming power of the Holy Spirit in my life. It has to be this way. I told Mel that I wasn't shunning them. The truth is that maybe that's exactly what I'm doing.

Chapter 35

Wednesday June 4th, 1997

"Look, Jerry, the two elite instrument techs are so very hard at work in their little kingdom," says Roger, as he and Jerry stroll into the Instrument shop and find Mark and I, not so very hard at work.

"And what the hell are you two even doing in here?" asks Mark. "It's not break time. This is the Instrument shop. Why don't you two just go to your shop.....uh....oh....I'm sorry, there's no such thing as a common laborers shop. Is there?"

"You've developed quite the acid tongue lately," says Roger.

"Thank you," responds Mark.

"Well, Don, he's taken over your duties quite a bit hasn't he?" asks Roger. "Smart ass mouth and all."

"Yeah, I've got myself quite a protégé there, don't I?" I respond. "He takes care of my light work. I just sit around and live off of the fat of the land."

"How is that different from what you've always done?" asks Jerry.

"Because I'm doing even less than ever," I say. "Don't be jealous."

"How the fuck did you manage to keep him off of night shift anyway?" asks Roger. "Did you convince Butch that you needed a fucking assistant or something?"

"Something like that," I respond.

"I didn't even think about that," says Jerry. "He never did have to do a tour of duty on night shift, did he?"

"No, I didn't," says Mark.

"It takes time to train someone correctly," I add.

"You are the milk man extraordinaire," says Roger. "You sure have milked the hell outta this one."

"Actually, it's all the work that's been going on the last few years, Max's plan to save the plant. I need the extra help to get all this shit installed," I explain. "And in the meantime, well, Mark gets to learn all this new automation shit inside and out."

"Well, I've got to say that we seem to be bucking the trend of closing textile plants," says Roger.

"Yeah, I didn't expect to still be open this long," I say.

"Jerry, what the fuck's up with all these damn tank tops you've been wearing in here lately?" asks Mark.

"He's trying to show off for the women. He's been working out," explains Roger.

"Yeah, he's been working out all right. He got those muscles one can at a time," says Mark, as he mimics a drinking motion.

"Yeah, I'm curious, Jerry, how does all that drinking jibe with this working out and trying to be healthy?" I ask.

"He has his own sort of logic on that one," responds Roger.

"Fuck you guys," says Jerry.

"But seriously, Jerry, how does that work?" I ask. "You can't be healthy drinking all the time."

"I've cut back. I've been going to church with Steph for a while now. I'm making some changes," explains Jerry.

"So, why are you trying to show your muscles off to all the women in here if you're getting all religious and shit?" asks Roger.

"I wear these because they feel good. They're comfortable."

"You didn't wear shit like that before," says Roger. "And how do you go to church when you're still drinking? You may be working on it, but I still see your ass in Ronnie's joint quite a bit. The only difference now is that you sneak in there."

"You don't have to be perfect to go to church," explains Jerry. "I'm like the apostle Paul. Paul said he had a thorn in his side, a problem he just couldn't get rid of all the way. I think mine is drinking."

"Nice way to excuse it," says Roger, rolling his eyes.

"Yeah, my thorn is that I like to fuck everything that walks. Can I be a member of your church?" asks Mark.

"I've read that passage. I'm not sure that the thorn Paul was talking about was a sin," I say. "I think Paul's thorn was some sort of illness or physical problem that just wouldn't go away."

"But do you know that it wasn't a sin?" asks Jerry.

"No, I don't," I have to admit. "It doesn't really say what it was."

"And besides that, there's the verse that says that if you bring one person to Christ, it will cover over a multitude of sins," adds Jerry. "Bringing people to Christ is the most important thing. You do that and God grants you mercy on any sins you may have."

"Get out of jail free card," jokes Mark.

"No, apparently it's a get out of hell free card," corrects Roger.

"Have you brought anyone to Christ though?" I ask.

"Not yet, but I'm working on it. I've been witnessing to some folks."

"Probably women," says Mark.

"I don't care what verses you recite, you aren't supposed to be going to church if you're openly sinning," proclaims Roger.

"Well, thank you, Mr. Biblical Scholar," says Jerry, with a certain sharp tone.

"Yeah, I don't know about that, Roger. The bible says that the sick are the ones who need a doctor, not the healthy," I say. "How else to be free of sin than to come to Christ? And that means going to church."

"Does it? Is that the only place you can find God?" asks Mark.

"No, I found God apart from a church," I say. "But you are supposed to fellowship with other Christians."

"But does that even have to be in a church?" continues Mark.

"I guess not. You can fellowship with other believers anywhere," I say. "But most people tend to do that in church."

"Well, maybe Jerry should be holding church down at Ronnie's then," says Roger.

"Wouldn't be anything wrong with that," says Jerry. "Jesus ate with the sinners. He hung around with the ones that the so-called religious leaders of that time refused to have anything to do with. If Jesus were here today, he would be in places like that."

"You have got to be kidding me," says Roger. "Jesus would be sitting at the bar in Ronnie's joint?"

"Yeah, read your bible. Jesus did that. Jesus hung out in dives," says Jerry.

"Maybe he went to the titty bar, too," offers Mark.

"Justify it all you want, but you ain't supposed to be going to church if you're living in open sin," asserts Roger.

"This idea that church is supposed to be all clean and whitewashed just doesn't seem right to me," I say. "It ignores what's in scripture."

"That's right," agrees Jerry.

"How else will sinners find God but if they come to church? Do we expect them to clean themselves up first?" I say. "Do we expect them to eliminate all sin before they come to God? That's the impression I get from many churches."

"Preach it, brother," jokes Mark.

"But he's right," says Jerry. "It's right there in scripture."

"Okay, but even if that's true, you can't just claim that your sin is never going to go away, like Jerry's trying to say," says Roger. "You can't just claim it's your thorn and then keep doing it. That seems very convenient. And understand that I am very far from being a saint. I just know how I was raised."

"The bible never says that we can't drink alcohol," says Jerry. "That was added by men."

"But it doesn't say that we're supposed to get drunk as a skunk every night at some dive bar," says Roger. "Now, does it?"

"No, but that's still a good point Jerry just made," I say. "So many churches go beyond what's written in the bible. And that's just one example. They say that we're not to drink alcohol at all. But the bible only warns about getting drunk."

"But there are even verses where it says that only the leaders should not be given to drunkenness. But that it's perfectly alright if the regular members get drunk," says Jerry.

"Bull fucking shit," says Roger.

"Sign me up. I'll be a regular member then," adds Mark.

"No, he's actually right," I say. "At least partially."

"No, he's not," responds Roger.

"There's a passage where the qualifications for being a leader in the church are laid out....you know, deacons and elders," I say. "Well, it's there as clear as day. It's says that they should not be given to too much wine or something like that. And one of them may actually say drunkenness. But it does make it sound like you could be a regular member and still indulge in too much wine, to use the language that's in the passage."

"You're twisting that. It's talking about leaders and you're trying to get something else out of it," says Roger.

"If it were just a given that no one in the church should be drinking too much wine, then why would he have to say anything?" I ask. "It would already be a given that if you're a member, that you would not be indulging in too much wine. So why say something specifically when it comes to qualifications for being a deacon?"

"Exactly," says Jerry.

"But Jerry, this still doesn't give you a license to just keep drinking," I add.

"I know that. I am working on it," responds Jerry.

"Yeah....you're working on it. Working on the next bottle,"

says Roger. "And what the fuck are you doing now? You're hoping to get one of these hot young things here at the plant to fuck you. That's what all of this working out bullshit is about. I know your ass. You ain't fooling me."

"Fuck you, asshole!" says Jerry. "I ain't trying to fuck anyone. I'm faithful to Steph."

"Isn't there a verse in the bible that says something about praises and curses coming out of the same mouth?" asks Roger. "You got that shit down pat."

"I ain't perfect," responds Jerry.

"We don't have to be," I say. "That's the point."

"It's a good thing," adds Roger. "Because Jerry is far fucking from it."

"Why are you so opinionated about this, Roger?" I ask. "You don't go to church. You're not a preacher. What's the deal? Why are you such a big defender of the faith?"

"I'm not a preacher but I know plenty from when I was growing up," responds Roger. "I just don't like it when people try to make their own rules."

"You may know whatever it was that you learned when you were a kid," says Jerry. "But I ain't going to no fucking snake handling church."

"We didn't handle no fucking snakes," says Roger. "But we were, well, they still are hard core. I can tell you that they threw people out of the church for shit. And there's a scripture for that, too."

"Yes, that's true, but that's only for someone who's just totally given over to a sinful way of life," I say.

"Sorry, but that's what Jerry seems like to me. He's making excuses for the drinking," responds Roger.

"But how do you know that he isn't fighting it? Unless you know, he can't be kicked out of the church," I say.

"So, you set the standard?" asks Roger.

"No....I'm just trying to interpret that scripture with common sense. It would seem to me that the only way you could kick someone out of church would be if you had absolute proof that they were sinning and weren't doing anything to stop it. For instance, say a man leaves his wife and is living with another woman. That's absolute proof that despite anything he may say, he's intending to keep sinning. But, no matter how many times you see someone drunk, you can't reach the same conclusion. It's a different sort of thing. After every episode of being drunk, that person could vow to not do it again. You can't judge whether they're sincere or not. But the case where the man's shacking up with his mistress, well, there isn't any question there."

"How is it that you two seem to know so much more than all of these theologians, preachers and teachers? Why do you think you have the answers?" asks Roger.

"God chooses the lowly things of this world to shame the wise," responds Jerry.

"Well, he's made a good choice then," cracks Mark.

"I just know what I see," I say. "I don't just go with the crowd. And there are plenty of scriptures that contradict what many Christians believe and do. I'll go with what scripture says even if no one else does."

"I just don't get how after a few years of reading the bible you think you know so much more than all of these established leaders in Christianity," adds Roger.

"I see what I see," I say. "And there are others that do, too. They're out there."

"Don't you consider Karen's church to be a part of established Christianity?" asks Roger. "But you go there."

"They have their own little establishment. They're not as uptight as more traditional denominations, but sure, they have their problems," I say.

"Church is supposed to be done is a whole different way," says Jerry. "They used to meet in people's houses. Now we have these huge cathedrals with stained glass and all of that shit."

"And you have to wear certain clothes," I say. "You have to have church clothes."

"So the fuck what?" asks Roger.

"I should be able to go like this," says Jerry.

"Karen took me shopping before I went to church with her the first time. She bought me church clothes. I didn't think anything of it at the time, because I was raised that way. You have to look a certain way to go to church."

"And even better for Easter," adds Mark.

"There's actually a verse that speaks about this, too, that everyone seems to ignore," I say.

"Oh God," exclaims Roger.

"There's a passage that talks about two men. It's a parable," I say. "But one man has shabby clothes. He comes into the church. Someone tells him to sit on the floor by his feet. Then there is this man who's dressed to the nines. Well, he's led up front and given the best seat in the house. Isn't that's really what we're doing today in church?"

"I don't think anyone's making anyone else sit at their feet. And I doubt anyone is running up to give Mr. Best-Dressed the best seat in the house," says Roger.

"No, not in an obvious way," I say. "But the effect is still the same."

"How?" asks Roger.

"I'll give you an example," I say. "Karen had become friends with and was helping this really poor family. They had the shabby clothes that are spoken of in that scripture. They wanted to come to church. Of course they didn't have church clothes. Sure, they wouldn't have been turned away, if they had shown up at Karen's church with those crappy clothes. But they resisted coming because they knew there was a certain standard when it comes to so-called church clothes."

"That's exactly what I'm saying," says Jerry. "We should be able to go in the dirtiest and most fucked up shit we have. Clothes don't fucking matter."

"Did they end up coming to church?" asks Mark.

"Not until the church helped them get church clothes," I say.

"See, it all worked out," says Roger. "They weren't shunned at all."

"But it's not even right that they had this image of what church is," I say. "The church projects this image that some people can't live up to. A formal sort of image, that's totally against what Christ stood for."

"We should be meeting in homes, wearing our regular clothes," adds Jerry. "Most of these church buildings sit empty the majority of the time. It's a big waste. The money should go to helping people. Let the homeless sleep in the damn church."

"The whole point of Christ coming was to abolish the whole temple worship system," I say. "But we just have a new form of it in the church."

"We are supposed to be the temple of God now," says Jerry. "Not some building."

"Then why keep going?" asks Roger. "Just stay at home and be your own little church."

"Well, actually, I am thinking of quitting Karen's church," I say.

"Why?" asks Roger.

"Well, they aren't as bad as some churches when it comes to ignoring scriptures that contradict their traditions, but they recently asked me to start participating in the services. I can't pretend that I'm something I'm not. They have all of that crazy stuff going on. I just don't fit in with all of that."

"So, you're not a holy roller after all," says Roger.

"People look at them as being kind of extreme or something but I probably have more radical views than they do," I say. "I don't think they go far enough, at least in some areas, but then they go much too far in others."

"What does that mean?" asks Roger.

"It just means live according to scripture," I say. "If you believe it's the truth then shouldn't you try to live it? I see them just disregard some things totally. But then put too much focus on others, even to the point of going beyond what's written, such as with the alcohol. They believe that you shouldn't have even a drop of alcohol despite the fact that scripture never says that."

"Maybe you two great prophets should start your own church," suggests Mark.

"And Ronnie's could be the temple," adds Roger.

"Not that bad of an idea," I say.

"Oh God," exclaims Roger.

"We'd have a hell of a church," adds Jerry.

"Yeah, send everyone who goes there to hell," jokes Roger.

"If there's drinking allowed, I'll be your first member," adds Mark.

"Jack Daniels in place of grape juice for communion," continues Roger.

"Maybe we ought to noodle with this a little," suggests Jerry.

"Something informal maybe," I add.

"Not a bad idea at all," says Jerry.

"God, please help us all," says Roger.

Chapter 36

Saturday August 2nd, 1997

"Hey baby, it's a nice day today, isn't it?" asks Karen, as she joins me on our porch.

"Yeah, it is," I respond.

"You did such a nice job building this porch. I've got me such a talented man."

"Yeah, it came out alright."

"Is something on your mind?" she asks. "You seem like you're deep in thought or something."

"Yeah....I do have something I need to tell you."

"Okay."

"I'm going to stop going to church."

"What? But why?"

"It's really a lot of things," I say. "I just don't fit in. I'm just not having the same experiences as you all are. I don't know. It just isn't working."

"You just need to let go and let God have his way with you."

"I know that's what you keep saying, but it just never happens for me. And it's been four years now. That ship has sailed."

"It's just the fact that you're so shy. God'll get through at some point."

"I don't know....maybe."

"No, he will."

"What really made the decision for me was when Claude asked me to help lead the praise service," I say. "I just felt like I didn't belong up there at all. I don't want to keep going if I'm pretending. And that's what I feel like I'm doing in church. I'm trying to act like I feel the same things that you feel. But I just don't. And I'm not sure I even want to."

"It isn't all about feeling something."

"Oh...I know. Believe me, I know. That's the problem. From the things I've been reading, I just don't see how a lot of what goes on at your church is right. I might be wrong, but it's what I see."

"What do you mean? We just let God lead the way. We ask for the Holy Spirit and he comes."

"But is the Holy Spirit going to contradict scripture?"

"How is that happening?" she asks. "I don't see how we're

going against scripture."

"Everyone's praying at the same time. Everyone's doing everything at the same time. I can't hear myself think most of the time. From what I see in scripture, it just seems wrong to me."

"Well, if you're asking if we always dot every "i" and cross every "t", no, I'm sure we don't. But we are human. Things may get a little wild sometimes, but that's just people being free in the Lord."

"So, I'm wrong because I see things differently?" I ask. "I'm wrong because I say that we should be following scripture?"

"No, honey, I didn't say that you're wrong. I don't know. But this is just what we're led to do. We trust the spirit."

"But don't we have to test things to see if they're of the spirit? We can't just let ourselves go and then just hope that it's all right. Scripture is what we say we go by. We have to follow scripture."

"And I think that we do follow scripture."

"What about speaking in tongues?"

"That's in the bible. What about it?" she asks, defensively.

"But aren't people supposed to do it one at a time? And isn't there supposed to be an interpreter? I've never seen an interpreter. Never! The bible very clearly says there should be an interpreter."

"That's a good point. I really don't know why there's never an interpreter."

"It's not just that," I say. "It's the whole tone of the service really. It seems like the idea is to get things stirred up enough, to build up enough excitement, so that the Holy Spirit falls on the church."

"Well, yeah.....but what's wrong with that? We're inviting the Holy Spirit to come in."

"I've done some research on this, and this seems very similar to what happens in a voodoo ceremony. It's like you're conjuring up spirits the way they do in voodoo. In my studying the movement, I've found that there are some connections to voodoo and how all this Pentecostal stuff got started, too."

"Studying the movement?" she asks. "We're just a little simple church."

"Yes, but what you believe and what you're doing hasn't always been around in Christianity. It is a recent movement."

"I just can't believe you believe that this is something anywhere near to voodoo. This is the spirit of God."

"It's just too similar."

"You sound like you've made up your mind."

"No, not really. I'm just saying that it's just so similar to voodoo, that it needs to follow scripture more closely. If it doesn't, how can you be sure that other spirits aren't coming in?"

"So, you think we're inviting other spirits into the church?"

"I don't know," I say. "I'm just saying that things don't quite add up to me."

"I can't believe you think that."

"Listen, I've seen from the beginning how much on fire you all are for the Lord. I've always wanted that fire. There's no question that you love God. But something just doesn't add up here. I can't quite put my finger on it, but something isn't right."

"But, if we're for God, how can we þe against him? We do all of this in the name of the Lord. We're raising up the name of the Lord in praise and worship. How can that be wrong?"

"I'm not saying you're against God."

"Then what are you saying?"

"I don't know," I say. "The whole thing confuses me. I know that you're all seeking the Lord. I believe that. But a lot of this just doesn't add up to me."

"Can I make a suggestion?"

"Sure."

"Why don't we go on a fast together and seek the Lord for some answers?"

"That's another thing. You and Claude have always hammered me about fasting. Fasting is so important and all of that. But it's barely mentioned in scripture. I'm not even sure it's actually meant for the church. It's something left over from Old Testament times."

"It's in the New Testament."

"It's in there, but it isn't emphasized as something that we definitely must do."

"Well, I believe that it's the only way for us to put aside the flesh so that we can hear what God wants us to hear."

"But why would we have to go without food to hear what God has to say? Isn't the Holy Spirit supposed to live inside of us now?"

"Yeah."

"How could we be any closer to God than that then? Why would we have to go without food?" I ask. "The Spirit's already inside of us. Isn't that what we claim as Christians, that the very spirit of God is right there inside of us? Why would we need any gimmicks to find answers? They should be right there. And take that even further. Why do you have to praise and sing and do all of this stuff to get the Spirit to fall on the church? He is supposed to be already inside of you. He doesn't have to fall on you if you already have him."

"Honey, what can I say? I've seen this work. I've seen God's power at work. Would I be able to say that if I were inviting in other spirits?"

"Actually, it is possible. Depending on what you're talking about."

"I've seen results when I go to the Lord with a fast. I've seen him do what I was praying to happen. I've seen it."

"I notice that you stop eating when you fast, but you'll still watch TV and stuff like that."

"So?"

"It would seem to me that to stop watching TV would be a better way to get close to God than to stop eating."

"But that isn't what fasting is."

"How do you know?" I ask. "It would seem that if you were so dedicated to getting some answer from God that you would cut out anything and everything that may hinder that. I would think that worldly TV would hinder you getting closer to the Lord."

"You may be right. I never said I was perfect. But fasting does work for me. I just wish you would try it."

"It just doesn't add up to me. I'm not going to do something blindly just because it's mentioned in a few passages of scripture. I need it to fit into my total understanding of what salvation is. And it just doesn't."

"So, you aren't going to try it?"

"It wouldn't be in faith, so no, I'm not."

"Okay.....but you still need to seek God."

"I'm always seeking God. Believe me, I'm constantly looking for answers."

"I wish you would keep going to church with us, but if you don't want to, I just encourage you to find a church home somewhere. You need somewhere to worship and fellowship."

"From what I see in reading and researching, I'm not sure that any church is right for me," I say.

"So, you're right, and the rest of us are wrong?"

"Hey, you're the ones who talk about all these dead churches out there. Do you want me to go to a dead church? Should I go back to my parent's church?"

"No, I don't want you to go to a dead church. But there are other ones out there that may suit you, but that are still in the will of the Lord."

"I don't know. I don't think I need a church. At least not the way churches are today. The early church wasn't like this."

"The early church?"

"The first disciples. The time when the church first started. When the faith was pure."

"No one's perfect. We're all human. I'm sure they had their problems just like we do."

"But we claim to have the Holy Spirit inside of us. How can that be true, yet we have so much error?" I ask. "That's what I don't get. We claim to have the very spirit of God inside of us, yet we can't get along with other Christians. We claim to have the spirit of God, yet we have gross error in all churches......I don't know. You say we aren't perfect. But anyone who claims to have the Holy Spirit inside of them should be closer to it than anyone I've ever seen. It would be different if we were just practicing some religion. But we claim to have the actual spirit of God living inside of us. The evidence just doesn't show that to be the case."

"Okay, honey, I don't think we're getting anywhere right now."

"No, I don't think we are."

"Just keep seeking God and it'll all work out. Trust in him. And remember, no matter what, I still love you."

"I know. I love you, too."

I really am confused by the whole thing. I know that I am very far indeed from being a pure and blameless Christian. But I just can't get away from all the error I see in Karen's church, and in the whole Pentecostal movement. I just know that I'm doing nothing but pretending when I go to church. I'm just acting like I enjoy it. The one thing that I am sure about is that I shouldn't be going if I'm really not into the whole thing.

I feel like I'm just sitting there judging them. I'm just sitting there waiting for them to do another outrageous thing that I can condemn. I need answers. I have to pull back from them to get some time to breathe. All I'm thinking about is this movement and how things just don't seem to fit. I know I need to focus on myself. I know that I'm far from who I need to be. Even with all their error, there's no question that they're living more like true Christians than I am. I guess that's why I'm so obsessed with them. I need to know what's happening here. Am I really just a lost soul with no connection to God? Am I the one who's in error? Or I'm I the one who really sees the truth? At this point I don't know.

Chapter 37

Tuesday August 12th, 1997

"Oh my God! Jim, please say it isn't so," I say, feigning seriousness.

"What isn't so?" replies Jim.

"That the great Drake Miller died today at 5:32 am."

"Oh....you mean what someone wrote out there on the blackboard?" asks Jim. "Who the hell is Drake Miller anyway?"

"He was a race car driver. He was killed in a plane crash or something. But it's like they think the President died or something, to put a message up like that. Only in the South."

"Where were you when Drake Miller died?" jokes Jim.

"I mean, it's too bad he died, but to put the time up there? You would think he was some world leader or something, someone who was actually of some importance."

"I'll bet there wasn't a message up like that when Martin Luther King was shot," adds Jim.

"This being the South, I'm not sure there was one up when Kennedy was shot."

"They probably threw a party," says Jim.

"How the fuck are you guys today?" asks Roger, as he and Jerry come into the Instrument shop for break.

"I'm sorry for your loss," I say, solemnly.

"What loss?" asks Roger.

"You know....Drake Miller," I say. "He passed away today at 5:32 am, you know."

"He was a great driver," says Jerry.

"But he wasn't the fucking President," says Jim.

"No, Jim, apparently he was God," I say.

"Fuck you guys," says Jerry.

"Hey, did you hear who our newest engineer's going to be?" asks Roger.

"No, who?" I respond.

"None other than Tricia Wortham," reports Roger.

"Wasn't she that black girl who worked here as in intern last summer?" asks Jim. "Was going to NC State?"

"Yeah, she's the fool who changed all the heaters on the motor starters on the dyeing machines," I say.

"Yeah, undersized them, and we had to go back and change them again because we were having them trip out all the time," says Jim.

"Now don't you guys talk shit about my black sister," says David, who walked in as Jim was speaking. "We need a little diversity around this joint here, especially in the engineering ranks."

"What do you think about this, Homer?" asks Roger, to Homer, who worked his way into the room at some point.

"I don't have a problem with it."

"But you gotta figure they did this just because she's black," says Roger.

"And a woman, too," says Jerry. "They kill two diversity birds with one stone. A black and a woman."

"Don't you mean a nigger and a broad?" asks David, laughing.

"Fuck you," responds Jerry. "I don't talk about women that way."

"But really, Homer, considering that this is almost assuredly because of her being black, you don't have a problem with it?" asks Jim.

"She ain't the first black manager or engineer though," I say. "This is more about her being a woman."

"But a black woman is the biggest minority of them all," says Jim. "Especially in this field."

"Jim, you know that textiles is pretty much the bottom of the barrel, especially when it comes to engineers," begins Homer. "What do the so-called engineers do here anyway? Do they really engineer? Do they design anything? No, all they are are supervisors with a fancy title. And like I said, textiles is pretty low down the ladder when it comes to manufacturing, low pay, basic technology. Let her have the damn job. She has to start somewhere. And this is about the lowest someone can start. The truth is, I'm not sure it is race. She's just another one of our dumbass engineers now. She fits right in, actually."

"That, she does," agrees Roger. "She fits in perfectly well."

"Yeah, it's not like the really smart engineers are going to come to this dump," I say. "As long as they insist on their managers having engineering degrees, we're going to end up with this type of shit. I mean, look at the idiot Bob is, yet he heads the whole damn shop."

"The funny thing is, they actually are making some decent decisions lately," says Jim.

"Decisions, yeah. But can they really design anything themselves," I ask.

"Max is behind all the changes going on here," says Roger.

"Who knows, maybe the girl can help us out some," says Homer. "If so, more power to her."

"David's just glad they hired her because he wants to fuck her," observes Roger.

"Or fuck her some more," says David.

"I seriously doubt you got into those pants when she was here before," says Roger.

"Yeah, she's got her nose just a little too high in the air to fuck someone the likes of you," adds Jim.

"She's just an entry level engineer in a shitty textile plant," says David.

"Yeah, but you're just a shitty electrician in a shitty textile plant," says Roger.

"We'll see," says David.

"The question is…. who wants to work for her?" I ask.

"I will," says David.

"Guys who want to fuck her don't count," says Roger.

"I would have a hard time working for a woman," I say. "I mean it just seems like any time you run across a female manager or supervisor they're a complete bitch. It's like they have something to prove."

"But they do," says Jim. "This is a male dominated field. When a woman does come along she does have to put up with a bunch of shit."

"Like wondering which guys aren't taking her seriously," I say. "And just want to fuck her."

"Exactly," says Jim.

"Well, you already know that she's an electrical engineer," says Roger. "So you know my ass ain't gonna be working for her."

"That's right," says David. "She may end up replacing Butch if his ass would ever retire."

"His fat ass will outlast all of us," says Roger.

"So, everyone ready for the fishing tournament?" I ask.

"We're going to kick your ass," responds Jerry.

"In drinking beer maybe," says Jim.

"David, I hear that your partner's going to break out the old bamboo poles," I say.

"Yeah, they're going to fish from the shore," says Roger. "They don't have a fucking chance."

"Oh, we'll give you boys a run for your money," replies David. "I've caught plenty of fish from the shore before. I don't need no fucking boat to beat you amateurs."

"Who you fishing with, Homer?" I ask.

"Your protégé, Mark."

"It's probably about time we drop the protégé thing," I say. "He has been here four years."

"It's just that you've truly turned him into another you," jokes Jerry. "Fucking off all the time and making more money than the rest of us."

"Homer, how the hell did you two end up together?" asks Roger.

"Well, we were kind of the odd men out, I guess. He offered the use of his boat, so, I said why not. I'll fish with the young kid."

"I like the fact that we're doing the partner thing," I say. "Combining the weights. It makes it more interesting."

"Why ain't Mark fishing on your boat, Don?" asks Jerry. "I mean with him being your partner and friend and all."

"Jim had already said something," I respond. "I didn't know Mark wanted to do it."

"Since when did the playboy pretty boy know how to fish?" asks Roger.

"Don't worry about me," says Jim. "I know plenty. Any lack of practice will be made up by the impairment that you'll be under."

"Impairment?" asks Roger.

"Alcohol.....dumbass. That's what he's talking about," I say.

"That's right. It'll be all that you can do to even manage to stay in the fucking boat," adds Jim.

"Boys, boys, there's no need to argue amongst yourselves, the winners will be Mark and myself, of course," says Homer. "You boys know that I've won this annual event of ours more than anyone."

"That's because you're so damn old," says Roger. "None of us has actually lived long enough to win as many as you."

"Yeah, it's time for the young guns to take over," says Jerry. "Step aside, old man."

"I ain't stepping aside for no one, son."

"It'll all be settled tomorrow," I say.

"We're gonna kick your ass," says Jerry.

"Will you stop saying that, dick?" asks Roger. "The more you brag, the less chance we have of winning."

"Yeah, just let your fishing do the talking, son," adds Homer.

Chapter 38

Saturday August 16th, 1997

"How long you had this thing?" asks Jim, as he looks over my aluminum hulled bass boat.

"Couple of years," I say. "I bought it off of Raeford, actually. He got a newer one. It does what I need it to do."

"There're a lot of people here today," observes Jim.

"Looks like a lot of skiers," I say. "We'll have to find us a nice quiet cove somewhere away from all the action. I know a few good spots."

"How are you gentlemen doing today?" asks Homer, as he and Mark drive up pulling the old boat that Mark's family used to go out on when he was a child.

"I see you brought the speedboat today," I say.

"What's she made out of, wood?" asks Jim. "She's a little ragged around the edges."

"Fuck.....there ain't nothing wrong with this boat," says Mark.

"This is a real boat," says Homer. "A real boat is made out of wood. This is the kind of work we used to do in this country, true craftsmanship. Now we just weld pieces of metal together and call it a boat."

"Yeah, you can enjoy that craftsmanship as you're treading water in the middle of the lake after that piece of shit sinks," adds Roger, who just arrived with his partner.

"It looks like you too are more prepared to drink than to fish," observes Jim.

"Whatever," says Roger. "We're going to toast your little fucking asses today."

"Look at Max and Bob pulling up," I say.

"Damn, look at that thing," says Jerry.

"Well, when you're the plant manager, you can afford toys like that," observes Roger.

"That's like those boats those pro fishermen have," says Jerry. "Bet it's decked out with all those fancy gadgets."

"They still have to catch the fish," says Homer.

"And here comes the backwoods boys," says Jim, as Boonie and Ray roll up, with Boonie's canoe in the back of his pickup.

"How the hell are you fellas doin?" ask Ray.

"Ray, you know that only fish can be weighed in today," I say. "No beavers, or skunks, or possums. None of that shit, okay?"

"Where's that possum cap?" asks Roger.

"No, it's a little hot for that," says Jerry.

"Fuck you guys," responds Ray.

"And no using dynamite," adds Jerry.

"Better check their canoe for a shotgun," adds Jim.

"Yeah, to be clear, this is not a backwoods redneck style fishing tournament," I say. "Fish only count that are caught with a pole and a hook. I won't say rod and reel because of Israel and his bamboo poles."

"We know the goddamn rules," growls Boonie.

"How you guys doing?" asks Israel, as he and David walk up.

"Goddamn, Israel, how long are those fucking poles?" asks Jerry.

"They twelve feet."

"You guys are really gonna fish from the bank with those bamboo poles?" asks Roger.

"Well, I did bring my spinning rod," says David.

"We see. You laugh now. But we show you," says Israel.

"Alright, we're all here, aren't we? Why don't we get started?" says Roger. "We meet back here at five for weigh in. We all know the rules. We're operating under the honor system. The winning team splits the pot of five hundred dollars."

"You know…..I wouldn't be surprised if Israel and David did win after all," I say, as Jim and I cruise out onto the lake.

"I hope they do, in a way," says Jim. "It would be worth losing the money to see the looks on the faces of those guys."

"As long as Bob and Max don't win," I add. "They don't need any more money."

"Well, most of the time all that technology and shit doesn't help all that much when it comes to something like this."

"Except for those fish-finders. Those things actually do help quite a bit. At least you know you're fishing in a good spot, because you can actually see the fish."

"Should have outlawed them in the tournament if everyone

doesn't have one."

"Too late for that now. But this cove right here has almost always given me results."

"Shit, and look at the scernery," says Jim, nodding in the direction of a pontoon boat on the opposite side of the cove."

"What.....where?"

"Over there, look at those two girls on the deck of that boat."

"Yeah.....I see," I say. "How old do you think they are though?"

"Not legal....I'm sure."

"Yeah, they probably are a little young."

"I mean just perfect," says Jim. "Nice full racks. And those asses......damn."

"You know, I hear people say from time to time, that they didn't grow them like that back when we were in school. Do you think that's true?"

"Listen, I don't remember girls being built like that where I grew up," says Jim. "Maybe one here and there, but damn, what you see today? These girls today are literally built better than many grown women."

"I mean they have the whole package. Those tits just couldn't be any nicer... just the right size....not too small and not too big," I say. "But it's those asses, that's what's different today. These girls today just have these nice sweet bubble butts."

"We better watch it, or their parents are going to notice us ogling their daughters."

"We'll be branded as perverts," I say. "Which we probably are, by the way."

"But how do you not look?"

"We have no choice in the matter really. Tits and ass come into our field of vision and we're compelled to look. That's an immutable law of nature. Too bad our women and the parents of hot teenage girls can't understand that."

"They may be underage, but they have all the parts that make them look like women."

"It's that whole Lolita thing," I say. "All the parts that make up the hottest woman you could conjure up, coupled with the innocence of being still somewhat a child."

"Yeah, but it's that child part that gets you in trouble, even though they're really very far from being children."

"Well, I have a problem with that whole underage thing

anyway," I say.

"I'll bet you do."

"No, seriously. They're women in every sense of the word, except for age. Those two have all the body features of women. It's not like they're twelve years old or something. They have to be sixteen or seventeen.....fifteen at the youngest. They aren't children."

"They definitely have the bodies of women," says Jim. "Most definitely. Most definitely, indeed."

"And they're capable of having children, I'm sure."

"What?"

"Not that that would be my intention," I say. "No, I'm just pointing out that their bodies are saying that they're women. But if I fuck them, I'm labeled a sexual deviant. I'd have a record and would be branded as a sex offender, even if they're totally willing."

"Well, it is against the law."

"And that's fine. Society has a right to make it illegal to have sex with a girl who's under eighteen, or whatever. My problem is that it isn't the same thing to fuck one of those girls, as it is to molest say a ten-year old. But we, as a society, tend to lump everyone into that one pervert category. But as far as I'm concerned, it isn't perverted at all to want to fuck either one of those girls over there. It's as natural as can be."

"And what you're talking about is definitely a societal thing," says Jim. "In some cultures, girls that age are getting married and having kids, even younger than that, actually."

"Exactly. The only thing saying that they aren't women is society. Their bodies are saying one thing, but society says something else. Age is just an arbitrary number. There isn't some cosmic law stating that girls shouldn't have sex until they're eighteen."

"But there are reasons for setting the age wherever it happens to be"

"I know that."

"I guess we just think there should be a certain level of maturity until they start having sex."

"But age determines maturity?" I ask. "I'm sure there are many young girls that are far more mature than many adults."

"And not to mention that girls tend to mature faster than guys."

"I'm not even sure that's really it. I just think parents don't want their daughters having sex because it's supposed to be some sign that the innocence of childhood is gone or something. They want to hold onto that child as long as they can."

"But the age has to be set somewhere. Actually it's different ages in different states. We could check to see what it is in North Carolina. Maybe we could bang them legally."

"Listen, I have no issue with the law. I understand that. But don't label me a pervert if I were to happen to have sex with someone that age, or simply want to, or really, just doing what we're doing now, looking at them. It may be against the law, but it ain't perverted. That's my point."

"Yeah, we'll just tell the father over there, 'Why shouldn't I be looking at your daughters, sir? Don't you see what fine asses they have?'"

"Don't forget the tits."

"No, never forget the tits."

"You know, speaking of something along these same lines," I say. "Why can't women just understand that men are visual? Why is it always such a big deal when we look at other women? Don't they understand that it's just a reflex? I see a fine piece of ass pass before my eyes and I just have to look."

"And even if she happens to be underage."

"Exactly."

"Men and women will never fully understand one another," says Jim. "At least I don't think so."

"But women can hear these researchers explain that men are visual creatures. We respond to what we see. Yet they still get so pissed off when we look at other women."

"Even get jealous when you look at some woman on TV."

"Exactly. It's just a girl on TV. I can't get to her. No chance to fuck her. Why is it such a crime to look?"

"But they say, 'Is that what you like?' or 'Is that what you want?'"

"Yeah."

"Well, this country's all repressed sexually anyway," says Jim.

"The hang ups we have about nudity really get me," I say. "Especially the way we look at the female breast."

"And don't we love to look at the female breast."

"The whole thing's just strange to me though. It seems as if it's alright to show the entire breast, as long as the nipple's covered, I mean literally. You can show the entire breast, as long as there's a little piece of fabric covering the nipple. As long as the nipple's covered, women can just let those big things flop all over the damn place."

"But men have nipples. So, we don't have a problem with

nipples, per se. We just have a problem with the female nipple."

"Exactly, I don't get that. The big fleshy part of the breast is what's different between men and women. We all have nipples. Yet as men, we can show ours all day long. But women can't."

"Yeah.....you're right," says Jim. "And what's the big deal about showing ass? We all have asses. Everyone knows what an ass looks like."

"Well, there it's almost the same deal. Women can show literally their entire ass, if they want to, just as long as they have a piece of string running up the crack."

"Yeah, I know. Their entire ass is out there basically. So what's the big deal in just having it all out there?"

"But what's the big deal about any of it anyway?" I ask. "Most everyone's going to have sex at some point in their lives. So, we're all going to see the naked bodies of other people. With it being so common, why are we trying to shield whoever we're trying to shield from this? Are we doing it for the kids?"

"The funny thing is......the more you try to hide it, the more enticing it is."

"We have all of these issues with nudity in certain circumstances, yet most Americans see nudity in porn or regular movies or where ever else," I say. "It's like we have two faces. In public, we want to appear proper and conservative, but behind closed doors we let loose."

Actually, I feel the same way about myself. Here I am talking about being able to fuck underage girls with Jim. But with other people I talk about God and salvation and all that stuff. I can't always seem to reconcile my more liberal views on things with the biblical morality for which I strive.

"We produce more porn than any other country in the world," says Jim. "And then we have Hollywood movies and all the sex and nudity in them. But we can't have it on TV."

"Or out here. Why shouldn't those girls be able to sunbathe in the nude if they want? Why should it be a big deal?"

"I think there's more lust produced by wearing skimpy bikinis than there is in being nude."

"Yeah, because you wonder what they'd look like with all that stuff hanging out," I say.

"And bouncing around."

"And a jiggling and a shaking, too."

"We need to stop thinking about those girls over there."

"I know, why look if you can't touch?"

"Well, you could touch," says Jim. "But there'd be consequences. Severe consequences."

"Isn't that how life is anyway?" I ask. "Nothing's ever easy. There always seems to be adverse consequences to anything that would give us pleasure."

"Not always, but yeah, a good amount of the time, that's right."

"Well, just think how fraught with consequences this scenario here is. Suppose that you did have the opportunity to fuck one of those girls over there. Let's just say for the sake of argument that the girl won't say anything. That's a given."

"So you're saying that you don't have to fear getting arrested?"

"Not quite," I say. "I'm just saying the she's willing and that she has no intentions of telling anyone, because she knows that you'd get into trouble."

"Okay."

"But just think of everything else that could go wrong," I say. "What if she gets pregnant? What if she wants more than a good time? What if she falls in love with you? But then you reject her, which of course you'd have to do, then she tells what happened."

"Then you're in jail."

"But how often do we think things through when it comes to sex? We just know that we want what we want. Now, it's easy for us sitting here, because we aren't in a situation where we have any real chance. But what about if a girl like that was the daughter of a friend, and she came onto you? What if she was right there for the taking?"

"Yeah....hard to resist."

"That's the thing though, there's always consequences. Eat too much, get fat. Drink too much, ruin our liver. Do drugs, fry our brains. Fuck a minor, go to prison."

"And most of the time it's all for a fleeting feeling anyway," says Jim. "But it's a damn good feeling."

"Just trying to escape reality for a little while," I say. "We're always looking for something different. But in the end, even if we get that something different, we get tired of it and want something different from that. Even if I were to be able to fuck one of those girls, even for a while, eventually, I'd want someone else. Not necessarily better, just different."

"Well, that's what women don't get, either. When a girl catches our eye, it's not necessarily that she's better than the one we have, it's just that she's different."

"If they would just let us sample a little, here and there."

"Fat chance of that."

"Especially with mine."

"I didn't quite expect to have this conversation with you today."

"Why's that?" I ask.

"Just with you being all religious or whatever."

"Well, I'm not sure how religious I am really. I stopped going to church recently."

"Crisis of faith?"

"No, I just don't agree with all of the stuff that Karen and they do in her church, all that crazy Pentecostal stuff."

"So, where does that leave you now?"

"I don't know really. I've never been what you'd call a conventional Christian anyway. I'm not sure what the hell I am."

"Did it not take or something?" asks Jim.

"No, I wouldn't say that it didn't take. I'm just not one to go with the flow. I actually think for myself. I'm probably not cut out for organized religion. But I do still believe in the bible, as strange as that may sound."

"But you don't necessarily abide by the standards of conventional morality I take it."

"Well....I don't know," I say. "There may be a difference in what I may believe in some philosophical way and what I have to live by."

"Playing both sides of the fence?"

"No, I'd just say that I'm in the process of sorting some shit out," I say. "I just doubt that God's concerned with some of the shit that religious people get all hung up on. I just think some of our rules have nothing to do with God."

"Does the bible say anything about underage girls? Is there any age mentioned?"

"No, there isn't," I say. "That shit was totally created by men."

"Yeah, I know."

"I just have a hard time with this shit that men just create out of thin air then act like it's some edict from God."

"So, if you're not cut out for organized religion, what are you doing?" asks Jim. "Are you making your own religion?"

"Who knows? Maybe I'll start my own church."

"Yeah," says Jim. "You know, we better get serious about fishing if we have any hopes of winning this thing."

"Yeah, but maybe we should find us another cove, where the scenery isn't so enticing."

"Yeah….I think so."

After hours of fishing, everyone assembles onshore for the official weigh in.

"Just as I expected, you guys look like you have more empty cans than you do fish," quips Jim.

"It's not the number, it's the weight," responds Jerry.

"Yeah, but that shitload of little fish that Israel and David caught is probably going to beat the few that you have," I say.

"We should have limited this to bass so that we could have gone by size limits," says Roger.

"Too bad….you can't change rules now," says Israel.

"Yeah, these two niggas done beat your white asses," adds David.

"I knew I shouldn't have gotten involved in some half ass fishing tournament like this," says Max.

"Looks like all of that technology couldn't touch those good old bamboo poles," says Homer. "Good job, boys."

"Yeah, it's fucking official. They won," says Roger, as he hands Israel and David their winnings.

"Thanks, guys. Easy pickings," says David.

"This is strictly a bass tournament next time," says Roger. "We just thought it would make it more interesting to allow other fish."

"And it did," I say. "We could have all fished differently and caught just as much as they did."

"I'm fishing for fucking mud cats next time," says Jerry. "They weigh a fucking shitload."

"Where the fuck are Boonie and Ray?" asks Roger.

"They too late now," observes Israel.

"They must be gone, Boonie's truck ain't here," says Homer.

"Why the fuck didn't they stay to weigh in?" asks Jerry.

"Who knows, probably found something floating in the water and got distracted," I say.

"Instead of road kill, maybe…… lake kill," adds Jim.

"Leave it to those backwoods dopes to just leave their money on the table," says Roger.

"Probably weren't having any luck, so said, what the fuck?" says Mark.

"I'm surprised that you two caught anything Mark, with all the bailing you had to do," says Jim.

"Fuck you, this thing is as tight as a goddamn drum," says Mark. "We didn't have to bail shit."

"No, we didn't have a bit of a problem out of the boat," says Homer. "I told you guys that it's a work of true craftsmanship."

"Anyone who wants to come back to my place is welcome," offers Jerry. "We can take these fish and fry them up and have us one big old fashioned fish fry. But, bring your own beverages, please."

"Sounds good to me, let's roll," I say. "That's what this is really about, getting to eat the fish."

Chapter 39

Wednesday March 11th, 1998

"Sprucing up the old front lobby, huh?" I ask, as I stroll up to Jerry and Roger.

"How'd you figure that out, Sherlock?" asks Roger. "Was it the paint? Or this new molding here? What gave it away?"

"Okay....smart ass," I respond.

"Jerry, Don must think he actually runs the plant now," says Roger. Turning to me. "I mean, you're going to stand around and fuck off right here by the front door?"

"Well, for one, I'm not dumb enough to stand around here but for so long. And secondly, I know that they would never fire me for something like this. You know how hard it is to get fired in this place. This isn't a union plant, but little Dickie McClean sure acts like it is sometimes. There are people that should have been gone long ago, but our poor excuse for an HR manager insists that we build a federal case in order to let anyone go. That's one of the reasons we're going down the toilet. Max will never be totally successful in turning this joint around if he can't see the problems Dick causes us."

"Like the time Raeford got caught jacking off in the warehouse," says Jerry.

"Twice, he got caught twice," I say.

"But he got away with it because it was only his word against the supervisor's," says Roger.

"And there's much more they could have thrown in there in Raeford's case," I say. "But it all wasn't officially documented."

"Well, looky here," says Jerry, looking out the front door. "Look who's driving in together."

"And late at that," adds Roger.

"Israel and Lisa," I say.

"A little late night action and they couldn't make it in to work on time," adds Roger.

"What's she see in him anyway?" I ask.

"She must see something for as long as it's been," says Roger. "But still no wedding bells."

"Well.....I think Israel's a decent guy," responds Jerry.

"And he's going for his engineering degree," says Roger. "He'll be getting out of this joint even if none of the rest of us do."

"So that's why she's seeing him?" I ask. "He's her ticket out of here or something?"

"I have no idea, really," responds Roger. "Why does this concern you so much?"

"No....it doesn't. I don't know......"

"I think he's sweet on her," offers Jerry.

"She's just a nice girl.....and I just think Israel has some old fashioned ideas about women.....primitive ideas, actually."

"But isn't that her business?" asks Roger.

"Of course it is," I say. "Just drop it."

"Gladly."

Yes, I do have a thing for Lisa. I've grown to admire her over the years. There's just something sweet and sexy about her. I shouldn't be letting anyone know that though. There's nothing I can do about it.

"So, you still doing your own thing when it comes to church?" asks Jerry.

"Yeah.....it's been about seven months since I quit going," I respond.

"What do you do then?" asks Jerry.

"Nothing special. I just study my bible. Seek God on my own. Do some research on the internet."

"I need to start messing around with that internet thing," says Jerry.

"It is cool," I say.

"How's Karen taking you not going to church?" asks Roger.

"Well, she just wants me to go to a church, any church. They're real big on this idea that you must assemble with other believers."

"There is a scripture about that somewhere," says Jerry.

"Yeah, there is," I say. "I believe that you should as long as the truth's involved."

"Here we go again.....you two bible scholars think that you have all the answers," says Roger.

"Don't jump down my goddamn throat," says Jerry. "I didn't say anything.....yet."

"I'm looking for something like what the early church had," I say.

"And what did the early church have?" asks Roger.

"They just had a much purer faith," I explain.

"They weren't caught up in all of this ritual and ceremony," adds Jerry.

"It was a lot less formal," I add.

"They actually met in each other's homes at the beginning. It was just like a bunch of friends getting together," says Jerry.

"Yeah, we've talked about this before," says Roger.

"It's hard to get people who want to be a part of something like that," says Jerry. "People are so set in their ways. They don't like change."

"Well, who knows what sort of cult you two have in mind," says Roger.

"We ain't talking about no fucking cult," says Jerry.

"More like a family," I say. "Being in the early church was like being part of a new family."

"You know.... Charles Manson called his little thing a family, too," says Roger.

"Yeah, funny," I say. "But what the early church had was beautiful."

"They were totally devoted to one another," says Jerry. "They sold their possessions and gave to those who had need."

"There was none of this ten-percent tithe crap that's pushed today," I say. "You gave everything. But you did it because you were so filled full of the love of God."

"The true message of Christ and what the early church was doing is actually very radical," says Jerry. "Your whole life is supposed to change."

"But what's church today?" I ask. "You basically live your life, except that you go to church for a couple of hours a week. These people looked at being Christians as a total way of life, not just this little part that they added on."

"I don't see a radical change in either of your lives," observes Roger.

"But that's what I want," I say.

"Me, too," concurs Jerry.

"Then what are you waiting for?" asks Roger. "Just do it."

"It's not that easy," I say. "The spirit of God has to work through you to do that."

"The flesh is too weak to give up all of the stuff of the world," says Jerry. "We need Christ to do that."

"If that's how it's supposed to be then why isn't the spirit doing it in your lives?" asks Roger.

"Because we're so corrupted with tradition and the old ways that we can't free our minds and spirits enough to embrace the truth," I explain.

"Selling possessions and all that sort of thing," says Roger. "That sounds like some sort of fucking commune to me."

"Great idea," I say.

"I'd love to live on a piece of land with other believers who wanted to live this way," says Jerry.

"Oh, God, you two are turning into a couple of commie pinkos."

"Actually, socialism, not capitalism, is closer to the way God wants us to live," I explain. "Except that we don't rely on the government to take care of those who need the help. We do it ourselves of our own free will, from the love that God has placed in our hearts."

"Now you're sounding like you already live in a commune," says Roger. "And the way you two keep finishing each other's thoughts…..have you rehearsed this or something?"

"Mock all you want," says Jerry. "But it's the truth. And there are other people who are buying into this, too."

"Jerry, why don't we start some sort of bible study ourselves?" I ask. "We can start to spread the word of what we'd like to do. We were talking about it one time before but never did anything."

"Yeah, we can start winning people over to the truth."

"We can have it at my house," I say.

"I'll ask a few people I've been talking to," says Jerry. "I think people would like something like this, without all the dressing up and formality of church."

"Exactly."

"And so the cult begins," jokes Roger.

"Why don't you try it out, Roger," I say. "You've been taking part in our discussions here at the plant. Could be fun."

"But I don't see things as radically as you two do."

"We're just getting together to talk," I say.

"Yeah….just a bunch of guys shooting the shit," says Jerry. "Except that we're talking about the bible."

"Well…yeah….I don't know….I may give it a shot. But you two are starting to scare me…just a little."

"That's the problem we face," I say. "People have such negative ideas when it comes to communes and that sort of thing. But there's nothing wrong with the idea when it's based in the truth."

"People are just brainwashed," says Jerry. "They think they know what church is all about but they have no idea."

"Well, I'm sure you two are prepared to show them," says Roger.

Chapter 40

Friday March 13th, 1998

"Typical hard day's work being put in by the instrumentation staff, I see," says Roger, as he enters the Instrumentation Shop to find Mark, Jim, Israel, Lisa, David and me all sitting around. "Oh....I'm sorry.....electricians, too."

"Yeah....be careful. Don't be calling me no instrumentation tech," says David. "I do have my pride."

"You can call me an instrumentation person if you want to," says Lisa, glancing at Israel. "I happen to like instrument guys."

"Oh God," says Roger.

"Did you two manage to get here on time today?" I ask.

"Who?" responds Lisa.

"You and Israel," I say. "We saw you two drive in together the other day."

"And late to boot," adds Roger.

"Yeah, Israel was getting some boot alright.....booty that is," says David.

"You guys shut up," says Israel. "That shit our business."

"Touchy about this, are we?" responds David.

"I didn't see them driving in together today," says Roger. "We were working up front this morning."

"No pussy for Israel last night," says Mark.

"You don't know what I got," responds Israel.

"Damn, you guys talk like I ain't even here," says Lisa. "The pussy....and the booty in question happen to belong to me."

She turns me on so much when she talks like that. I don't know why. I just seem to have a high sensitivity to women with dirty mouths.

"I'm sure you're used to it by now," I say. "You know how crude they can be."

"They?" asks Roger. "Who the fuck are they? It seems that you join in plenty of times when the crudeness starts to flow."

"I agree, Roger," says Lisa. "Don has no room to talk."

"What....little ole me, crude?" I ask.

"Yes, you, crude," responds Lisa.

"I've just been adversely affected by my surroundings," I say.

That's actually the truth. I didn't really use profanity until I started working here. It's not something you generally heard in my family, so, I didn't pick it up really until I came to work here.

"Yeah, that's my excuse, too," says Lisa. "I've been corrupted."

"I kind of like your crudeness though," I say.

"Do you now?"

"Hey, what's this shit I hear about you guys starting some bible study or something?" asks David.

"Yeah....I was meaning to tell you, Don," says Roger. "Our buddy Jerry's been telling people that there'll be beer served at the bible study."

"Well shit, sign me up," says Mark.

"Yeah....me, too. I've been waiting for that sort of thing," adds Jim, just as Jerry comes in. "That's a religion I could really sink my teeth into."

"Jerry, what's this Roger's telling me about some beer bible study that you have planned?" I ask. "You want to serve beer at a bible study?"

"I never said anything about serving beer. I just thought that since this is informal, why can't we have a few beers as we talk."

"Well....I'm not having any part of that," I say, dismissively.

"Why?"

"It just isn't right."

"You said yourself that the bible doesn't prohibit alcohol use, just drunkenness. Why are you backing up on that now?" asks Jerry.

"Because he knows that your intention is to get plastered," explains Roger.

"Everyone knows that," says Mark.

"Well, I don't want to start this thing up by imposing rules," says Jerry. "That's the whole problem with organized Christianity anyway, too many rules, regulations and laws. This ain't gonna be like that if I'm gonna be a part of it."

"There have to be some rules," says David.

"No....none. That's the point of Christ coming," says Jerry. "He freed us from the law. That isn't just halfway. It's everything."

"Prophet Jerry has spoken," says Roger.

"Don, you said the same thing yourself," says Jerry. "You've said that there's no law for the Christian."

"Even better…..lawless religion," says Jim. "What do you say, Mark?"

"Just my cup of tea."

"You know the verses, Don. Everything is permissible, but not everything is beneficial. You know what that means. There is no law for the Christian, none, even the Ten Commandments," preaches Jerry. "Christ abolished the law."

"Wait a minute. You're trying to tell me that the Ten Commandments don't apply anymore?" asks Roger. "You're just so thoroughly full of shit if you believe that."

"No….I believe the same thing….basically," I say.

"Then I guess you're both thoroughly full of shit," says Roger.

"I don't think I've ever heard anyone say that sort of thing before," says Lisa.

"The whole idea is that we don't need written laws because Christ is supposed to write the laws on our hearts," I say. "It's what the bible says."

"But what the hell does that mean?" asks Roger.

"It just means that the Holy Spirit changes you supernaturally," says Jerry. "We're turned into different people."

"When's he gonna do this?" asks Roger. "You seem like the same ole jackass Jerry I've always known."

"Fuck you."

"Case in point," says Roger. "Still cursing me like fucking always."

"Not needing the law just means that you don't need a law to tell you to not commit adultery, because your heart will be changed through Christ, so that you would never even have the desire to commit adultery to begin with," I explain. "No need for a law to say that you shouldn't kill someone, the desire to kill them will never be in your heart to begin with."

"No need for a law saying fucking underage girls is wrong," jokes Jim. "The desire won't be there to begin with. Is that the idea, Don?"

"Yes, that is the idea," I say, stiffly.

That ass! Taking a shot at me like that.

"That was a little creepy there, Jim," says Lisa.

"Just trying to keep up," says Jim. "Besides, I am known as the plant pervert. But I'm not the only one."

Lisa glances at me.

"We need no law, no commandments," I say. "We really don't

need the bible. All that truth is supposed to be implanted into our hearts, into our spirit. The whole idea is that this is supposed to be a supernatural transformation, not just some religion like other ones where you just do your best to live by some book."

"Then where is the law written on Jerry's heart to stop getting fucking loaded?" asks Roger. "Where's that truth?"

"God's working on me," responds Jerry. "But he ain't done yet."

"It isn't instantaneous. It's a process," I explain.

"Why would it have to be a process if it's supernatural?" asks Roger. "Why wouldn't God just do it? You say God implants this into your spirit. Why wouldn't he just fucking do it?"

"You're just a mocker and a naysayer," says Jerry. "The bible warns that there'll be people like you."

"I'm just asking a question," says Roger. "You think all this shit is just going to go unchallenged?"

"No, Jerry. He does have a point," I say. "Sure, you're right, it should be instantaneous. It should be. But it obviously isn't. But I have a theory on why it isn't."

"This should be good," says Roger. "Proceed, professor."

"We're supposed to be able to just stand back and let God do his work in our life. That's the way it's supposed to be," I explain. "But we've gotten so far from the truth that we have no idea how to just let God do his work. Instead, we try to do his work for him, through rules and regulations and all that shit. But that ain't the way. Religion ain't the way."

"But if it's supposed to be this supernatural transformation that you talk about, then how did everyone get so off track?" asks Jim. "If God just miraculously does this then how is it possible for it to go off the rails so badly?"

"It just happened," says Jerry. "Who knows? But at some point, manmade religion started creeping in and corrupted the whole thing."

"That's right," I say. "Religion fucked everything up."

"Well....religion usually does fuck everything up," says Jim. "But....I'm sorry....I know you meant it in a different way."

"No, no offense taken. I don't consider what I'm trying to achieve a religion anyway," I say. "Practicing a religion causes us to feel the need to impose all of these rules on ourselves to make ourselves seem so religious. But those rules actually short circuit what God's trying to do. I don't want a religion. I want a real experience."

"What gets me is that you two knuckle-heads think you have

this all figured out," says David.

"Be careful, David, we're in the company of two great prophets," says Roger. "God may strike us down for speaking ill of them."

"Mock if you must. But it's the truth," says Jerry.

"We get so loaded down with manmade rules that we forget how to really let God do the work inside of us," I say. "We join a religion instead of letting Christ truly come into our hearts. If I could just get to that place….."

It's hard to explain to people what I believe should happen. They don't get what it is I'm seeking. I happen to believe in the concept of true holiness. I believe in a supernatural transformation. It's what scripture says should happen. But it isn't happening to me. I just can't seem to figure out why. I'm not sure if it's happening to anyone really. And if that's the case, does it even exist?

"Those who live by the law will be bound by the law," says Jerry. "Those who live by the spirit will be set free by the spirit."

"Well, how are you supposed to live then?" asks Roger. "How do you know what to do and not to do?"

"God doesn't care," says Jerry. "That's the grace of God."

"What do you mean, he doesn't fucking care?" asks Roger.

"That whole mindset's wrong. That's the problem," says Jerry. "God isn't sitting up there keeping a checklist of our wrongs and rights."

"Thank God for that," says Jim. "I'm really starting to like your religion."

"Praise the Lord!" adds Mark.

"Mockers," says Jerry.

"I keep telling you. This is a supernatural happening, if it's the real thing," I say. "We're either indwelt with the spirit of God or we aren't. If the spirit's in us, then we're saved, no matter what we do. We're forgiven of all sins. There are no exceptions."

"So, I can do anything I want to do?" asks Roger.

"You can, but you won't," I say.

"What?"

"You won't want to sin because of the spirit inside of you," says Jerry. "There's no need for the law if you have the spirit. You're permitted to sin, but you won't have the desire."

"Love is the key to the whole thing," I explain. "If we're filled full of the love of God, then we won't sin. Most sin involves hurting others. Those who love won't want to hurt others."

"All we need is love…love is all we need," sings Jim.

"You guys need to stop," says Lisa. "They're just trying to share what they believe."

"Well, of course you like their message," says Mark. "You can still go to heaven even though you're fucking someone without the benefit of marriage."

"I have plenty of company," says Lisa.

"And don't forget that she's sinning against her race, too," adds Jim.

"No, it's not a sin now," says Mark. "In their cult, you can do no wrong."

"Oh yeah, my mistake."

"This is all a nice theory," says Roger. "But that's all it is. I still don't understand how you can think you have this great undiscovered truth that so many have failed to see."

"I'm not going to mock you, but I don't understand how you can say we don't need any rules, or even the bible. How do you know how to be a Christian then?" asks Lisa. "Not that I'm a practicing Christian or anything. I just don't see how you can just say that you can do what you want and just wait for the spirit to take away the desire. I could just say that the spirit hasn't taken away my desire to fuck someone outside of marriage, for instance."

"I've already said that," I say. "God imparts all of that to you through your spirit. It's supernatural. He just gives it to you. And some stuff is just common sense. We know what wrong and right is basically. And I'm not so sure that a marriage certificate issued by the state is what we should base anything on, as far as that issue's concerned."

"Then, like I said, how is it a process?" asks Roger. "How can it be a process if God just supernaturally imparts it to you?"

"Yeah…right….why doesn't it just come to you magically?" asks David.

"Do you understand how ridiculous this seems?" asks Roger. "You two think you have this great new truth that all of these theologians throughout the ages have somehow missed. And all these churches today are missing it. You have this great undiscovered truth, yet you're absolutely incapable of proving it. If it's true, then why isn't it happening to you? That's the bottom line."

"Well….I don't have an answer for that, except to say that it's possible that because we're all so brain-washed with the trappings of legalistic Christianity, that the truth has a hard time breaking through," I explain.

"But you two say you believe. You two say this is the way it's supposed to work," says David. "Why aren't you making the transformation?"

"Exactly....you believe....isn't that's all that's required of us?" asks Roger. "If we believe, doesn't God do the rest?"

"Well....maybe we don't believe enough yet," says Jerry. "Maybe we can't quite accept the reality of what no law means."

"It is a radical concept," I say. "And we are so brain-washed to think in traditional religious terms."

"But why would God make it so hard?" asks Roger. "Why would you have to believe this very specific truth to be able to receive the spirit? Isn't that what the spirit's for?"

"Exactly," says Jim. "You're saying that the spirit imparts truth, but you can't get the spirit because you aren't in the truth yet. That's contradictory."

"I don't think it's contradictory," I say. "This is a radical shift from what traditional Christianity tells us. At least the Christianity I've been exposed to. It's hard for me to explain how radical it is. It's hard for me to grasp myself. And maybe I haven't."

"Yeah, there aren't too many people saying this stuff," says Jerry.

"There are even verses that make it sound as if the early Christians, who were trying to be free from the Old Testament law, would appear to be sinning, at first, because of their freedom in Christ. They would be doing things that they weren't allowed to do before. Being free from the law is deep. It actually means the freedom to sin," I say. "It's not an easy concept to get used to."

"You can say that again," says Roger. "Freedom to sin?"

"No law, means absolutely no law," I state. "We have to be free to sin to be free of sin."

"Sin is a condition. It isn't an act or a series of acts," says Jerry. "It's like a disease. We all have it. Unless you're perfect, what's the point of trying to keep a list of rules. Christ makes us perfect without keeping the law."

"So, if we can't be perfect by keeping the law, why try at all?" I ask. "Christ is the better way."

"The bottom line is that neither of you is living this great new truth that you claim you have," says Roger.

"It's not new. It's right there in the bible," I say.

"Then why the hell hasn't anyone else seen it?" asks Roger.

"There are others out there," I say.

"Maybe the rest aren't meant to," offers Jerry. "God said that narrow is the way."

"Narrow is the way?" asks Mark.

"It means that very few find the truth path to salvation," explains Jerry.

"So….God has selected you?" asks Roger.

"I said before that God chooses the lesser things in this world," says Jerry. "Those who are smart, or rich, or comfortable in this life don't think they need anything from God. God chooses the lowly people of this world to share his truth with."

"There are verses to back that up," I add.

"Let's get back to the beer bible study, Don," says Jim. "If you say there's no law, then why would you be against beer at the bible study? Seems contradictory."

"That passage that Jerry mentioned earlier about everything being permissible? Well, the other part is that not everything is beneficial," I say. "It's perfectly legal, so to speak, for anyone to drink beer. But in this case, I don't see it as being beneficial. We're supposed to try to only do things that benefit us, not anything with the potential to harm. And with Jerry's history, it just seems like the wrong tone to set to drink beer. But it could just be me holding onto old ideas."

"Yeah, if Jerry was just a guy who enjoyed a couple of beers, then fine. But Jerry admits to having a problem," says Lisa.

"I admit to him having a problem," says Roger.

"Fuck you, Roger," says Jerry.

"Such language from the chosen one," jokes Roger.

"If drinking a beer is like drinking a coke is to me, then fine," I say. "But many people only drink to get that buzz. That isn't beneficial, to stick with the language of scripture."

"Wait a minute," says Roger. "You just said that we didn't need the bible any more…right?"

"Yeah," I say.

"Okay….so how can you judge what Jerry wants to do by that scripture? What if you didn't have it? What if Jerry feels as if the spirit inside of him is leading him to have beer at the bible study, while you say it shouldn't be there? Who's right?"

"That's what I'm saying," says Lisa. "You have to have some sort of written standard."

"It's not a huge issue to me," I say. "Now, if I go, and they started getting drunk, well, then I'd just leave."

"Why? Without the bible, who are you to say that anything's

wrong?" asks Jim. "You would have no basis to condemn drinking, drunkenness or anything for that matter."

"Yeah...see? You're building your shit on a house of sand," concludes Roger.

"Like Jim said, you're using the bible itself to make the case that you don't need the bible," says Lisa.

"Bingo," says Jim.

"I'm not claiming to have it all figured out," I say. "It's just what I see in scripture."

"Scripture that you claim to not need," says Roger.

"Okay....I get it," I say, getting a little angry.

"Some things are beyond our understanding," adds Jerry.

"That's a nice way to excuse a faulty argument," says Jim.

"We're at a disadvantage. The spirit came on the disciples so much more powerfully than he does now. They just knew how to live because it was so obvious," I explain.

"But you only know about that through scripture," says Jim. "What if it was how you say it should be and there wasn't a bible? How would you know what they experienced? How would you know anything about Christ or Christianity? The very doctrine that you're advocating is taken from scripture. Would you even be a Christian without the bible?"

Damn, I have to admit that that is an excellent point.

"Well, Jim, the answer I have to that, is that maybe the faith we ought to have, should be much simpler than what we have now. Maybe we should have a basic faith just based off of the complexity and beauty of creation," I say. "A faith based on a very simple but innate sense of right and wrong. Maybe that's the answer. To not think so much about what's the right way and what's the wrong way. I think I would still believe in God, but maybe it would be a very simple faith."

"Good answer," says Lisa.

"Reading is much more prevalent today. What did people do who couldn't read?" asks Jerry. "They had to have faith apart from the bible."

"That's true....the bible wasn't available to the general public for quite a while," adds Jim. "For centuries people didn't have bibles or any books for that matter."

"Those who believed in God would just have to have a basic faith," I say. "We're probably too educated for our own good."

"We complicate it," says Jerry.

"Some of them may have had this basic faith that you talk

about," says Jim. "But many of them just did what the church told them to do."

"Listen….we pretty much know the things that we should do and the things that we shouldn't. Most of us are programmed that way," says Roger.

"That's what I'm saying," I say.

"I think it has been complicated too much," says Mark. "You're right about that. All of the formality that many churches and religions have."

"You know….this has been interesting," says Lisa. "If this is what it'll be like, then I may like to come to some of these bible studies, beer or no beer."

"Listen….I can do without the beer," says Jerry. "It's no big deal. You guys may not buy it, but I am making progress in that department."

"If Lisa come…I come, too," says Israel.

"Good, we got ourselves a decent little group to start," I say.

"I've got a few more that may be interested," adds Jerry.

"I've got another question to pose about this little bible study," says Mark.

"What is it?" I ask.

"Well, with the way this group usually talks, will profane and obscene language be allowed?" asks Mark.

"Can't wait for this answer," says Roger.

"Why is that, Roger?" I ask.

"I just want to see what your answer happens to be," says Roger.

"It's not that big a deal to me," I respond. "I don't give a shit what words anyone uses. I have a big problem with the whole so-called dirty words shit anyway. I probably cuss more than I ever have."

"That's why I asked that," says Mark. "We've had those conversations before, about how stupid it is to consider some words wrong. I was just wondering if your views have changed since you've become a Christian."

"Obviously they haven't," says Roger. "Some of the shit that comes outta his mouth."

"No….still feel the same way," I say. "There isn't anything inherently wrong with most words. It's just the perception that it's dirty or something. But people will judge you on that shit. I know that firsthand."

"Yeah….but certain words shouldn't be said by a Christian,"

says Roger. "I mean….you shouldn't be saying goddamn, for instance."

"Yeah….but what's funny is that many Christians think that's the only way to take the Lord's name in vain. But it isn't," I say.

"What? What do you mean?" asks Roger.

"Taking the name of the Lord in vain just means that we shouldn't use his name loosely, we shouldn't use it unless we mean to," I say. "It doesn't just mean that you can't attach damn to it."

"Use his name loosely?" asks Roger.

"That means using it as an expletive, for instance," I say. "Karen does this all the time. Say she smashes her finger with a hammer. She blurts out 'Jesus'. She's taking the name of the Lord in vain. She's yelling out his name just like I may yell out 'damn' if I smash my finger."

"Or fuck," says Mark.

"I'm not sure I get that one," says Lisa. "She isn't cursing God."

"No, but is she actually calling on the name of the Lord? Or is it just an exclamation of pain and frustration?" I ask. "If you're not actually intending to call on the Lord, then you are taking his name in vain. At least that's supposed to be the idea behind it. But I don't think God is his actual name anyway. I'm just talking about what the traditional idea is."

"What you're essentially saying is that when someone says goddamn, the problem is not with the damn, but with the god," says Jim.

"Yeah….exactly. But most Christians are blind to that. They'll say 'god' in anger or frustration and never think anything of it, yet condemn someone for saying goddamn," I say.

"So, you think they're the same? God, goddamn, Jesus….any of it qualifies as taking the name of the Lord in vain?" asks Roger.

"Yeah."

"You agree with your partner in prophecy here, Jerry?" asks Roger.

"Yeah….I think he's right. I haven't really given it much thought, but yeah, it makes sense."

"So, you're now changing the definition of what constitutes taking God's name in vain?" asks Roger.

"We ain't changing nothing. We just see what's written and accept it, instead of just going with conventional thinking," says Jerry.

"We aren't just sheep being led by the nose. We think for ourselves," I add. "And the only reason I even give this any thought is because of the way so many people get offended by mere words. If you want to play the speech police game…well….let's play."

"I love the idea of a church where drinking and bad language is totally acceptable," says Jim, laughing.

"But most of the words that are considered bad by society are only bad because they're perceived that way," I assert. "Words are just words. They can't be inherently bad."

"Well, I'm not sure about that," says Lisa.

"Shall we go word by word?" I ask.

"Sure, let's have a deep discussion on the subject of profane and obscene words," says Mark. "Should be fun."

"Fuck, is this what bible study will be like?" asks Lisa.

"Let's start with fuck," I say. "Probably considered one of the dirtiest words."

"But increasingly common," adds Lisa.

"Yeah, fuck is bad, yet it has several acceptable replacements. Hosed, screwed, reamed….." I say.

"Dicked," adds Mark.

"But it depends on how you're using it," adds Jim. "There are many ways to use it."

"Very versatile word it is," agrees Mark.

"Those replacement words are really just for the most graphic meaning," I say.

"Yeah, that you're getting a dick stuck in you somewhere," says Mark.

"That's the point. You could be describing the same action, but because you use a so-called clean word, it's okay?" I ask. "The act is just as graphic, but okay to talk about if you use a clean word."

"I'm not sure I'm following," says Lisa.

"Well, say that someone cheated me," I say. "To describe that, some would say that I got fucked. When you get down to it, they're saying that I got fucked in the ass."

"But those who don't want to use the dirty word, would say perhaps, that they got hosed, instead of fucked," explains Mark. "They got hosed in the ass."

"But it means the same thing," I say. "They're still describing a very crude thing, but it's acceptable just because they didn't use the word fucked."

"Or take fuck in its most literal meaning….having sex," says David. "I would say that those two were in the back room fucking the shit out of each other. But someone else may say they were back there screwing their brains out."

"Or that Israel was fucking the shit out of Lisa," says Mark.

"Man....she right here," says Israel. "Show some respect."

"That's alright, babe," says Lisa. "I'm a big girl. Besides, you do fuck the shit out of me. Quite regularly, too."

"Damn!" says Mark.

I'm liking her more and more.

"You guys watch it," says Israel.

"Israel, it don't mean nothing," says Mark.

"I not used to women being spoken to that way," says Israel. "But for that matter, I not used to women talking that way, either."

"I like nasty mouthed women," says Mark.

"You always have hard-on for her," says Israel.

"He has a hard-on for every good looking woman," I say.

"Good looking, huh?" says Lisa.

"Of course," I respond.

"Okay, we've established that Lisa has a potty mouth," says Jim. "And that Mark has a hard-on for her. And that she's good looking. Can we please move on now? Before Israel totally loses it."

"Shit is the same way," observes Mark. "Replace it with crap, poop or dung, but it's still a pile of shit."

"And what makes that word so offensive? What is it?" asks Jerry.

"Ass is a good one though. Ass is in the bible," I say.

"Ass is fine as long as you are talking about a donkey, but not if you are referring to a rear end," says Roger.

"Lisa's rear end," says Mark.

"Stop talking about her," says Israel.

"So, there is nothing wrong with the word itself, just in its context," adds Jim.

"Damn and darn are almost the same, yet one is a bad word and one is a nicer replacement," says David.

"But damn is becoming almost accepted now," observes Roger.

"What about the middle finger?" asks Jerry.

"Yeah, can we give each other the finger during bible study?" jokes Mark.

"But think of the absurdity of it. It's offensive for me to hold up a certain finger?" I ask, holding up the finger in question.

"We can start our own tradition. Holding up the pinkie can be our way of saying fuck off. No one would know," says Mark.

"But it points out how absurd it really is. It's just a fucking finger," I observe.

"But they sure won't let it get on TV, if they can help it," says Jerry. "Blur it out in a second."

"Hell is a good one for Christians," observes Mark. "They use it all the time."

"Yeah, nothing wrong with the word itself, as long as you're referring to people ending up in hell," I say.

"I'm fine then," says Mark. "I tell people to go to hell all the time."

"But why is it wrong to say, for instance, that that was one hell of a game?" I ask. "What's so wrong about that?"

"Do you cuss at home, Don?" asks Jim.

"No, I try to respect Karen's opinion when it comes to this. I try not to cuss around her. But I even hate that we call it cussing. They're just words. I don't think God gives a rat's ass about these words."

"What about motherfucker?" asks David. "That's a heavier word than most."

"I personally don't use that," I say. "That word's pretty descriptive."

"Yeah, someone who fucks their mother," says Mark.

"Exactly," I say.

"What about pussy?" asks Lisa.

"Sure....I'd love some," jokes Mark.

"You watch it," says Israel.

"Just a little joke," says Mark.

"Well, it's funny. In Britain they sometimes refer to old ladies as pussies," I point out. "It's in some of the Agatha Christie books I've read."

"Or it can refer to a cat," observes Mark. "Can I please pet your pussy, Lisa?"

"I kick your joking ass, if you don't stop," say Israel.

"I don't have a cat, Mark," says Lisa.

"I know."

"But the point is that it's all perception," says Jim.

"Exactly, but people make such a big deal over what are nothing more than words," I say.

"Too many of these religious people have such a narrow view of the world," observes Jim. "They're just totally unaware that there's a world outside of their little circle. It doesn't occur to them that there could be these other perceptions out there that make their little hang ups seem so silly."

"I think some of them do know," I say. "But they just give into the pressure of their little group."

"Well, after all, is it really all that big of a deal to not use profanity?" asks Lisa. "Is it really necessary?"

"No, I agree," I say. "And that's why I refrain when I'm around Karen and her family. We shouldn't do stuff that'll offend others if we can avoid it. I'm speaking from the viewpoint of a Christian when I say that."

"Well, I love to go out of my way to offend others," says Mark.

"And you sir are a sick and demented bastard, and a motherfucker, and an asshole son of a bitch," I say.

"Yeah, what about bitch?" ask Mark.

"Yeah, what about your mom?" I ask.

"No...I mean that bitch is a female dog," observes Mark. "I heard the announcers say it on TV one time during one of those dog shows."

"You and your mom sit around watching dog shows together?" asks David.

"Wouldn't that be cool? Some dog walks by and I say come to daddy you little bitch," I say. "I mean, do it around Karen's family or something."

"You, sir, do not have the balls to do that." says Mark.

"How would that go along with your idea of not being offensive?" asks Roger.

"It wouldn't," I respond.

"Oh shit, here comes Bob," says Jim.

"Busted," adds Mark.

"Uh....do you all mind getting your asses back to work," says Bob. "Break is long over with. Don and Israel, you're senior here. I hold you responsible for this."

"What does that mean?" I ask.

"Just don't let this happen again."

"We just got a little caught up in a discussion," I explain.

"This isn't the place for town hall discussions," says Bob.

"Could have fooled me," cracks Mark.

"What was that?" asks Bob. "Be careful, son. Don't let your mouth write a check that your ass can't cash. Now get back to work. End of discussion."

Chapter 41

Saturday June 5ᵗʰ, 1999

"Guys, my buddies here at the club have graciously allowed us to have our tournament here today," says Max. "I ask that you please act with decorum and don't embarrass me, please?"

"Boy, does he know how much he's asking?" I say.

"I think he does, actually," responds Jim. "He just wants to be able to tell the guys that run the place, that he did say something to us if indeed there's an incident."

"Okay, we heard what Max said," says Roger. "Let's try to place some good golf and see who the better man is. We're playing in pairs, but we're in this each man for himself. All standard golf rules apply. The honor system is in effect. But remember that we also have partners to keep us honest."

"Unless the partner is a corrupt son of a bitch," cracks Ronnie.

"As far as pairings are concerned, those who wanted to be paired together are, but we had a few odd balls in the mix that we had to pair up," says Roger. "The pairings are as follows, Jim and Don, Max and Bob, Jerry and me, Ronnie and Mark, Jack and Butch, and last but not least.....uh.....Raeford and Israel."

"Real funny......asshole," says Raeford. "How'd you come up with that shit?"

"Well, everyone else had made arrangements to partner with someone, except for Jack, Don's dad, Butch, and you and Israel," explains Roger.

"Fuck it....whatever......big joke....haha," says Raeford.

"I not thrilled about this shit, either," says Israel. "We just make the best of it."

"They play golf in Africa?" asks Raeford.

"I learn to play here."

"Yeah, everyone.....Roger mentioned it, but for those of you who don't know him, that's Jack, my dad," I say.

"Glad to join you gentlemen today," says Jack.

"He doesn't know us too well, obviously," says Jerry.

"How the hell did Mark and Ronnie end up being partners?" I ask.

"Roger paired them up," says Jerry. "We wanted to put Israel and Raeford together, just to see if something would happen. But we knew that Raeford would feel like Ronnie was a logical partner for him. So, Roger lied and said that they had arranged to play together."

"Always trying to provoke shit," I say.

"I don't think there has to be much provoking to get something to happen here, with this group of idiots we have here today," says Jim.

"Well, since Max is a member here, he's most likely the favorite," I say. "He probably takes the game far more seriously than most of us do."

"And he can afford to play more than the rest of us," adds Jerry.

"Look at that personalized cart he's got," says Roger.

"I know....I bet Israel's playing with clubs with shafts of bamboo," jokes Jerry.

"I heard that," says Israel. "I got good fucking clubs."

"I wonder if they even have black members here," I say.

"Good point," says Jim. "Max probably had to get a special exemption just so we could have the tournament."

"Many of these southern country clubs are like that," I say. "Thing is, I'm not sure most of us could afford to be a member here anyway. We need to make a spectacle of ourselves, just for the hell of it. Show them how the other half lives."

"Like I said, I don't think that's gonna be hard to do," says Jim. "We won't even have to try all that hard."

"Okay, attention everyone, we have all pulled numbers out of a hat to establish the playing order," says Roger. "Ronnie and Mark will begin."

"Wanna go first?" asks Mark.

"No, fuck.....you go ahead," says Ronnie.

Mark tees his ball and takes a swing.

"Damn man, you shanked the shit out of that one," says Jerry.

"Does everyone have to fucking stand here watching?" asks Mark.

"Fuck.....let them stand there," says Ronnie. "I'll really shank one and bean their ass with my ball. They won't wanna watch anymore."

"Stop being a pussy," says Jerry. "That's the joy of being on the first tee. You always have a fucking audience."

"Alright man, how bout shutting the fuck up so that I can hit my goddamn ball," says Ronnie, who proceeds to hit a perfect drive.

"Damn, look at that," says Roger. "Get lucky? Or can you

actually play?"

"What? You think I'm just some biker dude that runs a bar and can't do the more genteel things in life?"

"Well, yeah," responds Roger.

"Might surprise your fucking ass then."

We all proceed to tee off and get the grand Raymond Mills Annual Golf Tournament under way.

"So, Don, tell me, when are you and Karen going to produce some babies?" asks Jim, as we wait for Ronnie and Mark to clear off of the green on the third hole.

"Damn, I'm getting so tired of that question. Is that all we're good for? Are we all destined to have kids? It's like it's just what you're supposed to do."

"Sorry if I struck a nerve. I just thought that's part of the whole getting married thing for most people. It's like the next thing in line. And it's been how long now?"

"Five years."

"Most people have done something by now."

"I don't know, Jim. Karen wants them, but I've never had the urge all that bad. And I don't think it's right to have them just to please her."

"No, that wouldn't be right. There's probably too much of that sort of thing happening anyway, people who don't want their kids."

"I know that people have to be wondering why we don't have kids yet. I get that it's considered to be the natural thing to do. But it still gets to me, this constant harping that people do about that."

"Okay man, I'll drop it then."

"It just irritates me anytime people want me to do something just because it's what everyone else does. I just hate the idea of conforming. It really gets to me."

"I was just making conversation."

"I know....sorry."

"I'm with you," says Jim. "Remember, I'm the guy with no kids and a vasectomy."

"Yeah, pervert playboy ladies' man on the hunt for all of our pure virginal girls," I say. "Speaking of that, seeing anyone right now?"

"Not anyone......a few."

"You dog."

"That's me.....woof, woof."

"I never really got to play the field like that."

"Yeah, the whole virgin thing?"

"I didn't have the fun most people have in high school," I say. "Girls, parties and all of that shit."

"Too bad."

"Yeah, it was, but you know…..now, it doesn't bother me like it used to. I'm kinda glad now that I didn't slip into that whole cycle of drinking all the time. Too many people seem to think that all there is to life is partying."

"I know. Some of my friends act like they're still in high school. That does get old for most of us."

"Even though the real reason I didn't do any partying in school was the shyness, I still never had this strong desire to use drugs or alcohol. Just never did. Except for a couple of times."

"This coming from someone who was growing pot once upon a time?"

"Trying to grow pot. We never quite succeeded," I say. "And we weren't really doing that for personal use. We had some big plans. I really wanted to have some sort of business doing that."

"Yeah, I remember you referring to that one time. I just never knew you were all that serious about actually doing it for a living or something."

"Jim, I absolutely cannot stand the thought of a conventional life. I know I've said this before, but this idea that you have to go according to some program. You have to do things by the book. You have your career. You get married. You have kids. You have your little hobbies or whatever. Then you retire and sit around waiting to die. I absolutely cannot stand the thought of that. I need something different."

I wanted something different. I still want something different. But I have a very conventional life at the moment. I'll never be happy like this. Deep down I know this is the truth.

"So, you wanted to be some sort of drug kingpin?"

"I was even planning on getting a gun."

"Damn."

"At least it would've been exciting," I say. "Not conventional in the least."

"Do you ever think about trying that again?"

"The idea still really intrigues me, but I don't think Karen would go for it."

"Yeah….obviously."

"It was just some stupid spur of the moment thing," I say. "The idea had been there before. Mark happened to have this book lying around that his brother had. Well, I just took it from there. Mark kind of just came along for the ride. I think he knew nothing would really come from all of my talk."

There's no doubt that I have big dreams. I can concoct any sort of plan in my head. But when it comes to following through and executing these plans I always seem to shrink back and fall short.

"Yeah, there's a difference between being unconventional and being downright dangerous," says Jim.

"Yeah…I know….it was stupid. But I still think I could do it."

"You'd need a better partner though, someone like me."

"You'd actually do something like that?"

"Damn right," says Jim. "If you ever decide you want to take a shot at it again, just let me know. I actually have experience growing the shit. Just never did it as a business proposition."

"I have to admit that I'm intrigued by the idea, just the challenge of doing it without getting caught."

"It'd be fun. I think we're both smart enough to pull it off."

"I guess we better go now."

"Shit, you're right," says Jim. "They're gone."

Just then, a cart comes careening towards us, seemingly from nowhere, and slides to a halt right beside our cart.

"That's right, you motherfuckers need to hit, or we'll gonna rain balls down on your ass," says Jerry. "Now if you want to keep talking, we can just play the fuck through."

"Get your ass back up to the tee, Jim's getting ready to hit," I say.

"Yeah, go drink some more beer," adds Jim.

"Fuck….I'm the designated drunk golf cart driver today," says Jerry, as he whips the cart in a circle before tearing back up to the third tee.

"Guess you'd better go ahead and hit," I say.

"I would, but some other asshole is racing towards us with their cart," says Jim.

"Give me a fucking ball," I say, as I hurriedly take a ball out of my bag and pull out my driver. "That's fucking Ronnie and Mark."

"What are you gonna do?"

"I'm gonna try to bean there fucking ass," I say, as I tee up my ball and take a shot at them.

"You're gonna pay for that, you fucker," says Ronnie, as he comes sliding up to and into our cart.

"What the fuck are you two doing?" asks Jim.

"We're backed up on the next tee, and we saw Jerry down here sliding around. We thought we'd come down and join the fucking party," says Ronnie.

"What were you two waiting for anyway?" asks Mark.

"You bastards were taking so fucking long that we just started talking and didn't realize you were done," I explain.

"Shit, here comes Max," says Mark.

"Guys, what the hell are you doing?" asks Max.

"We just came down to wake these boys up," explains Ronnie.

"But you're driving the carts like goddamn fools," says Max. "I've got a reputation to uphold here. Stop this shit. And get back to the fourth tee, where you fucking belong. And you two, please get moving. You're holding up the whole goddamn fucking shooting match."

"No problem, hoss," says Ronnie, as he proceeds to circle Max a few times before tearing off down the fairway.

"I knew this was a fucking mistake," says Max, as he and Bob drive off.

"We all knew it was a mistake," I say.

"Redneck party at the country club," adds Jim.

"Somebody must have said something to Max."

"Yeah, they're the last group. They wouldn't be able to see any of that."

"I'm sure they have people keeping an eye on us, if nothing more than the fact that Israel's with us," I say.

"Yeah, have to keep track of the dreaded black man to make sure he's not defiling any women on the course or anything like that."

"Wonder if they know that I'm married to a black woman."

"They wouldn't be all that fond of that, either."

"Look.....here comes Ronnie again," I say, as Mark and Ronnie come sliding to a stop.

"Come on, let's fuck with Max some," says Ronnie.

"What do you wanna do?" I ask.

"Let's have a fucking race," says Ronnie.

"We're going on a fucking rampage," says Mark.

"Let's back track and see how many of the guys'll join in," says Ronnie.

"Well, I can guarantee that my dad and Butch won't do it," I say. "My dad's driving. He would never do something like that."

"Well, fuck him," says Ronnie. "We know that drunk ass Jerry'll join in."

"That just leaves Raeford and Israel," I say.

"Come on, let's roll," says Ronnie.

"Fuck it," I say. "What do you say, Jim?"

"Fuck it, why not?" says Jim, as we take off on our little adventure of mayhem.

"Hey, fuck the golf," says Mark, as we all come sliding up to where Jerry and Roger are parked.

"What do you mean, fuck the golf?" asks Roger.

"Max came and told us to behave ourselves," says Mark. "We're gonna give him hell now."

"What are we doing?" asks Roger, laughing.

"I little racing," says Ronnie.

"Fuck, yeah......lets rip this course a new one," says Jerry.

All of us take off down the course in search of the cart carrying Max and Bob.

"Hey, you bastards, stop bumping us," says Roger, as Ronnie keeps bumping them in the rear end.

"Pussys!" says Mark.

"I'll take care of them," I say, as I come up on the other side of Ronnie's cart and start to bump him.

"So, that's how you bastards want to play it," say Ronnie, as they approach Max and Bob's cart.

Ronnie rams hard into the back of Jerry's cart by the rear wheel. Almost simultaneously, all three carts pile up together, get sideways and roll over, all right there in front of Bob and Max. Golf clubs, beer, ice and people go sprawling across the fairway in all directions. It was like one of those Nascar crashes where the cars just all crash at once, one taking out the others like dominoes.

"What the fucking hell are you motherfucking assholes doing?" shouts Max.

"Just a bunch of fucking hooligans," adds Bob.

"Goddamn, everybody alright?" asks a dazed Ronnie. "Shit, I think I broke my fucking arm."

"We fired his ass for a reason," says Bob.

"Fuck you, Bob, this don't have nothing to do with that shit," says Ronnie. "Hey, shit, Mark ain't getting up."

"Shit, look at the blood coming from his head," says Roger.

"He's fucking out cold," says Ronnie, as Butch and Jack come driving up.

"What the fuck did you idiots do?" asks Butch.

"Max, where's the nearest phone?" I ask. "We need to get help for Mark. He ain't waking up."

"Nearest place would be the clubhouse," offers Max. "We'll go make the call. I'll need to explain what happened anyway."

"What do we do?" I ask.

"Is he breathing?" asks Butch.

"Yeah," responds Ronnie.

"Then don't move him, keep him still," says Butch. "He obviously hit his head, may have affected his spine, too. Just make sure he keeps breathing. Other than that, just keep him warm."

"Goddamn it, I'm such a fucking dick," says Ronnie.

"We were all doing it," says Jerry, who's bleeding.

"You alright, hoss?" asks Ronnie.

"I'm fine," responds Jerry. "Just a bloody nose."

"How about everyone else?" asks Ronnie.

"I think Mark got the worst of it," I say. "Shouldn't we just get him to a hospital?"

"No, they're gonna have to do the backboard thing and stabilize his head and all of that," says Roger.

"Just so fucking stupid," says Ronnie.

Just then Israel and Raeford comes rolling up on the scene.

"Why the hell didn't you bastards let us in on the fun?" asks Raeford.

"It ain't fucking fun no goddamn more," says Ronnie. "Mark's fucking hurt."

"Shit, what the fuck happened?" asks Raeford.

"We wrecked, he must have hit his fucking head, cause he ain't waking up," says Ronnie.

"He ain't dead, is he?" asks Raeford.

"No, he ain't fucking dead."

"You guys shouldn't be playing like that," says Israel.

"It showed a total lack of respect for Max and everyone here, son," says Dad.

"I know," I say. "We just didn't think about all of that."

"It's all my fault," says Ronnie. "I instigated the whole goddamn thing."

"Well, it's done now," says Butch. "Let's just hope Mark's alright."

"This ain't good," says Jerry.

"No shit, Sherlock," says Roger.

"Here comes Max," I say, as Max and Bob roll up.

"Rescue squad should be here in a few minutes," says Max.

"But there's a doctor on his way. He was having lunch in the clubhouse."

"Good," I say.

Chapter 42

Same day.

"Where the fuck is my son?" says an apparently inebriated Diane Sinclair, at the front desk of the Franklin County Memorial Hospital emergency room.

"It's alright," I say, to the woman at the desk. "She's with us."

"Don.....uh.....what happened?" asks Diane. "How the hell do you get hurt playing fucking golf?"

"There was an accident with the golf carts."

"Cart....or carts?"

"Carts....it was three carts."

"How the hell did three carts wreck into each other?"

"We were just playing around, racing, bumping into each other....we just got tangled up and we all went flying," I explain.

"Mrs. Sinclair, my name's Max Bond. I'm the plant manager. I'd just like to say that I'm sorry about what happened here."

"How bad is it anyway?" asks Diane.

"He has a head injury. He was unconscious," I say. "They haven't told us anything else."

"Was anyone else hurt in this little three cart pile up?" asks Diane.

"Ronnie broke his arm," I say. "He was playing with Mark."

"Was he driving or was Mark?" she asks.

"Not sure it would have made a difference, but Ronnie was driving," I say.

"Fucking idiots," she says, shaking her head. "What about everyone else?"

"Just bumps, bruises and scrapes," I say. "And a bloody nose."

"Well, that's good?"

"Here comes Crystal, maybe she has some news," I say.

"Who's she?"

"She's a nurse in the brain trauma ward. And she happens to be my sister in-law," I say, as Crystal approaches. "Hey, Crystal, have any news? This is Mark's mother."

"Well, we have moved him to ICU. He isn't conscious yet.

There doesn't seem to be any injury except for the brain trauma. The doctor'll be out soon to brief you. I just thought I'd come out and let you know something."

"May I see him?" asks Diane.

"In a while, they're still getting things situated in there. But only family's allowed in ICU. And we'll need you to fill out some paperwork.....you know....insurance and all of that stuff."

"Thank you....I'll do that now," says Diane, as she follows Crystal to the front desk.

"Damn, does she always have that sort of mouth on her?" asks Roger.

"No, just when she's a little lit," I say. "Which is quite often, lately."

"What's the word, son?" asks Dad. "I saw you talking to Crystal."

"No injury, except the brain injury. Moving him to ICU. Not awake yet," I explain.

"Hey, baby, you alright?" asks Karen, as she arrives. "Crystal called and told me what happened. Why didn't you call me?"

"Well, I'm fine. I wasn't hurt. Just hadn't thought about it yet," I say. "Mrs. Sinclair just got here. Mark hit his head. He hasn't woken up yet. Crystal just came out and told us."

"She told me that there was one serious injury, but that you were alright," says Karen. "How did it happen?"

"We just had an accident with the carts."

"We should pray for Mark," says Karen.

"Anyone who wants to join us, we're going to pray for Mark," I say.

"Where's his mother?" asks Karen. "She should be a part of this, too."

"She's doing some paperwork," I say. "Then she'll probably get to go in there and see him."

"We'll wait."

"Hey, guys, any news on Mark?" asks Ronnie, sporting a cast on his left arm.

"He's in ICU," I say. "Hasn't woken up yet. His mom's here."

"Goddamn it....fuck.....I just can't believe this shit happened," laments Ronnie. "Why did I have to be so fucking stupid, ramming Jerry like that and turning him around?"

"So, it was your asshole driving that caused my boy to be laying in there in a fucking coma," says Diane, as she rejoins them.

"No.....we were all being stupid," I say. "We all got carried away."

"Why don't you fuckers just grow the hell up?"

"Please....Mrs. Sinclair, please calm down," says Karen. "You know that no one meant for this to happen."

"And you, mister fucking plant manager, why the hell did you let these nimrods do this?" asks Diane. "This is your fucking country club. You had to know that these fucking yahoos would do something stupid like this."

"Mrs. Sinclair, would you like to pray for Mark?" asks Karen.

"Pray.....what the fuck for?" shoots back Diane.

"All is not lost. Mark's still living. God can still intervene."

"I guess. Guess it couldn't hurt. You're right. Sorry"

"Let's all join hands please," says Karen. "Dear Lord, we come to you in Lord Jesus holy name. We ask that you please intervene on behalf of Mark. We ask that you touch him. We ask that if indeed it is your will that you heal him. We also ask forgiveness for the actions that led to this accident, Lord. Please soothe the consciences of those who may feel responsible. We ask all of this in the name of our Lord and Savior Jesus Christ."

"Amen," I say.

"Thank you, Karen," says Diane.

"Mrs. Sinclair?"

"Yes."

"You can come see you son now," says Crystal.

"Okay....I'm ready."

"Has anyone noticed that everyone's here except for Bob?" I ask.

"Uh....yeah....he said he had something to tend to," responds Max.

"What? What if the accident didn't happen? He would have been playing golf," I point out. "What was this pressing business that all of a sudden presented itself after the accident?"

"Listen....I don't know," says Max.

"Typical of him, Max," says Roger. "He doesn't give a shit about us. I think you need to know that."

"I'll have a talk with him," says Max.

"Max, we're sorry that we did this though," I say. "Besides Mark, we didn't make you look all that good at the club. I mean a three cart pile up on the fairway."

"I'm sure they've never seen that before," says Max. "And I

guess you already know that you'll never set foot on those grounds again? Hell, they may not let me back in after this shit."

"Sorry," I say.

"How the hell did you manage a three cart pile up anyway?" asks Max.

"Well, it started because you came up and scolded us for our behavior," I explain. "We decided to give you something to really complain about…"

"So, I decided that we should have a race," interrupts Ronnie. "And one thing led to another and we were bumping each other. Then I bumped Jerry's cart from behind and they whipped around sideways and the next thing we know, we're all flying all over the fucking place. It's basically all my fault. I drove up there to mess with Jim and Don to begin with. That started this whole thing. Fuck!"

"I couldn't believe it when I looked up and all I saw was carts and bodies and clubs flying all over the place," says Max. "I didn't know what the fuck happened."

"Might have been kind of funny, if people didn't end up getting hurt," says Jerry.

"I glad we not involved," says Israel.

"Ronnie….don't beat yourself up over this too much," I say. "Mark and I always play around with the carts. This could have easily happened any of those times. We've turned a few over."

"Remember that time when you were racing me and my friend Archie?" says Dad.

"Yeah….drove the cart so hard that I blew out the tire," I say.

"So that's where he gets this shit from," jokes Max.

"No, that was his friend Archie driving that time," I say. "I don't get my irresponsibility from my dad. We didn't even bother trying to get Butch and him to participate."

"You're fucking right I wouldn't have participated in those shenanigans," says Butch. "You kids today just have no respect for anything."

"Damn, boss, we just like to have some fun," says Roger. "We don't want to be some old stuffed shirts like you."

"Listen, I did shit like that when I was a fucking teenager," says Butch. "But there's a time to grow up and stop pulling shit like that."

"Hey, here she comes," says Roger.

"How's he doing?" I ask.

"Well, he doesn't look bad, except for the fact that he hasn't woken up," says Diane. "They said to just let him rest. I'll just come back tomorrow. There's no point in just sitting there."

"Let me know if you need anything," I say. "Grass cut, anything that you need."

"Okay, Don….thanks."

"Let's get outta here."

Chapter 43

Monday June 7th, 1999

"So, I hear you had quite the pile up on the golf course this weekend," says David.

"It's not funny, David," I say. "Mark's still in a fucking coma."

"I know, man…uh….I didn't mean anything by it."

"Well, you have to admit that it would have been funny as hell if Mark wouldn't have been hurt," says Roger.

"Yeah, it was a pretty dramatic wreck," I say. "All of that just exploding in front of Max and Bob."

"I'll bet Max just about shit his fucking pants when he saw that," says Roger.

"How is Mark?" asks Lisa. "Do they know how bad the injury to his brain is?"

"It wasn't all that hard of a hit, as these things go. It just has to do with what part of the brain. I don't know….it's complicated," I say.

"Have you been able to see him yet?" asks Lisa.

"Not until he gets out of ICU. I'm not a family member."

"Sometimes people come out of this stuff just fine," says Roger.

"We'll be praying for him, son," says Homer.

"Speaking of praying," says David. "My preacher was teaching something interesting the other night at bible study. I thought it may interest y'all."

"What, pray tell, was that?" asks Homer.

"He said that Jesus was black," says David.

"What?" asks Roger. "Where the hell did he get that shit?"

"It's in the bible," asserts David. "It says that his hair was like wool and that his feet were like bronze that had been heated in a furnace."

"Who the fuck cares?" I ask. "Your pastor is so far out of the will of God that it's pitiful. Shit like that has no place being taught in church."

"Why? You don't like the idea of a black Jesus?" asks David, indignantly.

"It doesn't fucking matter you son of a bitch," I say, getting increasingly angry.

"Oh.... and you're the perfect Christian in here cussing like a goddamn sailor," shoots back David.

"I'm more of a Christian than your so-called pastor," I say.

"Damn, I thought I'd get more of a rise out of Homer than you," says David.

"And why is that, son?" asks Homer.

"With your racial views and all, I'd think you'd want to shoot me for suggesting that Jesus was black," says David.

"Son, all you're spouting is ignorant babble," says Homer. "The point isn't what color Jesus was or wasn't. The point is that it doesn't matter. I don't care what color he was, son, he's our Savior. That's what matters."

"It does matter," continues David. "I don't want no blond blue-eyed Jesus forced down my throat, when it ain't the truth."

"You are just so fucking stupid," I say. "I could just wring your fucking neck."

"You wanna try," says David, as he gets in my face.

"Get out of my fucking face you...you...," I shout.

"You what?" shouts David. "You what? What were you gonna call me? You better not call me nigger."

"I'm married to a black woman, you asshole," I say. "You're the fucking racist. You're the one talking about what color Jesus was. You're such a dick."

"What the fucking hell is going on in here?" asks Bob, as he and Butch come into the Instrument Shop to see what all of the commotion's about. "We could hear you halfway down the corridor. I'm tired of these fucking town meetings you keep having in here."

"You know, Bob," I say, seething. "I don't give a shit what you think. I lost whatever shred of respect I had for your sorry ass, when you didn't come to the hospital the other day. Real class move."

"That isn't the issue here," says Bob.

"I'm making it the fucking issue," I say. "How about that?"

"Butch, you'd better rein your boy in here, and quick," says Bob.

"Bob, you've proven over and over that you don't give a shit about any of us," I continue. "Ass!"

"Don, calm down," says Lisa, as she steps between me and Bob. "This isn't worth it."

"Butch, can I see you outside?" asks Bob.

"Yes, sir," responds Butch, as they both step just outside of the room,

"Butch, he's done. I cannot have that sort of insubordination. And the fucker isn't even working most of the time. Catch him shooting the shit more than I find him working."

"Bob, we need him. He's my best guy. He's just a little hot-headed, a little spirited. That's part of what makes him good. Just give him another chance."

"Fine. But if this shit happens again, it'll be both of your asses out the fucking door. Do I make myself clear?"

"Yes, sir. Clear as a fucking bell," says Butch, as Bob walks off. Butch steps back into the room. "Well, I saved your ass."

"Let him fire me," I say.

"I will next time. Now, how about getting your asses back to work," says Butch, taking his leave now.

"Damn, man, didn't mean to get you so riled up that you almost lose your job," says David.

"That was an ass move though, not coming to the hospital," says Roger.

"Yeah, and notice that he still didn't ask about him, either," I say.

"Well, he was preoccupied with the idea of firing you, son," says Homer. "Don't imagine he had time to think about much else."

"Whatever," I say.

"Well, I guess we'd better get back to work," says David. "I'm sure that both Bob and Butch will be sticking their heads back in here soon to make sure we cleared out."

"Next time, we'll discuss whether or not Jesus was Chinese," jokes Jerry, as they all clear out, except for Lisa and me.

"Damn, man, what's going on?" asks Lisa.

"I don't know why I let David get to me like that," I say. "But Bob had that coming."

"Yeah, but you can only push him but so far. I think he would fire you if you were to do that again."

"I'm worth too much to them. It would leave too big of a hole if they were to fire me."

"Yeah, but everyone's expendable, even you."

"I know, but I think I would have to do far more than that. Bob can take a little abuse."

"I didn't know that you had that sort of temper."

"Certain things just burn me up."

"But you know that David's just doing that to get you going."

"It's just so stupid. I just get so tired of this race thing. But it comes from both sides."

"I know....but it doesn't mean anything," she says. "What David was saying doesn't affect anything. Most people just let that shit go in one ear and out the other."

"I guess I'm just already on edge a little."

"Mark?"

"Yeah, he's my best friend. I can't believe this happened."

"But it's possible that he'll come out of this with flying colors."

"I know....but it could also go the other way. There could be permanent brain damage."

"Do they have any indication of that?" she asks.

"They won't know until he wakes up.....if he wakes up. But the physical damage is slight."

"Well, that's a positive sign."

"Yeah....I guess."

"Listen, try to control yourself a little," she says. "I like having you around here."

"You do, huh?"

"You're a smart guy, funny. Yeah, I wouldn't like it if you were to get fired."

"That's nice to know."

"I have to admit, though, that I'm not too sure what you think of me, if you like me or what."

"Of course I like you," I say. "Why would you say that?"

"It's just that you don't seem to talk to me like you do the guys."

"Well, it's not like I have anything against you or anything like that."

"I'm not saying that we haven't spoken. We've had some banter over the years. We've even flirted some. It's just that I still feel some distance, even after all of this time."

"Lisa, believe me, it's not just you. I've just always had a hard time connecting with women. I'm kind of shy in general, but especially with women. Socially retarded with women is really the way I describe it."

"Shy? You've said some pretty flirtatious things to me in the past."

"I know, but hasn't it always been when there's a group of us?"

"Now that you mention it…"

"I don't have as much of a problem like that. But one on one with women is harder."

"But even after all of these years of working together?"

"I know….I can't explain it."

"Why are you like this?"

"I wish I knew."

"Well, you are married."

"That was almost like God put us together or something. The ice was broken, the path was made. It just all sort of fell into place."

"The ice isn't broken with us?"

"I guess it is."

"Then why?"

"Lisa, it may be because I'm attracted to you."

I can't believe I told her that.

"Well, I sensed that was the case."

"I don't know. I'm a real head case. I try to analyze myself. I seem to have a hard time just being friends with women who I find attractive."

"So, it's either lovers or nothing?"

"No, I'm not saying that," I say.

Damn, does she know how much that turns me on?

"So, we can be friends?"

"We are friends, Lisa."

"Glad to hear it. You're one of the good guys."

"What the fuck?" says Butch, sticking his head through the door. "Get the hell back to work, you two."

"Sorry, boss," I say.

"I hope we can talk some more, Don. I have a feeling that you have some interesting things to say. In fact, I know you do."

"Well, I don't know…..I guess."

"Well, back to work."

"I'll just find another place to hide," I say, as we both leave the shop.

Chapter 44

Saturday June 12th, 1999

"So, he's awake now?" I ask.

"Yeah, he's in a regular room, so you can see him now," replies Crystal.

"Can I come, too?" asks Karen.

"Sure," says Crystal.

"It's just down the hall here, room 423."

"Hey, Diane," I say, as we all three walk into Mark's room. "How's he doing?"

"Well, as you can see, he's awake now," responds Diane.

"He's got full motor function and his speech is fine, but he's not making much sense right now," explains Crystal.

"Hey, man, what's going on?" I ask.

"I gotta get the system set up and working," replies Mark. "The poles have to match the stratums."

"Oh, okay, maybe I can help you with that," I say.

"Good, I need to align the stratum with the axis," adds Mark.

"That's all it's been so far," says Diane. "Just a bunch of jibberish."

"Does he know who you are?" I ask.

"I don't think so," responds Diane. "Mark, do you know who this is?"

"Sure, this is my old buddy, Mike," responds Mark. "Mike's gonna help me fix the stratum."

"Should I correct him?" I ask. "Of will it upset him?"

"I think it's fine to correct him," says Crystal. "His brain is in the process of sorting things out after the trauma. He needs to have correct information."

"Mark, my name's Don. We've been best friends for years."

"Don? Your name is Don?"

"Yeah, Don. Don't you remember all of the fights we used to get into as kids.....usually over some wiffle ball game? You were always such a selfish bastard that I had to deliver severe beatings to you."

"Don!" exclaims Karen. "You shouldn't do that."

"It's alright. He'll get it. That's the way we talk to each other."

"If I remember correctly, you sir, are the selfish bastard," says

Mark.

"That sounds exactly like him," I say, laughing.

"I remember, we used to play bocce ball in the street," says Mark.

"No, we played wiffle ball in your back yard," I say.

"Wiffle ball?"

"Yeah, little plastic ball and bat," I say. "Just like baseball but only so that you couldn't break out windows and stuff."

"I don't know….sorry…..I don't remember that, Mike."

"Now I'm Mike again."

"It may take a while," says Crystal.

"If it happens at all," says Diane.

"The body can do some amazing things," says Crystal. "With brain injuries there's about a two year window for recovery. Wherever he is in two years is where he'll probably stay. It can take that long."

"Well, we'll be praying for him," adds Karen. "This is just God's will. We may not understand it all the time, but he must have a great purpose in mind for Mark to take him through this."

"I just fail to see the purpose in this," I say. "Why would this one family have to face so much tragedy? His dad died young. His brother is dead. His sister died of cancer. And now this? He was just getting his life straight. He was working at the plant and doing well. Now it's just taken away."

"But, honey, God can still heal him," says Karen. "We have to have faith."

"And remember that God never puts more on us than we can bear," adds Crystal.

"Well, I can't bear any fucking more," says Diane. "And why did I get more than my share?"

"Mrs. Sinclair, I understand how you feel, but God's ways are beyond understanding sometimes," says Karen.

"You can say that again," says Diane.

"Could you hold your committee meeting in another office, please?" asks Mark. "I have business to attend to."

"Yeah…okay man," I say, laughing. "At least he's entertaining."

"We should let him rest," says Crystal.

"Okay, do you need anything, Diane?" I ask.

"Well, the grass does need cutting, if you could see to that."

"Sure, and I'll come back tomorrow to see him."

"Yeah, keep doing that," says Crystal. "He needs the

simulation. It helps his brain in getting things working again."

"Okay, I'll try to keep thinking positively," I say.

"It's in God's hands now," adds Karen.

"Where were his hands out there on the golf course?" asks Diane. "That's what I'd like to know."

Yeah, I'd like to know that as well. I'm not sure I buy this idea that every single thing that happens is God's perfect and unquestioned will. I think some shit just happens. But then the question becomes, why does so much shit happen to one family, or one person? Is there a curse or something on the Sinclair family? I just don't understand how they just continue to get pummeled like this. It just seems so unfair, so unjust. No wonder Diane drinks.

Chapter 45

Later the same day.

"Hey, Jim, fancy seeing you here," I say, taking a seat in a booth at the diner.

"Yeah, funny."

"I'm surprised you don't have a booth named after you by now."

"That'll be next year."

"Nice spot to just watch people," I say.

"You'd be surprised how entertaining it can be just sitting here looking out this window."

"The food doesn't hurt, either."

"And the coffee."

"And the waitresses?"

"Well, yeah, a couple of them are kinda hot."

"That they are," I say. "Especially that Rachel, is she working today?"

"Yeah, just wait. She'll be coming by."

"This place is kinda like that diner in Seinfeld where all the waitresses have big healthy racks."

"And thank God for that," says Jim. "So, what are you up to today?"

"Just came from the hospital," I say. "Visited Mark."

"How is he?"

"He's conscious now, talking, not making much sense though. Doesn't really seem to recognize anyone."

"It is still early."

"Yeah, they say this is normal," I say. "His brain's just trying to sort things out now."

"Is his mother still as pissed as she what last week when it happened?"

"No, she's calmed down some."

"Does she always swear like that?"

"No, I don't know if you could tell, but she was a little toasted that day," I say. "I think we happened to catch her at the wrong time."

"She likes her alcohol, I take it?"

"Yeah, she's not real open about it. But yeah, she kinda gets a little buzzed sometimes. And she can get a little loud when she's in that state."

"I wouldn't know what to do if my mother raised hell like that. She's the epitome of the southern lady, even though she's not from the South."

"It is a little weird," I say. "I'm not used to seeing an old lady like her cussing like that."

"She must have had Mark kinda late in life, or else she aged like hell."

"No, she was in her forties, I believe, when she had Mark."

"So, that means she's in her seventies?" asks Jim.

"Yeah, that's about right. Somewhere in there."

"Mark have any other family?"

"There were four kids. But two of them are already dead."

"Damn, and then this."

"Exactly."

"What happened to the two that died?"

"His brother basically drank himself to death," I say. "His sister died of cancer."

"So, he has one living sibling?"

"Yeah, Matt, he lives in California. He's the oldest. Quite a bit older than Mark, too."

"Is he coming out?"

"I kinda doubt it. He's a bum," I say. "Probably can't afford the fucking plane ticket. Besides, they hardly get along anyway."

"So, it's just his mom?"

"Basically, and me, I guess."

"What about a girl?" asks Jim. "Was he seeing anyone regularly?"

"You know....I'm not sure. No one that I know about."

"It's too bad that this happened. Mark has really done well on the job."

"It just seems like things just don't work out for that family," I say. "Cursed or something."

"Well, it's probably too early to say how this'll turn out."

"That's true. Visually, you don't really see anything. You wouldn't know anything is wrong until he starts talking. It just fucked his brain up."

"A couple of stupid decisions and here we are."

"Exactly," I say. "All the stupid things we did as kids and somehow come out unscathed, then a stupid race with golf carts results in this."

"Yeah, but we can't live in a shell. That wouldn't be any fun."

"I know. If we analyzed the risk for everything we do we wouldn't come out of the fucking house."

"It's just the lottery of life," says Jim. "Sometimes you win and sometimes you lose."

"I'd like to think there's a little more rhyme and reason to things than that."

"I don't know.....seems pretty random to me."

"But, like I said, why has this family suffered so much loss, while others go through life with little or no real tragedy?"

"Who knows?"

"Take my family for instance," I say. "We're pretty much free of tragedy. But Mark's has just been wracked by one thing after the other."

"So, what do you think?" asks Jim. "Do you believe they're cursed or something?"

"But why would they be? Why would they be so cursed, yet my family is so blessed? What have we done that's so good?"

"I don't know what you believe but I have a hard time believing that some supposed sin by some ancestor causes a curse to fall on future descendants. That idea seems awfully primitive."

"I agree," I say. "I'm not saying that's what I believe. I'm just trying to make sense out of it. Why do some people just never seem to get any relief?"

"I don't know, man."

"Karen thinks that this is all God's perfect will. That this thing somehow fits in perfectly with God's plan for Mark."

"You see, that's where religion totally baffles me," says Jim. "How does that even make fucking sense?"

"It's always been something I've struggled with. It's what many Christians believe."

"If we're all just following a prearranged program then what's the point of any of it? You know what I mean? We should just go with however we feel because that's where we're going to end up anyway."

"I guess that's the point of finding Christ," I say. "You change your course."

"But do you? Aren't you just going the way you were always meant to go?"

"I do believe in freewill."

"But how is that the case if God just determines it all?"

"I know…..it doesn't quite add up."

"It just seems like that's the whole point of religion," says Jim. "It's like we're so desperate to figure this whole thing out. But the problem is that we try to force things to fit. We try to make it all make sense somehow."

"I don't know. I think it does make sense. It has to. There is a reality somewhere."

"Yes, that's most definitely true. There is one reality lurking behind everything else."

"And I guess that's what I'm looking for."

"I really don't give a fuck," says Jim. "I guess if I'm meant to know the meaning to all of this then it'll come one day."

"I think it'll come to all of us…..one day."

"I assume you mean judgment day or something to that effect?"

"Well…..maybe…..I just think that we will know the meaning of things at some point."

"If there's life after death then I guess that could be true."

"There has to be," I say. "I just don't see how this could be all there is."

"But it most definitely could be all there is."

"None of us has any real proof….that's for sure."

"It's too bad we don't know. It would make things much easier….especially if it were true that we just die."

"Then you could basically do whatever you wanted to do without fear of consequences."

"But….I'm not sure I really restrain myself all that much now."

"I think it's really more about not hurting other people than it's fearing some sort of judgment. But I think the judgment could be there as well."

"Well, I'll just go on thinking that there won't be a judgment. Works for me."

"Yeah, that's about what we all do…..find what works for us. But I want to really know."

"But how? How will you really know something like that?"

"I know….but I can't help looking."

It is hard to believe in a just God at times. So many things in life just don't make any sense. Too many people just live lives of complete and utter misery. Jim's right, so many of us who want to believe in God feel compelled to try to force this all to work somehow.

We try to make it all fit together. We try to convince ourselves that there is a purpose to everything that happens. But what could the purpose possibly be in most cases. I'm not speaking so much of just Mark's plight. There is far more severe suffering in the world than what his family has gone through. His situation just got me to thinking about all of this. How can a just God, a God that is supposed to be so full of love and compassion for us, allow some of the truly horrid things to happen that happen in this world each and every day? How? I can't make it fit. I just can't.

Chapter 46

Monday June 14ᵗʰ, 1999

"Look out, the gang's coming to visit," I say, as Roger, Jerry and I come into Mark's hospital room.

"Hey, Don, glad to see you," says Mark.

"He was calling me Mike," I say. "So that's an improvement."

"I was?"

"Yes, dear, you were quite a bit out of it when you first woke up," says Diane.

"Yeah, you were talking about having to fix the stratum and poles and crazy shit like that," I say. "You said this was your office."

"Well, I did take a hit on the head."

"Do you recognize these two lowly peasants?" I ask.

"Lowly peasants?"

"Yeah, that's what we call them at the plant."

"They work at the plant?"

"Yeah, they're carpenters, painters....whatever it is they do."

"Is it John.....uh....and Ralph?"

"Well, you got the first letters right," I say. "It's Jerry and Roger."

"Oh.....that's right."

"How you doing, man?" asks Jerry.

"Miss you down at the plant," adds Roger.

"Do you remember anything about the accident?" asks Jerry.

"No...not really," says Mark. "Mom tells me that we were fooling around on some golf carts."

"Yeah, we put on quite the show for Bob and Max," says Jerry. "Three car pile-up. Bodies and carts flying all over the place."

"Bob and Max?" asks a puzzled Mark.

"Two of the bosses from the plant," I say.

"Oh...okay....I don't remember."

"That's alright....you can't remember everything all at once," I say.

"Excuse me, guys," says Crystal. "It's time for Mark to eat. He's having to relearn some things. This is one of them."

"Should we go?" asks Roger.

"Not as long as Mark doesn't mind," she answers.

"I don't mind....I'm just eating."

"What's he have to relearn about eating?" I ask.

"Nothing, I know how to eat."

"But he doesn't know when to stop," says Diane. "If you don't say something, he'll just stuff his mouth. He forgets to swallow or chew or something."

"I suffered a brain injury, you know."

"Yes, we are all well aware," says Diane.

"He's having to relearn stuff like brushing his teeth and bathing and stuff like that," adds Crystal.

"Did you have to teach him how to wipe his ass?" asks Jerry.

"In fact, yes we did," answers Crystal.

"Is that common in brain injury cases?" asks Roger.

"It really depends on the area of the brain that's affected," answers Crystal. "But it is common to have to relearn some of the basics."

"Look at him shovel it in," says Jerry.

"Mark, stop eating and swallow," says Diane.

"Most of that sort of thing comes back pretty quick," says Crystal. "But functions having to do with the actual part of the brain with the damage could have permanent impairment."

"Sounds as if the entire brain is kind of scrambled up initially, but then   reorganizes itself, except for the part that may have permanent damage," I say.

"That's a good way to put it," says Crystal. "Well, I'll let you continue your visit. Just make sure he eats most of it."

"The way he's going, I don't think that's the issue," says Jerry.

"Fuck you guys," says Mark. "I've got a brain injury, you know."

"I can see it now. He's gonna use that as a universal excuse," I say. "I got a brain injury, you know."

"But I do."

"Hey....uh....what happened to the guy over there in the other bed?" asks Roger.

"He was in a car accident," says Diane. "He lost a foot. It was so mangled that they amputated."

"Hehehehhheheh.......sorry.......heheheheh.......I don't know why I'm laughing," says Mark. "It's not funny.....hehehehe......."

"That's something we've noticed," says Diane. "He seems to laugh at the most inappropriate times. He can hear about a murder on TV and he starts chuckling like that."

"I know it's not funny," says Mark. "I just start laughing."

"The doctor said that it's just part of the injury," says Diane. "It'll probably clear up."

"Diane....I'm sorry to tell you this, but that has nothing to do with the injury," I say. "Your son has always been a sick, sadistic and twisted bastard."

"Well....that may be true, but he never did this before."

"He's just taking it to a whole other level," I joke.

"Hey....I have a brain injury," says Mark, with a big grin across his face. "Weren't you aware of that?"

"Told you," I say. "It'll be his universal get out of jail free card to explain away any sort of anti-social or otherwise bad behavior."

"No, it isn't," says Mark.

"You, sir, are a sadistic and severely deranged brute," I say.

"And you, sir, are a sick and perverse bastard," replies Mark.

"Well, at least that part's back to normal," says Diane. "Your profane banter."

"Well, I guess we'd better be going," says Jerry. "Good to see that you're getting better, man."

"Yeah...hope to see you back at work soon," says Roger. "Or should I say back at the plant walking around acting like you're working?"

"Hey...I was trained very well indeed," says Mark.

"He's a true instrument man," I add.

"Alright, see ya," says Jerry, as he and Roger leave.

"I need to be going, too," I say. "Know when you're going home?"

"Uh....what did they say, Mom?"

"It'll be in a couple of days," replies Diane. "They just want to observe him a little more, then they'll release him to me."

"This is a nice hotel, I'd like to stay a little longer," says Mark. "Do they have a pool?"

"No....uh...this is a hospital," says Diane. "They don't have a pool."

"Gotcha!" says Mark, smiling.

"See, he's gonna use the injury just to mess with us," I say.

"I've got a brain injury, you know."

Chapter 47

Saturday June 26th, 1999

"Hey, Claude, how are things going?" I ask, as I let Claude into my den.

"Praise Jesus, things are great, son. How's your friend doing?"

"Well, we'll see. It takes time with those injuries."

"God can work miracles, son. Time don't mean nothing to Him."

"Well....yeah.....I'm just talking about the normal recovery time."

"You know, son, you have to be operating in the will of God for Him to heed your prayers."

"What does that mean?" I ask.

"Well, Karen was telling me how you were questioning how this could be God's will."

"Yeah, that's true, I don't see it."

"Could it be that you can't see God's will because you still don't have a place to worship, and that you aren't up under the teaching of a true man of God?"

"Where does it say that in the bible?" I ask. "Where does it say I have to have a place of worship? And this thing you always say about being up under the teaching of a man of God? It sounds like you think we all have to be under the control of someone else."

I'm normally not this bold with Claude. I have hardly ever really challenged the things he's said over the years. Claude has a way of intimidating people. It's not the typical way that people intimidate others. With Claude the intimidation has to do with the fact that he's always so sure and always so forceful when it comes to his spiritual views. For some reason I normally don't have the balls to stand up to him. I guess some of it is the fact that I know that I'm not living the life that I should be, coupled with the fact that the Lord really has brought a dramatic change in Claude's life. I think he's drastically wrong about a whole lot of stuff, but he just seems to have some sort of authority. Today is different though. I've just had it with all of this pressure to conform to something that I know isn't right.

"First of all, scripture very clearly says that we are not to forsake the assembling together of the believers," says Claude.

"Sure, but what does that mean? Does that mean I have to go to church services?"

"Yes it does, son."

"I do not forsake fellowshipping with other Christians," I say. "I just don't go to church. Some of us from the plant have been getting together and having informal bible studies. That's my assembly."

"You still need a church home."

"I disagree. Scripture doesn't say that."

"You're out of the will of God, son. You think you can just make your own way, but you can't. Karen tells me that you don't believe in the tithe."

"I let her tithe from what she makes, but no, I don't see that in scripture."

"Don't rob God, son."

They love to say that. How would I rob God? Doesn't it all belong to him? This idea that he needs us to give him money is just odd.

"I am very far from robbing God," I say. "I'm not trying to keep more money for myself. I'm actually saying that we should give more than the old ten-percent tithe thing. But that giving doesn't have to be to some church. It doesn't have to be to some organization. The early church just gave to those who were in need."

"You're still supposed to help support the house of God."

"Where does the bible say that, Claude? Who says I have to give that money to a church? What if there isn't one that I agree with? Who should I support then? I don't go to one."

"Are you saying that all churches are out of the will of God?"

"You say it about many churches. You love to call churches dead all the time."

"But do you think that you've found a special path to God that the rest of us have somehow missed?" asks Claude. "You don't need any church now?"

"Who are you to say that what I do isn't church? The early church met in homes. They didn't have special buildings to meet in."

"But you're still rejecting some basic truths, son. Do you think you have some special knowledge or something?"

"I could ask the same thing of you. I think you step outside of the word plenty."

"What I preach is the straight up Word of God."

"But most people who preach think they're doing the same thing."

"Well, the proof is in the pudding. What I teach and preach is right there in black and white in scripture."

"I agree that it's right there in black and white," I say. "But too much of what you believe and say is the truth, doesn't agree with a simple reading of scripture. In some cases, you fall short of what scripture says, while in other cases, you go well beyond what's written."

"Give me some examples and let's talk discuss this, rightly dividing it with the Word of God."

"Okay, you mentioned the tithe. The tithe is not for the church. It's something left over from the temple worship that the Jews had."

"Paul said to set aside according to what your income is."

"But did he ever say ten-percent?" I ask.

"Yeah, I believe he did."

"It's not there, Claude. What he said was that those who were in need should be provided for by those who had plenty. There's no limit. He never said to set aside money to present it to God in the church."

"No one said that you couldn't give more. You give to the church then you give to the needy. But that ten-percent is an obligation."

"It's not only not in scripture, but the whole concept of the tithe isn't consistent with being a Christian. That's why I oppose it so strongly."

"How do you get that?" asks Claude.

"We're supposed to be filled full of the spirit of God now, aren't we? Isn't that the whole point of being a Christian?"

"Of course."

"Okay, why would I need a law telling me what I needed to give if I have the very spirit of God inside of me? Wouldn't I just know what I'm supposed to do? You're the ones who are always talking about God leading you to do this or to do that. Well, why can't he tell you to give whatever it is you should give? Why must there be some rule telling us we must pay ten-percent?"

"But we always need rules, son," says Claude. "Scripture is there for a reason."

"And you know what I get from scripture?"

"What?"

"I get the truth that the law isn't for the Christian. And that means everything, even the tithe. So, you get one thing from scripture and I get something else."

"Many anointed men of God teach the truth of the tithe."

"If they're really anointed, well….. they should know better."

"But if you believe in giving more, why don't you just pay your tithe and then give the rest to those in need?"

"Because you act like it's some requirement," I say. "You're binding me under law when you insist I must pay my tithes, like I owe it or something. I refuse to be bound to the law. I will not live under a form of the old temple worship."

"Temple worship?"

"That's what the Jews did in the temple once a year. They gave their offerings to God. They gave ten-percent of all that they made in a year. We're not under that system anymore. That's the whole point of Christ coming, to eliminate all of that stuff."

"I know that, son, but some things are still in force."

"No law for the Christian, that's what I go by," I say. "We are under absolutely no law anymore. That is the truth."

"This isn't really a law, son. This is just about you getting your blessings from God. It's just how God has ordained it."

"I don't agree."

"Karen tells me that you've never fasted, either."

"So?"

"Fasting is essential to a successful walk with the Lord."

"You mean that his spirit living inside of me isn't enough?"

"Fasting is important."

"But why?" I ask. "Are you saying that without fasting I don't have access to all of God's spirit?"

"Some things only come but through prayer and fasting."

"I've seen those verses."

"Okay, so why aren't you abiding by them?"

"There's evidence that those scriptures were added later," I say. "The footnotes in my bible say that those verses did not appear in the earliest manuscripts of the bible."

"But they are there in the bible we have."

"I'm not basing it all on just the question of whether those verses belong or not. There are other things."

"Like what?"

"Even if those verses belong in scripture, fasting is not emphasized in scripture the way you emphasize it. There are only a few verses that really emphasize it."

"We can't pick and choose which verse to follow and which we do not."

"It's interesting that you make that point."

"What does that mean?" asks Claude.

"There are plenty of passages of scripture that you just explain away, yourself."

"Well, I don't think that's true."

"Claude, I've looked at fasting in the total context of what it means to be a Christian," I say. "To me, it just doesn't fit. It's Old Testament thinking. The spirit of God is all that we need now. We don't need to do special tricks to get God to act. He's either in us or he isn't."

"Son, it's in scripture. And I've seen it work."

"Can I ask you a question?"

"Fire away."

"Do you believe that if I don't fast that I'll lose my salvation?"

"No."

"What about if I don't tithe?"

"No, you may just lose some blessings."

"Then why are you trying to load me down with this?" I ask. "If it doesn't involve my salvation then why make such a big deal?"

"Because the farther from the truth you fall, the farther from God you fall."

"I'm not falling from the truth, I'm trying to get at the truth. Things just don't add up to me, Claude. I don't care if every Christian in this world believes something. If it doesn't add up to me, then I can't buy into it."

"You need to be up under the teaching of an anointed man of God, son."

"Who says? We all have to be taught?"

"How else do we learn?"

"Isn't there a scripture that says that we have no need for a man to teach us, because it all comes through the spirit?" I ask.

"Yeah, but you have to have a proper understanding of what these scriptures are saying."

"I think I do that better than many of you're doing. Just like that fasting scripture. I'm looking at that with the bigger picture of what salvation involves, so I don't think it belongs. But you, and others, have built up this whole ideology based on one scripture that maybe shouldn't even be there."

"But you're relying on men who say that it shouldn't be there."

"But you're relying on a bible that was interpreted by men," I say. "You know that English wasn't the original language. How do you know it's accurate? Men wrote it. We're all relying on men."

"God has revealed to me that the King James Version of the bible is the true word of God."

"Sorry, but I don't see how that's the case."

"You're going to doubt what God told me?"

"I'm going to doubt what you say God told you," I say. "Do you expect me to just blindly accept what you say God told you?"

"Well, I accept that the King James Version is the true word of God. And many other brothers and sisters in Christ see that, too."

"But those aren't the original words. Why would that version be the one?"

"I don't have the answer for that."

"Could it be that because it's in old style English that is sounds more religious or something?"

"I told you. God told me that it is the anointed version."

"English wasn't the language it was originally written in," I say. "How do you know that the king who made them make this translation didn't have them make some changes? You're gonna trust a king to make a correct version of the bible?"

"Son, you're just going way off on a tangent now."

"No, I'm trying to get at the truth. The truth that I've come to is that scripture itself says that we do not need scripture to lead a Christian life. It's supposed to be in our hearts. And that makes sense in the bigger picture of what being a Christian is supposed to be about."

"We don't need scripture? Is that what you said?"

"Didn't people go many years without having it? In the old times many people couldn't read anyway. And what about blind people? How can salvation rely on written words on a page, and we don't even have proof of their accuracy."

"And yet you're basing what you're saying on scripture."

"Sure, but scripture's telling me to not rely on scripture," I say. "How is it that we can keep claiming to have the spirit of God indwelling us, living inside of us, the very spirit of God, yet we have to keep turning to a book to know how to live? I look to scripture to understand what this is all supposed to be about, not for rules and regulations on how to live. There's a difference."

"I can see that this is going nowhere, son."

"That's probably true, Claude. We're very far from agreeing, yet, at the same time, painfully close."

"Just remember that we're all striving towards the same thing."

"I know that. But I don't happen to believe your way we'll get us there."

"We'll just have to agree to disagree on that one."

"I guess so, but there is only one reality," I say. "And that's all I want to find."

Chapter 48

Sunday July 4th, 1999

"Glad you could make it, son," says Dad, as we join Momma on the porch. "Karen's not coming?"

"No, even the fourth doesn't get in the way of her church stuff."

"But, it's the afternoon," says Momma.

"Haven't I told you before that church to them is a marathon event that lasts all Sunday?"

"They need to rest sometime."

"Glad you could make it, brother," says Mel, joining us on the porch.

"Are Grandma and Hugh coming?" I ask.

"Marie, not Hugh," says Dad.

"Your choice or his?"

"Both, I would say," responds Dad.

"I'm sorry Grandma has to be in the middle of this," I say.

"Hugh somehow kept himself straight the few times he came to things we had when Karen was here, but there's no way he could remain civil with Dan and Steve," says Momma.

"I'm sorry I stayed away for a while," I say. "There was just a lot going around in my head. I just needed to stay to myself."

"What's important is that you're here now," says Momma.

"So, I hear things are humming along quite well at the plant," says Dad.

"It appears that way," I say. "We seem to be booked pretty solid."

"The question is how long that'll last," says Mel. "There are still textile plants closing down right and left."

"I'm starting to think we may just be the exception," I say. "Some of these high priced specialty fabrics we're running right now seem to be doing the trick."

"And we definitely are spending less on labor than we used to," says Mel. "I see that for myself."

"They've automated where they could," I say. "And they finally started getting rid of some of the dead weight around there, especially in maintenance."

"How's Mark doing?" asks Momma.

"Well, he's supposed to finally come home from the hospital this week," I say. "They ended up keeping him a little longer than they originally expected. I'm not sure why really."

"That's good."

"Well, look who's here," says Mel, as Dan and Steve join us all on the porch.

"Hey, everyone," says Dan.

"Nice to see you all," says Steve.

"See you made it, Don," says Dan, curtly.

"Yeah, I made it."

"Too bad you couldn't make it to everything."

"No Karen?" asks Steve.

"No, church stuff," I say.

"Not for you though?" asks Steve.

"No, I don't go to church anymore."

"I didn't know that," says Momma.

"Guess it never came up," I say. "Actually, it's been a couple of years."

"But, are your beliefs the same?" asks Dan.

"We don't have to do this today, do we?" asks Momma.

"I would like to hear the answer to that one question, though," says Mel.

"Yeah…my beliefs are basically the same."

"But he's here," says Momma.

"Yeah, I can't argue with physics," says Dan. "He is indeed present."

"Yes, I most definitely am here."

"So, we all agree on that little fact," says Mel.

"I was sorry to hear about Mark," says Dan.

"Yeah, we don't really know what the outcome will be," I say. "I was just saying that he should be coming home from the hospital this week."

"Well, that's good."

"So, I'm interested," says Steve. "Why aren't you going to church anymore?"

"It's complicated," I say.

"I'm not sure what you mean by that but I agree that the whole church and religion thing isn't easy," says Steve. "The world is changing so much. Religion needs to change with it. But that doesn't always happen."

"I don't like the word religion anyway," I say. "I don't care if religion changes or not because I don't consider myself as being part of any religion anymore."

"You're not a Christian?" asks Momma.

"No, I'm still a Christian," I say. "I just find myself identifying with organized Christianity less and less every day."

"Well, that may be a good thing," says Steve.

"Listen, despite what you two may have thought, or still think, I've never been one of these rabid anti-homosexuality zealots," I say.

"But you didn't come to our wedding," says Dan.

"Because I don't agree with it," I say. "I can't help that."

"Can we please not do this?" asks Momma.

"I agree," says Dad. "Can't we just enjoy the day without dealing with these heavy subjects?"

"Sure," I say. "Let's just talk about the weather and work and all of that stuff. Small talk. That's us."

"What's that supposed to mean?" asks Mel.

"It just means that we never seem to really talk about anything meaningful," I say. "We never want to get too deep."

"Maybe it's because those sorts of conversations too often end with hurt feelings," says Mel.

"There's a time and a place for all of that," says Momma.

"When's the time? Where's the place?" I ask. "That's why I wrote that letter to Dan that time. I had some things to say and there wasn't a time or a place to say them."

"I happen to agree with Don," says Steve. "You do seem to never want to talk about anything that may result in hurt feelings. I may disagree with Don, but I want to at least try to understand why he believes what he believes."

"That's our family, Steve," I say. "We always hide ourselves from each other."

"I'm not sure that's true," says Momma.

"No, I think Steve and Don do have a point," says Dan. "That's why it took me so long to come out. We just don't deal with those sorts of situations all that well."

"No, we most definitely don't," I say.

"Well, maybe that can change," says Steve.

"Maybe it can," I say. "I seem to be more willing to lay in all on the line recently."

"Why is that?" asks Steve.

"I don't know really. I guess I'm just tired of hiding from the truth."

"The truth should never be feared," says Steve.

"Because truth is reality, and reality is just how things are."

"Exactly. Why try to cover up what is actually right there in front of us?"

"You know, Steve. I think it just may be possible that we could get along fine."

"Stranger things have happened."

Despite a few exceptions, in my family, we never seem to ever deal with any of the uncomfortable subjects. We try to ignore the elephant in the room. I'm just as guilty as anyone else. We've just never been the kind of family that can really share our deeper emotions with one another. It is easier that way. But it gets tiring to just sit around making small talk when there are these gigantic issues looming between us.

Why do we insist on forcing ourselves to spend time together when we obviously live completely different lives with hardly a thing in common? It just feels like we're doing what's expected of us. We're just doing our duty. I know how that sounds. I know they're my family. But the truth is that I feel like they only know me on a superficial level. They don't know anything beyond the surface. But, for that matter, does anyone really know the true me? Probably not. I've never let anyone in that far. The thing is, I feel the same is true for me. I'm not sure I know what really makes any of them tick. How well do I know my family? Not all that well.

Chapter 49

Saturday July 24ᵗʰ, 1999

"Well hello, Don! Come on in," says Diane, letting me into the living room.

"How are things going?" I ask.

"Well…he's still making progress. It's just slowed down some now."

"Hey, man, how's it going?" I ask, as Mark comes into the room.

"Oh…alright I guess. Still relearning things."

"Well, they said it would be a process," I say.

"It's been five weeks since the accident though," says Mark. "You know how impatient I am. I just want to get back to the plant and have everything be normal again."

"Yeah…I know, but the reality is what it is," I say.

"Reality sucks a big donkey dick," says Mark.

"Thanks for that," says Diane.

"Anytime, Mom."

"She's used to it by now."

"Uh….if you don't mind….before I forget to mention it…...could you show me later how to sharpen the blades on the mower?" asks Mark.

"Do you have them off?"

"No, I wasn't sure what to do."

"You just take a wrench and turn the bolt to get them off."

"I didn't know which way to turn them," says Mark. "I was scared that I'd mess something up."

"Okay….no problem."

"And we've been having this problem with the toilet," says Mark. "Could you take a look at it and see what you think?"

"Don't bother him with another list of things to do," says Diane. "He's over here to visit you, not to be a handyman."

"That's alright, Diane," I say. "What's the toilet doing?"

"The water's running all the time," says Mark.

"You just need to replace the float valve inside that tank," I say.

"I told you that," says Diane. "We got one but he wanted to wait to get your opinion."

"I just wanted to be sure," says Mark.

"Well, there really isn't all that much there," I say.

"Well, if I knew how to do this stuff before, I'm sorry," says Mark. "I just don't remember."

"But some of it's just common sense," says Diane.

"Hey….I had a fucking brain injury, you know."

"Yes…I am most perfectly aware of that fucking fact."

"It's no problem though," I say. "I'll help you with those things in a while."

"Hey, did we used to play that Sega video game that I have in the den?" asks Mark.

"It's been awhile, but yeah, we used to play the golf game all the time."

"I hooked it up the other day and messed around with it a little. Wanna play?"

"You know, that's probably a good therapy for you," I say. "Get your brain thinking about how to make certain shots and all of that shit."

"Yeah, that's what I was thinking."

"Let's go."

"So, did you remember how to play?" I ask, as we make our way to the den.

"Yeah, I hooked it up to the TV and everything," says Mark. "I'm gonna kick your ass all over that golf course."

"Are you still laughing at the news of dismembered babies and raped schoolgirls?"

"It's the brain injury. I can't help it."

"You sick and perverse bastard."

"Takes one to know one."

"Alright, let me open a huge can of whoop ass on you," I say. "I will take my golf club and beat you so severely that you'll cry for your momma."

"We'll see. You think you're gonna kick my ass because of the injury. Well, you couldn't do it then and you can't do it now."

"What do I have to do?"

"First you have to make your profile. You can create whatever avatar you want."

"I see that you made one that looks like you….but quite a bit better looking," I say. "Well, I'm going another way with it."

I create the most absurd looking avatar that anyone could

imagine.

"So….you're going with that?" asks Mark. "You're going to be black, but with blond hair?"

"Why not?"

"You look fucking ridiculous."

"Good. This is supposed to be fun."

"But why do you want to be black?"

"It's just funny," I say. "I have these white features, yet I'm black."

"Okay, whatever, I tee off first," says Mark, as he hits a perfect drive.

"Great shot. You weren't kidding when you said that it all came back to you."

"Yeah, I didn't have to look in the book or anything. It was all just there."

"Isn't this the game where the crowd lets out this groan or something when you miss a close putt?" I ask.

"Yeah….they go ahhhh."

"Well, my friend, they'll be saying that plenty today."

"Are you going to hit?"

"As soon as you refresh my memory."

"You line up the shot with the arrow keys, then you hit the A key to start the stroke, then hit it again to set the strength of the swing, then again to hit the ball," explains Mark.

"Oh….okay….I think I remember now," I say, as I take a swing.

"Damn….hehe…..you shanked the shit out of that one."

"Damn it! Uh…..do you remember that from the golf tournament?"

"What?"

"Shanked the shit out of that one," I say. "We were saying that the day of the golf tournament."

"I don't know….maybe I do. I just said it," says Mark, as he hits his second shot. "There you go, right on the green. Four feet from the hole. I'll be putting for birdie."

"I hit my drive farther than you though."

"Farther doesn't matter if you aren't on the fucking fairway."

"I am on the fucking fairway."

"Not the right fucking fairway though……you're on the wrong fucking hole."

"That's what she said," I joke.

"What?"

"A girl…..the wrong hole….?"

"Oh….okay….I get it."

"Look at that shot," I say. "On the fucking green."

"You lucky bastard. Go ahead and putt. I'm closer."

"In the hole," I say, as I putt.

"And the crowd goes ahhhhh," says Mark, mimicking the game. "You shanked the shit out of that putt."

"Damn it, I can't hit the button at the right time."

"I'll show you how….like this…..right in the hole…..," says Mark, as he putts.

"Ahhhhh….not so my friend…..you shanked the shit out of that one."

"Shit!"

"And the crowd went ahhhhh…..I love that sound," I say.

"Hehehehehe……"

Mark starts to chuckle.

"What's so funny?" I ask.

"The crowd going ahhhhh….hehehe."

"It was funny…..when you missed. Now go ahead and putt, you missed worse than I did. I'm actually closer."

"Be quiet then," says Mark. "I need to concentrate."

"You don't want to hear the crowd go ahhhhhh again?"

"No."

"Ahhhhhhh," I say, as Mark starts to putt, and also starts to chuckle.

Upon seeing that this makes him chuckle I continue with the absurd   sounds.

"Ahhhhhh…..ohhhhhhh..ahhhh…..ohhh…uhhhhhhhhhh…..ah hhhh, whoops, you missed again, and what a severe miss it was," I say.

"You bastard, you did that on purpose."

"Did what?"

"Started going ahhhhh just when I was putting."

"It worked, didn't it?"

"We'll see how it works on you," says Mark.

"I'm not the one with the laughter problem."

"That wasn't inappropriate laughter though."

"No, it was just easy to get you to laugh."

"That's cheating though."

"What is this, the Master's or something?" I ask.

"Fuck it, just go ahead and putt."

"It's your turn. You missed so severely that you're still farther away than I am."

"Stop saying ahhhh, and let me fucking putt."

"Ahhhhhhhhhhhhh.......ohhhhhhhhhhh.........ehhhhhhhhh.......ahhhhhhhhhh."

"Hehehehe.........stop it......hehehehe......."

"Are you going to putt?" I ask.

"You sound like a fucking mental patient."

"I'm not the one laughing at the perverse and gory things of this world."

"I have an excuse.....I have a brain injury."

"Go ahead and putt. I won't do it this time."

"Okay," says Mark, as he promptly sinks the putt. "See, you bastard, you can only win if you cheat."

"That's part of the game."

"It is not. You don't hear professional golfers doing that shit. They remain quiet when the other guy's hitting. You're breaking the rules of golf."

"Well, I think rules are made to be broken anyway," I say.

"Go ahead and putt."

"Here we go......in the hole," I say, as I promptly miss the putt severely.

"Not so," says Mark. "And what a sorry display it was."

"Damn it........shit!" I say, as I miss again. I slam the controller to the floor in disgust. "This piece of shit."

"What the hell are you doing?"

"This goddamn controller ain't working right."

"There isn't anything wrong with the fucking controller," says Mark. "It's the fucking operator."

"Game's rigged."

"Hehehehe....how's the game rigged?"

"It just is......I'm hitting the buttons when I'm supposed to.....but the damn ball won't go where it's supposed to fucking go."

"Well, you must not be hitting the buttons at the right time."

"Game's rigged."

"Stop being a bad sport," says Mark. "Pick up your controller and let's play."

"Bastard."

"It's just a game."

"Rigged game."

"Rigged by your incompetence possibly."

"Possibly."

"Well….you'd better get used to it this feeling. You're going to get a severe beating."

"Ahhhhhhh………ehhhhhhh……ooooooooooeeeeeeeeooooooo oouuuuuuuuuuoooooooooooooo…..ahhhhhh."

"You cheating bastard," says Mark. "Stop it."

"I've got to even the odds some way."

"What a friend."

"That's me."

"I have a brain injury, you know."

Chapter 50

Later that same day.

"Hey there," I say, as I stroll down Main Street after my visit with Mark.

"Hey, Don....how you doin?" asks Lisa, coming up beside me.

"Well, I just got done visiting Mark. I try to visit him at least once a week."

"How's he doing?"

"He's better......it's just hard to say.....there are still some issues."

"Want to get a cup of coffee or something?" she asks. "Unless you have something to do."

"No....Karen's at some women's church conference or something."

"Okay....the diner then?"

"Where else?" I ask, as we head for the diner.

"Well, look who's here," says Lisa, as we walk through the door.

"He's always here," I say. "He's leading the life of a bachelor....eating out all the time."

"That's right.....and loving every minute of it," says Jim.

I'm both relieved and disappointed that Jim's here, but probably more disappointed. It would have been nice to spend some time alone with her.

"Mind if we join you?" asks Lisa.

"Where have you two been?" asks Jim.

"We just ran into each other on the street," I explain. "I was telling Lisa that I just came from visiting Mark."

"How is he?" asks Jim.

"He's still got a ways to go. Every time I go over there he has this list of things he wants me to help him with, just things around the house that need doing. But it's things that he should know how to do."

"Well, it may take a while for some of that to come back to him," says Jim.

"Yeah....I get the memory part. But it's more than that. He doesn't seem to be able to figure simple things out. We all do things that we've never done before.....especially on the job. But we use our knowledge to figure them out. He doesn't seem to be able to do that. I'm just starting to wonder if there may be a permanent disability."

"But didn't you say that the recovery window is about two years wide?" asks Lisa.

"It is….but I don't know….I just feel like this is pretty much where he's gonna end up."

"But he's basically functioning," says Jim.

"Yeah….it's funny….such a seemingly slight injury can have just enough of an effect to fuck a life just totally up."

"But you don't know that yet," says Lisa.

"Yeah….and actually…..he did hook that video game of his up with no problem at all. And he beat the hell out of me in that golf game we played."

"See? It might not be as bad as you think," says Lisa.

"He's much farther from normal than he thinks he is. He thinks he can come back to work soon."

"They won't let him in the door unless he's one hundred percent," says Jim. "They don't want the liability of him getting hurt if he were not totally recovered."

"Yeah….you get hurt at the plant and they'll get you in there even if you're in a full body cast. But if you get hurt outside the plant, they want you completely right before you can come back."

"Besides not remembering how to do certain things, are there any other issues?" asks Lisa.

"I think the biggest thing is that it's hard to carry on a real conversation with him."

"Why?" asks Lisa.

"I guess it's the memory. But it's hard to get into anything too deep, because he keeps getting sidetracked by little points that have nothing really to do with the larger thing we're talking about."

"So he really can't follow any sort of conversation," says Lisa.

"Yeah, we could talk about anything before the accident. But now it's like it's hard to have any depth to our conversations. It's just shit about the injury and his recovery all the time."

"Well, it is understandable that all he would be concerned with is his recovery," says Lisa. "It is the most important thing in his life now."

"I know that. But he's different. There are traces of the old Mark. There are glimpses. But overall….well….he's different."

"How's his mom holding up?" asks Jim.

"I just hate that she has to go through all of this now…..with her age and all."

"Especially if it ends up being permanent," adds Lisa.

"That's the thing," I say. "If this is a permanent disability then where will he end up?"

"Listen, don't you think you're jumping the gun just a little?" asks Jim. "It's only been a few weeks. He has time to recover. You have no idea what level of functionality he'll end up having. He may just end up with some minor memory issues. And those are easy to work around."

"Yeah, I know you're right," I say. "I just don't have a good feeling about this."

"He may end up just fine," says Lisa.

"Shit, I hope so."

"So, changing the subject, Lisa, I've hounded Don about this before, but where's the baby at?" asks Jim.

"What fucking baby?"

"Well, you and Israel have been together for quite a while now. Don't you want to give him a baby?"

"Fuck no!"

"Damn….that was pretty emphatic," says Jim.

"I ain't having no more kids," says Lisa. "I don't care who the fucking man is."

"Any change in your answer, Don?" asks Jim.

"No, I'm probably farther from wanting them now than I ever was in the past."

"Why's that?" asks Lisa.

"Just too much shit going on in my head for that. Too much in my life is unsettled."

"Like what?" asks Lisa.

"I won't bore you too with all of that shit," I say. "Suffice to say that Karen and I just don't see eye to eye enough on much of anything. This is no time to start having kids."

"I don't think you ever want them," says Lisa.

"I think that's probably true," I say. "And that's one of the things that we don't see eye to eye on."

"Why did you ever get married?" asks Jim. "Don't you know that the secret to happiness is to never get into a serious relationship with a woman? Keep it light. Keep it open."

"Yeah, Israel's practicing that with me," says Lisa.

"I thought you didn't want anything serious," I say. "I thought you just wanted to have fun."

"I did…but I don't know….it could just be more, that's all."

"Yeah, I know the feeling."

"I don't," says Jim.

"Jim, why don't you just suck my dick?" says Lisa.

"Such crass language from a lady," I say.

"Good thing I'm not a lady."

"Yeah….it is a good thing."

"I'm assuming we're talking about your proverbial penis here?" asks Jim.

"Never know…..maybe I am carrying around a package."

"Tell you what," says Jim. "If you have a literal dick…..I'll gladly suck it."

"Me, too," I say.

"You guys are just so fucking nasty."

"You started it," I say.

"That, I did."

"Does Israel want kids?" asks Jim.

"Yeah, he has talked about wanting a family."

"Well, it sounds like you both may be with the wrong people," says Jim. "You may be more suited to one another than you are to the people you're with."

"This guy doesn't have a problem saying what he thinks," I say.

"Yeah, I see."

I must confess that what Jim said gave me some sort of thrill. Just the suggestion that Lisa and I should be together does sort of excite me. There's no denying the truth that we are compatible in several ways.

"Well, it's true," says Jim.

"What's your fucking obsession with who's having kids anyway?" I ask.

"Just making conversation."

"Just trying to stir up some shit, is more like it," says Lisa.

"Well, I just like to get people to think sometimes," says Jim.

"What does that mean?" asks Lisa.

"I don't know…..I just like to ask those probing questions. You'd be surprised what you can learn about people sometimes."

"And what have you learned?" she asks.

"Well, I've learned that it must not be all that serious with Israel if you won't give him kids when he wants them. And I've learned…..which I already knew….that Don and Karen are a mismatch, have been from day one."

"I'm not so sure that's true," I say. "We have some things to work out, but I still believe we belong together."

"It shouldn't be that much work," says Jim. "That's the point. This shit about having to work on your marriage…..it's just bullshit to me. If it works…great, but if it doesn't… then fucking move on."

"Or fuck the whole marriage concept from day one," adds Lisa.

"Well, I took vows before God," I say. "I happen to take that seriously."

"So, you're just going to try to force things to work just because you made a mistake and made those vows?" asks Jim.

"Jim, I don't care how it looked then, or how it looks now, but Karen and I are meant to be together."

"I don't buy that whole concept," says Jim. "There are many people that we can be compatible with. I don't accept this being meant to be together shit."

"I have my doubts, too," I say. "But I still think there's a spiritual purpose to us being together."

"Well, it's your life," says Jim.

"I think you just go with what feels right," says Lisa. "I agree with Jim, we shouldn't have to force things to fit."

"Unless it's my big fat dick," says Jim.

"Fuck, I guess I left myself wide open for that one," she says.

"Yeah, that's what we need……you wide open," I say.

"Damn, this conversation took a turn…..and quick," she says.

"Well, you said you weren't a lady….so we're just acting accordingly," I say.

"I don't mind at all," she says. "You two are a lot of fun."

"Yeah, this is nice, isn't it?" I say.

"We'll have to do this again," she says.

"Well, you know I'm always here," says Jim.

"And do you know why he's always here, Lisa?" I ask.

"No, why?"

"Because all the waitresses have big breasts."

"You guys are so pitiful."

"The food and coffee are alright, too," says Jim.

"But it's more the waitresses," I say.

"Well…..yeah," says Jim.

"Pitiful," she says.

Chapter 51

Thursday July 11th, 2002

"Hard at work here in the dyehouse, I see," I say, as I walk up on Jim, who is at his usual post behind a line of dying machines.

"Yeah, not much going on today. Everything's running good. Don't have any PM's scheduled today, either."

"All I've got today is that circuit I have to add to Frame 6, but that won't take all that long. Just waiting for them to run that lot they're on now and they'll let me have it."

"Need any help?" asks Jim.

"Nah…..it's nothing."

"So, how are things?"

"Things are alright, I guess."

"You guess?"

"Yeah, I don't know…..just going through some shit," I say. "Just not sure where my place is anymore, if I ever really did."

"Maybe you don't need a place."

"You know, I've always been somewhat of an oddball. I've never really totally fit in. And it seems like now it's getting worse. Whether it's religiously, politically or socially, I just don't seem to fit in with the crowd. Either one way or the other, I just don't fit. I can't seem to go with the program. And I really don't want to anymore."

"Well, I don't think I fit too nicely into most molds, either," says Jim. "I resisted the almost pathological need that most have to reproduce, even though many of them should refrain."

"Yeah, I have, too."

"Have you now closed the book on that issue?" asks Jim.

"I have. I'm not sure Karen has yet. But it ain't gonna happen. It's been eight years now."

"Yeah, I kind of figured that if it hadn't happened by now it wasn't going to happen."

"Well, besides my not really wanting them, we can't bring kids into our dysfunctional mess of a marriage."

"It's that bad?"

"We don't fight or anything. We never have. It's just that we're really living two separate lives now. I sit at home and do whatever while she's running around visiting her seemingly endless family or going to some church service or whatever. And the truth is that I think we both like it that way. It's a chore to be together when she does come home."

"I'm sorry to hear that."

"Well, it is what it is," I say. "I'm just not sure what the end game will be yet."

"You're like me in a lot of ways. I don't think you're cut out for marriage. Not wanting kids is a clear sign of that. You have the need to be free."

"That's why I like you. You buck against all these traditional things that we're all just supposed to do, getting married, having kids, all that shit."

"I try," says Jim. "I am stuck in this dead end job though. But hopefully I can extricate myself from this at some point, too."

"Yeah, me, too. I just don't know how to get out of here."

"They may still make that decision for us. I'm not sure this little miracle is going to endure much longer."

"I'd welcome the plant closing."

"This isn't a totally bad place to work," says Jim. "We fuck off quite a bit. The people are interesting. And we definitely have some lively discussions."

"That we do."

"Although lately I've noticed that you guys aren't talking as much religion as you used to."

"I imagine that you're glad of that."

"No, actually, some of what you and Jerry have said over the years has made some sense. You two are very far from being apologists for traditional religion."

"Yeah, I know. I'm really isolated now in the things I believe. I'm at odds with what Karen believes, and with what many Christians believe. The thing is though, that the things I believe are actually far more radical than the most fervent fundamentalists believe, different, but far more radical. I don't believe in all the legalistic shit that they do. I believe in a real supernatural transformation."

"And that makes more sense than some of this religious bullshit."

"I'm not sure how much sense it makes really. It ain't happening to me."

"I just think we're all tied together somehow," says Jim. "We need to stop worrying about whose god is right and whose is wrong. That's the secret."

"Well, I'm not sure that it doesn't matter. There has to be a truth."

"Maybe that is the truth."

"I don't know."

"We can disagree about that."

"Well, we may not be totally on the same page when it comes to religion but I believe we are when it comes to politics and that sort of shit."

"Yeah, I guess you could call us both pretty much libertarians."

"Although I tend to think that label carries negative connotations with some people," I say. "I think they think we're too radical or something."

"I'm just glad you didn't turn into one of those crazy right-wingers out to force Christianity down our throats."

"Never even thought of doing that," I say. "I don't believe there's one iota of evidence to suggest that Christians are supposed to use the government to force people to live a certain way."

"Plenty of them do though."

"I know. They seem to think that if something is made legal that we're somehow endorsing it. But I don't think that's the case. I think making some things legal makes it easier to deal with. Of course this position makes me not quite fit in with the conservative Christians."

"I imagine not."

I couldn't have said something like this a few years ago. It's not that I've ever stopped thinking for myself. But there's no question that back then I did kind of buy into that typical shit you hear from so many conservative Christians about how we have to take the country back for God and all of that stuff. I guess, back then, I wanted so badly to find a place to belong. But now, I'm actually happy not fitting in. I enjoy going against the grain. I love to stir the pot.

I can't help but to wonder if things would have been different if I wouldn't have slipped into that shell I was in when I was younger. Would I be the same person if it weren't for my condition, the shyness? Because there's no question that that really shaped who I am today. If it wasn't for that, I'm not sure that I wouldn't have just fallen lock step in line with the crowd. It would have been a much different crowd that I would have been conforming to, but I'm sure I would have nevertheless felt the need to conform. Most people do.

But I couldn't go with the crowd back then because I couldn't stand to be in the crowd. I was too shy. I led a very secluded existence as a teenager and to a lesser extent after that. But that caused me to be more introspective than most people. I think that's why I tend to see things in a much different way than the majority seems to see them. I like that about myself now.

I felt like I finally belonged to something when I became a Christian. But I was happy because I felt like it was something on the fringes. It was still something not accepted by the masses. I still felt as if I wasn't conforming to accepted standards. Not many people believe what Karen and her church people believe. Then I discovered that I really didn't belong there, either. But, as I said, I'm fine with that now.

"Well look at this.....caught fucking off by two bosses," says Butch, who is with Bob.

"Yeah, what are you doing over here, Don?" asks Bob.

"Yeah....Don, they're done with that frame. Do you have everything....uh....what the fuck?" says a startled Butch, as a loud boom is heard, as the power goes out to the plant.

"Where the hell did that come from?" asks Bob, looking around the dyehouse, now dimly lit from the emergency lights.

"Oh shit!" says Butch.

"What?" asks Bob.

"Look," responds Butch, as he points down the aisle of dyeing machines, to a staggering and dazed Raeford, who still has a drill in his hands.

"He was down there drilling holes in the main panel to mount something," offers Jim.

"Yeah....he was installing that new control system we're trying for the lifter reels," says Butch, as he runs towards Raeford.

"That idiot drilled into the power again," I say.

"What happened?" asks David, as he runs up.

"We done lost power," I joke.

"What was the boom, though?" asks David.

"Go down to Beck 34 and ask Raeford that question," says Jim. "But you may want to take a trip out to the substation and get us some lights first."

"Thanks for the help, guys," responds David, sarcastically.

"Hey, you're an electrician," I say. "And this is obviously an electrical issue. Handle it."

"I heard that," says Bob, walking back up to us. "This ain't no goddamn union shop, you know. You could turn the power back on, too."

"It was just a joke, Bob," I say. "But David's got it now."

"Damn it, I don't know why I put up with your shit," says Bob.

"Cause I don't drill into live panels, and make them go boom, perhaps?" I offer.

"That fucking idiot better have a good goddamn excuse this time. Max won't take this lightly, the way Lawson did when this happened the first time," says Bob, as he walks off.

"I must not have been here when he did this the first time," says Jim.

"No, that was when the plant manager was Mike Lawson. Didn't you know? That's why Raeford's missing the index finger on his right hand. Exact same thing. He drilled into a live panel, and it blew his fucking finger off," I say, as the lights come back on.

"I hope he doesn't have anything in his system, but knowing Raeford, it wouldn't surprise me," says Jim.

"And you know they'll do a drug test," I add, as Raeford comes by, along with Bob and Butch.

"You alright, Raeford?" asks Jim.

"Yeah, man....just a little boom," says Raeford. "No problem."

"What the fuck happened down here?" asks Max, who just showed up. "I was meeting with a customer then we hear this boom and the power goes out."

"Uh....sir....Raeford had a little mishap drilling into a panel," says Bob.

"Is he alright?"

"It seems so, but we'll take him to the nurse."

"No, take him to the ER, now," says Max. "And get him drug tested."

"Yes, sir."

"I've got a feeling that it's bye bye, Raeford, this time," I say, under my breath to Jim.

"Yeah, I think he's done."

"Hell of a way to go out though."

"Boom."

Chapter 52

Saturday July 13th, 2002

"So, you're joining the festivities, I see," says Lisa, as she takes a seat across from me at a picnic table at the pavilion at Riverfront Park.

"Yeah, I don't always come to these things, but thought I would this year," I respond. "Israel here?"

"Yeah, he's down there playing volleyball."

"That where everyone's at?"

"Yeah, wanna go down there?"

"No, I'm fine."

"You're not interested in playing?"

"I don't know. I'm not that fond of playing sports in front of a bunch of people," I say. "Too self-conscious, I guess."

"Nobody's standing there staring at you or anything."

"I know. I didn't say it was rational. It's just the shyness. Groups are hard for me."

"Is your wife here?"

"No, she doesn't like this thing...... because of the drinking."

"How long has the company done this thing?" she asks. "I know they've done it as long as I've been here."

"They've been doing this for ages," I say. "Kind of harkening back to the days where every town had a textile mill in it and everyone worked there. This was one of those company towns. The plant was the center of life here."

"Many still do work there, at least in this town."

"But the landscape's littered with towns with empty factories sitting in the middle of them now."

"Think it's going to happen here?" she asks.

"I think it's a matter of time. We've lasted longer than most, thanks to Max and the changes he brought. And I think we're in good shape because we sit on the river and process our own water. But I don't see how we're gonna make it long term."

"And things have been slowing down recently."

"It'll happen at some point."

"You have any plans to get out before then?"

"I'll probably ride it in to the ground," I say. "Stay as long as I can."

"I don't know if I can do that, having a kid and all."

"Yeah, but if the plant closes, me and Karen are both out of work."

"Well, remember, I don't have a husband in the first place."

"What about Israel?"

"What about him?"

"Wedding bells in your future?"

"It's been nine fucking years," she says. "You think I'm getting married now?"

"Just asking. Just thought it was a long engagement."

"You know….Israel's a decent guy, but there's never been a future there."

"Why?"

"Well, for one thing he has plans to return to Nigeria one day."

"I didn't know that."

"Yeah, he's getting close to getting his engineering degree," she says. "After establishing himself as an engineer and building up some money, he wants to move back to Nigeria."

"Why does he want to do that?"

"I can understand it. It's his home."

"But there's a lot of instability there from what I understand."

"Well, that's what he wants to do."

"Is he trying to sell you on the idea?"

"We're really not serious like that," she says. "We just enjoy each other's company. We're just having a good time."

"Nothing wrong with that."

"Yeah….we're shacking up. We're fornicating. What else?"

"Doesn't matter to me."

"I wouldn't care if it did," she says, smiling. "Is Mark going to come? I'd like to see him."

"He's kind of reclusive lately. It may be depression. He's only getting out of the house for doctor's appointments and that sort of shit."

"Does it have anything to do with the injury?"

"Who knows? He wasn't like this to start off. It's kind of developed."

"That's too bad."

"Yeah, it's a tough situation," I say. "I think part of this is that he doesn't have a purpose now. He needs to be able to come back to work. I'm gonna talk to Max and see if there's any way he can get him in the plant in some capacity."

"But he wouldn't be able to do the instrumentation stuff now, I assume."

"No, he has trouble figuring out the simplest household tasks. There's no way he could troubleshoot machines."

"That's too bad. He was really coming along well, wasn't he?"

"Yeah, he was on his way to becoming quite a good technician," I say. "It's amazing how something so seemingly small can have such an impact on your life."

"Well, maybe he can come back in some capacity."

"With the belt tightening that we've done, I'm not sure."

"How long has it been?"

"Three years."

"And they never did replace him."

"No, I think they just count it as money saved."

"You two should see what's going on down at the volleyball court," says Jim, as he sits down.

"Why? What's happening?" I ask.

"There's this new girl down there, April. Well, the guys are making fools of themselves over her. They're just fawning all over her. They're really smitten."

"Who's this April?" ask Lisa.

"Apparently she's the new librarian. But she's pouring it on thick herself, complementing the guys on their volleyball skills and all of that shit. She's flirting like hell down there."

"And is Israel in the middle of this?" asks Lisa.

"Well......yeah," says Jim. "But I can't say he's the worst offender."

"Who is then?" I ask.

"Let me see.....Harold, David, Jerry, Roger and Ray."

"Is Ray playing?" I ask. "He's a little old isn't he?"

"No, he isn't playing, but he's sure all up in her shit."

"And Israel's just being a good little boy?" asks Lisa "What does this April look like?"

"She's one hot black girl, I'll say that. She's got them eating out of her hand."

"Does she now?" asks Lisa.

"You should've heard them," says Jim. "They were like little school boys. When she left they were talking about how she said this or said that about them. It was like there was a competition to see who she said the most nice things about. Actually kind of pitiful really."

"Typical men, fawning all over a piece of ass," says Lisa.

"Yeah....let me go find her," I joke.

"Yeah, do that," responds Lisa.

"Hey baby, that was good game," says Israel, as he joins us at the picnic table.

"Yeah, we heard it was quite the game.....plenty of complements from the crowd," I say.

"What?" asks Israel.

"He means that there was a pretty piece of ass down there that you guys were fawning all over," says Lisa.

"Who....me?"

"You guys are pitiful. Wave a piece of ass in front of you and you all swoon," says Lisa.

"Speaking of a piece of ass, Israel....have you ever told Lisa that story about the girl you picked up that time right after you came to this country?" I ask. "I believe that was before your time, Lisa."

"No...I never tell her," says Israel.

"What story?" asks Lisa.

"Well, I go to this bar one time just after arriving in country," begins Israel. "I see this hot girl. She by herself. I by myself. So I say why not. So I talk to her. I buy her drinks. Well, one thing lead to another and we go to my place. We kiss. We start to feel each other up. Then my hand go down between her legs. I expect pussy. But I feel something long..."

"Oh my God," says Lisa.

"I say....what the hell is this? She said...I thought you knew. I said hell no.....get the hell out of here. I didn't know anything about that shit. We don't have that in Nigeria."

"At least that you know of....," I say.

"Yeah...it not in open," says Israel. "I just could not believe my fucking eyes. She was gorgeous. She had chest. She had nice round ass. But she a fucking man. She had dick. What the fuck?"

"Welcome to America," says Jim. "Land of the free and home of the transvestite."

"I mean...it fine, but let me know something. You can't go around looking like that and expect me to just know."

"What if April's one?" asks Lisa.

"Ahhh.....believe me...she not," says Israel.

"And what the fuck does that mean?" asks Lisa.

"It mean, it daylight and I can see clearly," says Israel. "She ain't got no dick."

"So, you looked that closely?" I ask.

"You guys try to get me in trouble," says Israel.

"No, I think you're doing just fine on your own," says Lisa.

"We guys, we just like to look," says Israel.

"Okay....you keep looking then......but I will, too," says Lisa.

"You know what's really interesting about that whole thing?" asks Jim, rhetorically. "It's that many of the guys fawning all over her are white, and she's black. Could you imagine that happening at this picnic in the 50's or 60's?"

"Yeah, things have come a long way," I say. "I actually thought Karen and I would have more of a problem than we have. We haven't really experienced the first bit of racism."

"Yeah, but like we've said before, you aren't the ones they're worried about," says Jim.

"Yeah, they don't want their nice white daughters to be defiled by these black monsters with the huge dicks," says Lisa.

"Oh my God," says Israel. "This girl got such a mouth on her."

"I love a nasty mouth on a woman," I say.

Lisa shoots me this wicked little grin.

"Lisa, what does your family think about Israel?" asks Jim.

"They don't have the trouble with him that they would if he were from here," she says. "I think the accent makes him seem exotic. He's not a brother from the hood. I don't think my Daddy would go for that as easily."

"So, is this your first black guy?" I ask.

"Yeah, I don't have a special thing for black guys or anything like that."

"But, you know what they say.....once you go black, you never go back," says Israel.

"Well, I may just go back," cracks Lisa.

"What about you, Jim? You ever been with a black woman?" I ask.

"Well, you know that I was in the Navy before I got this job. There were a couple of ports where I tasted a little brown sugar," says Jim, as he gets up to go over to the food tables. "And it was sweet."

"The blacker the berry, the sweeter the juice," says Israel.

"What does that mean?" I ask.

"It's just something I heard. The blacker the berry.....the darker the chick.....the sweeter her juice," explains Israel.

"Then mine must be downright bitter," says Lisa.

"No...no...only applies to black girl," says Israel.

"Hey, are you guys going swimming in the river?" asks Jerry, as he and Roger walk up. "A bunch of us are going down to the beach area."

"Well, I'm sure Israel will be going if April is," says Lisa.

"I'm sure that's why they're so enthused about going already," I say.

"Hey, I wouldn't get any of the mac and cheese they have over there," says Roger.

"Why?" I ask, as Jim walks up with a plate full of food.

"Well, Harold was talking up April over there...and well.....hehehehe....his fucking false teeth go flying out of his mouth and land in the goddamn mac and cheese."

"What?" says Jim, after spitting out some mac and cheese. "Why the fuck didn't he say something? Damn it....I just ate that shit."

"Shit, with as nasty as Harold is, do you really think he thinks his teeth flying into the mac and cheese is worth a mention?" asks Roger.

"Might have made it taste better," suggests Jerry.

"What does that old geezer think he's gonna get anyway?" asks Lisa. "I gather that this April is young and hot. Does Harold really think he's getting any of that?"

"It just makes them feel young again to get a little attention from a hot girl like that," I say.

"No, I think Harold and Ray have hopes of really getting a piece," says Roger. "They are delusional."

"Did you hear?" asks Jerry. "Raeford got canned."

"Did he fail the drug test?" asks Jim.

"No, he refused to take the drug test," says Jerry.

"Same result though," I say.

"Yeah, but he had to go" says Lisa. "There were times where I was scared to work around him. He smelled of alcohol a lot of the time."

"To fuck that up....what an idiot. Raeford was lucky to have that job," I say. "With his education, he won't equal what he had there."

"Guys like that figure they can handle it," says Jim. "They just consider it part of life. And I'm not sure that the drinking had anything to do with the accident anyway."

"He was just being a dumbass," I say.

"Well, it doesn't matter now," says Roger.

"He would've lost the job eventually, anyway," I say.

"What do you mean?" asks Jerry.

"When the plant closes," I say. "We know it's coming sooner

or later."

"Yeah, but Raeford comes out far worse this way," says Jim. "No unemployment, he loses however many more years of pay, and all of that extra contribution to retirement. These old guys have a lot to lose."

"But that's part of what's killing this company," I explain. "This retirement plan that matches five for one of what these old guys put in. They're cleaning up, while us younger ones are only getting one or two to one match."

"Yeah, they are stacking it up in piles," says Roger.

"So, how are you guys enjoying the cookout?" asks Bob, after walking up to our table.

"I think everybody's having a ball," says Jim.

"Especially the men," adds Lisa.

"Would you just drop it," says Israel. "It all just innocent flirting."

"You talking about that black girl that was down at the volleyball court?" asks Bob.

"Yeah, that's the one," says Jerry.

"Yeah, she's not bad, that's for sure," says Bob.

"Bob, do you have a second?" I ask.

"Sure," says Bob, as I get up and walk away from the table with him.

"Sorry to bring up the plant today, but I was wondering about Mark," I say.

"Mark?"

"Yeah, golf tournament, brain injury.....worked at the plant."

"Yeah, yeah....sorry. What about him?"

"I was just wondering if there was any way he could come back to work in some sort of capacity," I say. "There's no way that he's ready to have his old job, but I was thinking there was something he could do, just so he could have a job again, some sort of purpose."

"Don, in the old days...sure, it wouldn't be a problem. But these days it's just not a liability that the company wants. When the company was run by the Raymond family, of course we'd be able to let him come back. But now with these big megacorporations running things.....well....things are different."

"Would it do any good to talk to Max?"

"Don....you can if you don't trust me. I know that we don't have the best relationship. But I would love to bring Mark in to do something. Hell, I'm sure he could man the tool room, or something like that."

"Yeah…..something like that's what I was thinking."

"It just isn't going to happen. The guideline's pretty clear when it comes to getting injured off the job. You can't come back unless you're one hundred percent. If he has any impairment, then he's more susceptible to injury on the job. Or at least that's what the corporate people think."

"Well, I can understand that."

"I can talk to Max, or call corporate. But the result will be the same."

"Okay, Bob, thanks," I say, as Bob leaves and I rejoin the gang at the table.

"What was that about?" asks Jerry. "Doin a little bit of brown nosing? That's Roger's job."

"Fuck you," says Roger. "Asshole."

"Well, Roger, I have to admit that you seem to be in more offices than anyone else I know at the plant," I say.

"I am not."

"He's got his nose so far up Max's ass that it ain't even funny," says Jerry.

"If I were brown nosing the way you guys think then why am I still just a fucking carpenter?" asks Roger. "Why ain't I a manager or supervisor yet?"

"Must not be too good at it," says Jerry.

"He doesn't know how to deep throat yet," adds Jim.

"Yeah, you have to learn to go balls deep," says Jerry. "Then those promotions will just come rolling your way."

"You guys are nasty," says Lisa.

"Yeah…stop talking this shit in front of my woman," says Israel.

"I don't think it really bothers her all that much," I say.

"Yeah, she has to be tough to work in the same building as this crowd," says Roger.

"Yeah, it's part of the bargain of doing the job," says Lisa.

"Bargain, my ass! You've got a pretty nasty fucking mouth yourself," I say.

"She holds her own," adds Roger.

"Look, that fucker Boonie has his bag of cans," says Jerry. "He's digging them out of the trash."

"Why doesn't he just sit a can out so that people can just put their cans in it?" asks Jim.

"He must like dumpster diving," says Israel.

"How much could he really be making from that?" asks Lisa.

"Not worth it to me, but you'd probably be surprised how much he makes from all of that," says Roger. "He also takes every discarded piece of aluminum that comes out of the plant. That shit really adds up."

"Do you remember that time in the break room when he got in that little tussle with Joyce over a dime that was sitting on the floor?" asks Jerry.

"I've always wondered if he'd dig a coin out of a urinal," I say.

"Gross," says Lisa.

"But I bet he'd do it," I say.

"If it were at least a dime," adds Jim.

"Do you guys hear that?" asks Lisa, quietly.

"Hear what?" responds Roger.

"Over at the other table over there.....Harold and David are comparing notes on April," says Lisa.

"Harold's really a piece of work, isn't he?" I say. "His wife's a well-known figure in the community. She's a minister at a church. And he's always carrying on. You see him all the time on the street gawking at women. Not even trying to hide it."

"And don't forget getting busted for moonshine," says Roger.

"I mean just have some respect for your wife," I say. "Don't make it so obvious that you're staring at these women. I understand looking, but don't make a spectacle of it."

"Oh, you should have seen him down there when we were playing volleyball," says Jerry. "He was all over her. Brushing up against her....you know....trying to hit the good parts."

"He obviously has no respect for her and her position if he's doing all of this, and the moonshine?" says Lisa.

"But he's a deacon in their church, too," I say.

"I don't understand the outrage, Don," says Jim. "From what I see, this is par for the course behavior when it comes to many Christians. Preaching one thing and then doing another. Look at all of these TV ministers and their infidelities."

"Yeah, it seems like the religious ones act up worse than anyone," adds Roger.

"Isn't it always true that the kids of ministers are wilder than anyone else?" asks Jerry.

"It's unnatural to keep all of that pent up inside, the way religion makes you do," says Jim. "It has to get out some way."

"To me, it's more of an issue that he's disrespecting his wife than anything else," I say. "He's just so blatant about it."

"Yeah, but that's the case with many men," says Lisa. "You guys are just pitiful when a little piece of ass is waved in front of you. You can't control yourselves."

"I can," I say.

"Well, well, if it isn't Saint Donald," says Roger.

"No, I'm just saying that I'm not running after ass the way some guys do," I say. "I'm not saying I don't notice fine looking women."

"Or girls," adds Jim.

"Or girls….sure," I agree. "But I'm not out chasing them and leering at them in front of everybody."

"Or maybe you just don't have the game to do it," says Jerry. "After all, you've been with how many women?"

"Yeah, that's right….it's only been two," I say. "The point is that I have respect for my wife."

"So, you just leer at girls in secret," says Jim.

"Pretty much," I concede.

"Pervert," cracks Roger.

"Let me go leer at April for a while," I say.

"We'll all join you," says Roger.

"Just kidding," I say.

"I'm not," says Roger.

Chapter 53

Monday July 15th, 2002

"Join me at the diner for a bite to eat?" asks Jim, as we leave the plant after work.

"Yeah, sure, why not?" I say. "Karen's going somewhere with her aunt."

"Start up today wasn't all that smooth was it?" asks Jim.

"A little bit tougher than usual."

"Guess it was the hard shutdown we did for the cookout this weekend."

"Well, they like to give everyone an opportunity to go. Kind of nice of them to shut the plant down for that."

"Where the fuck is Jerry going?" asks Jim, pointing ahead, as we approach the diner.

"He's going right past Ronnie's. Has someone opened another redneck bar?"

"That fucker's going into the library," says Jim, as we go inside the diner.

"Could it be that he actually reads?" I joke, as we take a booth at a window with a view of Main Street.

"Not likely......hey, look who's going in there now."

"Roger......those fuckers. You know they're going to see that girl, April."

"Yeah, those two probably don't even know what the word library means."

"What the fuck is this? Look.....it's Israel and David."

"Well, at least with them it's possible that they actually read," jokes Jim.

"Doubt it. They're going there to sniff after April."

"Oh, believe me, I know. After the show they put on the other day, I know what they're after."

"But every single one of them has a woman," I observe. "What does this April have that's so intriguing, that these guys just go straight to her as soon as they can? I mean, they get off of work and go straight there?"

"Well, you saw her at the picnic. She is hot."

"Yeah, I'd have to agree with you there. But so hot that these guys are surrounding her like a bunch of hound dogs?"

"It's more than that though," says Jim. "I think it's all the attention and flirting she does with them. They really think they're getting some pussy out of her. That's why they're sniffing around. She's giving them hope that they can actually get a piece of that fine brown ass."

"What do you think's going on in there with all of them showing up at the same time?"

"Yeah, what do Israel and David want to do.....have a threesome?" asks Jim. "At least Roger and Jerry came separately."

"Well, you never know...... Israel did pick up a guy once before," I say. "Maybe he wouldn't mind another guy in the room."

"Not me. Maybe more than one girl...sure....but no other man in the room."

"I agree. I'm a little surprised at Roger, actually. The rest of them, sure, but I wouldn't expect Roger to go out of his way to hang around her."

"It is funny though....all of them there at the same time."

"Damn, Lisa was right the other day," I say. "This is just pitiful. These guys falling all over themselves...and each other, just for some outside hope of getting a piece of ass."

"It's unnatural for men to settle for one woman. It's just too bad women can't just accept that."

"I happen to think they have it all fucked up actually. They look at the whole relationship thing wrong. This whole idea of the perfect mate is what fucks things all up."

"The so-called soul mate."

"Exactly," I say. "It's great if that happens, but it hardly ever does. We usually end up settling for something short of that."

"Well, if I remember correctly, you said that Karen was meant for you."

"Yeah, well, maybe I'm having second thoughts on that," I say. "We have to basically settle for something short of the ideal, I guess."

"Absolutely, most of the time, in fact."

"And I don't mean that's bad. It's just reality."

"Yeah, we all have to make choices. We almost never get perfection in anything in life. We have to make compromises."

"A woman wants someone who can be all things to her and meet all of her needs. I think that's unrealistic," I say. "Why can't we get different things from different people, even if that different thing is sex? I mean, the woman we're with has most of what we want. We want to be with her. That's why we're with her. But there may be other women that have a little something we may want, too."

"But would you be able to let your woman have the same freedom? What if another man had a little something that she wanted?"

"Well, I don't know. I like the idea of it. But I'm not sure the reality would be the same."

"I do see what you're saying," says Jim. "Some women have no problem with their men going places with other women and having them as friends. But they have zero tolerance when it comes to sex. You would think that the other shit, the friends type of shit would be a bigger threat than the sex."

"Exactly. Don't they get that it's possible to just fuck a woman without any sort of emotional attachment at all? Don't they realize that it isn't a threat to the relationship?"

"It's just because we view sex differently. Men view it as a recreational activity, sometimes, not all of the time, but sometimes. But women put a deeper meaning on it than we do. Well, most of them do. Thank God for the ones who do view it as just a recreational activity."

"Yeah, to most women, sex isn't just sex," I say. "Especially when it's in the context of a relationship. Outside of a relationship....well....I see how that can work."

"Yeah...what was her name.....?

"Gina."

"Haven't forgotten her after all these years, huh?"

"No, I guess I haven't."

"But most women will never get that sex can just be like playing a sport," says Jim. "We're just wired differently."

"Yeah, most women wouldn't have a problem with their men playing tennis with a woman, for instance. So why can't the sport just be fucking?"

"It can definitely be a good workout."

"That's it," I say. "Tell the wife, 'I'll be back in a little bit honey. I'm going to work out.'"

"Yeah. And I'll come back smelling like pussy."

"Of course, I say all of this knowing that it doesn't exactly jibe with the biblical idea of morality."

"I just know that it's our nature to fuck more than one woman," says Jim. "We're made to roam around. We're made to spread our seed."

"Philosophically, I agree. But religiously, well, I'm not so sure."

"Didn't some of those biblical characters have more than one wife?"

"Sure, but we aren't talking about wives really. We're just talking about fucking around with other women. Recreational sex."

"True. Probably no way to make that fit into the bible."

"Yeah…I don't know," I say. "I seem to have these competing views bouncing around in my own head."

"The question is…..which ones are going to win?"

"I wonder sometimes myself."

"How did we get off on this?"

"Because of those clowns parading themselves to the library in search of some fine brown sugar."

"So, you do think she's a little sweet?"

"How do you not?" I ask. "But despite how hot she may be, I still think it's totally disrespectful for them to go flocking to the library where anyone can see them. Do they think this isn't going to get back to their wives or women or whatever?"

"It's a great excuse though. They can claim they had some business over there."

"At the library? Believe me, those women aren't that stupid. And especially if someone sees them in action fawning all over April."

"Well, that's their problem."

"Yeah, I know."

Chapter 54

Wednesday July 17th, 2002

"Excuse me….uh….I have a question," I say, somewhat nervously.

"Yeah, sure….how may I help you?" asks April.

"I'm interested in books having to do with Pentecostalism," I say.

At least I have some sort of pretense for being here in the library. But why in the hell did I pick that subject?

"I can help you with that," she says.

"I'm not familiar with this new computer system. I'm used to the old card catalog thing."

"I know….but this is much easier. Here….looks like we have fifty seven titles for you to choose from with Pentecostal or Pentecostalism in the title."

"How about charismatic?" I ask. "Can we add that to the search, or do another search? That may turn up some more books."

"Sure……uh……yeah, that adds a few more."

"I'm surprised there are so many titles on that."

"Well, with this being a regional library, we actually have quite a broad selection. And this is a really religious area, so….."

"Well, thanks for the help," I say.

"I was wondering when you were going to say something," she says. "You've been circling around for a while now. Wasn't quite sure what your game was."

"I know….I'm kind of shy when it comes to approaching people I don't know."

"I'm April," she says, extending her hand. "New to town actually."

I take her hand and it's like a charge shooting through me.

"I'm Don. I work down at the mill."

"I say I'm new to town. I feel like that's the case," she says. "I'm actually from here. But I've been living in Alaska for several years now. And before that, I was in the Air Force."

"Alaska? Quite different from here I would imagine?"

"Yeah, it is. You know, my mom works down at the mill, runs one of the frames, Susie....Susie Rogers?"

"Yeah....I know Susie."

"What do you do at the plant?" she asks.

"I'm an Instrumentation technician."

"So, you keep Momma's machine running then."

"Yeah...that's right."

"I was actually raised in a Pentecostal church. Very strict. But I'm a long way from that now.....if you know what I mean," she says, with such a sly, sexy smile.

Damn, she absolutely oozes sex. Does she intend to do that? Is it directed at me? Or does everyone get this treatment?

"Is your mom still into that stuff?" I ask. "I mean the Pentecostal stuff?

"That's a funny way to put it. Into that stuff."

"Well, I'm married to someone who goes to a Pentecostal church. But I quit going years ago. I'm kind of disillusioned with the whole thing now."

"Yeah, my mom and my sister are both still really heavy into it. They go to 5th Street Holiness Church."

"My wife's visited there before."

"You married to a sista?" she asks. "Cause that's a black church."

"Yeah, she used to be Karen Johnson, Karen Higgins now."

"Damn, my sister Hope is friends with Karen. I know her."

"You're Hope's sister?" I ask. "Well, of course you are, I knew that Hope was Susie's girl."

"Small world, isn't it?"

"Small town."

"So....is it true, what they say.....would you ever go back....I mean.....after having black?" she asks, as she kind of bobs her hair in my face.

Why is something as simple as her hair in my face so fucking powerful? Is she coming on to me with that question?

"Well.....hehehe.....I don't know, it would depend," I say.

"Depend on what?" she asks. "On how hot the black was?"

"I guess...but it's more than that though."

"Of course....but the sex has to be good, right?"

As she says this, she kind of nudges me with her hip.

"Well.....yeah," I say.

I'm less nervous than I thought I would be. She makes it so

easy.

"What else do you like in your women?" she asks.

"In my women? You act as if I have a stable of them."

"Who knows," she says. "Some men do."

"Well, not me....uh....I'm very far from that. Karen's only the second women I've ever had sex with. And the other was just a drunken one night stand."

And why did I tell her that? Her fucking sister is a church friend of Karen's.

"Drunken one night stands can be kinda fun," she says.

Well, that sure seemed like a clear signal. But now I think she's just fucking with me.

"Well.....it was," I say. "It was a pretty wild night. We fucked three times."

Now I'm getting into the game with a little talk of my own.

"But what's your deal, man? Why so few?" she asks. "You're a cute guy. There's nothing wrong with you."

She reaches down and rests her hand on mine.

"I can't believe I just told you that actually," I say "It's not exactly something that I broadcast to the world."

"People tell me I'm easy to talk to.....maybe that's it."

"Maybe."

"So, tell me....how did someone like you end up fucking only two girls in your whole life?" she asks.

"I just developed this shyness around the time of middle school. Don't know what caused it. Hate to be in crowds. Have a hard time introducing myself to new people. But the worst part is that it seems to be worse when it comes to women. I'm just a total mess around girls."

"Total mess? You seem fine to me."

"Well, it did take me a while to approach you."

"But you were just asking a question."

"Yeah....."

"Or....... did you have something else on your mind?" she asks.

She asks this like she knows absolutely what my intentions were. She sees right through me.

"Well....yeah, the question was just a pretext," I say. "I was intrigued by you, actually. All of the guys are just so taken with you that I had to see for myself."

"Hmmm, I see."

"The real issue is getting past that breaking of the ice stage," I say. "But you make it easy."

"I tend to relate to men more than I do to women. I know those guys hang around because they think they're getting some. But they aren't. At least most of them won't. Most of them are amusing to fuck around with. But I only fuck guys that can give me a little more than a hard dick. I need someone who can stimulate my mind and my soul a little, as much as I want the hard dick. But to be clear, I do want the hard dick."

"Understood."

How do I respond to that? Which one am I? Is she just fucking with me? Or does she want to fuck me?

"Good," she says. "I just wanted to be clear about that. Just want you to know what my intentions are."

Intentions? What the fuck does that mean? Shit, the way she's looking at me. She's just so damn hot. She's like a fucking drug. I've just about got that hard dick right now for her.

"So, you aren't impressed with any of your suitors?" I ask.

"Suitors? What is this, the nineteenth century?"

"What should I call them then?"

"Horny devils, perhaps?"

"Yeah….that's about the size of it."

"But no, I'm not really impressed with any of them," she says.

"You know…I feel like a fish out of water most of the time around here," I say. "I don't seem to quite fit in. I'm not sure I'm a small town type of guy."

"How so?"

"Well….you've obviously met many of the guys I work with. I don't have the same desires and drives that they do. I seem to be plagued with the overwhelming desire to do something meaningful with my life. That thought never crosses their minds."

"That's a good thing though. All these guys are interested in is beer, sports and pussy. And at this moment it seems to be my pussy that has them so fascinated. Or is it my ass? Or maybe my tits?"

"Damn…," I say, turning my face away from hers briefly.

"What?" she asks, moving closer.

"Just the way you talk."

"Gets you hot, me talking this way?" she asks. "You like hearing me talk about my pussy, my ass and my tits?"

"Yeah, I seem to have a thing for women with nasty mouths."

"But I'm sure Karen doesn't have a nasty mouth."

"No, quite the opposite actually."

"You say that you have different drives and desires than the typical men around here, but you still seem to be interested in at least one thing that they are."

"I'm that obvious, huh?" I ask.

"Yeah....that obvious. And...well....you actually admitted it, too. You said you were intrigued by me."

"I did admit that, didn't I?"

"Yes, you did."

"Well, that's kinda a universal desire, sex."

"I prefer the term, fucking."

"I've noticed."

"So, you like pussy just like they do," she says. "It's just the other things....the beer and the sports that you're not obsessed with. Is that it?"

"I guess that's an accurate assessment."

"So, you say you want to do something meaningful with your life. What is it that you're doing that's so meaningful?"

"Writing."

"Writing about what?"

"Religion and all its problems."

"What specifically?"

"The Pentecostal and the charismatic movements in the church," I say. "I feel like it's my mission now to expose the truth of this movement, so it doesn't suck other people in."

"Damn, pretty serious about this, aren't you?"

"Yeah, I am actually," I say. "But I also want the book to include all of the other shit that corrupts established Christianity. To me, the whole thing needs to be torn down."

"Tear it down, huh?"

"Well, I know that isn't going to happen, but that's what needs to happen."

"Wow, this conversation really took a turn."

"I'm sorry. I am kinda passionate about this."

"No, that's alright. I'm not exactly an established Christianity type of girl anyway. I just don't care for all the moral shit. I like to fuck too much for that. But what's your deal?"

"We're missing the real truth of scripture," I say. "A truly profound change should be occurring in those who accept Christ. Pentecostals know this. They think they have it, but they don't. If you think you have the real thing, but you don't, then you'll never get the real thing. And many Christians in the more staid denominations don't even believe in any sort of supernatural change. They're just part of some fucking club."

"I don't know….I may not want to live that way, but I've got to say that my mom and sister really love the Lord."

"I don't deal with motives. I don't question that these people believe in what they do. But they've been led astray. They're being fooled by these supernatural experiences that they're having."

"So, you believe in all of that stuff?" she asks.

"Yeah, real things are happening. It's just the source that's corrupt."

"You think it's evil spirits or something?"

"Yeah…..basically. The roots of the movement can be traced back and it's evident to me that voodoo somehow found its way into Christianity. The whole Pentecostal thing is rooted in error. It was a false spirit from the beginning."

"But that assumes that voodoo is real," she says. "That there are real spirits involved in that."

"Well, I happen to believe that spirits exist."

"Well, I don't know. I'm not sure I could buy into all of that."

"Sorry…I didn't mean to dump all of that on you. I just don't have anyone to really talk to about all of this stuff. Most people, well, their eyes glaze over when I start getting into this spiritual stuff."

"And I don't guess you could talk to Karen about this, since it's really about her."

"No, she believes what she believes," I say. "It has a grip on her that I could never break. No…I can't talk to her about anything really. I have many interests, but all she's interested in is church and God. And now we don't even have that in common any more, if we ever really did."

"I'm sorry."

"I have this friend. I used to be able to talk to him about anything. We used to have some really deep conversations. But that's gone now, too."

"What happened?"

"He had an accident. He has a brain injury. It's really impossible to have any meaningful conversations with him anymore. He just can't follow things the way he used to. I really miss that."

"But there's no one else?"

"I talk to some of the guys at work about some things. But it's like different people are only available for certain subjects. Some don't talk about religion. Some don't talk about politics. Some don't talk about the deeper philosophical questions. I could talk to Mark about anything. He would get what I'm going through with this Pentecostal stuff. But I think most everyone thinks I'm way out there on this one, including you."

"Well.....I don't know....I really didn't hear all of it."

"I'm sorry....don't you have some work to do. I shouldn't be rambling on like this."

I hate the way I do that sometimes. I'll just get going and keep going until I totally lose whoever it is I'm talking to. I just keep talking until I see their eyes start to glaze over and then I know I've said too much.

"No, there's hardly anyone here," she says. "There's some guy back there in one of the reading rooms, but we aren't disturbing him."

"Okay....it's just that I keep some of this all pent up, and when I have the chance, it just comes pouring out."

"Yeah, man, you don't seem all that shy, talking my ear off like this."

"Once the ice is broken....well....it's hard to shut me up sometimes. And you just seem to be easy to talk to."

"You interest me somehow," she says. "You think for yourself. But you're quite the contradiction, you know?"

"Contradiction? Me?"

"Yeah, you're all into this biblical shit, yet you like women who cuss like fucking sailors. And you like flirting a little, too, despite the fact that you have a wife, a wife that I happen to know."

"That's the two different natures, I guess. The spiritual and the carnal."

"Bipolar....are we?"

"No, if I am we all are," I say. "We all have those competing natures. I may be just a little bit in flux right now though. There's a lot of shit going around in my head."

"I see that. You obviously have some idea in your head about fucking me, yet you try to ply me with talk of religion."

"Shit, that does sound pitiful."

"No, not really. It kind of intrigues me," she says. "I tend to like guys who don't quite fit into any sort of mold. And I don't mean the typical rebel with his leather jacket and all that shit. Those idiots conform just like everyone else. They just conform to a different group. I like guys who truly think for themselves."

"Christians aren't supposed to fit into any mold that the world has to offer," I say. "There's a scripture that says that we should be like aliens and strangers in this world. We should be looking for a country to call our own. Basically, the idea is that this world isn't our home, that we shouldn't be too comfortable here. I feel like I fit that standard, at least some of the time."

"And yet, many Christians on the right are saying that this is a Christian nation and that Christians are supposed to take the world over for God or something like that."

"That's a real joke, that this is God's chosen nation," I say. "This country was founded by slaughtering the Indians and taking their land from them. Then we shipped African slaves over here and continued the cycle of abuse. Even the Revolutionary War was against Christian principles."

"What?" she says, with a slight laugh.

"Yeah, this country was founded on rebellion. Christians aren't supposed to rebel. We're supposed to submit to authority, no matter how much we disagree with it."

"So, that means we shouldn't have fought for our independence from England?"

"Wasn't it a rebellion against the established authorities?"

"Sure."

"Just think what was happening during the Revolutionary war," I say. "We had Christians killing other Christians. How was that right? All in the name of independence. Just because we didn't like getting taxed by the king?"

"You mean Christians on this side were killing Christians on the other side."

"Yeah, and vice versa. Were they evil because they fought for the British?" I ask. "I'm sorry......I just get going sometimes. That's just one of my pet peeves. This idea that this is God's chosen nation to rule the world or something is outrageous. It's not even in the bible."

"I have a hard time with all this Christianity is the only way shit anyway. Being in the Air Force and travelling around the world just gave me a different perspective on things. Sure, I was indoctrinated with much of that military shit. But I saw and met people with a variety of beliefs. And many of them were decent people that would do anything for you. They just happen to believe in a different God. So, they go to hell for their misfortune?"

"That's why Christianity has to be deeper if it's supposed to be the only way to God. It can't be as simple as being lucky enough to be born in a Christian country, or unlucky enough to be born into a

Muslim country, for instance."

"So, you believe that Christianity's the only way?"

"Christ, not Christianity," I say. "I think we've totally missed the boat. We're supposed to experience a true supernatural transformation. Otherwise, how can we possibly claim that Christ is the only way?"

"It seems as if many people need some perspective. They need to understand that there is a world beyond their little small town, that there are people who basically live the same life that they do, but happen to believe in a different God."

"I agree. What these Christians have is no different than what people of other religions have. How can you claim that your way is the only way, unless you show them that something is profoundly different in how you live as opposed to them?"

"I just don't see how God would limit himself to one very specific religion."

"I struggle with that one myself sometimes," I say. "But it's what I see in scripture. I have to go with what's there."

"I know….but it just doesn't make sense to me anymore."

"I don't claim to have all of the answers. Even though I may be very assertive or whatever, in what I say, that doesn't mean that I've closed my mind or anything. I just believe what I believe. But it's not like I'm living this great Christian life that I say should exist. It's really just a theory. I can't prove it."

"No…I admire that in you. You aren't just going with the crowd. You're truly seeking for answers that make sense."

"Well, that's easy. There isn't a crowd that believes all of the stuff I believe anyway. I have no choice. I have to kind of forge my own way."

"I really enjoy talking to you. Maybe we could get together sometime, maybe a cup of coffee or lunch, somewhere besides here."

"I'm not so sure that's a good idea."

"But, why?"

"I don't know……I'm attracted to you. It wouldn't be for the purest of motives, at least on my part."

"Well, who said I was giving you anything," she says. "I said talk. You're a married man. I'm not in the habit of fucking married men."

She says this with the most interesting smile across her face.

"Still….I don't know….maybe. I'd better go now."

"Aren't you going to look at your books?"

"No, like I said, that was just a pretense, a reason to strike up a conversation. See? I can't be trusted around you."

"Okay, man…..see ya around, I guess."

"Have a good night."

Chapter 55

Thursday July 18th, 2002

"Don Higgins, how the hell are you today?" asks Jim, as I come into the Instrumentation shop.

"Well....alright....I guess," I say, kind of puzzled by Jim's attitude. "Just another day in paradise."

"Guess where I was last night."

"No idea."

"Well, let's just say that some of us actually use the library for its intended purpose."

"You saw me there?"

"Yep."

"You son of a bitch. How do you do that?"

"Do what?"

"Always seem to be lurking in corners observing stuff you ain't supposed to see."

"So, you didn't want anyone to see that, huh?"

"No, actually, it was totally innocent."

"I was just at the library reading and who do I see.... but you," says Jim. "You come in and it's obvious from the start what you wanted. It took you awhile to talk to her, but when you did, you stayed a while."

"I was just researching something and she was helping me."

"Don't hand me that shit. You left right after you talked to her. Besides, you're as bad as the rest of the guys. You never use the library. I'm in there all the time and I've never seen you there. When I saw you walk in, I knew what you were there for, or rather, who you were there for."

"My curiosity just got the best of me. She was just so hot down at the river. There's just something about her that just draws you in."

"No, something that draws you in."

"Yeah."

"I'm not denying that she's all that. It's just....well.... after everything you said about the guys fawning all over her and their being married and all, then you go and try to get into her pants, too?"

"No....it wasn't like that at all," I say. "We had a nice conversation."

"Okay….but you know what you were there for. Isn't one public sex scandal enough for you?"

"I don't really know why I went," I say. "Sure, I guess there's some sort of desire or thought that something could happen, but not an expectation. I'm just not a player like that. I couldn't get her into bed if I wanted to."

"I don't think you have to do all that much to get a girl like April in the sack. I think she'll pretty much fuck anything that has a dick."

"That's pretty harsh."

"Well, that's the book on her."

"The book on her?"

"I'm sure you know that she's from Raymond," says Jim. "Her mom's Susie, out there on Frame 8?"

"Yeah, actually, she knows Karen, too. Her sister, Hope, and Karen are close friends, church friends at that."

"Well, some of the women have been talking, after the little spectacle down at the park. She's got quite the reputation from when she was a teenager."

"Oh, really?"

"Yep, quite a few men have been in a backseat with that thing."

"Listen…..we just talked."

"Are you gonna be a regular visitor to the library now?" asks Jim. "Should I reserve a table for you? Or will you be spending all of your time in her office, perhaps under her desk?"

"Yeah….funny."

"Hey, I'm not kidding."

"She's one hell of a flirt though. But she probably does that with all of the guys. Bobbling her hair in my face. Kept touching my hand. She actually wants to see me for coffee or lunch or something."

"I'll bet she isn't meeting Jerry or Roger for coffee."

"Well, probably not. But we actually had a good conversation."

"Better watch out with her. She's trouble. At least for a married man she is."

"Jealous or something?"

"No…I don't have any interest in her. I don't need someone who wants to fuck the whole football team."

"I'm not so sure she's that big of a slut."

"Well, maybe not the whole football team," says Jim. "She just wants to fuck the star players."

"I don't know….I don't get that from her."

"The signs are all there. She has a history of that shit."

"I think she just likes to flirt. She's just messing with those guys. And how do you know that all that shit those women are talking about her isn't just jealousy? Maybe they just hate the fact that guys like her so much."

"Yeah, she may be messing with them, but when she finds one she wants to fuck, you can be sure that she'll pounce. And that's what she's trying to do with you."

"Why would she want me though?"

"Why not? You're a decent looking guy, smart, funny. It doesn't take much, just something to make you stand out from the crowd. She probably likes it that you're more subtle than those other idiots."

"Well....I told her it probably wasn't a good idea to see each other. I admitted that I was attracted to her."

"See....now she knows that you're into her. Better stay away from her."

"Why are you so worried about it?" I ask.

"I don't know....I just don't want to see you fuck your marriage up, unless of course, you want to. You somehow survived the Gina thing. I don't think you could survive another one."

"I'm a big boy."

"But let's be honest. It's not like you have loads of experience when it comes to women."

"Thanks for pointing that out."

"But you don't"

"Feels good...... getting that attention."

"Just remember what you said that time. There are always consequences."

"Yeah....I know."

Chapter 56

Friday July 19th, 2002

"Need any help with research today, sir?" asks April.

"No, I'll be honest today and admit that I'm here to see you," I say. "Can we talk in your office?"

"Sure....follow me," she says, as she leads me into her office. "So....what's up?"

"Well....I've just been thinking about what you said."

"And what was it that I said that has you so interested?" she asks, as she bobs her hair in my face.

I love the smell of her hair. Shit, I just love the smell of her.

"That you wanted to meet me outside of here," I say.

"Yeah...to have coffee or lunch or something."

"What would the something be?"

I cannot believe I had the nerve to ask her that.

"You men have such dirty fucking minds."

"Uh...I'm sorry....I shouldn't have said that. I don't even know where that came from."

"No, Don.....it's alright. I am interested. I was just kidding about the dirty fucking minds. I happen to like men with dirty fucking minds."

"Okay."

"Damn, man, you really don't have any experience at this at all, do you? You look like a deer caught in the fucking headlights."

"No, I don't. No experience at all."

"So, you need me to be blunt?"

"Yeah...I guess so."

"You were fairly blunt just then though."

"Well.....I don't know...."

"You didn't get the hints the other day? Me kinda throwing my hair in your face....touching your hand.....kinda giving you a little bump with my hip?"

So all of that shit was on purpose.

"No....I guess I thought there was something there....but I wasn't sure if you were just like that with everyone," I say. "Like you said, I don't have much experience with this sort of thing."

"No, I'm not like that with everyone. I'm friendly with

everyone, but not interested in everyone. I may flirt with a lot of guys, but not like that with everyone."

"But why are you interested in me?"

"I don't know…..I just like you. I don't try to analyze that shit too much."

"Okay….I was just wondering. It's not like we spent that much time together."

"It doesn't always take all that much time to know that you want to get to know someone better."

"I want to know you better…so….I guess that's true."

"You just seem to have a self-esteem problem. You simply cannot believe that any woman would be that interested in you, that quick."

"Yeah, I guess that's about the size of it."

"So….you wanna meet me somewhere?"

"What exactly are we meeting to do?"

"Well….I'm not promising you a fuck……I'm just saying….it could happen."

"Do you want to go out or anything like that?"

"Can you really risk that? You are married."

"Yeah…I guess not."

"I just want to talk to you some more. Maybe fuck you. Talk some more. Fuck some more. Get the idea? Let's just meet away from here and see what happens. Maybe nothing will happen. Let's just see."

"How about we meet in Raleigh at some park? We could find a spot at the lake."

"That sounds good. No one from town should see us there."

"Exactly."

"You'll be able to get away that long without Karen knowing?"

"We live such separate lives now. She's doing church stuff most of the time. I can pick a time where she'd never know I left the house."

"Can I tell you something?" she whispers into my ear.

Damn, her hot breath in my ear makes me want to just bend her over that desk and fuck her right this very minute. She sure knows how to push all the right buttons.

"Sure," I say. "Tell me anything you like."

"Despite what I said the other night, I prefer to fuck married men."

I'm barely able to choke out my response. "Why's that?"

"Less complications. I get to enjoy your company for a while, get the shit fucked out of me, then she has to deal with you the rest of the time. And I get a little thrill out of it, too. I'm fucking her man."

"You get me so hot talking that way."

"Which way?" she asks, with an air of mock innocence.

"Talking about fucking me."

"You like to hear me say that I'm gonna let you fuck the shit outta me?" she asks, staring intently into my eyes.

"Yeah, very much so."

"I don't think you're one of those good little Christian boys at all. You wanna get a little dirty. You wanna get a little wild. You wanna taste what you've missed all these many years."

"Well....yeah...that may be true."

"Yeah.....thought so."

"So, what are we talking about here?" I ask. "How is this gonna work?"

"Well.....you slip your dick into my..."

"No, no....I mean....what is this gonna be?"

"It might not be anything. Do you think I just pick guys out of the blue and go fuck them in some park then move on to the next one?"

"No.....I don't know....this is just so sudden."

"I'd like more than one night of fucking. A regular arrangement would be nice, provided of course that you satisfy my needs."

"An affair?"

"An arrangement. We meet every so often, but no relationship, no entanglements."

"Good, because I have no intention of leaving Karen."

"I don't want you to, Don."

"So, what will this be......fuck....I can't believe we're having this conversation."

"I don't go around having one night stands. I prefer these sorts of friends with benefits arrangements. I don't want anything serious right now. I want more than sex, but I don't want too much. I'm not saying that we're going to have that. I just want to spend some time with you and see. You're a good prospect."

"So, it's some sort of interview?"

"If you want to call it that. Would you be interested in something regular anyway?"

"I do kind of like the idea."

"Most men do, actually."

"Okay....uh....well....can we schedule the interview for next

Tuesday?"

"You're funny." She laughs. "Why Tuesday?"

"Because Karen doesn't even come home till around ten those nights. She does her nursing home stuff that afternoon after work, then has bible study until nine or so. I can give you the whole evening."

"Sounds perfect."

"How about we meet at Northside park? That's on the Wake Forest side of the lake....off of 98."

"I know where that is. What do you drive?"

"A 1990 blue Toyota truck."

"I've got a gold 96 Camry."

"What time's good for you?" I ask.

"Five?"

"Sounds good."

"You aren't going to pussy out on me are you?"

"Not if you keep talking like that."

"You good at eating pussy?"

"Haven't done all that much of that. Karen decided that oral sex wasn't right, wasn't moral or something."

"So, you aren't getting your dick sucked?"

"No, afraid not."

"Well, if everything works out, I may just be able to take care of that for you. Every man should get a vigorous dick sucking on a regular basis."

"I agree."

"And I'll have to see what sort of oral skills you have. But we can work on that if need be."

"Umm....just the thought of having my head buried between your thighs. I'm getting hard right now."

"Oooooh.....you're coming out of your shell a little, I see."

"Hey, all I need is the ice to be broken."

"We're in the process of melting it," she says, into my ear.

"I can't believe we're gonna do this."

"That's the thing though. I'm not sure you'll have the balls to follow through."

"Well, after Tuesday, you'll know I have the balls. If you know what I mean."

"Yeah....I do know what you mean. You think I'll have those balls dangling on my chin."

"So....can you go balls deep?"

"Well, provided that your dick isn't the longest I've ever

seen…then yeah….balls deep. I can do that."

"We have to stop this. I could fuck you right here….right now. You're bad."

"I'm just trying to keep up with you. What am I unleashing here?"

"I'm just a shy innocent lamb being led to the slaughter."

"Hey…you're the one asking me if I can go balls deep. Shy, my ass."

"Your sweet brown ass," I say, as I rest my hand there, while staring into her eyes.

"And you may just taste this sweet brown ass Tuesday."

"I'll see you Tuesday at five. I'd better go."

"Can't wait."

"I hope I'm a successful applicant for this position."

"I think you will be, as long as you can back up that talk with action."

Chapter 57

Tuesday July 22ⁿᵈ, 2002

"Wasn't sure you'd show up," says April, as I come up to join her at a picnic table overlooking Falls Lake.

"No, you've got me hooked. I had to come."

"Hopefully, if everything goes well, we'll both come."

"What am I gonna do with you?"

"Maybe, just maybe, anything you want to do with me."

"What is it about me though? I still can't get over that."

"Well, first of all...don't fool yourself," she says. "I have fucked quite a few guys in my time."

"That makes me feel quite special."

"Wait a minute there. I'm not a slut. I just look at sex differently than some do."

"I didn't call you a slut."

"Like I told you, I don't fuck every guy I meet. I am somewhat selective. But honestly, I think you could say that I look at sex the way many guys do. I'm gonna get as much as I can, without being a slut, hopefully."

"I'm sorry....I'm not complaining, actually."

"Like I said the other day, I'd prefer some sort of arrangement. I want someone who I enjoy talking to and like to be around. When I'm in an arrangement with a guy, I don't fuck anyone else. But I do move from arrangement to arrangement quickly if the guys can't hold my attention. Understand?"

"I like the word, arrangement."

"It's an honest way of describing what I want."

"So, I definitely don't have to worry about entanglements?"

"No, most definitely not."

"So...why did I make the cut?"

"I don't know....you're sweet, intelligent. I'm kind of charmed by your inexperience, too. I just like you. I think you make a bigger deal out of it than it is. To me, it's like selecting someone to say....I don't know...play tennis with. You know what I mean?"

"Yeah, I do," I say. "But this is new for me. I'm just not used to women being turned on by me."

"Believe me, plenty are attracted to you. You just have

something going on with your self-esteem where you don't see it."

"Not sure it's self-esteem."

"But you don't see yourself the way others do."

"I know. The shyness puts a tint on everything. I know that logically. But it leaves me being unsure about what people think of me."

"Well, I think you're hot."

"Is this really gonna happen?"

"Do you want it to happen?"

"Yeah, I do."

"What do you wanna do? Wanna get in my car? Wanna find a secluded spot on the water somewhere?"

"I happen to have this fantasy about fucking out in the open...in public," I say. "But I really can't afford to get arrested."

"But it would be fun. I like that idea, too."

"Well, if we were to find a spot in the trees down by the lake...that would be kind of safe....but still in public."

"I have a blanket in the car. I'll grab it."

"I didn't even think about it. Never have the need. Do I need to wear a condom?"

"Are you scared of getting something from me? I'm clean."

"No, it's just that I can't have you getting pregnant. After my denying children to Karen there's no way she could handle me getting someone else pregnant."

"Do you really think I wouldn't be on birth control? You aren't exactly going to be my first fuck."

"Okay."

"I don't want anything between your dick and my sugar walls."

"God...you get me so fucking hot."

"Then let's get the blanket and find us a spot," she says, as we go over to her car and retrieve the blanket.

"There are quite a few people here today," I say.

"Worried about someone you know seeing us?" she asks, as we start down a trail.

"No, just can't believe we're going to be doing this with so many people around."

"I've fucked in public places before. Fucking on the beach is the best. As long as you watch the sand," she says, laughing. "It gets in all the wrong places."

"It's the thrill of getting caught, without actually getting caught."

"Exactly. The chance of being seen, but not really wanting to be seen."

"Over there looks like a good spot," I say, pointing to a little spot on the water, hidden by a stand of bushes.

"I like this," she says. "Nice quiet cove. Don't see any boats anywhere near, either."

"Yeah....nice spot," I say, as I lay out the blanket.

"Yeah, nice spot," she says, as she sits down. "You gonna join me?"

"Yeah...sure," I say, sitting down.

"Nervous?"

"Yeah...the closer we get."

"Well, let's just break the ice," she says, kissing me.

"Ummm.....yeah...ice is broken," I say.

"Isn't that what you need with women? Didn't you say you just needed an icebreaker?"

"Yeah...I said that."

"Now...let me give you what you're been missing," she says, as she unzips my shorts. "Oooh....already hard. I guess the ice is indeed broken."

"Hey, I thought we were going to talk some first."

"We already did."

"And you already know all you need to know?"

"No, I'm getting ready to find out more.....if you'd let me."

"Are you sure?"

"Goddamn it, Don. Will you please, please let me suck your dick?"

"Yes....definitely," I say, as she begins to tease me with her mouth, slowly going farther and farther down.

"Anybody ever tell you that you've got a big fat dick?" she asks.

"Don't stop....and go deep."

"Balls deep? Is that what you want?" she asks, looking up at me, smiling.

"Yeah.....please," I say, as she plunges down onto my dick, indeed going balls deep. "Ooooh......that feels so good. Hold it right there.....ummmm."

"Uh....excuse me, sir.....ma'am....what do you think you're doing?" asks a Wake County Sheriff's deputy, showing up out of nowhere.

"Oh my God," says April, as she comes up from me, wiping

her mouth.

"I knew something like this would happen," I say, as I struggle to pull up my shorts.

"How'd you know we were down here?" she asks.

"We've had a problem with people having sex in the open in this park recently. I've learned to read the signs. I was out in the parking lot observing."

"What gave us away?" asks April. "If I may ask?"

"You came in two different vehicles. You spoke briefly. Then you went into the woods with nothing but a blanket. I wasn't sure. But it was worth checking out."

"Are we getting arrested?" I ask.

"I could. It is illegal. There are kids who use this park, sir."

"I know....we even mentioned how many people were here today. We just thought that this was secluded enough," I say.

"Doesn't matter, sir."

"Please officer....let us go. We get the message," says April.

"Absolutely! We'll never do this again," I add.

"Well, you weren't as blatant as some of these people are. Many of them just do it in their cars. Tell you what...I'll let you off with a warning. But if I catch you again....."

"Don't worry....you won't," I say. "I've learned my lesson."

"Me too, sir," adds April.

"Might I add, sir...that you're a lucky guy. Just get a room or something."

"Okay," I say, as the officer leaves.

"I cannot believe that," she says. "He followed us out here."

"Yeah....but it sounds like they've been having problems."

"I think he's a pervert looking for a peek. Did you hear what he said to you?"

"But I am a lucky guy."

"That was his way of saying he wanted his dick in my mouth."

"I wonder how long he was watching?" I ask.

"What do you wanna do?" she asks. "Wanna go somewhere else? Wanna see about getting a room?"

"I don't know.....this is kind of a boner killer."

"I can coax you back to life," she says, giving me a kiss.

"I don't think so....at least not today."

"At least not today? What the fuck does that mean? You're having second thoughts just because we got caught? I think it was kinda hot that he caught me with your dick in my mouth."

"Damn, girl, you're just too much."

"Yes, I am."

"I don't know…..that just fucked up the mood for me."

"We could still sit and talk. You seemed to want to talk so bad anyway."

"Let's do it at the picnic tables, just in case our buddy's still hanging around."

"Fuck him," she says. "He ain't coming back."

"Why don't we just take a walk on the trail?" I ask. "We can find another spot to sit."

"That's sounds even better," she says. "Maybe we can find a more secluded spot. And this time make sure we aren't followed."

"Well, we'll see about all of that," I say, as we start walking on the trail.

"Come on, you must have gotten some sort of thrill out of getting caught. Must have made you feel like such a stud to be caught with your dick down my throat?"

"Well, once I knew we weren't getting arrested, yeah, I guess a little."

"I knew you had a little freak in you."

"If you don't mind me asking, how did you get such a free-spirited attitude when it comes to sex?"

"I really don't know actually. I've just always looked at sex as something to just fucking enjoy. Why do we make such a big deal about it? I just look at it as some sort of sport I happen to love to play."

"Why don't we go over here," I say. "There's a little side trail here that goes to a bluff overlooking the lake. It's very secluded."

"So, you do want more?"

"Well, let's just see what happens."

"Oh, using my line on me now, huh?"

"Yeah, I guess."

"Oh, this is nice and secluded," she says, as we come to the spot. "And we can even see the trail coming in, so we can see if anyone's coming."

"Exactly."

"You devious little devil."

"I might be planning on raping you."

"Rape away."

"Just kidding."

"Do you have rape fantasies? Is that part of your spank bank?"

"Spank bank?"

"You've never heard that term before?"

"No."

"A spank bank is whatever fantasies you guys have stored in your little brains that you jack off to."

"No, no rape fantasies in there.....but I do kinda like the idea of a woman that has to have sex with someone. It isn't forced. But she really doesn't want to do it. You know what I mean?"

"Like if she loses a bet or something?"

"Yeah, I use that one specifically, sometimes."

"Damn, the more I find out about you the more I like."

"Do women masturbate the way men do?"

"You mean as often?"

"Yeah."

"I think it depends on the woman. I, personally, can't keep my fingers out of my pussy. But some women just seem to have this uptight thing about masturbating where they don't think they should be doing it or something."

"It's like an essential bodily function or something for men."

"So, Don, why are you here? Why are you willing to have this arrangement with me? What void will I be filling?"

"I haven't really put any thought into it. You just kinda intoxicated me somehow."

"So, you're drunk on little ole April?"

"Yeah....you just seem to push all the right buttons."

"I told you that part of the reason I like fucking married men is the satisfaction of knowing that I'm fucking someone else's man."

"Yeah, I remember."

"It's not that I'm vindictive or sadistic or anything. I don't know....it just makes it more interesting somehow, more complicated, yet simple at the same time. I just wonder what makes men want to step out on their women. I just wonder what need I'm fulfilling that their wife isn't giving them."

"I never thought I'd cheat, really. This just kinda happened."

"You think some of it is that you have some wild oats left to sow from not getting any action all those years?"

"Probably so."

"You have to have so much pent up inside of you, just waiting to explode."

"Explode all over your face."

"Goddamn it, man. You're about wide open, aren't you?"

"Just trying to keep up with you."

"Yeah, you do have quite a bit built up inside you."

"Yeah, I have to admit that I'd probably like to fuck almost every woman I see."

"Then why the fuck did you get married?"

"That's a long story. I met Karen and got saved all at the same time. It just changed my whole life."

"When did this drunken one night stand happen?"

"It was actually after I'd started talking to Karen. We weren't dating yet."

"So, Karen wasn't your first?"

"No, this girl Gina was. And that was after I'd told Karen that I was a virgin. A statement I never bothered to alter, by the way."

"So, Karen thought she was the first?"

"Exactly. Word actually got around to her before the wedding. That damn Gina has a big mouth. But I denied it."

"Well, word won't get out about us.....I'll promise you that."

"Why is it that you don't want a relationship? Why is it that all you want are these arrangements?"

"Love isn't all it's cracked up to be, at least romantic love. It's just too possessive. Been there, done that."

"So, you've been in relationships where the man's controlled you?"

"Don't try to get too deep into my head. There just aren't too many men who're willing to let their woman have a little fun on the side. That's all it is. This is the best way for me to indulge my desires at this point in my life."

"And I would guess, with the man being married, that he doesn't have too much leverage in trying to control you."

"That's right. I have all the leverage. I have the control."

"It is too bad that we have all of these hang ups when it comes to sex. Like you said, why can't we just treat it as a sport?"

"A sport that I'm damn good at."

"I'll bet."

"So, you ready to really find out?"

"Yes, I am."

"Fuck me on the rock over there."

"I think you have a little unfinished business first."

"That I do.....that I do," she says, as she unzips my shorts.

Chapter 58

Wednesday July 30th, 2002

"Hey, man, how's it going?" I ask, as I come into Mark's den.

"About the same."

"Okay."

"Hey, I've been meaning to ask but when are those bastards gonna let me come back to work."

"Where is this coming from?"

"What do you mean? I need something to do. That's where this is coming from."

"I don't know," I say, as I sit. "They wouldn't even think of letting you come back unless you're one hundred percent. And it has been three years, you know?"

"What does that mean?"

"It just means that most places don't hold your job that long."

"Have they filled my spot?"

"No, but that's not the point."

"What is the fucking point then?"

"It just isn't going to happen."

"I know that me getting to a hundred percent ain't gonna happen. But I can do things. I just need a little help."

"It doesn't have anything to do with what you can and can't do. They're worried that you may get hurt and then sue them or something."

"I could sign something saying I wouldn't sue."

"It just ain't gonna happen."

"Those bastards. Don't they realize that my whole life is getting ruined?"

"There are other jobs you could get. There are places that would hire someone with a disability."

"I don't want to sit around somewhere doing some simple task over and over again. I want something that uses my mind a little."

"I know....but you may have to be patient."

"Well....at least I know there isn't any point sitting around waiting for them now."

"Yeah…you can close the book on the mill."

"They haven't even talked to me," he says. "How would they know how I was doing? None of those bastards has even bothered to call me since maybe the first few months after the accident."

"I asked Bob when we were at the town picnic if it were possible for you to come back. Then we even talked to Max. He said there was no way."

"Who are Bob and Max again?"

"Bob is the head of the shop. Max is the plant manager."

"Okay….I forgot."

"But the point is that I did talk to them."

"So, you told them I wasn't fully recovered?"

"Of course I did, because you aren't."

"You could have lied."

"You don't think they could figure it out?" I ask. "Besides, they would require something from a doctor saying you were one hundred percent recovered before they would let you back. You have to let this go. It's been three years."

"Well…whatever…..fuck em anyway."

"I say the same thing actually, fuck em!"

"So what's new with you?"

"Well, actually….I did something kind of stupid."

"What?"

"Well, there's this girl who's the new librarian."

"Which library?"

"The library downtown," I say. "We only have the one."

"Oh…okay."

"But anyway…..she was at the town picnic a couple of weeks ago…"

"Down at the park?"

"Yeah…down at the park. But she's really hot. She was flirting with all of the guys…."

"Which guys?"

"It doesn't really matter…..just some of the guys from the plant. But that isn't important really."

Mark is almost impossible to talk to anymore. He constantly interrupts to get clarification on some insignificant point or else he goes off on some tangent because one little thing you may have said spurs on some long lost memory.

"Okay….I just wanted to know who you were talking about," he says, sensing my exasperation.

"Anyway….I was making fun of them for fawning all over her. Then that next Monday several of them go to the library to see her. Jim and I knew that's what they were going for, because they don't read."

"They can't read……really?" asks a shocked Mark.

"No….they are able to read….they just aren't in the habit of reading. So we knew they weren't going to the library to get books."

"Oh…okay….I get it."

"So I'm making fun of these guys, even talking about how bad this is to do with them being married and all…."

"What….married and going to the library?"

"No, married and fawning all over this hot girl."

"Okay….uh…what's her name?"

"It's April."

"Pretty…..like the month."

"Yeah…I guess so," I say. "But I ended up going to the library."

"Did you need some books?"

"No….I went to see April. I just had to see for myself."

"You're not happy with…..uh…..your wife…sorry…I can't seem to remember her name…"

"Karen."

"Yeah….okay…Karen."

"I don't know….we don't do all that much together anymore."

"I'm sorry….I didn't know."

"I don't know why I was so interested in April. But anyway, I went and we talked for a while. She was flirting with me big time."

"What was she doing?"

"Bobbing her hair in my face….touching my hand. Stuff like that."

"Bobbling her hair in your face?"

"Yeah, she has long curly hair. She would whip it around so that it would get in my facc."

"That's flirting?"

"Yeah….I think it was."

"I don't know, man, I don't think she's as into you as you seem to think."

"Well, she said she wanted to see me outside of the library."

"Where? On the street or something."

"She was basically saying that she wanted to see me so that we could have sex."

"Oh…okay."

"So we met."

"Where?"

"It doesn't matter," I say. "It was at a park."

"A park? Why at a park?"

"I don't know…it's just what I thought about."

"Seems odd. Why not get a room?"

"Because we hadn't quite decided yet what we were going to do."

"Thought you said she wanted to fuck you."

"She did."

"Then why not get a room?"

"We just didn't. Anyway….we went to this park. We found a spot in the woods….near the water…."

"Water? What water? The river?"

"What difference does it make?"

"I just want to know."

"It was the goddamn lake."

"Which lake? Falls or Kerr?"

"Falls."

"Okay."

"So….we find this spot. So we start kissing….then she unzips my pants. She starts sucking my dick…"

"I would really like to get my dick sucked," he says, wistfully.

"Okay…fine….but just as she starts to work on it…this cop shows up. He just appeared out of nowhere."

"Fuck….what did he do?"

"He asked us what the hell we thought we were doing."

"He saw her sucking your dick?"

"Yeah he saw it."

"What did she do?"

"Well…she didn't keep sucking….that's for sure."

"Did you get arrested?" asks Mark, laughing.

"I'm sure that would amuse you quite a bit if I had been."

"So, he let you go?"

"Yeah…just warned us to not do it again."

"So you didn't get a piece of April's ass?"

"Well, actually……we just found a better spot."

"So, you did fuck her?"

"Damn, is she something," I say. "We did it all up on this bluff overlooking the lake."

"A bluff?"

"Yeah, you know, a cliff, rocks and all of that shit."

"Oh, okay."

"First, she finished the job on my dick. The girl has no gag reflex whatsoever. She took me completely down her throat. Balls deep."

"Balls deep?"

"Yeah, she had my dick in her mouth all the way to the balls."

"Wish someone would go balls deep on me."

"Well, after that, while I was recovering, getting ready for another round, I ate out her pussy."

"Was it good?"

"Damn right. Made the girl come."

"Come where?"

"No, come....as in ejaculate?"

"She ejaculated?"

"No, she came," I say. "She had an orgasm."

"So, what happened after that?"

"Then we fucked. I leaned her up against a rock and laid the pipe to her."

"And all of this was outside there in the open?"

"Yeah, but it was a secluded spot."

"Any cops show up this time?"

"No, we made sure we weren't followed this time. And we had a clear view of the trail leading to where we were."

"So, what's going on?" he asks. "Are you gonna leave Karen and be with this girl?"

"No, that's the thing. This girl doesn't want a relationship. She calls it an arrangement. She just wants to meet to fuck every so often."

"I need an arrangement."

"I do kind of like the idea."

"So, you're gonna do it?"

"I don't know, really," I say. "I know I shouldn't. But this girl is just so fucking hot. But, I really think she's trouble."

"I wish I had that sort of trouble."

"I really didn't think I would follow through with it. After the cop caught us, I was sure that I wasn't going to do it."

"Yeah, I'm amazed you did go through with it."

"Yeah, normally I would have taken that as a sign or something, something to break the spell I was under," I say, shifting gears slightly. "You know, I feel like I live a charmed life sometimes. It just seems like when I'm getting ready to make a wrong turn or something that something intervenes to make me go another way. But this time….well….I just ignored it."

"Well, it's easy to ignore any sort of sign if your dick's in a girl's mouth."

"Yeah, that had something to do with it. It was actually a thrill getting caught."

"I wish something would intervene to make me stop when I'm doing something stupid….like that goddamn accident."

"I don't know….things just seem to fall into place for me."

"My life is just the opposite. Nothing has fallen into place."

"But even with things working out basically….well….I'm still not happy," I say.

"Not happy? You've got much more than I do. How can you not be happy?"

"Maybe it takes different things for different people. We all have holes that need to be filled. Maybe you just have to keep looking until you find whatever it is that will fill your particular hole."

"Well, I would love to have your life."

"I know. By most measures I should be happy. But I'm not."

"So, what are you looking for?"

"I still want to do something different with my life," I say. "I'm not even sure what that means. I'm just stuck in a rut. It's been that way my whole life. I just know that I need some sort of radical change. But I seem to shrink back from every opportunity I've ever had."

"What kind of opportunity have you shrunk back from?"

"Well, our little pot business, for instance. I look at it in one way, as something intervening to stop me from being stupid, but on the other hand we could have tried again. I think we could have done it."

"Pot business? What kind of pots?"

"We were growing pot. Don't you remember?"

"Marijuana?"

"Yeah."

"When did this happen?"

"It's not important. I was just using that as an example of my aborted plans. It was years ago."

"Where did we grow it? Where did we get the idea to do that?"

"Just some book that your brother left behind when he died."

"What were we gonna do?" asks Mark. "We were going to be drug dealers or something?"

"That was the plan."

"Hmm….that's something that I could still do."

"It's a stupid idea. We would have just ended up in prison."

"Then why are you saying that maybe you should have followed through with it?"

"I'm just saying that maybe someone isn't intervening to save me from myself," I say. "Maybe I'm just too big of a pussy to make any major changes in my life, too shy to step out and really live my life, too scared to take any goddamn risks. Maybe I should just do this with April. Maybe that's what I need."

"I took risks and look where it got me."

"Yeah..I know…but not the same sort of risks."

"Not to change the subject, but what are you doing this weekend?"

"Why?"

"Just wondering if you wanted to go to the dam and do some fishing. I haven't been in a while. Thought it would be nice to get out and do something."

"Well, the guys are having this big football game Saturday."

"Are you playing?"

"Hell no, they're going to play tackle football. Jim and I thought it may be entertaining to watch those idiots kill each other."

"Tackle football….hmmm……think they'd let me play?"

"Why the hell would you wanna play?" I ask. "You have a brain injury, you know?"

"What harm could it do? Maybe I'll get hit and it'll jostle something in my head and improve things."

"Are you serious?"

"Yeah….it may work."

"I don't think it works that way."

"Well…fuck it…I wanna try. Where are they playing?"

"At Riverside Park…..uh….one o'clock Saturday afternoon."

"Tell them I'm playing."

"Okay….I think it's not the thing to do….but it's your life."

"Yes…it is my life," he says. "I'm gonna open a serious can of whoop ass on those boys."

"I'm at least glad that you wanna get out."

"I don't mind something like that. I just hate big public things with a lot of people there. I hate crowds."

"I'm not too fond of them myself."

"You should play."

"Fuck that….some of those guys are nuts."

"It's gonna be fun."

"Well, thanks for listening about April."

"Yeah….no problem…I hope I was some help."

"Well….I don't know….I'll have to figure it out for myself."

No, he really isn't any help at all. It's really an effort to have any sort of conversation with him anymore. It's not his fault, it's just the way it is. I really have no one to confide in. I think that's part of the allure of April, she listens to me. She's like me in some ways. We are on the outside looking in. I understand her and she understands me. I know that I'm scarred. I know that I'm damaged. April is scarred and damaged too. But I'm not sure she really knows that's the case yet.

Chapter 59

Saturday August 2nd, 2002

"So, are we ready to see these idiots severely injure and maim one another?" I ask, to Jim and Lisa, as we sit in the bleachers waiting for the game to start.

"Yes, we are," responds Jim.

"It shouldn't be that bad," says Lisa. "This is supposed to be light tackle. They aren't supposed to hit each other full speed or anything. They don't have pads."

"I know…that's what makes it fun," I say.

"They may say they'll keep it light," says Jim. "But once they get going it'll get ugly. Believe me."

"Yeah….we had a bunch of injuries from a golf tournament," I say. "How much more from a tackle football game?"

"The real issue is heat stroke," says Jim. "Why the hell are they playing football in the dead of summer?"

"Because they're idiots," I say. "Football practice has started so they're all in the mood to play."

"I hope Israel isn't hurt," says Lisa.

"Well….I can't believe he's playing, actually," I say.

"David talked him into it," says Lisa.

"And he and Tommy Cash are on opposite teams," adds Jim.

"That happened years ago," says Lisa. "Do you think Tommy still holds some sort of grudge?"

"Is he a racist redneck?" asks Jim.

"Do you see who else is out there?" I ask.

"Yeah…what the fuck he is thinking?" asks Lisa. "Even if this stays light contact, this isn't a good idea for someone with a brain injury."

"He actually thinks it may help him," I say.

"Seriously?" ask Lisa.

"I think he thinks it'll be like you hear with amnesia or something, that if he takes another blow to the head, it may reverse the damage or something."

"That's crazy," says Lisa.

"I doubt seriously that that even happens with amnesia cases," says Jim. "That's just some shit you see in TV or movies."

"Well, he does have a brain injury," I say. "So his thinking isn't as clear as it should be. I just wish I wouldn't have said anything about it."

"Why did you?" asks Lisa.

"I was just answering a question. He wanted to know what I was doing this weekend. He wanted to go fishing."

"That would have been much better," says Lisa.

"Thank you for stating the obvious," I say.

"Sorry."

"Kickoff," says Jim.

"That was one hell of a kick by Israel," I say.

"Soccer," says Lisa.

"David's receiving," I say. "See….look at that. That wasn't exactly a soft tackle that Ronnie put on him."

"Yeah, but he wasn't going full speed, either," says Lisa.

"But what is full speed for most of these guys, anyway?" jokes Jim.

"Why does that girl from the picnic keep looking up here and smiling?" asks Lisa.

"Who?" I ask.

"Her," says Lisa, pointing. "The skank who was coming on to all the men that day."

"Ask Don," says Jim, with a smirk. "She's probably looking at him."

"Don?" asks Lisa, turning to me. "What does she have to do with you?"

"He couldn't resist her," says Jim. "He went off to the library like the rest of them did."

"Rest of them, who?" asks Lisa, seriously. "Was Israel one of them who was sniffing around her like a dog in heat? I knew about the fucking picnic but what's this about the library?"

"Well…yeah…Israel was there," says Jim. "They all rambled over to the library that Monday. But it was Don who really hit it off with her."

"Damn it, Jim!" I say. "Do you have to broadcast this to the whole fucking world?"

"What does that mean?" asks Lisa. "What are you doing messing around with her?"

"I don't know…she just intrigued me. I just wanted to know

what all the fuss was about. So, yeah, I had a moment of weakness and went to the library and talked to her a little."

"And did you find out what all the fuss was about?" asks Lisa.

"She wanted to meet him," adds Jim. "Outside of the library."

"Please?" I ask.

I have to admit that I would do the same thing to him. It's fun to put people on the spot.

"Meet for what?" asks Lisa.

"She just wanted to talk."

"Sure she does," says Lisa.

"I didn't go and I'm not going to go," I say. "It was just a stupid mistake."

I shouldn't have told Mark about what happened. But no one else will know.

"Ooooh....look...a long pass from Ronnie to Israel," says Lisa. "Touchdown!"

"Israel's faster than anyone else out there," I say. "He and Ronnie are going to eat those guys for lunch."

"So...what had you so fascinated with the town tramp?" asks Lisa.

She isn't going to give up.

"Well....I wouldn't call her that," I say. "She is a little flirty. But I don't think she means anything by it."

"Look at it this way, Lisa, at least the library will get used a whole lot more with her there," says Jim.

"Well, I'm gonna nip this shit in the bud when it comes to Israel," says Lisa. "That bastard, panting after her like that."

"They're just weak and helpless men, at the mercy of this sex crazed vixen," says Jim.

"You guys are disgusting. That girl wiggles her ass around a little and you're ready to just forget the women that you've committed to and run around trying to get into her pants."

"Hey, I didn't do anything," says Jim, holding up his hands in surrender.

"Well, fuck, you're the one who should've been, because you don't have a wife or girlfriend," says Lisa.

"I don't exactly have puritan ideas about sex," explains Jim. "But I prefer to have a woman who isn't quite as friendly with men as she is."

"No, you're right, Lisa," I say. "I'm ashamed of it actually. I can't treat Karen that way. In this small town she would almost assuredly find out anyway."

"Yeah, like the town knew about Gina?" asks Lisa.

"Damn. So you know about that, too," I say.

"Yep, known for some time now," says Lisa.

"Yeah, I guess you would. I guess it's almost common knowledge."

I guess I knew Lisa would find out. I know the way people talk in this town. I just didn't want her to know. I guess it's kind of telling that what she thinks of me matters more than what Karen thinks.

"Yes, we all know the whole sorted story," she says.

"That's great," I say.

"Have you ever bothered to come clean to Karen about that?" asks Lisa.

"Hell no."

I really don't know why I don't tell her now. I'm sure she's known for years. I guess it's so far in the past that it doesn't matter now.

"What would it hurt now?" asks Lisa.

"Probably nothing," I say. "There's really nothing to hurt now."

"What does that mean? Is your marriage that bad?" asks Lisa. "And to go chasing after another woman?"

"I don't know. We just have nothing in common anymore. But I know that isn't an excuse."

"No, it's not," says Lisa.

"I'm just at loose ends lately," I explain. "I have a wife that I can't really talk to. I'm just really alone. I saw a chance to alleviate that a little with April....so....I did."

"Did what?" asks Lisa.

"I mean talking to her," I say.

Jim glances at Don.

"You're very far from alone," says Lisa. "You do have friends."

"Yeah, I guess," I say. "But a wife should be a confidant, someone who you can share just about anything with. I don't have that."

"You two don't really talk?" asks Lisa.

"Most of the issues I'm going through have to do with this church shit," I say. "That shit is all about her. So, no, I can't talk to her about that."

"Well....I do know what you mean," says Lisa. "That is

important. It's nice to have that person who you can go to with anything and everything."

"Look at that!" says Jim. "Israel's eating them up, another long play. Tommy's trying to guard Israel, but he just can't keep up."

"I love it," I say.

"One thing I want to know," starts Lisa. "How is it that a supposedly shy guy like you ends up chasing after that cheap piece of ass like that?"

"And so fast, too," adds Jim.

"You know….I'm not sure," I say. "She's just really easy to talk to. I did have a hard time approaching her though. Jim can attest to that."

"Yeah…he kept circling her in the library that day," says Jim. "It took him quite a little while to actually talk to her."

"Yeah, acted like I needed help finding a book."

"Little shy Don getting mixed up with the town slut," says Lisa, with a smile. "Thought I knew you, but now, I'm not so sure."

"Maybe you don't know me at all."

She glances at me.

"He's a mystery, an enigma," says Jim.

"Jim, you may be right," says Lisa. "There's a lot more to him than I thought."

"Oh shit!" says Jim.

"What?" I ask.

"Ronnie literally flattened Mark after he intercepted his pass," says Jim.

"He's alright," I say. "He got what he wanted. He wanted to get hit big and he did."

"It's been getting a little rougher," says Jim.

"Well, part of that is the fact that they're using beer to keep themselves hydrated," I say.

"Bunch of fucking idiots," says Lisa.

"That they are," I say.

"I want to get back to one thing about this April," says Lisa. "How into her was Israel?"

"He was right there with the other guys," I say. "But we don't know what happened inside the library."

"I think I've about had it with his wandering eyes," says Lisa. "Makes me wonder what else may be wandering."

"Well, he also had a problem with Don seeing Karen when they first started dating," says Jim, hoping to stir the pot a little.

"And that was after we were seeing each other," observes Lisa.

"Yeah….we wondered at the time why it bothered him, if he had you," adds Jim.

"But it's one thing to look, and to talk, but another entirely to actually meet and do something about it," I say.

"But it isn't a difficult journey," says Lisa.

"No, it isn't," I agree. "Not at all."

Jim smiles, while looking straight ahead at the field. The fucker knows.

Chapter 60

Saturday September 7th, 2002

Normally, I don't frequent bars or any of those sorts of places. I'm doing this for Mark. He needs to get out more. The football game a few weeks ago was good for him. But he hasn't really gotten out since. He used to play pool before the accident. He's had the itch to play again, recently. So, with there being no one else to take him, I agreed to bring him down here to Ronnie White's.

"I remember this place," says Mark.

"Yeah, this is Ronnie's place," I say. "He's the one who sold us the pot seeds."

"Pot seeds?"

"Yeah, remember I told you about our little failed pot venture?"

"I must have forgotten," says Mark. "But wait….wasn't this the place that we picked up Cheryl and what was that other girl's name…..?"

"Gina."

"Yeah……you were a virgin and you popped your cherry on Gina."

"Okay…okay…enough of that," I say. "Let's play some pool. And by the way, please don't say anything to anyone about that other girl."

"You mean the girl you fucked in the park?"

"Yeah, yeah. God…why did I tell you?"

"Don't worry. I'll keep it on the down low."

"If you can remember that you're supposed to keep it on the down low."

"I'll remember. Don't worry."

"I just don't want to hurt Karen. I can't have this one getting all over town."

"I know. Don't worry about me."

But I do worry about him. I should have never said anything about April to Mark. He isn't the same person since the accident. I can't rely on him as any sort of confidant. The judgment just isn't there. His memory just isn't good enough, either. He'll just forget that he isn't supposed to say anything. Thank God I do keep Karen and him apart.

"Okay, let's play some pool," I say.

"I'm gonna open a huge can on your ass tonight."

"I will beat you severely with the pool cue, son."

"You're dead meat," says Mark, matter-of-factly. "You know I used to play in a league. Played out of that bar….uh….Shooters I think it was."

"Yeah…I remember," I say, as we walk up to the pool tables where Raeford and Harold happen to be in the middle of a game. "Well, look who the cat dragged in."

"Hey, Don, how's it going down at the plant?" asks Raeford.

"About the same."

"Don't miss it a goddamn bit," says Raeford.

He misses the easy paycheck, I'm sure.

"Well goddamn, if it ain't the kingpins of weed," booms Ronnie. "Ain't seen either of you in this fucking joint in a while. Damn long time it's been."

"Yeah…it's been awhile," I say.

He can't let that weed episode drop, can he? I don't exactly want word of that getting around. Harold, especially, has such a big fucking mouth when it comes to that sort of shit. I guess it doesn't really matter now. It has been nine years. It's just embarrassing.

"Yeah, you haven't been in here since you got all religious and shit," says Ronnie.

"Well, since the football game, Mark's talked about wanting to get out more. And he used to play pool, so I thought I'd bring him down here. It's not like there are many places to play pool around here."

"Well, have a good time, man," says Ronnie. "Good to see you."

"Thanks, Ronnie," says Mark. "Could I have a Bud please?"

"Anything for you, Don?" asks Ronnie.

"Just a coke."

"Alright, I'll send Tina over with your shit. And, it's all on the house tonight."

"Thanks, man," I say.

"Nah, man. It's the least I can do."

"What about us?" asks Raeford.

"What about you, fucking what?" asks Ronnie.

"Where's our goddamn free shit?"

"You ain't getting shit free."

"You would think with how big of a fucking customer as I am, that I would get a free drink once in a fucking while."

"No, with as much as you're in here, you pay my fucking bills," says Ronnie. "No freebies for you."

"Fuck," says Raeford.

"Would y'all be interested in playing a little tournament?" asks Harold. "Maybe for a little money?"

"I used to play on a team," says Mark.

"Yeah, but it's been a long time since you played," I say. "And besides, you've had the accident since then."

"I ain't lost it," says Mark.

He thinks he hasn't lost it. But we don't know that yet. And we'll be playing with my damn money.

"Hey, if you're scared, then we'll just play for fun," says Harold.

"Here are your drinks, guys," says Tina.

I really love Tina's jeans. Or is it what her jeans are doing their mighty best to contain? Why is it that women think men love those little tiny asses? I sure don't. There's nothing better than a round, fat ass. And Tina's is as close to perfection as you can get.

"Whatcha got for me baby?" asks Harold. "With that fine hindquarters of yours."

See? Harold agrees. But isn't that just a fine example of a churchgoing man, deacon in his church, at that. I'll bet his minister wife is proud of him.

"Hindquarters?" asks Mark. "How old are you?"

"Not too old to wipe the table with your sorry, no pool playing, ass," says Harold.

"Are we gonna play or what?" asks Raeford.

"I'll play you any day, Raeford," I say. "You're probably too fucking drunk to do too much of anything."

"In your dreams. Remember....I live in this place."

"Well, that you do."

Yeah, I'd better just look at this as money spent to have a good time. Mark hasn't played since the accident. I haven't played since we had a table in my parent's garage when I was a teenager. Our only hope is that they are too drunk to play worth a shit.

"So, how much we playing for?" asks Mark.

"How about we all put in twenty dollars and we play until three people have two losses?" proposes Harold. "The winner of the first match keeps playing until he loses one."

"Sounds good," says Mark.

"I guess," I say.

"Sounds like someone's scared," says Raeford.

"No, no…..let's do it," I say.

"Who's going first?" asks Harold.

"Maybe it should be our best against your best," I suggest. "Even though we're playing each man for himself."

"Okay, then it's me against Mark," says Harold.

"Who the fucking hell said that you were better than me?" asks Raeford.

"I'm better than you cause I ain't fucking drunk," responds Harold.

"Go ahead and play….it don't matter no shit to me," says Raeford.

"You do the honors, Mark," says Harold.

"Honors?" says a puzzled Mark.

"He means you can break," I explain.

Because of the injury, even seemingly obvious and everyday terms or expressions can cause Mark to draw a blank.

"What are we playing anyway?" I ask.

"Eight ball?" suggests Harold. "Have to call the pocket for the eight."

"Okay," I say, as Harold racks up the balls and Mark prepares to break.

"Well, goddamn…..look who's coming in," says Raeford.

"Shit….it's April," says Harold.

"Hey, Don," says April, as she comes strolling up to us. "How you doing, guys?"

Everyone shifts their attention to April, except for Mark.

"Hey, baby….what's shakin?" asks Harold, as Mark breaks. "Although, I think I can see all the parts that are shaking."

"Yeah, you wish you could shake those parts," says April, smiling, shifting her gaze to me. "If you know what I mean?"

Damn, she has such an effect on me. Just the way she looks at me makes me want to take her out back and just fuck the shit out of her.

"Damn, baby. I sure do," responds Harold. "Bouncing and a shaking all over the place."

"Your shot," says Mark, oblivious to the banter going on. "I didn't sink anything. It's your choice."

"Alright, man," responds Harold, as he prepares to shoot, still distracted by April.

"So, how you been doing, stranger?" asks April, to me.

"Uh….nothing out of the ordinary," I say, nervously. "Are you a regular here or something? What are you doing here?"

I cannot have these guys knowing what happened with her. What is she trying to do?

"Are you a regular here?" she shoots back. "Am I not allowed in here or something?"

"Oh no, baby.....you can come in any time you like," says Harold. "Anytime at all."

"Yeah...any time you like, sweetheart," says Raeford. "Believe me, we can use the change in scenery."

"I just came in here because I saw Don in here as I was passing by," she says, as she touches my hand.

Now I just want to kill her. Discreet, my ass!

"You here to see Don?" asks Harold, obviously stunned.

"I just have a question for him."

"It's your shot again," says Mark.

"Okay, man," says Harold, distracted as hell now.

"Are you gonna keep fucking me or not?" she asks. "Because if you ain't, well, I can find someone else."

And there it is. I knew she was trouble. Jim warned me. I just couldn't stay away from her though.

"Uhh....what....," utters a flabbergasted Harold. As he says this, his false teeth come flying out of his mouth and land on the pool table.

"What the fuck!" shouts Mark, as he proceeds to vigorously smash Harold's dentures with his pool cue.

"What the goddamn hell did you do that shit for, you asshole!" shouts a perplexed Harold. "Do I need to kick your fucking ass?"

"Uh....I don't know.....what is it?" asks a puzzled Mark. "What are they?"

"They were my goddamn false teeth, you motherfucker. Why in the fuck did you smash them?"

"What seems to be the fucking problem?" asks Ronnie, as he comes over.

"This jackass smashed my fucking teeth to bits," says Harold.

"Well goddamn, Harold, if you'd keep the motherfuckers in your fucking mouth then this wouldn't have happened," says Ronnie, starting to laugh. "But I have to ask, Mark...heheheheh...why the fuck did you smash the fuckers teeth?"

"I just didn't know what they were," explains Mark, truly at a loss. "They just came flying out onto the table. I don't know. I just didn't know what the fuck they were."

"But don't they look like fucking teeth?" asks Harold, holding some of the remnants up for Mark to see.

I believe I can explain this. I know Mark and his injury better than anyone else.

"Listen, the guy had a brain injury," I begin. "It does some strange things. That's probably what happened here. His brain just interpreted that in some strange way where he thought the teeth were a threat or something."

"A threat of bacteria maybe," says April.

"I think it's funny as shit, myself," says Raeford, laughing. "He busted those motherfuckers into a thousand goddamn pieces."

"Fuck it, it ain't no big deal," says Harold. "I need another pair anyway. Maybe the new ones will fit better. I guess I understand what you're saying, Don."

"Yeah, man, he just thought they were some wild animal that came out of your mouth or something," adds Raeford.

"I'm sorry," says Mark.

"Forget about it," says Harold.

"Don?" asks April, with an expectant look on her face.

"Yeah?" I respond.

I do know what she wants. I guess I'm hoping for a miracle or something.

"I'm waiting for an answer to my question."

"Oh....uh...," I utter, totally embarrassed now.

It's too bad circumstances aren't different. It would be great to just be able to glory in the fact that I fucked such a hot piece of ass as April. I would love to just rub that little fact right in Harold's face.

"If you don't want to fuck me, I can find plenty of men who will."

"I'll help you out, sugar," offers Raeford.

"Damn, man, what the hell's going on here?" asks Ronnie. "You married to one black chick and you're fucking another one?"

Thanks for pointing that out so clearly, Ronnie.

"No, that's the problem," says April. "He fucked me once but now he acts like he doesn't know me. Sucked his little dick for him and everything."

Despite the scene she's causing, she still gets me so hot talking like that. But what's the comment about sucking my little dick?

"Well, come on, man," says Ronnie. "Don't do the lady like that. Give her what she wants. Or somebody else sure the fuck will."

"It... was a... mistake," I somehow manage to get out.

"What....putting your dick in her sweet little mouth...or fucking her?" asks Ronnie.

"Ever getting mixed up with her," I say. I have to try to minimize this.

"Getting mixed up with me?" asks April, really pissed now. "What exactly the fuck does that mean?"

"I'm married, April."

"And we both were well aware of that when we went to the park. You were well aware of that when you let me start sucking your dick...... before the cop walked up."

She had to add that.

"A cop walked up?" asks Harold. "This just gets better and better."

"Yeah, a cop walked up and caught him with his dick in my mouth ," says April.

I wish a dick was in her mouth now, so she'd stop talking. And by the way, she knows what this does to all of the guys, too, this talking about my dick in her mouth. I guarantee that all of them are getting a little hard with all of this going on.

"Damn, man, I didn't know you had it in you," says Harold.

"What exactly does he have in him?" asks April. "Not so impressive to me."

"I'll leave an impression on you, baby," says Harold.

"Old man, please," says April, raising a palm towards Harold.

"April, I'm sorry, it was just a mistake," I say, hoping to placate her somehow.

"Well, maybe Karen needs to know about our little mistake."

"Well, man, I think I'd fuck her before I'd let her tell my old lady," says Ronnie. "I think I'd fuck her no matter what the deal was."

"No, I'm not begging him," says April. "And don't worry about me telling Karen. I'm not that low, despite what some people may think. There are plenty of fish in the sea. Aren't there, Ronnie?"

"Yeah, baby, you can believe that," says Ronnie.

"You can catch me anytime, sugar," says Raeford.

"I'm outta here," says April. "Don, have a nice life. Learn to follow through on things. It's a good quality to have. Believe me, I would have followed through, and followed through and followed through once again. See ya, guys."

"Damn, Don, I just don't know what to fucking say," says Ronnie.

"He's the man," jokes Mark.

"Great Christian example I'm setting here," I say. "The whole fucking town will know now."

"Hey, she's something, man," says Harold. "Hard to resist. I'm saved too…but damn. I'd fuck that fine brown ass in a second."

"She sure has one nasty mouth on her, doesn't she?" observes Ronnie.

"I like them like that though," says Raeford. "A nasty mouth girl lets you do nasty things to them. How did that mouth feel on your dick, man?"

"I don't want to talk about it," I say, wanting so bad to be able to talk all day long about it.

"She went balls deep on him," says Mark.

"You remembered every detail of this particular thing, didn't you?" I ask.

Memory issues with everything else, but he remembers details of my tryst with April. And I thought he wasn't half listening.

"I've never had a woman that could do that," says Raeford, lost in thought. "Go balls deep, I mean."

"How was it, Don?" asks Harold.

"I'm not talking about this."

"I think we need to drop it," says Ronnie. "The guy's trying to do the right thing. Let's not fuck with him."

"Thanks, Ronnie. And I might be asking a bit much, but could you guys not spread this shit around."

"I think you are asking a lot there, chief," says Raeford. "This is just too fucking juicy. And besides, unless you put a dick in it, she's gonna run that mouth, no matter what she says."

He's right, of course.

"I bet she gives one hell of a fucking blow job," says Ronnie. "That girl's got spirit in her."

"I'll be back in a few minutes," I say. "I need to say something to her. I can't let her leave all pissed off."

I leave Ronnie's quickly, hoping to catch April. I spot her walking down towards the diner. I sprint down to catch her. This is stupid in itself. What if someone sees me running to her?

"April, wait!"

"What the fuck do you want?" she asks, as I catch up with her.

"Not out here," I say. "I can't have any more public spectacles."

"Why the fuck should I want to talk to you?"

"Please? Can we step over there in the alley?"

"Fine."

I get her over in an alley behind the auto parts store.

"I thought I didn't have to worry about you running your mouth about this the way that damn Gina did?"

"You haven't fucking called. You haven't come to see me. Listen, I could've come to your goddamn house."

Her anger even turns me on.

"Listen, despite what I said in there," I say, moving in more closely. "I do want to have our arrangement."

"Then why the fucking silent treatment?"

"Because it's been a tough decision? Can you at least get that? And now you really make me question it with this shit."

"It wasn't so tough that day at the park," she says. "You were quite eager to fuck me that day."

"You're right, but's it's a totally different thing to have an ongoing thing, than it is to just have one encounter."

"But this isn't anything serious."

"Really? Then why the fuck are you making such a goddamn big deal about me not calling you?"

"Because you're ignoring me. I don't have a fucking issue with you not wanting to do it, but at least just tell me that."

"But I hadn't decided not to do it. That's the point."

"You should have said something. You made me feel like a cheap piece of ass doing shit like that."

"That's the last thing I think you are."

"So, what are you saying? Are you telling me you're gonna do this then?"

"Yeah, I want to. I want to so bad. It just drives me fucking crazy even being around you. I guess that's why I stayed away. I wanted to make the decision when I was not exactly in the heat of your passion."

"Sometimes you just need to fuck all the reason and logic and just go with the passion."

"I'm not used to that."

"We'll have to work on that."

"Yeah, I do want to change that about myself. I need to just cut loose sometimes."

"Okay, so, I guess I don't need to start interviewing new candidates?"

"Harold or Raeford would be glad to fill your slot."

"Yeah, fill my slot, funny. I wouldn't fuck those old coots, but that Ronnie....well."

"Maybe you can fuck him after you're done with me."

"Yeah, maybe I will."

"Okay, I'll call you or come by the library. Promise. But we have to keep this discreet."

"Yeah, I'm sorry about that," she says. "I hope those bastards don't tell anyone. I just want you so bad, Don."

"Fuck, I'm not sure I give a shit anymore, actually. But let's still be careful."

I really don't want Karen to hear this from someone on the street. But there's a part of me that just loves the illicit nature of the whole thing. I just felt so alive that day with April in the park.

"I think you like looking like a stud to those guys," she says.

"Not something I'm used to."

"But it suits you. You absolutely did not disappoint me that day in the park. I just wanna get you into the comfort of my bed next time."

"I can't wait to bury my face in that sweet pussy again."

"I don't know how you're so good at that, but damn if you didn't make me come with that tongue of yours. To not have any practice at it and be able to do that to me?"

"Actually, I do have some practice. I was pretty good with Gina that time."

"Karen doesn't know what she's missing out on."

"Yeah, I know. It's stupid."

"Seriously, though. You have some mad skills there."

"You inspire me to do great things, I guess."

"You're funny."

"Well, we better break this up," I say. "I'll call you soon, okay? Or, I'll just come by the library."

"I'll be looking forward to it. Can't wait to feel that big dick pounding the shit outta my pussy again, after you've made me come with that tongue."

"I can't wait. Now, let me get back to Mark. Hope he hasn't smashed anything else."

"That was fucking funny as shit, smashing that old fool's teeth to pieces."

"Yeah, I know."

"Okay, man. I'll be expecting to hear from you."

"You will."

"Can't wait to feel that dick up inside of me."

"I can't wait to feel it down your throat."

"Yeah, shy little Don......my ass!" she says, as she takes off down the alley.

Yeah, shy little Don has indeed come a long way. It's just that the timing was a little off. Why couldn't I run across a girl like April, who doesn't want anything more than a fuck buddy, about ten years ago? Things would have been so different. I have come a long way, but have so much farther to go.

Chapter 61

Later that night.

"What the fuck?" I say, aloud to myself, as I pull into my driveway. I mean, really, what the fuck is this? There's a fucking bonfire going in the yard between my house and the house of my sister in-law, Crystal, and her husband Kevin.

There are people gathered around the fire. I can't seem to make out who they are. As I pull up to my house, Karen walks up, coming from the direction of the fire. Because of the shadows, I still can't tell who everyone is over there. And I have no plans to find out. I have a feeling I'm not going to like what's going on here.

"What in the world's going on?" I ask. "What is this?"

"I'll explain," says Karen. "Maybe we should go inside."

"Okay..." I say. "I can't wait to hear this."

I follow Karen into our house. I turn to see Claude following us.

"Mind if I come in, too?" asks Claude.

"If you're going to help explain why you're out here with a bonfire in my yard in the middle of the night," I say. "What are you burning out there anyway?"

"We're burning things from Crystal's house," says Karen.

"What?"

I really am amazed. I don't know why really. I just never thought I'd see this sort of thing first hand.

"Well....you know that Crystal's been battling an evil spirit lately," says Karen. "She's been chased from the house several times."

"I knew that something was going on," I say. "You told me that."

There's no doubt that the girl's been tormented by something. I heard her outside wailing and screaming bloody murder one night. And Karen isn't kidding about Crystal being chased from the house. One night they left so quickly that they left the front door wide open. I found it that morning.

"Well, son, we found the source of the spirit," says Claude.

"Stuff in the house?" I ask, not believing my ears. I kind of figured that this was what was going on, but to hear it is something else entirely.

"Stuff in the house that's associated with Sister Carrie," says Claude.

"Sister Carrie, the pastor of your church?" I ask.

"No, baby, I told you, we stopped going there a while back," explains Karen. "But Kevin and Crystal kept going."

I've actually spoken to Sister Carrie. We agree on quite a few things, actually.

"I tried to tell my son that Sister Carrie was a false teacher," says Claude. "But Crystal wanted to keep going."

"Sister Carrie is the one that took over for you," I say.

"No, her family decided that I didn't need to be pastor anymore," says Claude. "I was ousted. I knew then that something wasn't right with them."

"I still don't understand what you're burning though....and why," I say.

"Sister Carrie gave Crystal and Kevin some bedroom furniture," says Karen.

"So...you're burning that furniture because you think it has evil spirits from Sister Carrie?" I ask, sounding agitated, I'm sure.

"It does, son," says Claude. "This is completely scriptural. Evil spirits can hide in objects."

"Wow....I can't believe this is actually happening," I say. "You have got to be kidding me."

"It's all biblical, son," says Claude.

"You know....while you're at it, you might as well burn all of my stuff, too," I say. "Because I've heard the things that Sister Carrie's saying and I think she's right on the money."

"She's peddling a false message that's destructive to the body of Christ," says Claude. "You shouldn't be listening to her."

I'm actually not listening to her. I already believed the things she's teaching before I heard what she was teaching.

"Do you really want to talk about false messages?" I ask. "Then what about this? Is this really biblical? Do you really think that we have to fear evil spirits hiding in furniture?"

It really is the most primitive of ideas.

"Don't doubt the existence of spirits, Don," says Claude. "They are very real."

"I don't doubt the existence of spirits at all. But we don't have to burn things to be protected from them. Do you really believe in a God who would leave us at the mercy of spirits living in all kinds of objects? I believe in a God who protects me no matter what's around me."

"I see what you're saying, but in some instances this is what needs to be done."

"The simple truth is that I believe in a God that is more powerful than that," I say. "Besides, there are verses in scripture that speak directly against this sort of thing. And they're in the New Testament. You may want to read that sometimes."

"No need to get shitty with me," says Claude.

What did I just here?

"Why are you so surprised?" asks Claude. "Aren't you the one saying that cuss words don't matter?"

I can see that Karen is stunned.

"Yeah, well, I do believe that," I say. "I'm just surprised to hear it from you."

Maybe there is hope for him.

"Where are these verses you say speak against what we're doing here tonight?" asks Claude.

"The verses that say that food sacrificed to idols has no power over us."

"No, that's not the same thing."

"Of course it is," I say. "If food that was sacrificed to idols was alright for Christians to eat back in the day, then we can surely sit on furniture that was once used by a supposedly false teacher."

Why is it that these people cannot seem to connect the dots? They always take things so fucking literally.

"It's not, supposedly. She is most definitely a false teacher."

"Not in my book, she's not," I say. "What does she teach? She simply teaches that holiness is possible, that we can live a sin free life."

I feel like such a fucking hypocrite right now. But I can't just lay down and take this nonsense.

"She's putting an unattainable burden on people," says Claude. "They think this is possible, then when they can't live that way, they fall away from God. That teaching is from the devil."

"It's from the bible," I say. "I see the same thing she does."

"She's corrupted you then."

"No, I came to that conclusion through the simple reading of scripture. No special revelation necessary. This is what scripture says."

"Your mind has been influenced by deceiving spirits, son."

"I'm more in line with scripture than you are."

At least this is true in what I believe, not so much in how I'm living right now.

"You're in error, son. You don't even go to church."

"I think I've made this point before. There's a passage of scripture that says we have no need for any man to teach us. We get everything we need from the holy spirit."

"But you are not to forsake the assembly of God's people. That means going to church."

"No, the scripture says that we are to make sure we do not forsake fellowship with other believers. It says nothing about going to a church. We've had this conversation before."

"You're in error, son."

"Whatever."

"Okay....I'll just leave," says Claude, as he heads for the door. "It's obvious that you're deceived, son. You may not realize it now, but you are."

"That's fine, Claude. I'll just be deceived then."

Just as Claude's leaving, Crystal and Kevin come to the door.

"Don, I have a word from the Lord for you," says Crystal.

"Oh, you do?" I ask.

My irritation with this is surely showing on my face. How can she presume to have a word from the Lord for me, after this shit they're pulling out there?

"Please, baby, just hear her out," says Karen.

"Okay, go ahead," I say.

"I just want to let you know that the Lord loves you, but he wants you to know that you're in error," says Crystal.

This is actually true. But I'm sure she means something else entirely.

"What does that mean?" I ask. "In error about what?"

"That's all I was led to say," says Crystal. "That you're in error. You need to get on the right track. The Lord sees all. The Lord knows all."

"Okay...whatever," I say, trying to sound dismissive, but actually feeling a little freaked out by what Crystal just said. The Lord knows all? The Lord sees all? Yeah, he does, doesn't he?

"I'm just telling you what the Lord gave to me," says Crystal.

"Just make sure the fire's out before you go to bed," I say. "Unless of course you want to burn this ole heretic's house to the ground, while you're driving out the evil spirits."

"Don!" says Karen.

"Goodnight, and God Bless," says Crystal, as they leave.

"I cannot believe that you're a part of this thing," I say to Karen. "I thought I was starting to get through to you some."

"I don't totally agree with it," says Karen. "I just went along, just being supportive."

"I just cannot explain to you how unscriptural this whole thing is…..and then for Crystal to come in and say that I'm the one in error? But….I know where that's coming from. I dare to speak ill of some of the great TV preachers that some of you love so much. I dare to call a spade a spade. So…well….I guess I am in error. I'm really surprised that I wasn't included in this little witch hunt."

I would have been if they really had any sort of real supernatural gift. The spirit obviously isn't letting them know that I'm fucking April.

"It wasn't a witch hunt," says Karen.

"But can you imagine what Carrie and her family are going to think if they hear about this?" I ask. "You went to church with those people for years. And now you're burning their furniture like they're some sort of devil or something. Do you know how much that'll hurt them?"

"I hope they don't find out."

"I hope so, too," I say. "God, no wonder people think Christians are nuts."

"We aren't nuts. That's not fair."

"You know what's so funny?" I ask. "Is that I'm the one who's looked at as being the charlatan or whatever, but you're the ones who believe all of the false stuff. I'm just saying what I see in scripture, but I'm the one in error, all because I don't have the anointing. As long as I don't have this anointing that you talk about, you'll never accept what I say as being the truth, even though it's right there in scripture for everyone to see."

"I never said that. I've never said that I thought you were a false teacher or something."

"But I know it's what you all think. Why can't Don just get with the program? Why can't he just believe what we believe? I know that's what goes through your mind."

"But don't you think that when so many people believe something that that has to mean something? Are you saying that we're all wrong? Are you saying that all of these great men of God are wrong?"

Just imagine how wrong and absurd this would seem if she knew what I did in that park that day. Me, the great prophet of God, with my dick in April's mouth.

"Well, I'll tell you that, yes, most of these TV preachers are absolutely false teachers. And the thing is that anyone can see it. People who aren't even Christian can see it. They peddle the word of God for money. They live in luxury. They make false prophecies. They teach things that a little kid could tell you isn't consistent with scripture. It's obvious. But because they have this so-called anointing, some feeling that you have, well, they have to be men of God. I don't accept that and never will."

"I'm not saying they're right about everything."

"But they're more right than I am?"

"Well...."

"How about actually living according to the book that you all say you believe in? I'm not claiming to have any special knowledge. I just read, and believe what I read. It's just simple understanding. But too many of these preachers claim that you have to have some special gift to understand what's written in the bible. They then try to explain away the difficult passages, the stuff that they don't want to live. Explain away the stuff that tends to punch holes in the little kingdoms that they've set up for themselves."

"It's not just about the written words on the page. It's also about the spirit leading us to truth."

"Then why does the spirit that you all claim to have never seem to lead you to the simple truth that I see? Why does the spirit let you do something like tonight? This was so far from the truth that it makes me sick. You're burning furniture because it belonged to someone who you believe is teaching something that isn't right? Are you gonna do that to everyone that believes the wrong thing?"

"Crystal was being tormented by evil spirits. That's different."

"But you really believe that those spirits came from Sister Carrie?"

"Well....I don't know."

"But you participated anyway. Because...I guess....the group can't be wrong? Is that it?"

"I'm not a pastor. I trust what my pastor says. I trust where the spirit was leading him."

"Just think about this though. Do we know who made any of the things in our home? How do we know that some devil worshipper wasn't working in the plant that made our TV? That's why this is so stupid. Do you really think an all-powerful God would leave us exposed to attack like that?"

"Honey, I don't know."

"Well, that's the thing…I do know. This one just isn't open to debate."

"Why don't we just go to bed now? It is late."

"I'm gonna watch TV for a while. I'm a bit wound up right now."

"Okay, honey. But I'm worn out. I'm gonna go lay down."

"Fine."

This might just be the last straw. This is just so outrageous. This is the kind of shit you see in movies. It's like they were on a witch hunt. Sure, I'm far from the perfect one to be trying to talk some sense into them. This is especially true after my telling April that I was prepared to be her regular fuck buddy. But I just can't let them win. I just can't. I just cannot stand the self-righteousness any longer.

Chapter 62

Thanksgiving Day, 2002

"Well....who we waiting on?" asks an impatient Hugh, as my family prepares to sit down for Thanksgiving dinner.

That's right. Hugh is back. I guess we're giving him another chance to not make a total ass out of himself. We're just doing it for Grandma, I'm sure? Otherwise, we'd probably just take him out back and beat the shit out of him.

"Dan and Steve are on the way," answers Dad.

"Steve, who's that?" asks Hugh.

Hugh has been banished from family functions for years now. This recent thaw is out of respect for Grandma's advancing years. We obviously don't want to deny her the chance to be with her family as much as possible. And it's awkward for her to leave him at home all the time.

"He's Dan's partner," says Momma.

"Partner....business partner?" asks Hugh. "Why would he be coming to Thanksgiving here?"

That ass is up to it already, unless, of course, dementia has set in. I'm sure Grandma has told him who the fuck Steve is by now. He's just doing this to stir up shit.

"Steve is his life partner," says Momma. "They were married several years ago."

"Oh....well.....damn," utters Hugh.

"Hugh, you're invited because you're married to my mother, we wanted to give you another chance, but you had better not make any comments," says Momma. "Dan is our son and we support him fully."

"Why wasn't I invited to the wedding?" asks Hugh. "I don't remember the first thing about it."

He really is such a dick.

"Hugh, we knew how you'd feel," says Momma. "What was the point?"

"Well...I don't..." starts Hugh, before Momma cuts him off.

"No, that's fine. You can have your viewpoint. But just respect ours as long as you're in this house."

"That's fine," says Hugh. "I do have some manners, despite what some may believe about me."

Manners? Is he really serious?

"There they are now," says Melody, as Dan and Steve come through the hall into the family room.

"Hello, everyone," says Dan.

"Nice to see everyone," says Steve. "But I don't think I've met you."

Steve extends his hand to Hugh. Surprisingly, Hugh takes it.

"I'm Hugh, Marie's husband."

"Well, I guess you know that I'm Dan's husband."

"Husband?" says Hugh, under his breath to Grandma. "What the hell is that? Does that mean that Dan's the wife?"

"Hugh, please?" pleads Grandma, in exasperation.

"Just a little joke, honey."

"Shall we eat now?" asks Momma.

"And then some football," I say.

"That's right," agrees Dan.

"You like football, Steve?" I ask.

I should know that already, but I have to admit that I haven't made all that much of an effort to get to know Steve. I really don't know all that much about the guy.

"No, that's something we don't have in common," says Steve. "I don't care for sports all that much."

"No, he's the wife," whispers Hugh, to Grandma, as we all take our places around the table.

"So, Steve, what do you do for a living?" asks Hugh. "Sorry, that's kind of predictable, isn't it?"

"Yeah, a little, I guess," says Steve. "I'm the CEO of a firm in Raleigh, advertising firm."

"Wow….we know who's got the money in this family then," says Hugh. "Both of you are hauling down the big bucks."

"Well, we do alright, I guess," responds Steve.

"That's one thing I'll say about you guys," says Hugh. "Gays seem to have better jobs on average than the straights. Maybe it's because you ain't got kids to worry with. Can focus more on the career."

"I'm not even sure that's true," says Dan. "Do we really have better jobs?"

"Better jobs than these two here," says Hugh. "But they'll have to do something soon. That plant's doomed."

Notice that Hugh totally ignored the fact that Karen works at the plant as well as Mel and I. There are three of us here who work at that plant.

"I certainly live to make you proud, Hugh," I say, sarcastically.

"Well, you're certainly doing a shitty job of it," says Hugh, glancing quickly at Karen.

"Speaking of kids," starts Grandma, hoping to stop the current line of conversation. She directs a question at me. "When are we gonna see some kids from you two?"

"Who? Us?" I ask. I know she wasn't talking about Dan and Steve.

"Miss Marie, I've been trying to get him to do it, but maybe you can do some good," says Karen. "I would love some kids."

Here we go with this fucking relentless pressure to conform. The truth is that I never want kids. But Karen doesn't know that yet. It's been nine years. I would have thought that everyone would have gotten the message by now, including Karen.

"You've been married for almost ten years now," says Grandma. "When am I getting some great grand babies?"

It might be a while, Grandma. Mel isn't married and Dan's gay.

"I just don't feel like we're ready yet," I say. "Or maybe I'm the one who isn't ready. I don't know."

I do know. I just don't have the courage to say so.

"You'll never be ready, not really," says Momma. "There is no perfect time."

"Well, sorry, I just feel like it's such a big decision," I say. "I have to be fully committed before I can do that....before I can take that step."

I realize as I'm saying this how empty it must really sound. After all these years, how can I not be ready? How much more committed could I be? Can they all see how dysfunctional my marriage really has become? Don't they see that this is the real reason there are no kids?

"Are you two planning on adopting some children?" asks Hugh, to Dan and Steve.

"We haven't really talked about it, but who knows?" says Steve, with a smile to Dan. "I think we could offer a great home to kids."

"Hmmmm....," utters Hugh. "Different world we live in today."

"Yes it is, Hugh," says Dan. "And I'm glad of it."

"No....I don't mean any harm," says Hugh. "Just don't think

it's right to raise a kid in that environment when there are normal families available."

Normal? What is normal anymore?

"What environment?" asks Dan. "A loving and supportive environment?"

"An environment with an alternative lifestyle, as they say," says Hugh.

"It isn't a lifestyle, it's who we are," says Dan.

"It's not a choice," adds Steve.

"Hugh, why must we always go down this road with you?" I ask. "Anybody with an ounce of sense would know that nobody would choose to be gay. With all of the crap that comes with it, why would they choose it?"

"Are you saying they're born that way?" asks Hugh.

"This isn't the place for this," says Dad.

"No, but I do know that it isn't a choice," I say.

"Enough," says Dad. "Can we please have a nice dinner without all of this?"

"Fine," says Hugh. "I'll shut up."

"If only you would," I say.

"Donald, end it now," warns Dad.

After this, dinner proceeds without incident. After getting our fill, we all scatter to different parts of the house. Most of the men meet in the family room for the traditional Thanksgiving Day football games on TV. I'm not too sure what the women are doing.

"Don, can I talk to you a second?" asks Dan.

"Sure," I say, as I get up to follow Dan into one of the bedrooms. "What's up?"

"Well, I'm just trying to get some understanding about where you're coming from here," says Dan.

"Where I'm coming from?"

"Well, you refused to come to our wedding, you even shunned us for a while there… and now here you're defending Steve and me to Hugh. I just want to know which brother's real."

Good question, actually.

"They're both real," I say.

"What?"

"See, you want me to accept you on your terms. But right now at least, I can't do that. I can only accept you on my terms. And I've done that. It's really as simple as that."

"I'm not following."

"You just assume that because I didn't come to your wedding that I was someone like Hugh, a total bigot and homophobe. But that isn't me. Never has and never will be."

"What am I supposed to think?"

"That maybe there's a middle ground somewhere."

"What the hell does that mean?"

"Well, to start off with, I can't ever see myself calling homosexuality normal, whatever normal means anyway."

"Great way to start."

"But that doesn't mean I hate or despise you.....or Steve."

"Well, I guess it's good to know that you don't despise us."

"I guess that's the wrong way to put it," I say. "It's just that it always seems to be one extreme or the other. I'm just saying that I'm somewhere in between."

"Why is it that you seem to be the only one, well, besides Hugh who can't seem to accept us for who we are? Everyone else seems to be able to accept us without any sort of qualification."

"Do you really think I'm the only one who doesn't accept it all the way?"

"Yes, I do, actually."

"Dan, Karen's more opposed to you than I am. Do you really think her church even comes close to accepting homosexuality? And believe me, she's in lockstep with that crowd."

"I don't believe that. She's been nothing but the picture of love and acceptance to me."

"Well, it's true. She isn't ugly about it. That just isn't her."

"She puts on a pretty good front."

"Most do. I'm just a little more honest with what I believe than others happen to be. I would think you'd rather have someone not attend at all, than to have someone attend who isn't fully supportive. That's why I stayed away."

"Stay away? You wrote a whole dissertation on why you weren't coming. I could have really done without that."

"I thought I owed you an explanation. But, in hindsight, I do understand how that came across to you. It wasn't the right way to handle it."

"You said something about people coming that didn't fully support me? Did you have someone in mind? Who came that you say wasn't supportive."

"I'm not gonna name names," I say. "And really, it's not just one person. I'm just saying that do you really believe that everyone in this family, who all live in the South, and are mostly religious to one extent or the other, are absolutely and totally accepting of homosexuality? Do you really believe that's possible? Do you really believe that they all accept you without reservation? Do they accept you as fully as your gay friends do?"

"I think I know who you're trying to hint at."

"No, I don't have a particular person in mind. That's the point. You don't really know who believes what. I would just say that the older ones would seem to have a harder time accepting it than the younger ones. I just don't think everyone is as enlightened as you think they are."

"More enlightened than you."

"Not really."

"Seriously?"

"Yes, seriously."

"You are the definition of a homophobe."

"I hate that word with a fucking passion."

"If it fits…."

"I'm not a homophobe," I say. "I don't have an irrational fear of homosexuality."

"It doesn't seem rational to me."

"It's logical. My beliefs are driven by logic."

"Really?"

Dan sounds skeptical and condescending. But I understand. I would too, in his shoes.

"Yeah, the whole thing is just simple logic."

"Great! Dazzle me with your logic."

"You sure you want to get into this?"

"Yeah, go ahead, enlighten me."

"Okay," I say. "If God intended for you to have sex with a man, why not make you a woman? It's really as simple as that."

"Like that's a new argument. Please don't use the Adam and Steve line."

"Being an old argument doesn't make it a bad argument. It's simple logic. Why would God make us male and female and then give you the desire to have sex with men?"

"But how do you explain what's inside of me with your simple logic?" asks Dan. "Why do I have the desire to love men and not women?"

"Don't get me wrong," I say. "I understand that it feels natural to you. And I believe that it does. I really do."

"Well, thank you, but I don't need your confirmation."

"Despite that though, logic doesn't support the idea that it's intended by God or anything like that. I just can't go that far."

"Then where the fuck did it comes from?" asks Dan. "It wasn't a choice, but it wasn't natural, either? How can you have it both ways?"

"Because being natural and being intended by God are two different things. People get those two mixed up all the time."

"Oh, continue to teach me, please?" asks Dan, sarcastically.

"It's just that we all have our imperfections in this life. Nothing is totally how it should be in this world. At least that's what I believe. We're all born with those imperfections."

"How does that apply here, though?"

"It's as simple as this. Just because it exists doesn't make it the Lord's perfect will."

"How can anything exist without it being in the will of God?"

"Maybe that's not quite the way to put it," I say. "But God allows many things to happen in this world that we would have to agree are very far from how they should be. There's a difference in how this world is and how it would be without sin. God lets many things happen that he only lets happen because of this world being corrupted and very far from perfect."

"So, there we go again with that, calling it a sin."

"No, I'm not so sure I believe in that concept anymore. We're all imperfect. That's all I'm saying. We aren't born perfect. We know that. We can very clearly see that. So, with that being the case, why do we assume that however we were born is the way God wanted us?"

"I'm not sure I want to be taken to bible class."

"It's not really bible class. It's related. But it's just what makes sense to me."

"Well, ok. But I still don't want to hear a lecture."

"It's not a lecture."

"Feels that way, brother."

"But that's what frames how I feel about this. It's who I am. Well, it's at least who I want to be. I'm very far from perfect myself. Believe me."

"How does this affect our relationship?"

"I don't know really," I say. "I just want you to know that I'm not out there campaigning against gay marriage and all of that stuff. I'm not a hate filled homophobe. Like it or not, there is some basis for how I feel about this. The bottom line is that I just can't accept what you're doing as natural."

"It's natural to us."

"I get that. I really do. But this isn't even about the bible to me. Like I said, this is just logic. And I just can't get away from that."

"But you're talking about logic when this is about love."

"I'm happy that you have someone. I really am. I don't know what else to say."

"I just feel like there'll always be this little cloud hanging over our heads. This little doubt about where you stand."

"I just don't see why this issue has to be painted in this way that makes it seem so black and white," I say. "Why does it have to be all or nothing? It's either total acceptance or you're labeled a homophobe who has no reason or intelligence. There is middle ground. And that middle ground is where I'm at."

"The other side of that coin is that you either renounce homosexuality or are sent to hell as an evil sodomite."

"Yeah….exactly. I don't see it as an all or nothing thing. This is a complicated world. There are a lot of screwed up people in it. We all are really. We're all fucked up. We're all trying to find our way."

"You know, Steve's a great guy."

"I'm sure he is."

"I'd like you to get to know him."

"I haven't burned all those bridges, yet?"

"No, I think there may be at least one standing."

"I hope you have a great life together."

"I'd like to believe that."

"Listen, I know you're not going to miraculously wake up tomorrow and start liking girls," I say, smiling. "I do want you to be happy."

"I guess I have to take what I can get."

"I wish life weren't so complicated, but it is."

"Yeah, especially for me."

"I can only imagine what you were going through as you were growing up, knowing that you were gay."

"Yeah, I knew at a pretty early age. Tried to fight it like many people do."

"Mel and I knew before Mom and Dad."

"Well, they were probably just in denial."

"Well, look at the family they have. There's nothing normal about it. I'm married to a black woman and you're married to a man. And to top it off, she isn't getting any grandchildren any time soon."

"She isn't?"

"Not unless you deliver."

"You don't want kids?"

"I just can't seem to get on board with the idea. Too much is unresolved in my life."

"What does that mean?"

"Uhh….nothing….nevermind. You should adopt. I think you'd make a great father….the both of you."

"Who knows…maybe. Not sure I would want to put a kid through that though."

"Better than not having any parents at all. Besides, the world's changing every day. Things that were once outlawed are now openly practiced. Things that weren't talked about are now in the open. It's becoming less and less of a big deal."

"Doesn't bother you?"

"Christians aren't supposed to be fighting all of this stuff. We're supposed to serve God and love others and let God sort all that shit out."

"Didn't know you saw it that way."

"I have, what some would call, crazy views, but I'm not one of these right wingers who think we have to legislate morality and take the country over for God or any of that crap."

"So, not like Hugh."

"Well, that guy….hmmm….he's in his own category altogether."

"Agreed."

"Let's hope that the day ends without there being any more fireworks," I say. "But with Hugh getting a few drinks in him, I wouldn't be surprised."

"Yeah…I know."

"I really hope things work out for you and Steve. Seems like a nice enough guy, for someone who doesn't like football."

"Yeah…I know. That is one strike against him, isn't it?"

"He'll have to be on probation. Maybe we can get him to like it."

"I doubt it."

"Well, the Cowboys are kicking off soon, so let's go watch some football."

"I'm glad we had this talk."

"I am, too," I say, as we hug and head back out to the family room.

"So, what's this all about?" asks Mom, seeing us come down the hall together.

"We were just talking," I say.

"Everything alright?" she asks.

"Yeah….I think we at least have a better understanding of one another now," says Dan.

"That's good. I need for my sons to get along."

"Don't worry…it'll work out," I say, as we head back into the family room.

"Where have you guys been?" asks Hugh. "It's almost kickoff time."

"I'm ready to see the Cowboys wipe the field up with the Deadskins," I say.

"Don't you mean the other way around?" asks Hugh.

"No….I don't."

"Where's Steve?" asks Hugh. "All the men are in here. I was right, he is the wife."

"Hugh….." I warn.

"What? I call then how I see them."

"You'd probably be surprised to know that some of your beloved players are gay."

"Bullshit! Only real men play football. And real men don't take dicks up their ass."

"Consider whose house you're in," says Dad. "I don't want to hear this kind of talk in here. Dan and Steve are welcome here. Is that clear?"

"I get it. I get it. You support this little unholy sodomite union they have here."

"Goddamn it, Hugh. Could you just shut you fucking mouth for once?" I shout. "You drunk bastard. No respect for anything or anybody."

"Don! What's going on in here?" asks a stunned Karen, stepping into the room.

"Hugh, it's time for you to go," says Dad, as everyone comes to see what's going on. "Sorry, Marie, but he's no longer welcome in this house. This is it. No more chances."

"He's just had a little too much to drink," explains Grandma.

"That may be so, but I can't have this anymore," says Dad. "He's not disrupting this house any longer."

"Sorry, Momma, but Jack's right," says Momma. "We just can't excuse this behavior anymore."

"I just can't believe you were using that sort of language, Don," says Karen. "Taking the name of the Lord in vain?"

"He's just a heathen like me," says Hugh. "Y'all gonna throw him out on his ass?"

"Hugh, I wish I could say it's been nice knowing you…..but it hasn't," says Dad.

"To hell with all you fag lovers anyway. Come on, Marie, we're leaving."

"Well…..I'd much rather be a fag lover, than to have anything to do with your sorry bigoted ass," I say.

"Wouldn't expect anything different from a nigger lover," adds Hugh. "You're married to one and then apparently you're fucking one on the side, too."

"You son of a bitch," I say. "Lying sack of shit."

"My momma won't no bitch," says Hugh. "You'd better take that shit back."

"Make me, old man."

"What's he talking about, baby?" asks Karen.

"Don't listen to him. He's just trying to cause trouble."

"Go down to the library, honey and you'll see what he's been sniffing around."

"Hugh, get your ass out of this house, now," says Dad, standing in his face.

"Fine…..this ain't no family for me anyway. Do you know how utterly fucked up this whole thing is? A far cry from the South I know."

"Thank God for that," says Dan, as Hugh and Grandma head out the door.

"Can we go now?" asks Karen.

"Why? The troublemaker's gone," I respond.

"We need to talk."

"There ain't nothing to talk about. I want to watch some football."

"Okay, but I'm leaving," says Karen.

"Suit yourself," I say. "But I'm staying."

"Want me to come back to get you?"

"I'll run him over," offers Dad.

"Okay. I'll see everyone," says Karen, tearing up slightly. "Sorry….I just need to leave."

"Don't guess she cared for my choice of words," I remark.

"That makes two of us," says Momma.

"What a Thanksgiving," says Dan. "Welcome to the family,

Steve. You haven't witnessed one of these yet."

"Yeah, wasn't quite expecting this," says Steve. "Although, you had warned me about Hugh.

"We should have done that years ago," says Dad. "We just tolerated that guy because he's married to Marie."

"At least that ass won't be a part of any more family functions," I say.

"Don, could I talk to you?" asks Melody.

"Wow....I'm popular today. Both brother and sister want a private chat....and my wife's left and gone home, too."

"Sorry about that," says Melody, as we step into the living room. "But I just want to know what's going on with you."

"Dan asked the same thing."

"Probably for a different reason, I imagine."

"I don't know."

"The thing Hugh said about the girl at the library, well, that's gotten around."

"What?"

"Yeah....I don't know if Karen's heard it or not, that is, before today."

"I doubt it. I think she would've said something."

"So, it is true."

"Well, something happened. I'm not sure what the rumors are, but yes, something happened. But I didn't have sex with her."

I can't admit that to my sister.

"What's happening here? I mean....you're messing around with another woman.....you're cussing like a sailor in front of Momma and Daddy. What's happening?"

"I don't know, Mel. Maybe I'm finally just coming out of my shell."

"Coming out of your shell?"

"Mel, there's just a lot going on. Things aren't good, at least in some ways."

"Are you and Karen having trouble?"

"As far as she's concerned, not much. Maybe now, though. I'm just drifting away from her. And then there was April. I almost did something really reckless there. I don't know what I'm doing really."

"What's the deal with this April? Are you still messing around with her?"

"No, not really. We've talked a few times."

That's actually somewhat true. We fuck more than we talk, though.

"Is there anything I can do or say to help?"

"I don't think so. It'll sort itself out, one way or the other."

"Karen's too good of a person to hurt with something like this. Okay? I'm not sure what you're doing with that woman, but word will get to Karen. In this town, I can promise that."

"I think it just did. Even though it isn't true."

"At least, not entirely."

"I have to admit that much. There is at least some basis to the rumors."

"She may not believe it coming from Hugh, but chances are that she's heard it elsewhere, too, or will soon."

"I know that."

"Okay, enough said. Just watch it, brother."

"Let's enjoy our Thanksgiving now."

"Yeah, and we kind of have a reason to celebrate now."

"Celebrate? Really?"

"We're finally getting rid of Hugh. I think Daddy's done with him this time."

"I hope so."

"Yeah, he's done, alright."

"Go watch your beloved Cowboys now."

"Yeah, that would be nice."

Wow, what a scene that was. But, amazingly, I'm actually a little glad this all happened. It's like everyone saw a glimpse of the true me. I feel like the wheels are in motion now. Things are going to change now, one way or the other. Whether the change is easy or hard, change is coming.

Chapter 63

Friday April 4th, 2003

"Guys, before we have our meeting, Max wants everyone back in the warehouse," says Butch, to his assembled crew in the Instrumentation shop.

"Everyone, who?" I ask.

"The entire shift," answers Butch.

"This ain't gonna be good," says Jim, as we all take the short walk back to the warehouse.

"What do you mean?" asks Lisa.

"He means that this is it," I say. "We're done."

"They ain't shutting it down," says David.

"Have we ever had a meeting like this?" asks Jim. "Look, the whole shift is coming. The whole fucking plant."

"We'll soon find out," I say, as we assemble in the warehouse in front of a catwalk in front of the warehouse offices. Max is standing by, waiting to speak to his troops.

"I just have a few words to say," begins Max. "I was hoping with all my will that it wouldn't come to this. But I have to make the announcement today….that the decision has been made to close this facility. If I would have had my way, we would have been given some more time to turn things around. But management has overruled me on this. Competition from foreign companies and domestic companies who have set up shop overseas is making it virtually impossible to keep this plant open any longer. We cannot compete. I thank you all for all of your hard work. This isn't your fault. There will be resources put in place to assist in your transition into hopefully brighter and more fulfilling opportunities. Your supervisors and managers can give you more information as we move towards the close date. And speaking of that, we will begin to phase out production at this facility almost immediately, with all operations ceasing approximately five months from now."

"We're reopening a small plant in Statesville. I believe we may have some who transferred from there when it closed. There will be opportunities to transfer to that plant once it's operational. However, that will only be a temporary measure itself. Statesville will not be open more than a couple of years. Management may not want this to be said, but I owe it to you. The majority of this operation will eventually be transferred to a facility in Mexico. An existing facility is being expanded. I'm sure many of you had no idea that there was a plant down there. But it's been there since the forties, I do believe. The truth is that Raymond Mills is struggling for its very life. Fast action is required to save what's left. I know that I can count on you to assist in this difficult transition. Thank you for you service," concludes Max.

"Assist them with the transition to Mexico?" asks David, in disbelief. "He wants us to help them ship our jobs down there?"

"I had no idea we even had a fucking plant down there," I say. "It doesn't show up on any list of facilities that I've ever seen."

"It probably just served the market down there," says Jim. "I don't think it's some deep dark secret."

"Yeah, but we've sent machinery to other plants before," says David. "I don't remember ever having sent anything down there."

"But they probably have some of them," I say. "They just didn't want us to know."

"Well, it doesn't matter now," says Lisa, as we make our way back into the Instrumentation shop. "They're getting the whole damn plant now."

"Come on in guys," says Butch. "I have a few things to say before we get to work."

"Work for what?" asks David. "I already know I'm getting fired, boss."

"Yeah, but it may come quicker than you thought if you act up," I say.

"Max mentioned the plant in Statesville," begins Butch. "Work on that will begin almost immediately. Basically we're looking for volunteers. We need one electrician and one instrumentation tech. They're offering a small incentive.....an extra three dollars an hour. But they'll want you up there almost every week."

"Where the hell is Statesville anyway?" I ask.

"It's about three hours from here," says Butch. "Out past Greensboro."

"What about this Mexico deal?" asks Jim. "Are they gonna want any help from us with that?"

"Sure are, the same incentive basically. And who knows, they may offer a permanent position if someone was willing to move down there," says Butch.

"And I'm assuming that the same would be true of Statesville," says Lisa.

"Yeah, but Statesville's temporary," offers David.

"But with mouths to feed you have to do what you need to do," says Lisa.

"It be alright," offers Israel.

"Well, I ain't so sure," says Lisa.

"Well, scratch me off the fucking list right now," says David. "I ain't helping them to open up no plant that's putting us out of business."

"We'd be out of business anyway, numbnuts," I say.

"Alright, just let me know something soon," says Butch. "As far as today is concerned, I'm sure you ain't gonna do all that much. We ain't got any issues right now. Let's try to be professional about this. Let's try to remain classy and keep doing our jobs to the bitter end. Just keep the plant running…okay?"

"Sure, boss….we'll do our best," I say, as Butch leaves.

"You sure called it, Don," says Roger, as he and Jerry come into the room. "You've been saying ever since Max got here that this was going to happen."

"Even if it took ten fucking years," jokes Jerry.

"Even so, I wasn't expecting it now," I say. "I thought other plants would go down before this one."

"Yeah, we always thought that us being on the river with our own water source gave us an advantage," says Jerry.

"Guess that wasn't the case," I say.

"What gets me is this plant in Mexico," says Roger. "They participated in this 'Buy American' campaign and they have a fucking plant down there."

"They're still an American company," says Jim. "You can't expect them to locate every single plant here. We sell to people around the world. Why can't we have plants around the world?"

"Listen, the truth is that textiles is a dying industry in this country," I say. "It's really a fucking miracle that it's 2003 and this company is still even here. Many textile companies are gone."

"Well, we're still all losing our jobs," says Lisa.

"Most of us in this room can do much better anyway," I say. "Now, that's not the case with some of the operators and people on the floor. Many of them will never find anything this good again. But those of us with more knowledge and skill, we'll all do fine."

"Well…I hope so," says Lisa. "But it's a little more difficult with my being a woman in a male dominated field."

"I know….but you'll get something," I say.

"So, are any of you going to help with Mexico or Statesville?"

asks Roger. "Bob told us that they just needed electricians and instrument guys for the moves. But after they get the plants in place they may have more openings."

"Well, my intention is to ride this thing into the fucking ground," I say. "I'm gonna milk it as far as it'll go. So I may help with Statesville. But I ain't moving there permanently."

"It won't be permanent anyway," offers Jerry.

"Exactly," I say. "If I wasn't married, I'd really consider working in the Mexican plant for a few years, depending on the deal they're offering."

"Karen wouldn't want to move down there?" asks Roger.

"Are you kidding? She can't be away from her family for hardly any time at all. She'll always stay in Raymond. I can promise you that."

"Well, I may have to do the Statesville thing with you, Don," says Lisa. "I can't afford not to, at least until I get another job."

"Bob was telling us that you may be able to get government assistance going back to school if you wanted to," says Roger. "We qualify because we're going out of business because of foreign competition."

"Ain't that some shit," says Israel. "I almost finish with school. Now they want to pay."

"Apparently they'll pay you unemployment benefits while you are in school," explains Roger. "They pay you to go to school."

"Well, I think I might just bite on that Mexico deal," says Jim. "If they're willing to just pay me what I make now I'll clean up. With the lower cost of living....damn....I'll really fucking clean up."

"It's perfect for you," I say. "Nothing and no one to tie you down."

"This hits you doubly hard, with Karen working here," says Lisa.

"I'm not worried. Things'll work out fine. Why worry about what you can't change?"

"Maybe there's another plant we could transfer to," says David. "Besides the little temporary deal in Statesville."

"Why would you want to do that?" asks Jerry. "They'll eventually close them all. It'll just prolong it a little."

"Just get out now," I say. "You can do better than this. Textiles is pretty much the bottom of the barrel when it comes to the maintenance field. Get into pharmaceuticals or something high tech. Cleaner plants, not as hot, better technology, better pay. I'm telling you, this is gonna be good for all of us."

"Glad you're so positive," says Lisa.

"We can't change it," I say. "Besides, I was getting tired of this place anyway. I actually feel a funny sort of freedom. Like this will be a new stage in my life."

Chapter 64

Later that day.

"Now, if there was ever an occasion to go to Ronnie's, well, this is the day," says Roger.

"And do what?" I ask, as we walk out of the plant.

"Have a bull session about the plant closing," says Roger. "At least it'll be entertaining. All the usual suspects are coming."

"Yeah, this is big news for the town," adds Jerry.

"It's going to change a lot of things for a lot of people," I say.

"So, join the discussion," says Roger.

"You goin, Jim?" I ask.

"I'm going to be the voice of reason."

"Okay, let me tell Karen to go on without me and I'll be there."

I walk the short distance to Ronnie's place and find quite a group already gathered around the bar.

"Don, how the fucking hell are you," booms Ronnie. "Gonna drown your sorrows with the rest of them?"

"Shit, I don't have any sorrows to drown," I say. "I've been needing to get another fucking job anyway."

"Ain't that the fucking truth."

"Oh my God, this is a bad day," says Roger. "Look who's coming in."

"Pop, what the hell?" booms Ronnie, as Homer strolls up to the bar.

"Well, gentlemen, I just thought this was enough of an occasion to visit my son's place here and to commiserate with my friends," says Homer.

Homer would normally not be caught dead in a joint like this. From what I understand, he does enjoy the occasional drink. But he prefers to do that at home. This place is very far from the image he wants to project as a good upstanding Christian man.

"At least you got to retire before they shut it down," says Jerry.

"Hate to see the plant close though. I have so many years of memories in that place," says Homer.

"And one of them's your son here getting busted smoking pot," says Roger.

"Thanks for pointing that out, hoss," says Ronnie.

"Hey, that ain't no big deal to me," says Homer. "Ain't nothing I mess with, but to each his own."

"Thanks, Pop."

"Homer, can I talk to you a second?" I ask.

"Sure, Don," responds Homer. "I haven't talked to you since I retired."

"Yeah, I know," I say, as we settle down into a booth.

"So, what's on your mind?"

"I always regretted that we never got a chance to clear the air before you retired."

"What's there to clear the air about?"

"I've been pretty hard on you over the years, you know, about the racial stuff?"

"Yeah, I thought we were alright after I came to your wedding and all, but you did kind of give me hell there right before I retired. I don't even remember what started it."

"Who knows?" I ask. "I don't remember myself what it was all about."

"That's all water under the bridge now, at least as far as I'm concerned."

"No, I just wanted you to know that I see what you're saying now."

"About what, specifically?"

"I see in the bible now, where you were getting the stuff about the races not marrying and that sort of thing. It is there. And I'm starting to see the validity."

"But you also see that in Christ it doesn't matter."

"Yeah, but I'm not so sure about that now."

"Why's that?"

"Karen and I.....we just don't have anything in common," I say. "And much of it is cultural. About the only thing we had in common was our faith and now that's changing."

"But, how is that changing? Don't you both still love the Lord?"

"Yeah....but it's just that whole Pentecostal thing that she's all into. I just don't get it. In fact, I happen to think that it's just plain unbiblical."

"I think you may be on the right track there, son. There is indeed something wrong with that whole deal."

"I'm starting to think the whole thing's demonic."

"No, I wouldn't go that far," says Homer. "I know Claude and his family. There's no question that they're not totally in the will of God when it comes to that stuff, but no, it's not demonic."

"I'm confused by the whole thing. They're mixed up in so much that's unbiblical, but at the same time, they seem to be really godly people."

"And they are. Deception just has a way of creeping in sometimes. But that's a trick of the devil, son. He wants it to look like true Christianity. That way, people are lured into it. But he still has his hooks into you."

"I'm just really confused…..but….I didn't mean to get into all of this. I just wanted to apologize for blowing up at you that time. Actually, we had words several times."

"Well, like I said, that's all water under the bridge now."

"I just wanted you to know that I see now what you were trying to say back then."

"No, listen, I know that scripture says that. And life will go more smoothly if we live according to scripture. But you were right when you said that it didn't really matter what people did if they weren't saved. If they aren't saved, then that's the only problem I should be worried about fixing. I have to admit that some of my views on race were shaped by the time I grew up in. The scripture's there to back it up, but my bias may have caused me to fixate on something that wasn't all that important."

"Homer, you're so much more gracious than I could ever be, I'm afraid."

"Don, that comes with age. The older you get the less some of this shit matters anymore. You took some of what I was saying in a much worse way than I intended it. I believe in scripture. I can't help what the text says. If you have an argument, then it's with scripture. You made the mistake of inferring meaning from what I was saying. I have black friends. You have to understand that this is what we were brought up into. Wanting a certain level of separation or whatever, doesn't mean that we hate one another. Many older blacks actually agree with some of what I say. But, like I said, how much does it really matter? People need to be saved first, or nothing else matters."

"Well, I just wanted to set things right."

"Don, let me just say one thing more. You're very passionate about the truth. And that's a good thing. But you have to live it too, son."

"Okay, what does that mean?"

"It means that you know it isn't right to be screwing around with that harlot over at the library. The Lord's given you a passion to strive for the truth. Don't mess that up by doing something like that."

"Homer, it's true that I was talking to her. But that was it. She wanted to meet me, but I never did."

"What I heard is that she came in here one night saying that you two had sex."

"Yeah, she did say that, but we never did. She wanted me to. I wouldn't. So she was pissed, wanted to get back at me. Besides, that was last fall. I can't believe that one little story like that has such legs."

"Okay, let's say that that is all there is to it. It still shows that you were getting just a little too close to the fire, son. You know you shouldn't be messing around like that."

"Yeah, I know. Just by letting myself flirt with her I've caused this huge rumor to spread."

"Does your wife know?"

"What do you think?"

"Yeah…..you ain't gonna have no secrets in a town like this."

The thing is, I kind of do.

"Why don't we rejoin the discussion?" I propose.

"Sure," says Homer, as we move back over to the bar. "Just remember, son, you have a gift for seeing the truth. Just don't squander that."

"Okay, Homer."

The thing is, I'm not so sure that's true anymore.

"Have a little private bonding time, did we?" asks Roger.

"Just had something I needed to say," I say, as the conversation continues.

"We have to stop all of these jobs from going overseas," says Raeford. "These bastards are going to put us all on the street."

"But these are low skill jobs that are leaving," says Jim. "Do we really want to save them?"

"Why the hell wouldn't we want to save them?" asks Raeford.

"You already fucked up your job," says Ronnie. "What the fuck are you talking about?"

"I'm fighting for the people," proclaims Raeford.

"A case could be made that this is good for this country," I point out.

"How is it good when one plant after another is closing?" asks Raeford.

"Cheap goods, for one thing."

"But how does that matter if nobody ain't got no fucking job?" asks Raeford.

"Not everyone works in a plant," points out Jim. "Plenty of people have jobs, chicken little."

"I ain't no goddamned chicken little," says Raeford. "This shit just ain't good."

"Are we all supposed to pay more for everything just so the people who work in plants can keep their jobs?" I ask. "Do we pass a law making companies stay here?"

"You're fucking up people's way of life," says Raeford. "These plants are the heart of the community."

"But there isn't a promise written somewhere that says that every small town has to have a factory in it," I say. "That's part of the issue here. People expect the jobs to just come to them. It's not that there aren't jobs. It's that people think that they can just sit in the same town they've always lived in and have a job. But who's to say that's how it should be."

"It's the same way with these fucking farm subsidies," says Jim. "We have to pay more for food just so people who have always farmed can keep farming, instead of allowing them to fail like any other business that can't succeed on its own."

"We do that so that we have a food supply," says Tommy Cash.

"But if the prices for food are so low that these farmers can't make it, then that means we have plenty of food," I say. "All that shit is just to preserve this ideal of the family farm."

"My family has always farmed," says Tommy. "It is a way of life. And it's probably the most important business there is."

"Sure, we need food," says Jim. "But we have all we need. Why should I have to give my tax dollars to someone who owns huge amounts of land just so they can keep living the way they always have? Do I get the same support if I start a business and can't make it work? No, I lose it. So why should farmers have that safety net."

"How the fuck did we get to talking about farmers?" asks Roger.

"Listen, it's all gonna even out in the end," I say. "The wages in China and other places are real low now. But as the standard of living rises the wages will rise. They will be able to buy more, which will raise demand."

"And as their wages rise, the less incentive there is to relocate a factory there," adds Jim.

"You two sound like the goddamn politicians," observes Raeford.

"We should be looking to high tech jobs rather than these low-skill factory jobs," says Jim. "We should be the technology leaders."

"And why is it that we think it's perfectly alright to sell our products all over the world, yet the jobs have to stay here?" I ask.

"The more people who are successful in this world, the better it is for all of us," concludes Jim.

"I will guarantee you that a good number of people will end up in better shape after this," I say. "Especially if people take advantage of this displaced worker program and go to school to be trained for something else."

"But some people just don't have that capability," says Tommy.

"I'll probably just go back into construction," says Jerry. "It's the only thing I know really. I just took this job because of the benefits. I was still doing basically the same stuff."

"I'm applying for this job with the state," says Roger.

"That was fast," says Jim.

"I was already looking into it, actually," explains Roger.

"What sort of job?" I ask.

"Director of maintenance for parks in the eastern sector of the state."

"Sounds important," I observe. "You really think you can get something like that?"

"Don't forget that I do have management experience," explains Roger. "I just took this job because I was out of work and I needed something."

"Hope you get it, man," I say.

"I know what Boonie's gonna do," says Jerry.

"What?" asks Jim.

"You'll see him on the side of the road collecting cans," says Jerry.

"I wouldn't laugh at that, actually," I say. "You could earn a living collecting and cashing in metal. He just needs to expand beyond cans."

"He'll probably walk out the door with half the plant if he can manage to hang on long enough," says Roger. "Just imagine the junk he could haul off after they shut down."

"And they are gonna need some sort of skeleton crew to stay on while they clear all the machinery out of the building," I point out.

"Well, fuck me blind," says Ronnie. "The riff raff just keeps blowing in."

"Shut your fucking pie hole you long haired hippie freak," says Butch, as he walks up to the bar. "I knew you candy asses would be in here crying in your beers over the news."

"Actually, boss, I don't mind one little bit," I say.

"But you won't have any problem getting something better," says Homer. "You should have been out of that joint years ago. You're too smart for that place."

"Look at the love just flow," says Roger. "Did you two kiss when you went off together?"

"I guess with your old ass, you're just going to go ahead and retire," says Ronnie.

"Who the fuck you calling old?" asks Butch. "I'll kick your ass any goddamn day of the fucking week."

"Simmer down, boss," says Ronnie. "Shit, you're more pissed than you were when you caught me smoking the pot."

"It's just that if those bastards weren't asleep at the wheel they could have saved that plant," says Butch. "They've been caught with their pants down and now they're scrambling to save the company. They didn't need to be in this position. They were making the right moves for a while. I guess they thought they had it figured out. But they didn't."

"But how are we supposed to compete with cheap overseas labor?" asks Tommy. "I'm amazed it lasted as long as it did."

"By running a lean operation," says Butch. "We have far too many people to do what we do. Technology is another thing. We could have automated far more than we did. There are things that could've been done. They did some things, but didn't keep at it."

"They could have consolidated plants," says Jim. "Instead of having all of these small plants scattered all over the place they should have consolidated them and had just a few megaplants."

"That's right, what other manufacturing company has a plant in every goddamn town in the South?" asks Butch. "I mean of course besides other textile companies."

"Well, they were on that road," I say. "They just weren't aggressive enough."

"They waited until plants stopped being profitable," says Butch. "They never got out in front of it. Now this whole scheme they have to save their ass in Mexico. They'll manage to drive that in the ground in short order. They're just chasing their tails at this point."

"That hefty retirement deal that they have is part of the problem," I say.

"Yeah, matching five dollars to every one for people Butch's age," adds Jim.

"Yeah, exactly," agrees Butch. "I'll do fine. I've got the military retirement and then all the money I racked up the last few years here. But yeah, it's part of the problem."

"I know, Butch, why don't you get a job as a greeter at Walmart," says Jerry.

"Yeah, some poor soul has the nerve to actually ask him a question, and he sends them away with a 'fuck you asshole'," says Roger.

"I ain't gonna be no goddamn greeter at no fucking Walmart," says Butch.

"I could use a bouncer to kick the likes of Raeford out of here when he gets out of line," says Ronnie.

"Well, now that may be fun," says Butch. "To be able to throw some people out on their asses."

"You'd have to submit to a drug test though," say Ronnie, with a sly grin. "I have to run a tight ship here."

"Yeah, cup your hands," says Butch. "I'll give you the goddamn piss."

"Don, can I talk to you a second?" asks Jim.

"Sure," I say, as we start to make our way to the wall by the pool tables. "What is it?"

"I think I'm gonna do the Mexico thing," says Jim.

"Gonna help them move the machines down there?"

"I'm thinking of moving down there permanently, well, somewhat permanently. I have an idea, I was wondering if you may be interested."

"What is it?"

"You know that they're gonna come to you with this offer first. You're the senior instrumentation tech. I have to be honest, you're much better on this shit than I am at this point."

"You're being too hard on yourself."

"No, you're being too modest. But this is what I propose. Why don't we use this as an opportunity to go into business for ourselves?"

"How? What do you mean?"

"We can start by agreeing to help them set up the expansion in Mexico....as a start. But then when that's done we could start a consulting business and just work our way through Central and South

America. With the low cost of living, we could really clean up."

"And we know that whatever textiles doesn't go to China will end up in Central and South America."

"We already know that Raymond has a cut and sew operation in Honduras."

"Yeah, I know. They were considering doing the cutting and sewing at our plant at one point."

"Would you consider it?" asks Jim. "I think we could make a great team. I'm used to dealing with people from other countries from my time in the Navy. And you would supply the technical expertise."

"It's an intriguing idea."

"Then let's talk to Max and get this thing on the road."

"You know, I would absolutely jump at the idea if it weren't for Karen. She would be like a fish out of water in another country. She can't stand to be in another state than her family, much less another country."

"She could do missionary work while we're doing our thing."

"Well, she would like that."

"I'm sure we could find some sort of missionary group for her to work with in whatever place we happened to end up."

"I was actually thinking about doing the Statesville thing," I say. "Not permanently….I know it's not permanent anyway. Just to help get it set up. Then just see where I want to go from there."

"Just think about this….okay? We could have a great time. Live in exotic places and make a bunch of money."

"I will, Jim. It does sound cool….I have to admit."

"Let me know something quick. I want to jump on this before they go another way with it."

"I know."

"When do I get my one on one time with Don?" asks Roger, as he strolls up to us. "I see a pattern developing and I want my turn."

"I just had a proposal for Don," says Jim. "Nothing to concern your little government worker head with."

"What shady deal do you two have cooking?" asks Roger.

"Nothing that you would be able to do," says Jim. "I'm sure they have plenty of painters in Mexico."

"Ohhh….so you two are cooking up a scheme to help move the plant to Mexico."

"Maybe," I say. "Who knows what the future may hold. It's all up in the air now. Change is coming whether we want it or not. But we have to decide what that change will be."

There is one change that needs to be made before others can occur. I just can't quite bring myself to do that yet.

Chapter 65

Saturday April 19ᵗʰ, 2003

"Who the hell came up with this idea, anyway?" I ask.

"My son's played paintball for years now," says Lisa. "I thought it would be a good way to blow off a little steam, you know....with the plant closing and all of that."

"I can't wait to open a severe can of whoop ass on someone," says Mark.

"Just keep in mind that there's actually a lot of strategy to this, too," I say. "You don't just go charging around like Rambo blowing people away."

"Uh, Don, do you see who's here?" asks Lisa. "I forgot to tell you that her son plays, too. But you may have already known that, considering, well, you know."

"No, I don't know. Who are you talking about?"

"April," says Lisa. "The whole town knows you're fucking her."

"That's bullshit," I say, doing my best to sound dismissive. "That all came from that time she came into Ronnie's. I've never fucked her. Not even once. She was just pissed because I was flirting with her and wouldn't fuck her."

"So, she was just so pissed that you wouldn't fuck her little skank ass that she decided to embarrass you? Is that what you're saying?"

"Exactly."

"I was there that night," says Mark. "That was an ugly scene."

"It's funny though," says Lisa. "She has this one little detail about you getting caught by some cop. Why would she add that?"

"I don't know. Maybe she just thought that was funny or something."

"Hey, I remember you telling me about that," says Mark. "Didn't the cop catch you with your dick down her throat?"

"No, I didn't tell you that," I say. "That was what April said."

"I thought you told me."

"You're just remembering it wrong."

Sometimes I have to use his faulty memory to my advantage.

"Seems like an odd detail to just make up," says Lisa.

"Maybe it just happened to her with another guy."

"And you said that you fucked her up against a rock or something," adds Mark.

That fucking brain injury. He has absolutely no filter on that goddamn mouth.

"Now, I don't know where that came from. She didn't say that down at Ronnie's," I say. "But I did not fuck the girl."

I think that little part makes it seem like I'm being forthright and truthful. I didn't try to explain away the little detail about my fucking her on that rock. I just let it hang out there as something I knew nothing about.

"I don't know. If you say there's nothing going on, then I guess I believe you. Lord knows I have no faith in that bitch."

I do have a better reputation than she does. Undeserved?....perhaps, but better.

"I just wish this shit wasn't running rampant all over town," I say.

"Has Karen said anything?"

"No, not yet."

"You know she has to have heard it."

"I know she has. My fucking step grandfather or whatever said something to her Thanksgiving. Boy was that a fucking scene."

"What the fuck did she say?" asks Lisa.

"I denied it. Told her the truth. Said it was lies. He hates the fact that she's black anyway."

"Does she believe that it's all lies?"

"I have no idea. We haven't really talked about it."

Karen and I have always seemed to avoid talking about all of these difficult issues. That's probably due to my fear of confrontation more than anything.

"See what you get for even giving someone like that the time of day?" asks Lisa.

"I know. I just couldn't help chasing after her like the rest of the crowd."

"You fucking men. Just can't resist that jiggling ass, can you?"

"Actually, normally I can."

It's not so much that I have the power to resist a jiggling ass. I just have no game at all when it comes to jiggling asses. If it weren't for that, I would be the biggest dog of them all. April was just different somehow. It just happened, despite my insecurities and dysfunctions.

"Yeah, I will give you that," says Lisa. "You aren't normally a hound dog, at least that I know of."

The truth is that I would love to get Lisa into bed. Maybe that's why I seem to be so worried about what she thinks of me. I know she wouldn't spread this around like the guys would. I could admit the truth to her about April if that's all I was worried about. But there's more to it than that. I want her to like me.

"Hey, there's Roger and Jerry," I say.

"Hey, guys. Ready to get whipped by the master today?" asks Jerry.

"Masterbater," deadpans Mark.

"Yeah, that's funny," says Jerry.

"Jerry, you're just going to get your ass plastered with paint today," says Roger. "Why do you even bother coming to something like this if you're going to get lit?"

"Don't worry about me baby.....I...I gonna kick ass today," stammers Jerry.

Yeah, Jerry has been drinking already. The progress he made several years ago has vanished. He's back to the old Jerry.

"Look for him under a tree somewhere," says Roger. "Passed out."

"Any word on the job, Roger?" asks Lisa.

"Yeah, I got it," says Roger. "Pay of course isn't but so good. It's a state job after all. But I get the use of a company truck. And of course I get loads of vacation time."

"Never seen anyone as lucky as this bastard," I say.

"I don't know what I'm gonna do," says Lisa. "It's tough for a woman in this field. I won't even get half the interviews that you guys would."

"Unless they're shooting for more diversity," says Roger. "That's a big thing today."

"Yeah, that's great," says Lisa, rolling her eyes. "I'll get hired as the token woman."

"Do you want to do the Statesville thing?" I ask, as the guys leave us to go get their equipment.

"Bob keeps putting me off," says Lisa. "He never has had any confidence in me."

"I think I may do it," I say. "I'm sure I can get you onboard. If I say I need you, they'll let you do it."

"I thought you were thinking about going to Mexico with Jim," says Lisa.

"I'm not sure about that yet," I say. "I'll do the Statesville thing if that'll help you out. I'll think about Mexico in the meantime. Jim has to see what the terms are before he'll commit to it anyway."

"You would do Statesville just so I could get it? I was hoping Israel would do it with me, but he's got a chance to get on with an engineering firm. Guess that's more important than me."

"Of course I'd do that for you. It would buy you a little time at least," I say. "And I have to do something myself anyway."

"Maybe you do have some redeeming qualities after all," says Lisa, smiling.

"But oral sex would be a requirement," I say, taking a stab at a joke.

"Giving or receiving?"

"Both."

"Hmmm…..in that case…..it's a deal."

Where did that come from? I figured my little joke would just fall flat. People think I'm a gentlemen or something because I don't make comments like that to women. No, I'm not a gentlemen, the shyness is what keeps me from acting like any other guy on the planet. Despite the thing with April, I remain socially retarded in the company of women, at least when it comes to flirting or anything of that nature. The thing with April was just magic. That's the only way to describe it. But maybe she's unleashing something inside of me that's always been there. Besides, I know that Lisa can joke like that. She isn't easily offended.

"Are you thinking of transferring out there?" I ask. "To Statesville, I mean?"

"I don't know…..I may have to if nothing else happens before then."

"I doubt any other electrician from here is going to want it, so it should be yours for the taking," I say. "It would give you a definite foot in the door if you were to assist in setting the plant up. I'll talk to Bob first chance I get. No….actually…. I'll just go to Max. Bob doesn't like me very much, either."

"I really appreciate it."

"I would really love to bite on Jim's idea of starting with the Mexico plant, then moving on to some sort of consulting business and hopscotching across Central and South America. But I don't see Karen wanting to do something like that. She doesn't have much of a sense of adventure."

"You and Jim could really make that work, I bet. It would be a great opportunity."

"I know. And there's only one thing holding me here."

"Just one?" asks Lisa.

"Yeah, just one. Karen."

"You wouldn't miss your family?"

"I'm sure I would. But it's different with a wife. They have to come. You can't just leave a wife for months on end and then just come back for visits."

"People do that, actually."

"Karen would never go for it though."

"Well, that's the thing isn't it? Sometimes choices we make keep us from making others choices."

"Yeah, that's so true. And sometimes events or conditions beyond your control cause you to make choices that fuck your whole life up."

"Fuck your whole life up?"

"Nevermind. I was just being hypothetical."

"You sure?"

"Yeah, doesn't mean anything."

It actually does mean something. Actually, it means everything. One little condition caused me to make a choice that has altered my life so dramatically.

"So, how do we decide who's on what team?" I ask.

"They do it by drawing our names out of a hat," says Lisa. "They think it's more interesting that way. They'll do the kids first so that they're divided evenly."

"So, you may be on opposite teams from Brett?"

"Yeah, so what?" says Lisa. "I'll blow him away like I would anyone else."

"And I'm sure he'd be glad to return the favor."

Soon after the action begins, I slip away from everyone and lean up against a tree to think. That's the best thing about something like this, the chance to be out in the woods. It's the same way with hunting. I've always loved the idea of hunting. Not hunting itself, just the idea of being out in the woods on a crisp fall day, a chance to get some perspective on things. After a while, my thoughts are interrupted by a familiar voice.

"Hand's up, enemy," says April.

"They're up," I reply.

"This is what's gonna happen," she says, in that soft sexy voice of hers. "I'm gonna take you captive. Then I'm gonna tie you up, strip your ass bare, then…..well…. I'll just have to tease and tempt that dick to life. Once it's nice and hard, I'll just rape the shit outta you."

"It's not rape if you want it to happen."

"And I know you're kinky ass wants it to happen."

"Yeah, but out here?"

"Well, we have managed to fuck in quite a few public places since we started this little arrangement," she says, getting right up into my face.

She's still so intoxicating after all of this time.

"We have been quite adventurous," I say. "But I don't know about out here."

"Why not out here? Maybe someone'll see us and plaster my bare ass with paint. The pain of those balls bursting on my ass may just enhance my pleasure, if you know what I mean."

"Yeah, I do. You love that ass slapped, don't you?"

"Yes, I most definitely do."

"But there are kids out here," I say. "We can't do it out here."

"I was just kidding, numbnuts. I know there are kids out here. One of them is fucking mine."

"Yeah, I know. Sorry."

"What's going on, man? You seem like something's bothering you."

"It's just Karen. Everybody fucking knows what I'm doing. I tell them that it's just lies and rumors. But who knows who believes what."

"What are you doing?"

"I mean that everyone knows that I'm fucking you."

"You sure they know?"

"I keep getting asked about it."

"Fuck, it has to all be from that night at Ronnie's," she says. "I promise that I haven't said a word since then. And we've been very careful. There's no way anyone knows shit, I mean, not for sure."

"They might not know it, but they do happen to have it right. We are most definitely fucking one another."

"You don't regret it, do you?"

"Are you kidding? I can't get enough of your sweet pussy."

"I am sorry I said that shit that night at Ronnie's," she says. "I've just got this thing about being ignored."

"I know. I was just scared. I'd never done anything like that before."

"Well, no use talking about it now. I am very far from being ignored. You've seen to that."

"I can't keep doing this to her though. What have I fucking become, that I'm carrying on with you, pretending to be some Christian, and treating the woman who loves me this way?"

"I notice that you refer to Karen as the woman who loves you," she says. "Why didn't you refer to her as the woman you love?"

"Hmmm......that's a good question."

"I think so."

"Honestly, there probably isn't anything left now. I don't know."

"We've hardly talked about Karen before. Talked about plenty else, in between fuck fests, but never her."

"Well, talking about your wife is not exactly the thing to do when you're fucking another woman," I say. "At least it's never occurred to me to do that."

"Yeah, I know. A fuckbuddy is just that, someone to fuck. And boy do you wear a girl out."

"No, you're more than some fuck toy. Like you said, we do talk. We just don't talk about shit like that."

"No, I'm not offended or anything," she says. "I like what we have. I don't want your heart, Don. At least not in the way people typically mean when they say that. I want your dick, your tongue, and sure, a little bit of your mind. I know I'm more to you than some toy you play with and throw to the side."

"What's that about not wanting my heart the way people typically mean when they say that?"

"It just means that I do love you, Don. I love you like a friend, a good friend, a special friend."

"A friend that you fuck?"

"Yeah, but not just a friend that I fuck....you're the friend that I fuck, the only friend that I fuck."

"I feel the same about you," I say. "I do care for you."

"I just tend to resist this whole soul mate, true love sort of ideal. I just want to kind of redefine it a little."

"You know that you scare the shit out of me, don't you?"

"Why would I scare the shit out of you?"

"I'm just scared that this will somehow just blow up in my face."

"And you think I would do something to cause this?"

"Well, you kinda did already, if you remember."

"I know, but not since then."

"No, but I'm scared that you'll get too attached or something."

"Me? Attached?" she asks. "Why the fuck would you think that of me?"

"Well, you are pretty intense," I say. "You have a lot of passion."

"And that's bad? I thought you kind of liked my passion, especially my passion for that dick of yours."

"Yeah, I do, of course," I say. "It's just that I don't know what to make of you sometimes."

"Not much mystery here. I'm an open book."

"No, it's not that I think you're hiding anything."

"Then what are you scared of?"

"I'm just not used to women who can look at sex the way you do," I say. "How you can just separate it from emotions like that. I'm just scared that's going to change all of a sudden."

"But you see, I'm not really doing that. If I were separating it from emotions, then I would just fuck the best looking hottest guys and leave it at that. I want more than that. I don't look for that perfect ideal of true love. But I do want something else there to engage me, except for a hard dick, and a skillful tongue."

"Well, damn, I thought I was the hottest guy."

"You are pretty hot. But some of what makes you that way is in your soul. My point, is that I don't just go for the hottest piece of meat. At least, usually, I don't."

"But sometimes you do just fuck a guy because he's got a great body?"

"Sure, sometimes sex is nothing more than recreation to me," she says. "And sometimes it is for us. We've met sometimes, fucked like rabbits, and then went our separate ways."

"That's true. There have been times when we've barely spoken."

"And what's wrong with that? I think it's great. I think it's kinda hot to just meet, fuck, then go our separate ways. It's raw, nasty, illicit."

"But it's not considered proper behavior for a so-called respectable woman."

"Fuck respectable then. Why is it alright for a man to treat sex as a recreational sport, but not a woman?"

"Actually, I think you're right about that. I'm living the dream that many men have, with you."

"A guy can dream of fucking the entire cheerleading squad, and he's a stud, but if I fantasize about fucking the football team, I'm a skank or a whore."

"So, you do know what the women think of you," I say, smiling.

"Sure, but I have to take some of the blame, I guess. I do prefer to fuck married men. Like I've told you, less entanglements. I can understand how that may piss them off. But maybe I want to piss them off."

"What if the guy falls in love with you?"

"Don, you'd better not be saying what I think you're saying."

"No, April, I'm not in love with you. I may be in lust with you though. Big, hot, steaming lust."

"Lust is fine. Lust is pure. Lust is easy to deal with. But love, not so much. At least not the in-love sort of love."

"Like I said, I do care for you, I guess you can call it love, but I'm not in love with you. Fuck, I'm not even sure what that means anyway."

"All being in love means is that that person is supposedly your true love. They are the one. I'm just not so sure that there should be just one."

"Yeah....I know."

"Don, the reason you're scared of me is because I look at sex and love the way you wish you could. So many men think they want women with open ideas about sex. Many men of course want a woman who'll let them fuck other women. Some men are actually so gracious as to permit their woman to fuck other men. But most men can never seem to go all the way. They just can't seem to free their minds to a new way of looking at the whole thing, a less possessive way."

"Go all the way? What does that mean?"

"Well, totally disassociating sex and love," she says. "Although, that may seem kinda extreme."

"Yeah, it kinda does."

"It all goes back to this concept of the perfect mate. Most people look for that perfect mate."

"Yeah, a flawed concept, to me at least."

"But what does that mean? How do we define that term? What is it that people are looking for?"

"A person that can be all things."

"I think they want a best friend, basically, but someone who they also want to have sex with," she says. "Boil it down and they want a best friend that they can fuck."

"That may be a pretty accurate way to put it."

"But what if the person who happens to fulfill the qualifications for a best friend doesn't fill them when it comes to sexual desirability? Or, what if our best friend, or whatever happens to be of the same sex, assuming that we are heterosexual."

"Oh, I think we've firmly established that we are both heterosexual."

"Yes, firmly indeed," she says. "A firm dick."

"Firm nipples."

"But seriously, what if your best friend is the same sex."

"Like Mark and I used to be."

"Exactly. Why try to find a woman to fill that role?" she asks. "Instead, why don't we just separate the two? We end up trying to force someone into that role. We want them to fulfill both requirements. But what if they can't?"

"Then we go looking elsewhere."

"You may think you're enlightened. But you're still really conventional, if you ask me."

"Well, the thought has occurred to me before that we shouldn't try to make one person fit this mold of the perfect mate."

"But you still think you have to fuck whoever it is that you love the most," she says. "You just want to be able to fuck other women in addition to her. What I'm saying is why do we force ourselves into these relationships? Why can't we just let our relationships go wherever they want to go, whether sex is involved or not, whether love is involved or not?"

"We don't have to fuck everyone we love and we don't have to love everyone we fuck."

"Excellent way to put it."

"But most of us are programmed to have that special someone."

"I just don't understand why we look for that though," she says. "Why can't we just take different things we need from whoever it is who happens to have those qualities, whether it's sexual or not? Why does there have to be the one special person?"

"So, just kind of let things happen? Just let the chips fall where they may?"

"Yeah, when I hook up with a guy I don't know if it'll be for a night, a month, a year, a decade, fuck….who knows? Sometimes you just have to go with it. Why set ourselves up with all of these expectations? Just let shit lead wherever it leads."

"I think that's what scares me the most about you….I'm not

sure where it's gonna lead."

"It'll lead wherever the hell it wants to lead, wherever it's supposed to lead. Why try to put restricitons on it? Why try to label it?"

"No expectations."

"That's it."

"Just enjoy ourselves and not worry about anything else."

"Why the fuck not?"

"I don't know," I say. "Sometimes pleasure has to take a back seat to doing the right thing."

"So, we're back to Karen again?"

"Well, she's still my wife. And she isn't a party to this little arrangement. She would far from approve of this."

"Obviously."

"And now she knows…."

"Is it to the point that you'd consider leaving her?" she asks. "And I don't mean leave her for me, just to be clear."

"I don't know. I can't say that the thought isn't starting to cross my mind."

"Then maybe you need to really start thinking about doing something about it. Like I said, life is far too short to deny yourself pleasure when it's right there for the taking. Of course, you've had no problem up to this point taking me, and taking me, and taking me some more."

"This goes deeper than just wanting to keep fucking you."

"Of course it does. I know that. You need to be happy. Don't let some vows you made when you were probably a totally different person decide your fate for the rest of your fucking life. Things change. People change. When that happens…well….a change has to occur."

"Yeah….I know."

"And Don?"

"Yeah."

"I would keep seeing you even if you weren't married."

"Why?"

"I don't know. I just feel like we look at this the same way. I think what you really want is what I have. I think you have a side of you that's just dying to get out, a side that doesn't want to conform to society's standards. I feel like we could just keep on doing what we're doing and just see where that leads. I'm not afraid of getting entangled with you. You've got a free spirit. You just need to set it free."

I've had more meaningful conversations with April than I've

ever had with Karen. And the truth is that I probably love April more than I loved Karen. But, at the same time, I don't consider myself in love with April. Was I ever in love with Karen? I'm not sure I'm capable of being in love the way women seem to be in love. I'm not sure I want to be able to have that. I don't want a woman to be my everything. I don't want my whole life to rely on that one relationship. I'm not sure that idea itself is even a healthy one.

Chapter 66

Sunday April 20th, 2003

"Well, how you taking this, son?" asks Dad, as he, Momma, Melody and I sit in the family room. "Kinda rough with both of you working at the plant."

"Karen already has a job lined up," I respond.

"Well, that's good," says Momma. "Where at?"

"Some place in Youngsville that makes plastic bottles. One of her uncles works up there."

"Any chance of you getting on there?" asks Dad.

"I'm not really looking yet," I say. "I have a couple of things going that could keep me with the company for at least a little while."

"Statesville and Mexico?" asks Mel.

"Yeah, I'm definitely going to do Statesville. But I'm still thinking about Mexico."

"How would that work with Karen already having a job?" asks Mel.

"Well….the truth is….uh….I'm probably gonna be making a change."

"You mean involving Karen?" asks Momma.

"Yeah….I don't think it's going to work out."

"Sorry to hear that, son," says Dad.

"What's the issue, if you don't mind me asking?" asks Momma.

"Well….really it's the religious stuff. We just don't see eye to eye anymore. I just don't think I can stay any longer. I guess the plant closing has kind of woken me up a little."

"Well, I have noticed some tension lately," says Momma. "Nothing big, I could just tell that there wasn't that closeness that used to be there."

"And don't say anything to her if you happen to see her," I say. "I haven't gotten up the nerve to actually tell her yet."

"Maybe the Mexico thing would be good for you then," says Mel. "A way to make a fresh start."

"What's this Mexico thing about?" asks Dad.

"The company's had a plant in Mexico for years," I say. "None of us knew that until they announced the closing. They're going to expand that plant and move some of our stuff down there. They want a few people to assist with the move. And then there could be an opportunity to stay down there. Well...Jim, this guy I work with is going to do it. He wants me to do it with him, but to take it a step further and start a consulting type of business where we start with the Mexico thing and then start working our way through Central and South America. We'd just go wherever the work takes us."

"Doesn't sound like a bad plan to me," says Dad.

"I think it would be a good partnership," I say. "Jim is kind of a wheeler and dealer, where I'm really good on the machines. It could really work out."

"Maybe you ought to go for it," says Momma.

"I have to do the Statesville move first," I say. "I'm doing that mainly so I can bring along Lisa for the ride. She's worried about finding another job and they wouldn't talk to her about Statesville. So, I told her I'd do it and bring her along."

"Do you have...uh...something with this Lisa?" asks Momma.

Thanks for the bluntness, Momma.

"No....it's nothing like that," I say. "We're just friends."

"Sorry...I just thought that she may have something to do with your leaving Karen," says Momma.

"No, nothing at all to do with it," I say. "There isn't anyone else. I just want to help Lisa out. She's a single mom. She's just worried about finding another job being that she's a female electrician. There are many places that wouldn't even give her a chance based just on that."

"That's a nice thing to do," says Momma.

"Well, it does extend me with the company just a little bit, too."

"What about transferring to Statesville permanently?" asks Dad. "Are you considering that?"

"Statesville isn't going to run all that long," I say. "It's just a temporary measure to keep certain customers supplied while they get Mexico into full swing. It'll only run a couple of years. Upper management didn't want anyone to know that, but it's what they have planned."

"Yeah, Max wasn't supposed to tell us that," says Mel. "I know that he took some heat for that."

"He has more integrity than that," I say.

"I know he hates that he couldn't keep the plant open," says Mel. "After the announcement, he went in his office by himself and closed the door. It really hit him hard."

"What are you gonna do, Mel?" I ask.

"I'm gonna take advantage of the displaced worker program and go to school."

"What are you gonna take?" I ask.

"I'm not sure yet. Probably some sort of business classes."

"I've been saying that this will actually help many people at the plant. They'll end up in a better place than they are now. I know that I needed to get out of there a long time ago. I'm actually kind of excited."

"But some people don't have the options that you have," says Momma.

"Yeah, they sure aren't looking to transfer any of the machine operators to Mexico," says Mel. "Or office personnel, for that matter."

"Yeah, I know," I say. "But there are options for many more of them than you'd think. It's just easy to get comfortable and complacent. I don't want that anymore."

"But you need to be practical, too," says Dad.

"Yeah, I know. I'm too grounded to do anything too stupid."

I know what I want to do. I want to just leave all this behind and go to Mexico with Jim. There are so many reasons to do it, and really none against it, except of course for the impracticality of it. My parents have raised me to be so cautious and careful. Or rather, is that just something that developed in me over the years? I'm not sure. But is the Mexico option really all that impractical? It is true that it's a little risky. Who knows what will happen down there. But I need some adventure.

Chapter 67

Tuesday May 6th, 2003

"So, do you have an answer for me?" asks Jim, as we sit in a booth at the diner. "Are you coming aboard for the Mexico deal?"

"Does that mean that it's all set?" I ask. "Are the terms acceptable?"

"Yeah, I think so. They're willing to take both of us on permanently down there. Pay us what we make now, but on salary. We would get a three-year guaranteed contract."

"Shit, that does sound sweet."

"With the cost of living being so fucking low down there we will literally be cleaning up by making what we make up here."

"I know."

"So, are you in?"

"I know for sure that I can't do it just now," I say. "I'm gonna help with the Statesville startup. I should have told you that. I decided that a couple of weeks ago."

"Sounds like you've made up your mind."

"No, not really. I'm assuming that Mexico will take longer than Statesville. It involves far more machinery. I could come in late and still not miss a beat."

"But if you are considering it, why not just come in on the ground floor?"

"I'm doing Statesville for Lisa more than anything," I say.

"Doing it for her?"

"Yeah, they weren't giving her the time of day when she asked about it, so I agreed to do it and take her along with me. She's really worried about getting another job. So this will buy her some time and give her a leg up if she wanted to transfer out there."

"In another five years there won't be any more domestic plants left in the Raymond Mills portfolio."

"I know. She knows it's temporary. She has to do it for her kid."

"So you are still considering Mexico?"

"Yeah, I am."

"What about Karen?"

"I've all but left her."

"I didn't know."

"I just can't take it anymore," I say. "We just have nothing in common. All she's concerned with is her little narrow view of the world that's totally shaped by the church she goes to and the people who are around her."

"I wondered about the whole thing when you married her. It just seemed to happen so suddenly."

"Well, there were reasons for that. But I'm changing. I'm a different person than I was back then. I need someone that I can really connect with. I think that's why I chased after April like some damn fool. Sure, she has a great body and is as sexy as hell. But she's also intelligent and can actually talk about something besides church."

"Did you ever fuck her?" asks Jim.

I'm not really sure why I kept this a secret from Jim. He's not one to run his mouth.

"Actually, yes, and well, we're still seeing each other," I say.

"I always thought those denials were bullshit. But I didn't think you were still seeing her."

"It's just one of those comfortable things. It's casual. She has a very liberated way of looking at things."

"Are you leaving Karen for her?"

"No, we aren't in love or anything," I say. "We're just friends who fuck."

"The best kind of friends."

"Absolutely. I really love her attitude towards the whole relationship thing."

"And then there's Lisa."

"What does that mean?"

"It would seem to anyone with half a brain that your volunteering for Statesville for her, just for her, could have a deeper meaning."

Jim is admittedly pretty sharp.

"Deeper meaning?" I ask.

"I'm just saying that you taking her to Statesville seems like the perfect opportunity to develop a little romance."

"If that thought's there, it's just a sliver of a thought."

"But there is a sliver?"

"Sure….but who knows what she's thinking."

"I'm sure she's pretty appreciative of you for taking her along."

"Listen, the last thing I want to do is to jump from one relationship right into another," I say. "Besides, she has a kid, and there's a reason I don't have kids."

"What about your thing with April?"

"I told you, that isn't a relationship. She calls it an arrangement. No expectations. No entanglements. Just fucking and talking. And sometimes we don't even talk."

"Sounds like you have it made. You aren't afraid that she'll want more after you leave Karen?"

"I really don't think that'll happen. I guess we'll be more out in the open about things, but I really don't think it'll turn into a conventional relationship."

"Just remember that the best laid plans of mice and men are laid waste by the wiles of the female," he says.

"I think I can handle myself."

"So, you don't see yourself with Lisa?"

"I don't know if I even want to think in terms of relationships anymore."

"Well, Lisa has been pretty much just messing around with Israel for years now. And she's even said she doesn't see a future there."

"Listen, it's not like I'm scheming to get into her pants or anything," I say. "She's a nice girl. Lisa's like the complete opposite of April, quiet, much more reserved. She doesn't have the beauty or the body of April, but there is something sweet about her that's hard to resist."

"Well, no matter what you say, I know you're hoping to get her into bed out there in Statesville."

"I'm sure you'll be hooking up with some hot little Mexican babe as soon as you get down there."

"Naturally."

"When are you going down there?"

"I'll be going back and forth a few times before I go down for good. You know that we're taking a few dying machines loose now. Once they're down there, I'll take a trip down to oversee them getting hooked back up. And I guess I'll start looking for a place. I was hoping that we would both be going."

"They providing any money to move?"

"Yeah, that's all covered. I forgot that part. They're even gonna give me a monthly housing allowance. I'm telling you, man, you need to do this."

"You're coming real close to talking me into it."

"If you're gonna leave Karen then what's holding you back?"

"I don't know."

"I'm not sure you're going to be able to actually leave her."

"I haven't told her yet, but it's gonna happen."

"If you say so."

"I am gonna leave her," I say. "That's not why I'm hesitating about this. I'm just not really sure I want to keep doing this type of work. Factory work isn't what I really want to do."

"But this is totally different from working here. We'd be like supervisors. We'd have plenty of Mexicans around to do the real work. And once we start our own business, it really gets good. And you alluded to it yourself.....think of all the hot latina pussy we'll get a hold of?"

"I know, man......I've just got some things to think through. The plant closing is the opportunity for a totally fresh start. There are several possibilities. I just need to make sure I go the right way."

"Okay, man, but just think about it. I could really use you down there. But I'm going, one way or the other."

"I know you are," I say. "You're much more adventurous than I am."

"Being in the Navy kind of gets one used to being in different places around the world. It just whet my appetite for more."

"I am intrigued. If I were to say yes, are you sure they'd take me?"

"I'm in tight with Sam Irving, he's the guy running the show down there. You may have seen him up here. But I mentioned that you may be interested and he said he would be glad to have someone of your caliber."

"Okay, so I know the option exists if I want it."

"Yep, the door is wide fucking open."

"Good to know. I'll let you know."

Chapter 68

Monday, May 19th, 2003

"Well, I can see now why they're reopening this place rather than keeping a portion of our plant open," I say, as Lisa and I take our first look inside the Statesville plant.

"Yeah, it sure is small," observes Lisa.

"I guess the overhead of keeping the utilities running at our plant was more than the cost of getting this place operational again."

"Shouldn't be that much to starting it back up," she says. "It's only been down for a couple of years."

"Yeah, we had a couple of people that transferred to us when they shut this down."

"Yeah, one was that supervisor in tubular…..Wesley."

"Yeah, that's right."

"Well, I guess we need to find Gene," says Lisa.

We start to wander through the plant trying to find the maintenance shop. Gene Cook is the divisional engineering manager. He's Bob's boss. Or he was Bob's boss. I'm not sure there's too much of a division to manage now. Right now, his job is to get this plant operational again, with our help of course.

"He's taking a hell of a demotion," I point out. "Went from being division engineering manager to maintenance manager at this little dump."

"He's just trying to hang on to something until he can retire."

"He better be able to retire in a couple years because that'll most likely be the end of the line for him," I say, with the last part under my breath.

"Hey, Gene, we made it," says Lisa.

"Gene, how you doin?" I ask. "This place is smaller than I thought it would be."

"It's kind of a relic of how we used to do things," says Gene. "Many small plants instead of a few big ones."

"Yeah, kind of part of the reason for the trouble that the company's in, I gather," I say.

"Yeah, that's true to an extent, but this cheap foreign labor just took us by storm. It's proving very difficult to stay ahead of. "

"I'm not sure we are staying ahead of it," I say. "I feel like we're chasing our own tail at this point."

"Might not be a bad way to put it, actually," says Gene. "Well, why don't you two start by familiarizing yourselves with the plant. And I'd like to get the shop in order as well. I'll introduce you to the two guys we've hired so far. One of them worked here until we shut down. He can kind of show you around and get you up to speed on what needs to be done to restore the plant to working order. Okay?"

"Sounds good," I say.

"Let me show you to the shop," says Gene.

"Well, what do you think?" I ask, as Lisa and I relax in my hotel room after having dinner together.

"About the food?" asks Lisa.

"No, about the plant....the whole thing."

"It would be an easy job, if I were to take it."

"That's true," I say. "Not enough going on in there to keep my interest up though."

"What do you mean?"

"I just get bored with the same old shit going on. I need something to change to keep me going, either some new machinery or some sort of project. When things slowed down and it was just the day to day boredom of keeping the plant going.....I just hated that."

"Yeah, you know there won't be any major changes to this place after it gets running."

"No, two years isn't enough time. They wouldn't bother putting any more money than is absolutely necessary into a place that's only a stop gap measure."

"I'm starting to doubt that it would be a good idea to move down here. I mean for that? I just didn't know it would be so small. Just brings home the reality of how temporary it really is."

"You'll get something."

"I know I will eventually. But I need it now."

"Is it possible that you could do the displaced worker thing and go back to school?"

"I could swing it, with a little help from my family."

"It couldn't hurt to add some training to your resume," I say. "Classes of some kind."

"Maybe I should go for my electrical license."

"That's a good idea. That would help a lot."

"Do you know what you're going to do yet?"

"No, I'm not sure," I say. "It's like my life's getting thrown into full upheaval right now. Everything's happening at once. Guess I'm just going to see where it all lands."

"What does that mean?"

"Well, in addition to the plant closing.....I probably shouldn't tell you.....but I'm gonna leave Karen. Haven't quite told her yet, but yeah, I'm moving on."

"Wow. Sorry."

"No, it's what needs to happen," I say. "The hardest part for me is getting up the nerve to actually tell her. I'm not fond of emotional situations. I tend to avoid and put off those sorts of encounters."

"I think you know that you shouldn't be telling me before you tell her."

"Didn't I just say that?"

"Sorry.....I guess you did at that."

"I'll do it when we go back."

"So, why are you leaving her?"

"It's a little complicated. I guess I'm having some sort of crisis of faith or maybe it's just a midlife crisis.........I don't know...I don't know what it is. I just know that I have to do it."

"Crisis of faith?"

"I don't know if that's really true....if it's really the way to explain it," I say. "I just need to pull away a little. I need to stop being so intense about the spiritual stuff. I'm trying too hard to make things fit. It just isn't working."

"Sorry....but I really don't think I'm following you."

"Well....Karen and I have been at odds over the church stuff for a while now. I never really bought into that whole Pentecostal thing. I pretended to for a while, but I never got it. It never took root in me. Which I believe now is a good thing."

"Yeah, I remember hearing you talk about that here and there over the years."

"Well, because of that, I started researching and studying scripture. I came to realize that my views don't seem to fit in too well with those of most of practicing Christianity, not just the narrow little world of Pentecostalism."

"Yeah, you and Jerry, the two lone voices of reason in the vast world of Christianity."

"Yeah, I know. It does seem kind of stupid to me now, too," I say. "Jerry and I thinking we have all of this truth that no one else can see."

"I didn't say it was stupid. But it is kind of funny that you two thought you had all the answers, and these great theologians are all wrong."

"Actually, I still believe that. I won't back down from what I believe. I just see now how foolish it was of me to be so sure of it, to be so cocky. I had no authority to be like that."

"Well, that you were," she says. "You were quite sure of yourself."

"Yeah, I've been kind of aggressive about it. I've tried to get through to different people, including Karen. But I've come to realize that I'm preaching about something I don't possess myself. I'm probably the greatest hypocrite of all time. I need to just pull back and shut my mouth for a while. And that's if I ever open it again."

"Well, that's a little strong, don't you think? I don't see you that way at all."

"Yeah, but when you hear what I've been doing, you'll agree," I say, looking away.

"What? It can't be all that bad. None of us lives that perfect life."

"No, this is more than that."

"Oh my fucking God, it's true," says Lisa. "You have been fucking that slut April."

"Yeah…… actually………… for about a year now."

I'm not sure why I feel compelled to tell Lisa this really. I guess with my planning on leaving Karen it doesn't matter anymore. It doesn't matter who knows. It feels kind of nice to say it.

"Wow, I can't believe it," she says. "But in some way, I knew it was true all along."

"Yeah, not only have I been carrying on with her, but I've also been lying to everyone about it. Great Christian example I've set."

"Why the fuck didn't you just end it with Karen a long time ago?" she asks. "I just hate it when you guys can't just be honest with us. Why do you have to find someone else when you're still with us?"

"I didn't leave Karen…. because I still loved her….actually I still love her now. I just can't be with her anymore. I guess you could say that I'm not in love with her anymore."

"So, what's this thing with April about?" asks Lisa "Are you in love with her?"

There seems to be more passion than one would normally expect behind these questions. There's just something in her voice that makes me think that this matters to her somehow.

"Actually, no," I say. "We're basically just friends with

benefits. I guess that's why I didn't feel the need to do anything. I felt like it was just harmless sex."

"So, it wasn't cheating, because it was just fucking?"

"Well...I don't know....I don't think it's quite the same thing as having a full-fledged relationship....affair...or what the fuck ever."

"Typical male bullshit reasoning."

"I guess I know, that to you, and probably to Karen, there is no difference."

I don't know why I like it, but it seems to turn me on that she's pissed off at me.

"Well, you may just be the biggest hypocrite ever," she says. "Maybe that was an accurate statement after all."

"I know I said that...and in some ways I feel that way. But in another way.... I don't. I'm a totally different person than what I was, that is, if I ever actually was that person. I pretended to be religious. I wanted to be religious. I tried like hell to be religious. But that just isn't who I am. So, maybe I'm not really a hypocrite after all, maybe I'm just being true to what's really inside of me. Maybe this is just who I am."

"An adulterer?"

"Ouch!"

"Well...."

"I'm just talking about being a hypocrite. If you don't claim to be religious....well.... it's kind of impossible to be a hypocrite."

"What does that mean? Do you not believe in God now?"

"No, I wouldn't say that," I say. "Not exactly. I'm just pulling back from religion and this shit of trying so hard to conform to what's expected. The religious thing just isn't working for me."

"So, this is why you're leaving Karen? She's religious and you're not anymore, so you have to leave?"

"My life with her has become a prison," I say. "But it isn't really her fault at all. I'm the one who's changed..... no.....actually the real truth is that I never changed into the perfect little Christian that she expects."

"A prison? Is it really that bad?"

"Yeah, actually it is that bad," I say. "I can't be who I really am with her. There are just so many things that I'm suppressing because she thinks they're sins. Things that she thinks don't go with being a good Christian."

"Like fucking other women?"

"Hmmm......thanks."

"I'm sorry," says Lisa. "I know these are cheap shots. I just can't seem to help myself."

"Listen, I'm not proud of that. I know that April and I shouldn't be sneaking around like that."

"No, you really shouldn't be."

"But she isn't a slut," I say. "She's just different than most women."

"Yeah, I'll bet she is."

"She just has a different idea of what's right and what's wrong. She's doesn't have conventional views when it comes to sex and all that shit."

"Well, that's obvious. She's fucking a married man," says Lisa. "But, come to think about it, that happens all the time these days. She may be more conventional than you think."

"I'm starting to question our ideas of conventional morality myself. And this was even before I started seeing her."

"Question in what way?"

"Well, are we even supposed to be monogamous?" I ask. "We take all of this for granted because it's in a book, or it's just the accepted way, while our minds and our souls and our spirits are telling us other things."

"Or is it just your dick telling you this?"

She still turns me on talking like that.

"No, this isn't just about sex," I say. "I just question this whole notion of one person being our true love, our one and only, this whole soul mate thing. This isn't just me wanting to fuck other women."

"Okay, but despite these ideas you have now, Karen expected monogamy. You can't just change the program in the middle of the game. You can't just redefine what your relationship is on the fly."

"Yeah, I know that. And that's the thing. I'm not being true to myself. I'm not being true to what I believe. And I can't be as long as I'm with her."

"And besides being able to bed all the women you want, what does being true to yourself mean?"

"Do you really want to know?" I ask. "I don't really need all these snide swipes you're taking at me. You know, I ain't fucking around on you."

"Damn right you're not. I'd cut your fucking balls off if you were to carry on with April behind my back."

"I guess I'd better not cross you then."

"No, you'd best not," she says. "But yes, I do want to

understand what you're talking about here."

"Well, I haven't really told anyone about any of this….not even Karen….but I have all of these things I want to do…..creative things," I say. "I always have, really. And for some reason they're starting to blossom lately."

"What sort of creative things?"

"Music's always been the big one. I've dreamed of being a rock star since I was a teenager. In many ways, I guess I never really let go of that one. At this age it's kind of stupid, but it's still there, not the rock star fantasy, just the desire to do something with the music."

"A lot of people have those sorts of fantasies."

"I know….but I got so worked up about it that I bought a guitar and all of that," I say. "I was really trying to do something about it."

"Are you any good?"

"Now…. I'm kinda getting there…..but back then….well…not so much. I was more worried about all my fantasy world shit than I was actually learning to play the instrument well."

"What kind of fantasy world shit?"

"Back when I first began playing I had all these plans. I was going to move out to Los Angeles and make it big….or at least take a shot at it."

"But you obviously never did."

"Well….deep down I just knew that I was too shy to do any of that," I say. "For some reason, despite the shyness, I think I could have gotten on stage and played. But I would have had a problem with meeting people and starting a band and all of that shit. I was just so withdrawn and shy and in my own little world."

"So, you never really pursued it?"

"That fucking shyness has altered my life in so many ways. So many lost chances and wasted opportunities because I was too frozen by it to do anything," I say. "I've always said that shyness is probably too tame of a word to use for this. This is actually a disorder or something. It's a phobia. I don't know."

"It probably is some sort of disorder. It seems to go beyond what they call being a little bashful."

"I was writing songs. And I think some of them had potential to be good, if an entire band could get a hold of them. But I just knew that it wouldn't happen. I could never really reach out to people. Still can't really do it now. The shyness won't let me."

"You said you wrote some songs?"

"Yeah, I did. But who knows how good they really were. I was just trying to crank out some material for the hypothetical band I had in my head. Only recently have I really developed a passion for just making good music."

"Yeah, I think, in most cases, that you have to have that passion to be successful. You need something driving you besides the desire to be rich and famous or whatever. There are some exceptions to that. There are entertainers out there who really don't care about the music at all. You can tell by the shit they put out."

"Yeah, so, I let the deadline pass that I had set for myself to make the move to LA. I knew there wasn't any point to it."

"You were actually planning to just move out there?"

"Yeah, I was serious about that," I say. "Do you remember that mechanic that used to work here.....his name was Mike Swain?"

"Yeah, I think I do."

"Well, Mike was going out to LA to visit a friend. I asked him to bring back a newspaper so I could see what apartments rented for and jobs and stuff like that. Just to get a little taste of it. This was before the internet, of course."

"I do remember the long hair you had back then. You were trying to play the part."

"Yeah, that was all part of it. I feel like a real dick now. I was trying to act like someone that I was very far from being."

"Butch didn't like that long hair," she says. "He used to call you and Steve long haired hippie freaks."

"Ronnie was in there, too, when he worked up there."

"Yeah, I know."

"But anyway, I chickened out. I let the deadline pass. I somehow knew that I couldn't just move out there and expect to do the things I wanted to do. I actually like to refer to it as being socially retarded. That's my condition."

"I still don't quite get that."

"It's as simple as this, Lisa. I can't just go up to someone and start a conversation. I simply cannot do it. Even with April I had to have the pretext of trying to find a book."

"You just don't seem that bad to me."

"But you weren't at the plant when I started," I say. "Believe me, it took quite a while for me to settle in there."

"I mean I know that it took a while before you really spoke to me. But even then, it was really just work related stuff for the longest time."

"That's just the way I am with women. I don't know why.

There are probably women at the plant who think I have something against them, because I don't really talk to them, even now."

"It's funny that you're sitting here talking about being so dysfunctional with women and you've managed to bed the girl the whole fucking town was talking about. And you're still fucking her."

"Yeah, I know, but there's just something about her that just drew me in. Whatever magic she has just seemed to overcome all of that shyness shit. She just seemed to melt it all away."

"Yeah, I'll bet she did."

"It's strange, actually. If I can manage to break the ice with women, I know that I can be somewhat charming or whatever."

"Even if you do say so yourself," she says, rolling her eyes.

"Yeah, yeah, I know. But seriously, I know logically that I have a lot to offer, but the shyness, or what the fuck ever it is, just seems to override that most of the time."

"You are a nice guy. There isn't anything wrong with you."

"There's nothing wrong with me? Well, thanks for the glowing review."

"You know what I mean."

"Do I?" I ask. "I have a disorder, you know."

"It sounds to me like you're fishing for a compliment."

"No, not me."

"Well, despite that, I will say that you are indeed a very desirable man. You're funny, smart, and you aren't all that hard on the eyes, either."

"There you go with that again."

"What do you want me to say, that you're a god or something?"

"Yes, that would be nice."

"I'll just conclude by saying that there isn't any reason that I can see that would justify the way you feel. You are a very attractive man."

"Thanks. I guess I'm kinda figuring that out now. Just too bad I couldn't have figured it out, earlier. Maybe things would have turned out differently."

"It is what it is," she says. "All of us have things we would have liked to have changed in our past."

"Yeah, I know that."

"I'd like to get back to the music thing. I have a passion for music myself."

"What about the music thing?"

"You said that you discovered a passion for the music later after you realized all that rock star shit wasn't going to happen?"

"Well, it was funny really. After the self-imposed pressure of trying to make myself into a rock star overnight was gone, yeah, I started to play just for the sake of playing. I messed around with it in spurts, off and on, until I met Karen."

"What happened then?"

"Well, after meeting her and discovering the Lord and all of that, the rest just didn't matter all that much. It just kind of faded into the past, at least for a little while."

"But it never really left you."

"No, I never really lost the desire," I say. "The thought's always been there."

"I know. I was actually in a band when I was younger."

"Really? What did you do?"

"I was the singer."

"Any good?"

"Damn right. At least I think so."

"I have a thing for female singers," I say. "I would love to play in a band with a woman singing."

"Well, who knows, maybe we could do something someday."

"Why did you quit?"

"I don't know," she says. "It wasn't a serious band. We got older, had to get real jobs, started having families. Shit like that. It just kinda ended."

"You know, it's funny, like I said, I stopped playing guitar for a while, didn't touch it for a few years. Recently, I picked it up and started playing again. Now, after some practice, I'm noticing that it's like I took this huge leap in my playing. It's like I really believe I could be good enough to actually play in a group now. It's like something's blossoming in me."

"That's the second time you've used that word, blossoming."

"But that's what it feels like though," I say. "All of a sudden these creative juices are just flowing. I really believe that something can come of this now."

"Sure, there's no reason it can't, for both of us. I've always wanted to sing again."

"I'm not naïve enough to think that the whole rock star thing will happen now. But I look at it differently anyway. I just want to make music."

"You get me excited just talking about it," she says. "I never really got all into dreaming about fame and that shit. I just enjoyed the experience of performing in a band. There's just a magic that can happen."

"Yeah, I want to experience that magic. I think there's something almost supernatural that takes over when a band really gets in the groove."

"Yeah, that's what I always wanted. I never really cared about getting a record contract and all that shit. It was always just the feeling of playing live."

"That's all I really care about now," I say. "Before, I was obsessed with being famous and making a bunch of money. But that was just me compensating for the shyness. I know that now. I guess I thought that if I were famous, that the people, well, the women would just come to me. The shyness wouldn't matter anymore. The fame would just wash the shyness all away."

"That's good that you're so self-aware that you realize that's what it was about."

"Well, one thing about being in a shell, is that you have plenty of time to think," I say.

"You seem very far from being in a shell now."

"God….. in high school…… yes, I was in a shell. I never went anywhere. And that was true even after I started working at the plant. I never had a social life before Karen."

"Actually, don't you mean before that tramp Gina?"

"Yeah, technically that's right," I say. "It's great having so many people knowing your sexual history."

"Yeah, I know the feeling."

"Now, the fame or whatever isn't what I'm after. I just want that experience of playing live. There's magic that can happen when you play music with other people. I want that feeling."

"Yeah, you're right too in what you said, it's like something supernatural happens sometimes."

"Exactly! I can't believe I'm talking to someone else who believes that," I say. "It's not an idea everyone can grasp."

"It's obvious though, to anyone who knows anything about it."

"That's what attracted me to the guitar and guitar players early on. It just seems like something else takes over when they're playing. They reach this point and pass off into this other zone or something."

"Yeah, there is something that happens. I could get to that place sometimes myself."

"You see, I have all this passion for music, but Karen doesn't support it at all. If it's not church music or gospel then it's worldly music and isn't of any use. What I play is rock and blues, and to her and her church people, it's the devil's music."

"Yeah, that must be hard. You kind of expect your spouse to support what you do."

"I'm having a real breakthrough and she doesn't seem to even notice. It's not like she criticizes me or anything. But she doesn't say anything about it at all."

"So, how do you know what she thinks?"

"I know her views on music," I say. "What's so bad is that some other people have made comments about how good I sound. Just recently, I've been able to play in front of other people....well....at least when they're in the house. I could never do that before. I had to be by myself. Now I'm getting compliments on my playing, but nothing from her."

"I'd love to hear you play. Why don't you bring your guitar next week and play for me."

"Only if you sing along. Maybe we could write a song."

"What is it about the music and these people who think it's so evil?"

"You know, I'm not convinced that they're wrong actually," I say. "I just have a problem with the inconsistency. They're absolutely and completely against worldly music, yet they watch TV and movies and that sort of shit. If music's corrupt then isn't all that other shit, too?"

"Wait a minute. What do you mean that you're not convinced that they're wrong?"

"Well, that may be going a little too far. I don't think it's evil like they do," I say. "But I think good music comes from a dark place, whatever that means."

"I'm not sure I totally agree with that either."

"Well, consider that I like rock and blues. For that to be good it has to at least have some sort of spirit of rebelliousness behind it."

"Well, yeah, I guess I can buy that."

"That's why Christian rock is such bland shit.

"Christian rock is sort of shitty."

"Most music that I call good, music that touches you on a deep level, music that moves you, has that darker root to it, or just a rebellious, aggressive vibe."

"It depends on what you like."

"Real music comes from the soul," I say. "Not just the lyrics, even the rhythm and music itself comes from a deep place inside, rebellious, against the grain, at least that's what I think."

"Blues, especially, good blues comes from a deeper and maybe darker place, a place of pain."

"And to me, all good music is rooted in the blues."

"I would have to agree since that's a lot of what I sang."

"Hmm....that's the best of all.....a woman singing the blues."

"You like that, huh?"

"There's just a sensuality that can be conveyed through a good song, sung by a good singer."

"Men can do that too."

"Not like women can."

"To be a great singer, wouldn't I have to be troubled the way so many seem to be?"

"Not if you're able to channel something else."

"What?"

"You know how I was talking about guitar players being taken over by something when they play?"

"Yeah."

"Well, some of them actually talk about channeling some sort of spirit when they play."

"You believe that happens?"

"I do, actually," I say. "But then you have to wonder if bad things don't come with these spirits that take them over. So many of these great musicians are plagued with all kinds of problems, drug addictions and whatever."

"Do you believe in this concept that some of these people make a deal with the devil, so to speak, to have the talent they have?"

"It sure seems that way sometimes. Much of our better music comes from dark and disturbed people, or at the very least, troubled or damaged in some way."

"Is that why you identify with all of that, because you consider yourself damaged?"

"I'm not normal. I can tell you that."

"Who is?"

"I know, but I'm not really."

"If it were possible, would you make that deal, you know.....the deal with the devil?"

"That's an interesting question," I say. "I'm not sure. Not to actually give my soul to the devil to burn for all of eternity. But if having that talent were to mean that other things would be taken from me then….well….I don't know…that's a different thing altogether."

"You just don't seem like the type to me. You're too normal."

"That's the funny thing though," I say. "I am a misfit like many musicians seem to be. Despite what it looks like on the outside, I hate conformity. I hate it with a fucking passion. I'm just not addicted to drugs or any of that shit. But I do feel like I have the temperament of a musician. I just don't show it on the outside."

"I'm not sure you qualify for dark and disturbed though."

"But I am troubled and damaged."

"I don't see that, either."

"Does having an unhealthy desire to literally fuck everything I see qualify?"

"What?"

"Yeah, if it weren't for the shyness, I'd be almost literally fucking every woman I see, at least the hot ones," I say. "Seriously, it's like a sickness sometimes. I can't just see women as people. I have to imagine what it would be like to fuck them."

"Do you want to fuck me? Is that all you're thinking about as we lay here and talk? Are you just picturing how I would look naked?"

"Is that an invitation?"

"No, it isn't," she says. "Keep your dick in your pants. I just wanted to know."

"Yeah, actually, I've been attracted to you since you came to the plant."

"And you never said a fucking word."

"Would you have been interested?" I ask.

"Maybe."

"You were married when you started, anyway."

"Yeah, but by then he was fucking around and I was, too."

"So, I had a shot?"

"Probably so."

"See how fucked up it is for me because of the goddamned shyness?" I say. "And there are so many other missed opportunities, too."

"So, that's all I was….just another missed opportunity to get a little piece of ass?"

"No, more than that…..there's just so much that I missed out on."

"You know, you can't worry about the past now. Just focus on the future. You can't change any of that. Just don't make the same mistakes as you move forward as the new you."

"I know. And I just feel like the possibilities are endless now," I say. "As stupid and as trite as that may sound."

"No, it's true, you have a whole lot of living left in front of you, hopefully."

"I really want to take a shot at the band thing. I mean, who knows what could happen. At the very least I would get the chance to play live."

"Do you feel like you're channeling anything when you play? Do you ever feel anything taking over?"

"Nothing to the level of those guys, but yeah, there are little moments here and there where I'll play something, and I'm like, where the hell did that come from? It's like it came from somewhere else."

"Yeah, I think it's just below the surface," she says. "You just have to lose yourself in the music and it starts to happen."

"I think most art is inspired that way, if it's inspired at all. At some point the inspiration just shows up."

"Are you looking for your muse?"

"Yeah, I kind of believe in that concept," I say. "I've heard stories where musicians have explained that songs almost wrote themselves, that they were just there. The song just somehow appeared out of nowhere."

"I believe in the spiritual stuff. There has to be something more to this world than the physical. There has to be some sort of magic behind all of this."

"Yeah, to me, none of it would make any sense, otherwise. There has to be a spiritual connection. There just has to be supernatural shit going on that we just can't totally comprehend."

"You just seem to be fascinated with this idea that it's dark or something," she says. "I'm just not sure I believe that music has to come from a dark place for it to be inspired and beautiful."

"Well, I guess it may depend on one's definition of good music. Maybe it's just that the stuff I'm attracted to has a dark source? And I don't mean Satanic sort of dark. I just mean from a deeper part of our soul or spirit, a place where secrets are hidden away. Music can be good to me, but doesn't move me. But the stuff that does move me, seems to move me on a visceral level. It comes from a deeper place. Know what I mean?"

"Yeah, I guess so."

"You know, it's not just the music," I say. "I've got ideas for several different things."

"Like what?"

"It may sound really stupid, but I've been playing around with an idea for a TV show. Just for kicks. I know it's dumb."

"No, I guess that's not too crazy," she says. "What's it about?"

"Actually, it's about the plant, and the town. We've said from time to time that someone ought to write a book about everything that goes on in town. But instead of that, well, I decided it could be a TV show."

"You don't dream small, do you?"

"Yeah, I know that I have almost no chance of it ever being made. A factory worker in a small southern town has very little chance of selling an idea for a TV show."

"Maybe you ought to write a book then. Books are easier to get published than it is to get a TV show made."

"Great minds think alike, I guess. That's exactly what I started doing. I'm writing a book with the same basic story."

"What does Karen think of the book idea?

"I've never told her about any of it."

"Why?"

"Because, like everything else, she would never approve."

"Why would she not approve of a goddamn book?"

"For one, I want it to be realistic, so there is a healthy dose of profanity in it, or will be," I say. "But the real thing is that I want to include something based on my spiritual journey as well. All this shit that her church believes is tied up in that."

"So, this isn't going to be totally fiction."

"No, there'll be elements that are autobiographical, for sure."

"That's a little risky, don't you think?"

"They say you shouldn't do that for a first novel."

"I just mean that aren't you afraid of offending people?"

"Good art should shock and offend."

"You know what I mean," she says. "These are friends, and family. How are you gonna do that?"

"I'm gonna be careful, that when it involves other people, that I make it fictional enough, where people would know that it wasn't real, so that the real life actors wouldn't be embarrassed."

"Am I gonna be in there?"

"I hadn't planned on it….but I don't know how it's gonna end yet."

"So, I have to do something worthy of getting into your book."

"Yeah, there would have to be something."

"I couldn't imagine how I could be interesting enough to get into your book."

"Let me let you in on a little secret," I say, not sure that I should say what is to come next. "I only took this job so that I could spend some time with you."

"What?"

"Yeah, I just wanted the opportunity to get some alone time with you."

"You wicked little schemer," she says, with a smile. "I kind of wondered if there was some ulterior motive."

"You're not offended? Or worried? Or pissed?"

"Of course not. I'm flattered, actually. Why me though? I'm not exactly in the same category of your girl April."

"She's not my girl."

"But, she's hot enough to fuck for a year, and counting."

"There's no doubt that she just exudes a certain sexual energy."

"Obviously. That's why she has half the guys in town panting after her."

"But that's not all there is when it comes to attraction," I say. "Different women have different things that draw my attention."

"That's just a polite way of saying she's hotter than me."

"No, not really. She may be hotter in one sense, while you may be hotter in another."

"Listen, I really don't give a shit. I am who I am. I can't change that and I don't want to change that."

"Didn't I just say that I did this whole thing because I wanted a chance to be alone with you?"

"Yeah, you did."

"All things considered, I like you more than April," I say. "She may be the type that gets an instant response out of men. She's the type that you just want to take to the nearest alley and fuck the shit out of. But a woman like you....well....there's just something interesting about you. Something sweet. Something deeper."

"That's a sweet thing to say."

"It's true though."

"But, wait a minute, you agreed to do this before I even broke up with Israel."

"Yeah, I'm not saying I had some master plan to seduce you," I say. "I'm incapable of doing that anyway. I just wanted to be with you."

"But you were, and still are hoping that something will somehow happen?"

"I can't make those things happen. I just have to hope they do."

"Well, you got me right where you want me."

"I'm sorry for all this," I say. "Now I seem like a stalker or something."

"No, listen, Don, it's alright. I really am flattered. And besides, I needed this Statesville opportunity. I wouldn't have gotten it without you agreeing to come. And the truth is that I am available now. Who knows what may happen?"

"Hmmm....okay."

"I'm not giving you an invitation into my pants just yet."

"I know."

"You know, I do understand the whole thing with April. I get the whole thing with guys and the hot piece of ass. Shit, Israel was chasing that girl, too."

"In our defense, she is hard to resist," I say. "The girl just drips sex."

"I get all of that, but still, why are men so ready to throw everything away for the first piece of hot ass that crosses their path?"

"See, I don't think infidelity should carry the death penalty. Why should something that's really nothing more than sex just end a marriage....or whatever the relationship happens to be?"

"So, if it's just fucking, you expect us to give you a free pass?"

"Not necessarily free....but just some sort of leeway."

"Plenty of women do take back men who've cheated."

"I guess it's the idea that it's cheating at all that's my point," I say. "Why can't we look at fucking as just another sport? Because with most men that's all it is when it involves a woman that we aren't in love with. The problem is that too many women believe that there must be love there if sex is taking place. That's not always the case."

"I'm not so sure that's true. Don't be so sure you know what women think. Even if it were just sex, and I knew that for a fact, I'm not sure I could accept that my man was fucking another woman."

"I just think women are asking something of men that's against how we're programmed. We're made to wander. We're made to have sex with more than just one woman."

"Damn, it's pretty apparent why you're leaving Karen, now."

"Yeah, I know. I have some different views on things. This is very far from conventional Christian thought."

"That's putting it mildly."

"It's just that it's so easy for men to stray," I say. "We're visual. Dangle a piece of candy in front of us and before you know it, we've tasted it. I just think it's ridiculous to end a relationship for that sort of thing. Why must we resist every urge we have?"

"I can somewhat see what you're saying. But in most cases, it isn't like the woman is going to just drop her pants and let you fuck her on the spot. There is some time to think. There is time to consider what you're doing. Most women don't just spread their legs and wave you in."

"I kinda wish they would though."

"My point is that there is usually some time to cool off a little and think," she says. "You know what I mean? Most people can't really follow through on an urge the second they get one."

"Yeah, that's true."

"You didn't just walk into the library and fuck April right then and there."

"No, not the first time we met," I say. "But we have fucked in her office a few times since we've been seeing each other."

"You're kidding."

"No, we both kinda get a kick out of fucking in somewhat public places."

"The point I was making is that you guys aren't as helpless to the wiles of someone like April as much as you may think you are. You do have time to think about what the fuck you're doing."

"Not to pry, but did Israel's roving eye have anything to do with y'all breaking up?"

"No, you know I'd mentioned before that his plan was to move back to Nigeria. And that day's getting close. He started a job at an engineering firm that does work over there, so he'll get to move soon. I don't want to do that. I knew our thing, whatever it was, was never going to be permanent. Besides, I'll most likely be moving out here. He can't move out here now. So, we just ended it."

"You were together for a long time for it not to be permanent."

"I've been married twice. I've been disabused of the notion of permanence."

"So, you're not looking for that?"

"No, I don't look at it that way," she says. "If it works, then let it ride. See where it leads. Know what I mean? It lasted ten years. Ten years that were mostly good. They were much better than any of the years I spent with my two husbands."

"I like the sound of that," I say. "Just see where it leads, without any expectations."

"Not very traditional, now, am I?"

"No, you definitely aren't. At least not for living in a small southern town."

"I don't know. Does every relationship have to have to promise of eternity attached to it?" she asks.

"It may be an unrealistic goal this day and age. I think expecting that sets us up for failure and disappointment."

"Besides all that, Israel has some views of women that must come from Nigeria. Very traditional view of what a woman's role is. I can only imagine how my life would be if I were to move to Nigeria with him."

"Yeah, I've heard him talk about that before," I say. "That's typical though. Many of these foreign countries do treat women pretty badly."

"So, I knew nothing permanent was ever going to come out of that. Israel's a nice guy. He's smart. It was fun. He filled some needs for a while. But I kept him just where I needed him, but no closer."

"So, you just used him and threw him away when you were done?"

"Oh, he got plenty in return."

"I'm sure he did."

"I don't want to be what someone else wants me to be," she says. "I want someone who wants me for who I already am, or who I want to be."

"Who you want to be.....I like that," I say. "That really describes my situation perfectly. I simply cannot be who I want to be if I stay with Karen. I'm just suppressing so much of who I am with her."

"You can't live like that. That wouldn't be good for either of you."

"I never even considered leaving until recently. It was like I just had this epiphany that I couldn't do this any longer."

"I know the feeling. That's how it was with John, my ex. I tried to stick it out for Brett, but I just couldn't take it anymore. John thought it was bullshit that I wanted to be an electrician, you know, being a woman and all."

"How did you decide to do this anyway?"

"I imagine the way many of you did," she says. "I just wanted something that paid well and all of that. Plus, my dad works in the Vestal plastics plant in Raleigh."

"Was he supportive?"

"Yeah, he just worried about my being a woman, with all of you blue collar, less refined sort of men all over the place."

"Yeah, I know. I feel out of place there quite a bit of the time myself. I'm not the typical blue collar rough neck type at all."

"Well, I don't know," she says. "If your little thing with April is any indication, you may just fit in perfectly with them. They'd probably look up to you for being able to bag her."

"I guess I deserve that."

"No, I'm starting to think that you deserve them less and less, actually. It's just fun."

"That's me....I'm just a toy here for your amusement."

"A toy, huh, that could be interesting."

"Yeah, you can play with it anytime."

"Okay, enough of that," she says. "What was this great epiphany that caused you to decide to leave Karen?"

"This may sound kind of stupid really."

"I'm sure it won't"

"Well, I've wanted to shoot a low-budget film for years," I say. "Movies and how you make them has always intrigued me. But I didn't have an idea until recently. An idea that was practical to shoot on a really low budget. It just appeared in my head one day. Kind of almost like it's meant to be...... or something. You know, inspired."

"What is it about?"

"It's actually somewhat biographical. It's about Mark's brain injury. I had his character married and they came to live with my wife and I. But right after they arrive, he suffers the injury. Because of the injury, Mark's wife and the character based on me start to get closer. They kind of support each other. They've both lost something. My character's lost his best friend and the girl's lost her husband, or at least they've lost the person they knew. So, they end up flirting with each other. But in the course of writing this, I started adding things about how my marriage was leaving me unfulfilled. It was like as I was writing this, it was dawning on me how true this all was. I need an entirely different life."

"Who would have thought that you had all of this inside of you?"

"I know it may just seem like a silly dream, but it's entirely possible to shoot a movie today for next to nothing."

"No, I think it's great," she says.

"The way I look at it, I'd rather try and fail then to be sitting on a porch when I'm seventy or whatever and regretting that I never took a shot at any of this. This plant closure is actually invigorating me. It's like the new start that I needed. It's scary, but fun."

"It's just scary for me. I kinda have to be cautious. Having a kid and all. I just have to get a job."

"That's one thing that I don't have to hinder me."

"I've never looked at Brett as a hinderance."

"Yeah, I know. That was a blunt way to put it. But I guess that's why I don't have kids."

"Do you regret that? Not having kids?"

"I may one day, if I end up old and alone," I say. "But no, I've just had this stuff bouncing around in my head for so long now. I just couldn't bring myself to have kids. Karen wanted them, but I just couldn't do it. I've just never felt settled and content with my life. I just have this feeling that I'm destined for more than what I have now."

"So, the age old question.....can you go back after having gone black? In fact, you've gone black twice."

"Yeah, of course I could. The question is....could you go back?"

"Yeah....I might have to get used to a smaller dick....you know what they say about black guys," she says, smiling. "But yeah....I could go back. I don't have some special thing for black guys, like some of these country girls seem to. Israel was just interesting, exotic, being from Nigeria and all that."

"Well, just to address the dick issue, I've never gotten any complaints."

"The dick issue?" she asks. "And as far as complaints are concerned..... how many women are we talking about here?"

"Yeah, yeah, there haven't been many. But none of them have ever complained. And like you said, two of them are black, so they know all about the gigantic cocks that black men are supposed to have."

"So, I guess you measure up."

"Seems so."

"So....why so few women?" she asks. "I know you've mentioned your shyness a few times, but you've only had sex with three women?"

"Yeah, only three."

"I really don't know why I said that," she says. "Why would I just assume that you should have fucked a ton of women?"

"Well, it is kind of the norm today to have sex with many women."

"Okay, I'll rephrase that...sex with three women?"

"Yeah, I was a virgin when I met Karen. But by the time I

married her, I wasn't. And it wasn't with her that I lost my virginity."

"How did that thing with Gina happen anyway?"

"I was drinking and told Mark that I was still a virgin. No one knew, not even him. I was upset because Karen turned me down for a date. When Mark found out, he took me to Ronnie White's and we hooked up with some girls that he knew. So, my first time was drunken sex with a girl I'd just met at a bar."

"But I'll bet you liked it."

"It was good," I say. "She did everything, if you know what I mean."

"Is that a big deal to you? I mean....getting oral? Getting your little dick sucked."

Damn, my little dick turned into a big dick with that one little comment.

"What's this shit about my supposed little dick?" I ask.

"It's not?"

"Wanna see?"

"No, that's okay....at least not right this second."

Not right this second? Is something going to happen here?

"Now, if you want to show me something....well....I'm all for that," I say.

"Seriously, though...is getting your dick sucked such a big deal? It seems like all you guys fucking think about."

"It's more the idea of it. It's dirty, nasty, you know."

"Yeah....I do know," she says. "I just love the sixty nine position. The two of us just feasting on one another."

"The two of us?" I ask, grinning.

"You know what I mean."

"I don't know....maybe you think you mean one thing when you really mean something else. Freudian slip, perhaps."

"Look at you....just coming on so strong."

"Actually, the oral was something that I was missing....until April of course."

"Karen won't suck your dick?"

"Damn, you're turning me on talking like that."

"Maybe I need to stop then."

"No, don't do that."

"But does Karen just not like it..... or what?"

"We did it in the beginning........but then, all of a sudden, she just announces that she thinks it's a sin or something...... so we stop."

"Ummm.....I couldn't stop that."

"You actually like it?"

"Fuck yeah," she says. "And how can I expect my man to eat my pussy if I don't return the favor. But yeah, I love getting my man off with my mouth. Women think it's submissive or some shit like that, but hell, as far as I'm concerned, if you give your man that, he's fucking putty in your hands."

"There's no doubt about that."

"There's nothing nasty about it if it's with the man you love."

"Well, Karen must think it is."

"That's why it's a very bad policy to not have sex before marriage," she says. "We need to know these things first."

"Sex before marriage? Shit, we couldn't even talk about sex before we were married, much less have it."

"I've never quite understood that whole thing anyway," she says. "You and Karen. It just seemed like a mismatch from day one."

"Lisa, you just have no idea how much the shyness has determined my path in life. The truth is that I married Karen because of the shyness. I had never had a girlfriend of any kind before her. I just figured that this was my one chance for happiness. I kind of knew that I was making a mistake, but just hoped for the best."

"The drunken fuck with that girl didn't make you realize you could get women? I would have thought that would make you feel like a stud or something."

"I guess something dawned on me when that happened," I say. "If it wasn't for the fact that this religious shit was all mixed up in it, then sure, I probably wouldn't have stayed with Karen. I just looked at the thing with Gina as some mistake, some sort of sign that I was on the wrong track and needed saving. Instead, I should have looked at it as a sign that I wasn't some socially retarded basket case."

"Well, I think that happens more often than you may think. People making bad decisions because they believe that it's their best or only option."

"I just can't believe how one little thing….which I guess isn't that little….but how one little thing so profoundly altered the course of my life, so many things that I didn't pursue, so many missed opportunities, and I got into a marriage that was doomed from the start….just because of that."

"I had no idea that you had went through all of this."

"Well, that's part of being shy," I say. "You don't want to reveal anything about yourself."

"You seem to be wide open with the guys."

"Yeah, but I don't talk about most of this with the guys. We bullshit around. We talk religion and politics and that shit. But I've never talked about all of this stuff. You may be the first to know of all these things, the music, the shyness, all of these dreams I have."

"Why are you telling me all of this?"

"It's just pouring out. I don't know why. It's just bottled all up I guess."

"Well, I'm glad you are."

"Like I said, the shyness has always been much more pronounced with women. I don't know why it would be….. but it is."

"I don't know….I can understand that," she says. "With someone who has a hard time relating to people, it makes sense that it would be harder with the opposite sex. People who aren't shy even have trouble with that."

"Yeah, I guess that could be part of it. I don't know though….I think part of it's sexual. I just cannot seem to look at women as just people. I see tits and ass….you know….it's like sex is right there on my mind all the time."

"See? You're normal after all. You're a typical male."

"No, I know what you're saying. But I don't think all men are like me."

"Think it's because you never sowed your wild oats when you were younger?"

"Could be, I guess."

"So, all you're doing is laying there thinking about how it would be to fuck me?"

"Well…. I can't help but to notice your curves, your breasts, your ass."

"My huge ass."

"No, it's just the right size for me."

"No, it's too big."

"Why is it that you women don't listen to men?" I ask. "Most men I know really like nice full asses. I've admired your ass for years now."

"Oh really? For years? Pervert."

"Sorry. I can't believe I said that."

"I'm just kidding. I don't mind if you've been admiring my ass for years. But can we please take the focus off of my ass now? I'm not as enamored with it as you seem to be."

"Sorry, how about we focus on you rather plump breasts?" I ask, with a grin.

"They may be plump, but not as perky as they used to be."

"I get so distracted sometimes when I'm around good looking sexy women like you. I find myself trying to sneak peeks at the good parts, staring, if I can get away with it."

"But, it's like I said, most men do that shit. I know. I'm a woman. I see where the eyes go."

"I just feel like I'm obsessed though, sometimes. I just feel like that's part of the issue when it comes to my relating to women. I don't think this shyness shit is all there is to it. I'm so distracted by the physical that I can't ever get to know the person."

"Well, I feel like we're getting to know one another. So, what if you're a sex maniac obsessed with my body," she says, laughing.

"Yeah, I'm kind of surprised I'm saying all of this to you, actually."

"Well, like I said...I'm glad you are. I've actually admired....or I don't know....I've been intrigued by you for years now, not your ass, just you. But you're a hard person to get to know."

"I know. The shyness is really a vicious cycle. Because of the shyness, I tend to put up a wall.....which makes me seem abnormal or weird or something. People don't know what to think of the quiet guy. And, of course, that does nothing to help the situation."

"Yeah....I do hear people talking about you, I have to admit. But I don't think you're weird or abnormal or anything like that. I just looked at you as quiet, or mysterious.....thoughtful. You definitely aren't like most of the guys at the plant."

"That's why I don't share my creative side with them. They wouldn't understand. I don't fit in around here at all. That's why it's been so hard accepting Mark's injury. I could share anything with him."

"You definitely don't fit in with most of the guys at the plant. You are far too refined and nowhere near crude enough to fit in with that crowd."

"I don't know....here I am talking to a woman about dicks in mouths and shit like that."

"I don't mind. I have kind of a nasty mouth myself."

"Yeah....I like a woman with a potty mouth."

"Guess you've been missing that."

"Yeah, that's for sure," I say. "You know....I kind of value some of what came from the shyness now. I like the fact that I'm more introspective, that I'm more thoughtful. I like that I don't just go with the crowd, that I think for myself."

"Who knows what sort of ass you would have turned into if it wasn't for that," she jokes.

"Could have been one of these good ole boys, swilling beer and watching football all the time."

"There you go."

"I feel like I'm starting to just ramble on now. Once I get going I tend to talk too much."

"No, that's not true. I'm interested."

"Why?"

"The shyness....coupled with the outbursts of anger....then you go off the rails totally with April. I mean, getting your dick sucked in a park and getting caught by a cop? Yeah....I'm intrigued. You're hard to figure out."

"You know....I had doubts about the book for a while, but as I outlined it I realized that my life has been interesting enough for a book."

"Some people do say that we all have a book in us."

"And that's probably true. I'm gonna make this book about my journey and how the shyness so thoroughly changed my life."

"This must cause you to see yourself in a totally different light," she says. "Because I can tell you that you had no reason to feel like no woman wanted you. You may not think so but you are quite the catch."

"You know.....I know that intellectually. I know it's true. But the shyness just tempers all logic. It's like I'm looking through a pair of tinted glasses that makes me see myself and the reactions of people around me in a distorted way."

"Have you always been this way?"

"No...actually I was nowhere near like this in elementary school. This all came on me somewhere around the time of middle school."

"Do you know why?"

"For the longest time I associated it with the fact that I had to get glasses....either in the sixth or seventh grade. I thought that was the cause."

"Why would that be the cause? Many kids have to get glasses."

"It's because the glasses became a symbol of how the shyness caused me to be scared to make changes in how I looked," I say. "I was always afraid to make any changes to myself, because I didn't want to draw any attention. When I first got glasses they were these nerdy horned rim things. Well, that was fine for back then. But I kept wearing the same frames all through high school. I never got the courage to get a more modern or stylish pair until after I graduated. Then I remember one day sometime after I got the new glasses.....I happened upon my old pair. I got so upset with myself.....remembering the pain.....that I broke those things right in half....I knew those glasses made me look like a nerd....but I just couldn't change them."

"They may have looked nerdy.....but I'm sure you weren't the butt of jokes maybe the way you thought you were."

"I know that now. I know that it wasn't rational."

"I'm so sorry you went through all of this."

"The glasses actually weren't the worst part."

"What was then?"

"I had a bowl haircut until the summer between my junior and senior years."

"Bowl haircut?"

"Yeah....I had the Moe Howard special."

"Moe Howard?"

"Moe.....from the Three Stooges?"

"Oh....okay....never really been into the Stooges."

"Well....they say that it's a guy thing."

"But you mean you had a little boy haircut until you were in the eleventh grade."

"Thanks for that."

"Sorry."

"But I knew that was ridiculous for me to keep wearing my hair that way," I say. "God, that was so hard to do. I went to the barber one Saturday....I almost didn't tell him what I wanted. And then I had to hear the comments. Even though they were positive....God....I just hated it."

"So you associated the shyness with this stuff having to do with your appearance. But you don't think that was it?"

"Well, the more I thought about it the less I believed it was the glasses. And the main reason it couldn't have been the glasses was that I actually like the glasses when I first got them."

"So...do you know why now?"

"I actually think I do," I say. "I started thinking...isn't shyness about wanting to hide who you really are? Isn't it about not wanting people to see the full you?"

"I guess so....."

"What I'm going to tell you I've never told another living soul. I mean my family knows....because they were there.....they were in the house. But I never even told Mark about this…..."

"But you're going to tell me?"

"I'm not sure why I feel so free to tell you.…I guess it's just time."

"That's up to you."

"I wet the bed. And I mean I kept wetting it until the seventh or eighth grade. When I was in elementary school I was of course embarrassed that I was doing it. I remember not wanting to have anyone sleep over, because I was afraid I would wet the bed with them there. But I guess it took on a much bigger significance when I got older. I'm convinced that's what it was. I knew no one could know. There was no way they could. But I think that subconsciously I was scared that someone would find out. That's the part of me that I wanted to hide from the world. So.…I went into a shell that I'm still struggling to come out from now."

"Wow.…that's incredible that you figured that out. It has to be it. It makes perfect sense."

"Well, that's what happens when you have plenty of time to think."

"Most men don't have the desire or that capability to delve that deep into anything."

"Well, it's kind of ironic though.…the ability to be thoughtful and introspective enough to discover the cause of the shyness was actually caused by the shyness," I say. "Without the shyness I wouldn't need to have the ability to delve that deep."

"I'm glad you are who you are though."

"I am, too, now…..increasingly…….. I am."

"Increasingly?"

"I'm just starting to embrace these dreams that I put to the side because of the shyness. That one little thing changed my life in so many ways."

"How did you eventually stop wetting the bed?"

"My parents took me to doctors. They had my take these pills, but nothing worked. Well, because of the bed wetting, my mother had this rubber mattress cover. One day, she took that off and just put a regular one on. I never wet the bed again. I guess in my subconscious I knew that there wasn't a safety net there anymore. I don't know if she did that on purpose. I never asked, because the whole thing was just too embarrassing. But I've always wondered if that was done on purpose."

"Kind of sounds like it to me."

"I think so, too."

"You should ask her though."

"I wouldn't want to make her feel bad if perhaps she didn't do it on purpose."

"I wouldn't worry about that."

"Maybe I will," I say. "I would like to know."

"Well, I think you do have plenty of material for a book."

"There are just so many decisions that have been affected by this, so many missed opportunities, so many paths I could have taken if it weren't for this."

"I think everything happens for a reason though. Maybe this was just what you had to go through to be who you're supposed to be."

"I don't think I am who I'm supposed to be yet."

"Are you coming out of it now?"

"Yeah, some things are easier now of course," I say. "But I still hate going into crowded rooms. People think I'm early for plant meetings just because I like to be on time, but the main reason is that I hate to walk into a room after everyone's already there."

"And I guess public speaking's out of the question."

"Yeah, forget about that. And that eliminates quite a few jobs there."

"Yeah, but you're going in the direction you want to be now, aren't you?"

"I'm getting there. I'm starting to move. That's the most important part. Shyness kept me frozen all of the time. Part of leaving Karen is that I have to embrace the true me. That's the only way to come out of the shell. I haven't been my true self with her.....in so many ways. So I'm still hiding elements of myself. I can't do that anymore."

"I believe that as you continue to embrace the real you, the more the shyness will fade away."

"That's what I feel, too," I say. "It was so surreal when I came to that conclusion that shyness was about hiding something about who you were, being afraid to let it all hang out. Then I realized that I was living a lie in my marriage. I was suppressing the true me in so many ways just because of what Karen expects. I can't live like that. I simply can't"

"Well, at least you understand that's what's going on. Too many people stay stuck in the same rut their whole damn life. Look at me for instance."

"What kind of rut are you in?"

"How about the rut where you're a mother, but you don't think you were cut out to be a mother?"

"So, what are you saying?"

"I think I just went along with the crowd," she says. "I just did as I was expected. Don't get me wrong, I love my boy. It's just that there are times.....many of them....where I wonder why the hell did I do this. I get married to a bum. I pretty much knew he was a bum. I let him knock me up....and now I have a kid by that ass. And you know, you said how you had unfinished business that you didn't want kids interfering with. Well, sometimes I feel like he is limiting me. God....I hate to admit that.....I feel like that's a horrible thing to say. But it's the fucking truth. I wish I could just take off to Mexico and work with Jim. I wish I had that freedom. But I have to think of my son. Because of him I have to worry about what comes next. I can't be free to just do what I want to do. I have to do the responsible thing."

"Exactly, I like being able to be somewhat irresponsible."

"Talk about one decision affecting the rest of your life, try having kids."

"Think you'll have any more?"

"At this age? No, I seriously doubt it. But if I were to meet the right man, before my clock winds down, and he really wanted a child, then I would consider it. And I probably shouldn't do it for that reason. It should be something that I'm wholeheartedly behind. But we do that, we make decisions for others."

"I'm glad that's one thing I didn't give in on.....but it really bothers me that I'm leaving her with no kids," I say. "She loves kids so much. But I denied her all these years."

"I think you did the right thing."

"I just never pictured myself with kids. You know how you imagine how your life will be? Well, I never pictured kids as part of my life. I wasn't meant to have them."

"I kind of imagined having kids....but I don't know."

"I feel like I have a destiny. I feel like I'm meant to make my mark in this world somehow. I feel like things have fallen into line so that I'm clear to accomplish whatever it is that awaits me. Or.....I could just be fooling the shit out of myself."

"No, I believe in fate or destiny or whatever you want to call it," she says. "I'm just not sure what mine is."

"Well, some people are meant to just live a simple life, with simple pleasures, and simple contributions. Others are meant for bigger things. Not better things necessarily, just bigger....on a larger scale. I think the real tragedy is when you don't allow yourself to fulfill your destiny. I would hate to be nearing the end of my life and feeling like I was supposed to do certain things and never took a shot at them. At least if you take a shot and it doesn't happen you can comfort yourself with the idea that it just wasn't meant to be. But if you refuse to walk in what you were meant to do, how do you know that you didn't just stop yourself."

"Not to question all of this, but are you sure that your desire to be well known and to accomplish something big isn't just you overcompensating for the shyness all these years?"

"I think that very well may have something to do with it," I say. "There are many famous people who suffer from shyness. It seems to be a pattern actually. But I don't think that means I wasn't meant for it. The shyness was just part of getting me to that place."

"I probably am one of those simple people, as you say."

"But there isn't anything wrong with that. In some ways I wish that I could be happy just working a decent job, having a family, having a few hobbies, just living a regular life. In some ways life would be simpler. But because I do have all of these creative desires, I'd be miserable if I didn't pursue them."

"Yeah, I can see what you're saying. It basically comes down to the idea that we all have to be true to ourselves. We have to live the life that's meant for us. Otherwise, we won't be happy."

"Yeah, in a nutshell, that's it."

"I sure wasn't expecting meaning of life sort of discussions when I came out here with you."

"I'm kind of surprised myself. I don't normally open up like this. I'm only used to having conversations like that with Mark. At least before the accident I was. I guess the floodgates were waiting to open."

"You don't have these sorts of conversations with Jim? I thought you two were close."

"I don't know. Jim's pretty enlightened. He's definitely not a typical mouth breathing man. But he doesn't get into the deep meaning of things like I like to do. Not many men do. And, of course, I have a hard time getting close to women. So, there isn't much opportunity for me to discuss these sorts of things."

"You're not having a hard time getting close to me."

"Is that what we're doing?"

"I would say so."

"I don't know.....I guess you're just easy to talk to....I don't know what it is."

"Maybe it's just the new you starting to emerge from your

shell."

  "Ummm……that just may be it."
  "And you know what?"
  "No…what?"
  "I like the new you."
  "I like you too Lisa, the old or the new."

Chapter 69

Friday, May 23rd, 2003

"Hey, honey, missed you, how did it go in Statesville?" asks Karen, as she gives me a hug and a kiss, as I come in the door.

"Things went pretty well, I guess. It's a small plant."

"I start my new job at ProPlus next Monday. I beat them to the punch. I quit before they could fire me."

"Yeah....that's good."

"Is there something on your mind?"

"Yeah....there is...uh....I've given this a lot of thought," I say.

"Okay, what is it?"

"I think we need to go our separate ways."

"Separate ways?"

"Yes, separate ways."

"Do you mean break up?"

"Yeah, I want a divorce."

"But why, honey? I thought we were doing fine."

I can't believe she thinks we've been doing fine. I guess for her it has been fine. She gets to do everything she wants to do. She can be who she wants to be. So, sure, life must seem pretty good to her. I can't really blame her for being surprised, I guess. I do a good job of hiding the truth from people.

"We're not doing fine from where I'm standing," I say.

"Is there someone else? Is that it?"

"No, that isn't it. That's not why I'm leaving you."

Of course, there is someone else, but she isn't the reason I'm leaving. I feel as if the plant closing is what pushed me over the edge.

"But you didn't deny that you're seeing someone," she says.

She did pick up on that little subtlety.

"No, I didn't," I say.

"Is it Hope's sister, April?"

"Actually, yes, that whole thing was true. Well, it is true."

"Are you in love with her?"

"No, not really. It's just sex."

I'm actually amazed that I can be this frank and open with her.

I'm usually so worried about her judging me. I guess I really don't care anymore.

"Donnie, what are you doing?" she asks. "You need to repent. I just can't believe that you're doing this with her."

"This thing with April.....I don't know....it's actually just a symptom of what's going on with me. Like I said, I'm not leaving you for her. I'd be leaving even if she wasn't in the picture."

"But are you gonna keep having sex with her?"

"Probably."

"Oh, Don. The devil really has gotten to you, hasn't he? He used April to get to you."

"No, don't blame it on her," I say. "It's bigger than that."

"You don't have to leave, honey. We can work on this. I don't wanna give up on this marriage yet."

"What's there to work on? We've been basically living separate lives for a long time now. This isn't the way marriage is supposed to be. Why do we want to save it?"

"Oh, honey. Why would we want to save it? Because God put us together."

"I'm not sure about that anymore," I say. "The main thing we had in common was God, and now that's not even true."

"But that's because you stopped going to church with me."

"But that's because I just don't see things the same way you do anymore."

"You don't believe in the Lord anymore?"

"Of course I do."

"Don't you think it's a reasonable question to ask? I mean, the thing with April, hanging out in a bar, the language you use."

It actually is a reasonable question to ask. I am very far from being a model Christian, that's for sure.

"That's a perfect example of what's happening here," I say. "Yes, I cuss like a sailor at work. But I don't in front of you. But you know what? I don't think there's anything wrong with those words. I'm having to change who I am when I'm around you. I can't have that anymore."

"So, this is about you wanting to use cuss words?"

"That's just one example. You brought that up. Music's another one. I can't listen to the music I love because it offends you."

"I never made you get rid of those CDs," she says. "You made that decision."

"Yeah, I tried to convince myself that there was something

wrong with that music, but it was because of what you and your church people think about it. But that music is a part of me. I want to be in a band. I want to play blues and rock. Even if it's the devil's music, yes, I want to play it. I need to play it."

"Oh, baby….don't say that."

"Do you know how much it hurts for you to have never said the first thing about my guitar playing, while so many other people have? You're my wife. But you let your beliefs get in the way of that."

"I can't help what I believe. It doesn't matter what other people think. I have to be true to what I believe. I have to be true to myself."

"I'm glad you said that," I say. "That's the whole issue. I simply cannot be who I'm supposed to be with you. I'm pretending on so many levels and it has to stop."

"It sounds like you're backsliding on the Lord."

"Well, even if that were the case…..I have the right to do that if I want to."

"What happened? How did you get to the point of throwing away our marriage? And it sounds like you're throwing your salvation away, too. That's what makes me really sad."

"I've been waiting for that miraculous moment that all of you have claimed to have," I say. "But it just isn't coming. I've tried this and I've tried that. I've come to the conclusion that that's the whole problem."

"What's the whole problem?"

"The trying. You shouldn't have to try so hard for God to be in your life. Your way isn't the way for me. Keeping rules and laws isn't the way. Thinking that everything's a sin isn't the way. I believe in holiness. I believe we can live a holy life in the Lord. But we're missing something. You don't see it that way. But I do. You think you have all the pieces. I don't. I think God values honesty above all else. And I'm not being honest with Him or with you or with anyone else about who I am. I need to pull back some. That's the only way I'll ever find whatever it is I'm looking for."

"I don't know how you ever think you'll find what you're looking for if you keep fornicating with April."

"Well, you could be right," I say. "But I'm gonna stop judging myself."

"I just don't think I know you anymore."

"Maybe you never did. I'm not sure you ever did."

We remain silent for a few moments.

"I think there's something else you need to know," I say.

"Okay."

"That rumor…..before our wedding…..the one about me having sex with someone…"

"That was true?"

"Yeah, I was disappointed because I thought you turned me down for a date. So, I got drunk and ended up having sex with Gina at Mark's house."

"Were you a virgin? Was that the truth?"

"It was when I told you about it. Gina was the first. I'm not proud of it. It just happened."

"So, our marriage started off with a lie."

"Yeah. I just didn't think you'd still love me if you knew," I say. "You were so excited that I was a virgin and all."

"The lie was worse than what you did though. Can't you see that?"

"I was just so convinced that what we had was of God that I didn't want to mess it up."

"God doesn't need lies to accomplish his goals."

"Like I said, I guess you never knew me."

"Well….I won't try to stop you," she says. "The bible says that if our spouse wants to leave we're to let them go. If you want a divorce, then just tell me what I have to do."

"You may not see it now, but it's what's best for both of us in the long run. We hardly do anything together anymore. And I think we both liked that. We liked being apart."

"I know…..but we took a vow before God."

"I have to be happy. I'm not much use to God if I'm not in a good place. And I'm not in a good place."

"I don't know what you're looking for. I think you want perfect Christians and that just isn't going to exist."

"No, I don't want perfect Christians," I say. "You know what the last straw really was? It was that night when y'all had that bonfire. I saw how far apart we were that night. You all reminded me of the Pharisees in the bible. You were on a witch hunt. And you weren't even right, were you? Crystal ended up having post-partum depressions or whatever. That was the cause of all her so-called demonic torment."

"You're saying that we're the Pharisees?"

"What were they known for? They were known for being so pious and religious on the outside, but on the inside they were full of corruption."

"Full of corruption? We're full of corruption?"

"I'm not the one pretending to be all pious and perfect the way y'all are," I say. "I know what I am. The Pharisees didn't. They were blind."

"So, we're blind Pharisees?"

"Sure, you may not be quite as bad as them but you act the same way."

"I really can't believe that you think we're as bad as the Pharisees, or even close, really."

"You make people feel guilty for all of these so called sins on the outside, but on the inside you aren't as big of Christians as you make yourself into being," I say. "You say we shouldn't go to the movies, but you watch the same stuff on TV. You say we shouldn't cuss, yet you'll gossip and talk about people all day long. That's exactly what the Pharisees did. They made sure they looked all religious on the outside, but if you looked close, you saw that they were just like everyone else. You claim to have the spirit of God, yet you miss basic truths of the bible."

"Well, I must say that with the things you've been doing I doubt you have the authority to speak for God."

"I don't claim to. That's just it. You're the ones who claim to be so full of the spirit, but you miss stuff in scripture that anyone who can read can see."

"But, we are all human, aren't we? We aren't perfect."

"No matter what you say, the truth should be there if the spirit of God is there," I say. "You can claim you have the spirit living inside of you, but the spirit will lead you to all truth."

"I think we are in the truth."

"It's all based on these hollow experiences. All the stuff that you claim the spirit's doing to you in the church. It's only skin deep."

"I know what I feel. I feel the presence of the Lord."

"The truth is that few people, if any, ever have that true miraculous experience that the bible says we should have when God comes into our lives. Our entire lives should change, not just parts here and there."

"My life has changed."

"But not enough."

"Who are you to say enough?" she asks. "You're fornicating with that girl. You've lied about it."

"You sound like a Pharisee right there, talking about fornicating."

"It's the truth though."

"Nevertheless, the bible says what I'm saying. For you to claim to be led by God the way all of you do, you should have that total and complete change that occurred in the disciples."

"You've said that there isn't any law for the Christian, even the Ten Commandments. How do you justify that?"

"What do you mean? If Christ came to abolish the law, then it would stand to reason that he meant the entire law."

"But the Ten Commandments? That's going too far."

"That's just it. Someone who is filled with the spirit would go too far," I say. "Christ went too far. That's the whole point. Christians are supposed to be extreme. If you fit into this world just a little too well then that's a really bad sign."

"I believe people in the world can see how different I am."

"Listen, what I'm looking for is Christ, not just some religion based on Christ. Christ, not Christianity."

"So, you're right and everyone else is wrong?"

"You call plenty of people wrong, calling this church and that church dead. I don't see where you have the authority to judge like that. To judge the way you do you had better be really living as Jesus did."

"Well, I guess we're just going to have to agree to disagree on this."

"That's not the way it works.....but alright."

"Can I ask you something?"

"Yeah....sure."

"Did race have anything to do with this?"

"Why would you ask that?"

"I don't know. I just always wanted to prove everyone wrong. I just don't want it to be about that."

"I love you and I love your family. This just has to do with my being able to be free to live how I need to live. I just can't do that with you."

"I won't stand in your way. Are you going to move out now?"

"Yeah, I'll probably just stay at Mom and Dad's for the time being. It's only the weekends anyway, at least as long as this Statesville thing is going on. Actually, I may end up going to Mexico with Jim to work at the plant down there."

"Oh....okay. Just remember....I'll always love you, honey."

"I'll just get a few things together and be going, I guess."

Chapter 70

Tuesday May 27th, 2003

"So, how was your holiday?" I ask, as Lisa and I drive out to Statesville after the Memorial Day weekend.

"Just had a little cookout at my parent's house. You?"

"Well, I was supposed to go to the big event that one of Karen's uncles always has, but I just spent it with my family instead."

"Why's that?"

"Because it's over. I told her. The reason I spent the holiday at my parent's is because that's where I'll be living."

"Wow.....okay."

"Yep, quick and easy," I say. "I didn't wait or put it off."

"Why are you at your parents? Are you gonna let her have the house?"

"I haven't really thought that far in advance yet. I don't know."

"You did the right thing telling her."

"I told her everything, too."

"Everything?"

"Told her about April....and Gina," I say. "Even told her that April was just for sex."

"Is that true? Is April just for sex?"

There she goes with those pointed questions again.

"We talk. But it is pretty much just sex.," I say. "Well....I guess it must be a little more than that. But April isn't interested in a relationship."

"Are you?"

"No, actually, I like what we're doing now."

"Don't be surprised if she may be interested in some sort of real relationship now," she says. "Once she finds out you've left Karen, she may want more."

"I kinda doubt it."

"Well, it kinda sounds like the way's clear for you to go on your little Mexican adventure with Jim now."

"The way's clear, there's no doubt about that."

"Is that what you're gonna do?"

"I have no idea," I say. "It would make it easier to just let her have the damn house if I were to go down there. I wouldn't need a place to live up here if I were down there."

"Why do you want to let her have the house? You had that before you met."

"With the education and skills that Karen has she'll never have but so good of a job. And this isn't her fault. This marriage being in shambles is all my doing. I'm not the person she thought she was getting. I owe her something. Shit, I denied her children. I have to do something."

"Most guys wouldn't be that charitable."

"I know. But this is a different situation. We never fought. It was never like that. This will be the epitome of an amicable divorce."

"The only way mine could have been amicable would have been if the bastards would have just fucking died."

"Damn, remind me to never cross you," I say. "Some of the things you say….."

"Yeah, but I can't imagine myself being able to hate you."

"Hmmm…..really. What a thing to say."

"Yeah, anyone can see it. You're one of the nicest guys I know. Well, as much as I do know you."

"Well, believe me, you do know me now better than probably anyone," I say. "I've told you things that I haven't told another living soul."

"Why did you choose me to tell all of that to?"

"It all just came pouring out that night. I'm not sure why really."

"I almost wondered if that wasn't by design," she says. "I think you may have more game with the ladies than you say you do."

"No, I already admitted that I wanted to be alone with you."

"Exactly, you schemed to get me alone with you."

"Sure, I admit that, I wanted to spend some time with you. But no, I didn't have some master plan to reveal all of that stuff in an attempt to get you into bed or anything."

"It's interesting that you're aware that something like that could work on some women though."

"Did it have that effect on you?"

"See, it's comments like that that make me wonder," she says. "How can someone as supposedly shy as you be so forward?"

"Well, maybe fucking April has had some sort of effect on me."

"Yeah, apparently. What sort of monster has she unleashed?"

"You didn't answer the question."

"What question?"

"Are you being coy with me, Miss Delaney?"

"Me, coy?"

"Yes, you know perfectly well which question I meant."

"Remind me, please?"

"Did my pouring out my heart to you have any effect?"

"What effect in particular would that be?"

"Getting you into bed."

"Damn, I wasn't expecting you to come out and say that."

"Well?"

"I didn't fuck you that night, now did I?"

"No, you didn't, but did the things I shared with you have any effect as far as inching you in that direction?"

"No, it wouldn't have that effect if I thought for a second that it was just some calculated move."

"It seems as if you're dancing around the point here," I say. "Of course you wouldn't respond if you knew it was a calculated move. That goes without saying."

"Does it? Because some women would be turned on just by the idea that you put so much effort into it."

"But not you?"

"No, not me at all."

"But I think you know that I was sincere that night."

"Yes, I do think you were."

"And....?"

"What do you want me to say?" she asks. "Do you want me to say that I got all wet and weak in the knees because you revealed some of your deepest secrets to me?"

"Yes, that would be nice."

"All kidding aside....it did touch me, Don. There aren't many men, no, there aren't many people who're in touch with themselves the way you seem to be."

"I would never admit this to any of the guys, but I think I have a lot of feminine qualities in me."

"See, how many men would be willing to admit that?"

"Yeah, but I wouldn't admit it to them," I say. "Except for Mark, maybe. I think he would've understood, before the accident."

"They say we all have varying degrees of both masculine and feminine in us. There's nothing to deny or admit, it's just the truth."

"Yeah, but I find that I have more feminine in me than many men."

"Why do you say that?"

"Well, one is that it's pretty easy for me to tear up," I say. "I probably tear up more than some women. Just some sentimental story on TV and I'm fighting back tears."

"I'm not sure how much of that is actually being more sensitive and how much of it is just upbringing. So many boys are raised to be hard and unemotional, so they end up suppressing that. You must not have been raised that way."

"No, my Dad definitely isn't one of those types of men who demand that their sons be tough and never show any sort of weakness, well, supposed weakness."

"Brett's jackass dad is one of those types," she says. "He's always tried to push him into hunting and that sort of shit, but Brett just doesn't want to kill things. Of course, he blames me for making the boy soft."

"Yeah, that's another sign to me that I'm not the typical male. Well, at least not typical as far as many men are around here. That whole hunter mentality just seems so foreign to me. I just couldn't do that. And some of those hunters are just so proud of the fact that they killed this animal or that animal. I just couldn't do that."

"But there are many totally feminine women who love to kill things."

"I know, but I still associate a kinder and gentler spirit with the feminine. And that's me."

"How did it go telling Karen that you wanted a divorce?"

"I was really surprised how easy it was. I think I tend to build things into something bigger than they are anyway. I avoid difficult discussions like that, but in the end they usually aren't that bad. At least not as bad as I had thought they would be."

"Must not have been considering that you told her about April and Gina."

"Well, she did kind of ask about April," I say. "But I offered up Gina."

"What did she say about April?"

"She said that we were fornicating and that I'm basically a backsliding Christian."

"Well, you are most definitely fornicating with her."

"Yeah, I sure am," I say. "And that's basically what I said to her. I told her it was just sex and that it's what I was gonna do."

"Damn, you laid it on the line, huh?"

"You know, the truth is that I'd bet that what bothers her more than the end of the marriage is that she thinks I'm on my way to hell."

"Why would you say that?"

"I just know her. Salvation is more important than anything else. And she knows that we've hardly been spending any real time together lately. She knows it wasn't good."

"It will be better for both of you in the long run."

"I know. It really will be. She'll meet her a nice church going man who believes everything that she believes and they can be happy. I really hope she gets that."

"And what do you want?"

"I don't know. I told her I may end up going to Mexico."

"No, I'm not talking about that," she says. "What do you want when it comes to women?"

"Women? Well, to start off, I like the sound of the plural....women."

"So, that's what you want? You want to live the life of the playboy like Jim. Go to Mexico and fuck one hot Mexican chick after the other?"

"That does sound good."

"Yeah, I'll bet it does."

"Despite some of the changes that I'm going through, I'm still not equipped to play the ladies like that. It just isn't going to happen."

"I don't know," she says. "I think you're getting there faster than what you think."

"April has said that she'd be willing to go with me."

"Oh really? So, I guess that sweetens the pot considerably?"

"I guess. She wants to keep our thing casual though. We live together. We keep fucking each other, but we also get to have the freedom to fuck other people."

"Is she fucking other guys now?"

"I don't know."

"Don't you want to know?"

"It doesn't really matter to me," I say. "I kind of like the idea of an open type of relationship."

"Well, I guess it's all lining up nicely for you then."

"Yeah, I don't know. I'm not sure that's what I really want. The open relationship idea is great. I mean, that I'm not sure about Mexico. It's a great opportunity. I could save quite a bit of money. I could have a great time. Live in a different culture. But I'm not sure it's what's best for me as far as what I really want to do with my life."

"What do you mean?"

"I don't want to keep doing this sort of work. I want to do something creative. Writing books is probably the most realistic way to achieve that."

"Yeah, but you could still write if you went to Mexico," she says. "It sounds like from what Jim has been saying that the Mexicans are doing most of the real work and all he's doing is supervising."

"Yeah, I know. I'm not saying that it'll be all work. I'm just worried that I'll get sidetracked with other pursuits down there."

"I thought you said you didn't have any game."

"Well, that's true, but I would imagine that the opportunities would kind of present themselves for someone like me. You know, an American that's making good money?"

"Yeah, I can imagine that a guy like you would have them lining up to be with you down there."

"I mean....that would be great," I say. "I just don't want to get sidetracked."

"You're taking this writing seriously, aren't you?"

"I really am. I just cannot imagine myself doing this sort of work the rest of my life. I'll go crazy if that's what happens."

"But you have to do something now. You can't make a living writing yet."

"No, that's true."

"So, maybe do the Mexico thing and build up money, like you said?"

"Oh, I definitely haven't taken it off of the table," I say. "How can I? It's a job right there waiting for me."

"And with a hot fuck buddy to come along for the ride."

"I'm really not sure why she wants to come. It's not like we have a real relationship or anything, at least not enough of one to just follow me to another country."

"Maybe to her it is."

"Well, whatever I decide to do, it'll wait until after this Statesville thing's over."

"That would be a short term option for you, too," she says. "Now that you've left Karen you could come out here for a couple of years."

"Yeah, that's true."

"I'm kind of thinking that's what I may have to do now."

"I thought you were having second thoughts, after you saw

how small it is?"

"The reality is that I have to keep working. I may have to just let Brett stay with my sister so that he can stay in school. He's at the age now where he would throw an absolute fit if he had to change schools."

"You wouldn't have a problem being away from him like that?"

"I could still see him like every other weekend and on holidays," she says. "Shit, he hardly wants to spend any time with me as it is."

"I guess that's pretty common for kids his age."

"Yeah, exactly."

"You know, I mentioned last week that I feel like the possibilities are endless for me now....well....after telling Karen I was done, it's really starting to feel that way. I have two possibilities when it comes to jobs. I just have to take my pick. I'm free of all that religious baggage now. I can be who I really want to be now."

"I can't imagine why you would take the Statesville job though," she says. "Mexico seems much better."

"And why would Mexico be better than Statesville?"

"You don't have a fuck buddy in Statesville, yet."

"I don't have one there, yet?"

"Well, you don't, do you?"

"No....I don't," I say. "Of course I don't. What caught my attention was the word yet."

"Yet? It's just a word."

"Okay, it's just a word."

"Yeah, it is just a word......but...well, it may mean, it could mean what you want it to mean."

"And what do I want it to mean, Miss Delaney?"

"Who's playing coy now, Mr. Higgins?"

"Me, coy? Never."

"Well, let me just say that...well...I'm not like April," she says. "I don't think I am quite that liberated when it comes to sex. But I'm also no prude. Your charms are doing their trick on me, Don. And we're both free now. And we're spending all this time together."

"And this is going to last for a few months, at least."

"Yes, it will. So....well.....what do you think?"

"I think that sounds like a marvelous idea, Miss Delaney."

"Seems your plan worked out better than planned."

"Seems so."

"I'm glad it did," she says. "It was really all I could do to resist fucking you last week. But I kind of didn't like the idea that you hadn't said anything to Karen yet."

"What about April?"

"Well, you really aren't going to have that much time for her now, are you?"

"Yeah, that's actually true."

"I'm not gonna say that you can't see her. I have no claim on you. We haven't even done anything yet."

"But we will?"

"Yes, we most definitely will," she says. "You have no idea the effect you have on me, do you?"

"Well, I have picked up a few signs."

"It's not like it was only what happened last week. I've had my eye on you for years."

"The feeling's mutual."

"There's even something about you voice."

"My voice?"

"Yeah, it may be stupid, but I could just listen to you talk for hours. Doesn't even matter what you're talking about. I just love the sound of your voice. It's soothing somehow."

"Really, my voice is soothing?"

"Yeah, there are other things, too," she says. "I have to admit that I was thrilled when you said you would do Statesville just so I could do it. I guess I had some hope that you did have an ulterior motive in doing it. I wanted to believe that you had a real interest in me."

"Even though I'm married and fucking April."

"I'm just saying that the idea thrilled me. You can't control that. Circumstances determine if you act on urges or desires, but urges are just there or they aren't. You know what I mean?"

"Yeah, I do. Believe me, I do."

"But, now it seems as if the circumstances and the desires are lining up. And that's what we want, isn't it?"

"Yes, it most definitely is."

"The Statesville gig is starting to look pretty good now, isn't it?" asks Lisa.

"Should we just get one room?"

"Hold on a second. It's possible that either one of us may be repulsed by the other," she says. "I think we'd better just see what happens before we start making plans."

"I'm pretty sure I'm not gonna be repulsed by you."

"Yeah, I don't think that'll be a problem for me, either."

"Did we just seriously agree that we're going to start fucking one another?"

"I guess we did."

"It's just that it wasn't the way I would have pictured it happening."

"What do you mean?"

"I guess I just thought that it would happen in a much more romantic way," I say. "But we just kinda agreed that we are going to do it."

"Anything wrong with that?"

"No, I guess not."

"Alright then."

"How are we gonna get through the work day now?" I ask. "This is all I'm gonna think about."

"Haven't you ever heard that denying yourself pleasure makes it's fulfillment all that more rewarding?"

"But you're all I'm gonna be thinking about today," I say.

"Hmmm.....I like the sound of that," she says. "But we do have work to do first."

"I know.....delayed gratification."

"Exactly."

Chapter 71

Saturday June 14th, 2003

"Hey, Claude. Karen said you wanted to talk to me," I say, as I take a seat in Claude's den. "I think I know what you're gonna say."

"Just let me say what the Lord has led me to say," says Claude. "If you don't mind."

"Okay….whatever."

"Son….do you realize how serious divorce is?"

"Yeah, I think I do."

"You think? Well, I know," he says. "You made a vow before God. It's a serious thing to go against God."

"Do you think I do this lightly?"

"Well, I happen to know that you've been fooling around with that tramp April."

"Yeah, that's true. I'm not exactly proud of it, but it happened."

"Is it a godly thing to have your dick in another woman's mouth and out in a public park, at that?"

"Wow, such language."

"Better the language than fucking other women."

He's starting to lose his composure just a little. He doesn't like his supposedly God given authority questioned.

"I've still fucked less in my life than you ever did," I say.

"Okay, son. This is starting to get uncivil. I'm sorry about that. I just wanted to make the point that you're very far from being in the will of the Lord."

"I know that, but I'm not the one claiming to be led by the spirit all of the time. That's you."

"I want to share some scripture with you."

"No need," I say. "I probably know it better than you do."

"So, you know it, but you're just going to ignore it?"

"I'll ignore this scripture while you continue to ignore the scriptures that you ignore. How about that for a deal?"

"I don't ignore any scripture."

"That's your view," I say. "I know differently."

"Care to name chapter and verse."

"How about anything having to do with still living under the law? The tithe? How about burning furniture that belongs to a great woman of God? I could go on and on, Claude. You're very far from being in a position to judge me, very far indeed."

"You have an argumentative spirit. We aren't going to get anywhere here."

"Now you've finally spoken the truth," I say.

"Why are you so full of venom, son?"

"Because you have the nerve to summon me over here to give me the great words of the Lord, so that you can pronounce judgment on me."

"God will judge you, son.

"And God will judge you for all the damage you've done with the false teaching you've done throughout the years."

"I've never knowingly taught anything false."

"But you're wrong about plenty of stuff that's right there as clear as day in scripture," I say. "So clear, in fact, that anyone who can read can see it. But you claim to be filled full of the spirit of God, yet you fail to see it."

"And you think you can, when you obviously don't have the spirit?"

"It's just as obvious that you don't."

"Well, of the both of us, you're obviously the one in error."

"Well, so be it.....whatever," I say. "I know the truth. We aren't under any law. I will not live around this anymore. I feel like I'm living in a prison. Are any of us perfect? Don't we all break some law or rule or something?"

"Sure, son, none of us is perfect."

"So why can't I be forgiven for this, just like anything else?"

"Forgiven for what?" he asks. "Forgiven for fornicating with that girl?"

"Sure, that, divorcing Karen, all of it? Does God's forgiveness have limits?"

"No, well, of course you can be forgiven."

"Then why are you making such a big deal about this?"

"You aren't repenting," he says. "You're still doing this. You're defying God."

"You don't understand what repenting means. You're either living in Christ or you aren't. Repenting isn't an act that you must do every single time you make a mistake. Repenting is a state of being."

"No, son, there are certain serious sins that you must repent of separately. There is a difference between sin and what are just everyday weaknesses and mistakes."

"This just goes into what I've been saying for years," I say. "If we're no longer under law, then that includes everything. You always want to make exceptions. But those exceptions are always the things that don't affect you. Well, we're either under law or we're not. Which is it? You can't pick and choose."

"Of course we aren't under law anymore. I'm just saying that some things are more serious."

"No, it's all the same. There aren't degrees. We either break the law or we do not."

"You don't have a proper understanding of scripture, son."

"The proper understanding of which parts to ignore and which parts to instead obsess over?" I ask, of course, sarcastically. "You know....really, this has as much to do with you as it has to do with Karen. I'm tired of being looked down on as the poor little one who doesn't get it. No, I don't get it. I don't get what you believe. And I'm tired of trying to get through to you. I just have to get away from all of this. If I don't, you'll be burning my stuff in a bonfire someday, because, after all, I don't have the anointing. The anointing means everything. A man has the anointing and you just bow at his feet."

"No, son, I don't bow at anyone's feet.....only to Christ."

"Claude, I just believe in a bigger God than you do. I believe in a God who isn't worried about all of the small and insignificant things that y'all get hung up on. I don't believe in a God that's just sitting around waiting for us to slip up so that he can just drop the hammer on us. That just makes no sense to me. And I don't see that in scripture. What's salvation for if we have to still walk around worrying about slipping up all the time? The grace of God allows us to make mistakes, many mistakes, as many mistakes as we want. That's the whole point. We can't be perfect, so he gives us the right to be totally and completely imperfect."

"You're going in the wrong direction, son."

"The thing is, Claude, I'm looking for something that you don't have, I don't have....well....I'm not sure anyone has. You probably think that you're radical and extreme. But that's the problem....you aren't extreme enough. That's what I'm looking for. I'm looking for what the disciples had, a radical and complete change. A change that's supernatural. Maybe I'm searching in vain. Maybe the fact that no one seems to have that, suggests that it doesn't exist. You think I'm backsliding. No, I'm just trying a different route to get what none of us seems to be able to lay hold of."

"I've laid ahold of it. Don't let anyone fool you, son."

"Not according to scripture, you haven't."

"Well…..I've tried my best to get through to you. All I can say is that I'll always love you, son. And I hope you find your way back before it's too late."

"I hope you find your way."

Chapter 72

Sunday June 15th, 2003

"Hey, man, what's happening?" I ask.

"Oh, hey, thought you'd forgotten about me," says Mark. "Haven't heard from your ass in a while."

"Well, there's been a lot going on."

"Come on in and have a seat."

"You know, you could call me or come by my place," I say.

Mark has had this habit of never calling or coming by to visit, but then he complains that he hasn't heard from me. Since the accident, Mark seems to like to play the victim. This is just another way to do that. He can complain about how I've abandoned him like everyone else has.

"I just don't know when the best time to call you is," he says.

"You can call anytime. If it isn't a good time, then I'll just say that I can't talk to your sorry ass."

"You biatch."

"Just stop waiting for me to contact you then complain that you haven't heard from me," I say. "You're just creating a self-fulfilling prophecy."

"Self-fulfilling prophecy?"

"Just means that you're making happen the very thing you said would happen."

"I don't understand."

"Don't worry about it."

"Okay," he says. "So, what's been going on that kept you so fucking busy that you couldn't fucking call me?"

"Well, for one, I'm sure you've heard that they're closing the plant."

"Yeah, Mom did mention that."

"Well, because of that I've been going to Statesville to help open a plant there."

"They're closing one plant and then opening another?"

"They're just reopening Statesville," I say. "They shut that down a few years back."

"But why close one and reopen another?"

"Statesville will only stay open a couple of years. They're only opening that to service a few customers until they can get the Mexico plant in full swing."

"Mexico plant?"

"Yeah, it turns out that they've had a plant in Mexico for decades," I say. "None of us knew about it. But they're expanding that and moving much of our operation into that facility."

"Bastards! All of these companies are moving overseas today."

"It really doesn't bother me."

"But you're losing your job, aren't you?"

"Yeah, I am. But there are some opportunities out there."

"Like what?"

"Well, like I said, I'm helping them set up the plant in Statesville," I say. "I've been going out there every week since the middle of last month. Just come back home on the weekends."

"Statesville......where is that?"

"It's out in the western part of the state. It takes about three hours to drive out there."

"How long do you have to do that?"

"We'll probably have the plant set up by the end of August, if not earlier. But I may just take a job out there and stay for the little time the plant will be open."

"Does....uh...is it Cindy, your wife..."

"No, it's Karen."

"Yeah, that's right, I forgot. But does Karen want to move out there?"

"Karen's not a factor in my life now."

That sounded kind of harsh. Of course she's still a factor in my life, but will be less of a factor as time passes by.

"Karen's not a factor?" he asks. "What does that mean?"

"It means that we're getting a divorce. I left her."

"Oh....I'm sorry. I thought you had a happy marriage."

"It may have appeared that way on the outside, but no, it was far from happy."

"I didn't know things weren't good."

"No one really did, I guess."

"Did you move out or did she?"

"I'm living with my parents until I decide what to do," I say. "Like I said, I'm at Statesville every week any way. I'm only home for the weekends."

"Do you mean that you're going to stay with your parents until you decide to go to Statesville or not?"

"Actually, I have another choice."

"What?"

"I can move to Mexico and work in that plant."

"Why would you want to go down there and live, there are enough of them invading this country?"

"Listen, after what Jim has been telling me about those guys down there, I'm not going to talk shit about Mexicans. He says they're working there asses off. They're doing work by hand that we would normally have equipment for."

"Who's Jim?"

"You knew him," I say. "He worked down at the plant. He's helping with the Mexico move. He wants me to come join him down there permanently. He wants to start in that plant then eventually start our own consulting business and travel wherever the work takes us."

"Consulting? Consult for what? They pay people for that?"

"Yeah, our expertise is in textile equipment and textiles is going to be big in Central and South America."

"Yeah, because they're taking all of our fucking jobs."

"So what? We get cheap clothes because of it."

"What's Karen going to do?"

"She already has a job."

"Well, that's good."

"Yeah, it makes it easier to leave, in some ways."

"I kinda hope you don't take the Mexico option," he says. "I'd miss you. Who would I talk to, besides my Mom?"

"I keep telling you that you need to get out and do something. You need to meet other people."

"I just don't feel like being around a bunch of people most of the time."

"But you need to."

"I was going to that brain injury support group, but after that ass Mike, who I met over there showed he wasn't a good friend at all, well, I wanted to stop going. I don't want to see him again."

"So, you're just going to write off the whole idea of meeting other people because this one guy didn't live up to what you wanted him to be?"

"I don't know."

"What did he do anyway?"

"He just kept saying he was busy when I wanted to go play pool and stuff like that."

"But did he go with you sometimes?"

"Yeah, we went a few times," he says. "I thought he had a good time."

"Okay, well, then maybe he was busy those other times. Is that a possibility?"

"No, he was just an ass."

"Listen, from my experience, you tend to be a little clingy when it comes to people who want to do things with you."

"Clingy? What the hell does that mean?"

"It just means that you've tended to bug the shit out of people to do things," I say. "You act sometimes like we don't have anything else to do. You've done that to me. That's why you need to have more friends. You tend to latch onto one person and some people may not like that, so they pull away. And then of course, you also tend to get all pissed off and push them away."

"Well, I don't think I'm like that at all."

"I've seen it. I'm telling you that you've done that with me."

"Well, I don't have a life like the rest of you do. I just sit at home with my Mom and watch TV."

"That's my point," I say. "You need to stop that. You need more friends so that you don't try to rely on any one person."

"You can't rely on anyone anyway."

"Well, you can't if you expect perfection. And you seem to be ready to kick people to the curb for the least little transgression."

"People always do let me down. People always do seem to find a way to fuck me."

"I've seen you write people off for one little thing. And this doesn't just apply to friends. I've seen you blacklist a particular store or restaurant because you had one bad experience."

"Fuck em! If they can't do their job then they don't need my business."

"But people make mistakes. Don't you?"

"Yeah, but I just hate incompetence."

"You need to lighten up on people."

"I'll try…..but those bastards just keep fucking with me."

"Well, just try."

"I wish you weren't going anywhere."

"Well, we'll see," I say. "It may just be Statesville."

"How are you gonna make the decision?"

"Well, actually, it may come down to which girl I want to be with."

"Does that mean you have more than one?"

"Yeah, well, remember when I told you that I fucked that girl in the park?"

"April."

"That you remember?"

"Yeah, you fucked her up against a rock," he says. "And didn't a cop catch you with your dick in her mouth?"

"Yeah, you've got that down pat. Well, I've been seeing her since then. She's what you call a fuck buddy."

"I'd like to have a fuck buddy."

"But she's offered to go to Mexico with me."

"Okay, but what about Statesville?"

"Well, there's this girl, Lisa," I say. "You know her. She works at the plant."

"Yeah, I think I remember her."

"Well, she's helping me with the Statesville plant. And, well, we've started seeing each other, nothing serious, yet. We just talk and have plenty of sex."

"Damn, you're one lucky son of a bitch."

"It does seem as if all the pieces are falling into place after the plant closing was announced."

"I'd like to have a girlfriend, but who'd have someone as fucked up as me?"

"As far as your brain injury is concerned, you aren't that fucked up," I say. "It's more about your attitude. All you want to fucking do is to stay in the house. You won't get out into the fucking world."

"What do I have to offer a woman? I'm on fucking disability. I can't give her anything."

"Well, maybe you can find a woman who's in a similar situation. She would understand what you go through and you could help each other through life."

"You mean find someone else with a brain injury?"

"Could be....or she could have a physical disability.....or no disability at all. It's just a suggestion."

"I just have a hard time getting out and doing that. I don't like crowds anymore."

"Get on the fucking internet," I say. "I've tried to get you to do that before."

"What good would that do?"

"There's a whole world out there to explore. You could be in contact with so many people who share interests with you. And the great thing is that you can keep them at a distance until you decide you want to meet them…..if you wanted to meet them at all."

"I guess I could try it. Could you help me get set up and teach me how to do it?"

"Sure. And this will be a way that we can keep in contact as well."

"Good, because your sorry ass waits long enough to call or come over."

"Well, this will be a way for you to harass me."

"And you know I will."

I really worry about Mark and what his future will hold. He seems to have no desire, or else no ability, to try to live any sort of real life. His life now consists of sitting at home and watching TV with his mother. He tends to push away whatever friends he does manage to make. Either they offend him in some way, or else they feel as if he's clinging to them too much. Mark has always been very unforgiving of the imperfections that we all have. But after the injury this trait seems to be functioning at a really unfortunate level. He seems to push away anyone who shows any interest in doing things with him. I just worry what will become of him when his mother passes away. But I can't make my decisions based on his condition. I just can't do that. I'd like to be there for him, but that just may not be possible.

Chapter 73

Monday June 16th, 2003

"I can't believe you even agreed to see him," says Lisa, as we lay in bed naked, in the Statesville Holiday Inn, of course, after having fucked our brains out.

"I don't know....I guess I just thought I owed it to him or something," I explain.

"Well, I don't think you owed him shit."

"It pissed me off more than anything. They're all just so fucking smug about what they think they know."

"And you know that, yet you submit to it anyway."

"I guess I just have this idea that somehow I can still get through to them."

"I doubt it," she says. "Why do you even care?"

"Because, despite appearances, I'm still a Christian, and I do care about the truth."

"You say, after fucking a woman who's not your wife, and fucking me quite well, I might add."

"Yeah, yeah.....I know, I'm a shining example of biblical morality."

"And....to add to that, you've fucked yet another woman, for a whole year, who wasn't your wife."

"Another notch in my belt of apostasy."

"But it's some good fucking, isn't it?" she asks. "I can work magic with my mouth.....and....by the way....you can, too. I've never come like that in my life. You make me just explode every time we do it."

"I've been told I'm quite good at it."

"And to think I've been missing out on that all this time."

"Israel couldn't do that for you?"

"I've never had a man who does what you do down there."

"I'm glad you're pleased."

"It wasn't practice that got you here," she says. "So, what is it?"

"No, I have been practicing on April, remember? There was no oral with Karen but plenty with April."

"Did you have to learn with her? Do I owe this all to her? Did she teach you, or are you just a natural?"

"No, she was pretty pleased to start off with."

"So, you are a natural."

"I just love doing it. I just love being between your thighs."

"Well, believe me, I love you being between my thighs, too."

"Good."

"What is it?" she asks. "Something seems to be on your mind, lover."

"One thing you'll learn about me is that I have a hard time letting shit go."

"What did I do?"

"No, it's not you. I'm thinking of Claude and Karen and that whole crew," I say. "It just burns me up that they're sitting there thinking that I'm this big sinner. I've backslidden. I've turned my back on the Lord. It just burns me up when they're so fucking self-righteous."

"Why do you worry about that shit?"

"What they don't get is that I haven't given up. I'm still seeking the truth. I just realized there's a different path I have to try."

"What are you looking for anyway? Why can't you just be happy in the moment? Aren't we having fun? I know I am."

"I'm sorry. Sure, we are having fun," I say. "But I have to have it mean more than that. Life has to mean something. There has to be a reason for our existence. I believe that there's a hole inside of all of us that's only meant to be filled with God. The trick is to find out how to do that."

"I don't know.....I think you're tormenting yourself over something that you aren't even sure about. You say yourself that no one you know has had this miraculous experience that you say should happen. So how do you know that it should?"

"It's in scripture."

"And what if scripture's wrong?"

"But the concept rings true to me somehow."

"Or.... do you just want it to be true, because you want so desperately to find meaning in life? Maybe there isn't any meaning to be found."

"Even apart from scripture, that just doesn't seem likely."

"So, what's the plan then?" she asks. "Are you gonna join a monastery or something?"

"I've actually had that thought before. Also thought of starting a commune where we could try to build the perfect little Christian community."

"Okay, Jim Jones Jr."

"I wish I could be like most people and not look for meaning. It would be easier. But maybe that's my destiny. Maybe that's what I'm meant for, to seek for answers and help the world see the truth."

"Wow, what am I getting myself into here?"

"Yeah, I know," I say. "Bold words for some fool who works in a textile plant."

"No, if that's what you feel, well, you have to go with it."

"I think in addition to the book, I'm gonna create a website."

"What's the site gonna be about?"

"Whatever comes to me," I say. "Spiritual topics, politics, whatever I want to write about."

"That's the great thing about today. Anyone with a computer can get their viewpoint out there."

"I think there are people out there who would like to hear what I have to say."

"I know there are. I'm one of them."

"See, it's things like this that I have to think about when I consider what I want to do."

"You mean in whether or not to go to Mexico?"

"Yes."

"Seems like a no brainer to me," she says.

"No, it's far from a no brainer."

"So, what are the factors keeping you here?"

"Well, one that I hadn't thought about until the other day is Mark."

"What about Mark?"

"He just doesn't have anyone in his life except his mom and she isn't going to make it but so much longer."

"So you think you need to stay close to help him?"

"At first I didn't think his disability would be as bad as it is, but he's really gonna need supervision the rest of his life."

"No other family?"

"An uncle who's older than his mom, and a brother that he cannot get along with."

"So, it's just you."

"Yeah."

"You're willing to give Mexico up for him?"

"No, it isn't just him."

"Then what?"

"I think you know," I say.

"Do I?"

"Yes, you do. It's only been a few weeks, but you know that we're hitting it off."

"Yes, I would say that's quite true."

"Well, I kinda want to see where it leads."

"You would give up the chance to romp around Mexico in some sort of open relationship with April?"

"The idea is enticing," I say. "But I'm not so sure the reality of it would be."

"What do you mean?"

"I don't know. It would be different if April and I were in love or something. There isn't a real deep bond there. I get the feeling that I'm just her ticket down there. I'm just her free ride to a little excitement."

"But with me, you know….you aren't gonna be able to fuck other women."

"I know that," I say. "But I'm not so sure that matters as much as I may have thought. Sex is just a momentary and fleeting high anyway. Love is deeper."

"Is that what we have?"

"Well, I want to be cautious…..but yeah, I think we're going in that direction."

"Going in that direction?" she asks. "Does it even work that way?"

"I don't know. Maybe it does for me."

"I think I may already be there."

"Wow….I wasn't expecting that."

"And I'm not saying that because I expect anything from you. I'm just telling you what's going on. I'm just telling you how I feel."

"Well, I did say that we seem to be going in that direction."

"It's never…..as you say….gone in that direction with April?"

"You know…it's funny….we seem to get each other on a level that is definitely deeper than the superficial," I say. "It's definitely more than just sex. But…I don't know….I'm not sure if it's me, or her, but no, it isn't love. There's some sort of disconnect there. But that could be my fault."

"I doubt it's your fault."

"But you don't know that."

"You seem very capable of loving someone," she says. "I don't know her, but it seems as if April is the one with issues in that department. She's the one who seems to want to keep her distance."

"That's true. There is some sort of scar there. Someone has hurt her at some point."

"Yeah, I'm sure you're not the problem."

"I don't know, Lisa. I'm not sure what being in love is sometimes. I'm not sure I want to be in love the way some people are in love."

"Why?"

"I just can't accept this idea that one person is gonna be my everything," I say. "You know what I mean? This idea that this one person that we love is going to be the center of our life. I'm the center of my life. I have things that I want to do. Those things are more important than any woman could ever be. Maybe I'm different than other people in that regard. I can love a woman. I can imagine myself loving you. But I just can't imagine myself ever loving anyone to the point that nothing else matters."

"Does this apply to Karen?"

"Of course it does. But that whole situation was complicated by the fact that I was a virgin and then all that religious shit got mixed in, too. But no, I never felt like Karen was the center of my life. I don't want that. That's just who I am."

"I think I've been a little hardened by my failed marriages," she says. "That's why I kind of kept Israel at arm's length."

"Are you going to keep doing that?"

"I think it kinda depends on the man."

"Okay."

"Why....do you want me to keep you are arm's length, too?"

"No, I'm not saying that."

"I think I actually agree with what you're saying," she says. "I don't think it's healthy to fall for someone so thoroughly that if for some reason it ends, your whole fucking life falls apart. But that's who I tend to be. Actually, I probably didn't intentionally keep Israel at arm's length. I just never fell for him that way."

"I just don't see how it's good to rely on someone so thoroughly that your life does fall all apart if that ends."

"But sometimes you can't control what you feel," she says. "I can say logically that I don't want to fall for someone like that, but if I do....oh well. And like I said, that's what I tend to do."

"I know," I say. "But I don't think I even open myself up to that possibility. Or maybe I'm just not wired that way. Maybe I'm just incapable of that."

"Or….maybe you've just never run across a woman that could work that sort of magic on you. You may think you aren't wired that way. But just maybe no one has ever connected those wires just the right way."

"I do have somewhat limited experience in this area."

"Yes, you do."

"But that's most definitely changing."

"Yeah, you've left one woman and you've got two to choose from to take her place."

"Well, I don't know if I'd look at it quite like that."

"In other words, no one can take her place."

"No….I'm not saying that at all," I say. "I just mean that I'm not looking to jump back into a marriage."

"Okay….well…me either actually."

"I'm kinda surprised that you can be so casual about April."

"Well….I don't want you to choose her," she says. "But on the other hand, I don't know where this will lead anyway."

"Yeah, I know. But you know…..I told you that you know me better than any person on the planet. And you still want to be around me."

"Be around you? I think it's more than that. In fact, I know it's more than that."

"I know. I'm just saying that you seem to accept me for who I am. And you do this after understanding what really makes me tick. You do this after seeing the true me."

"Well, I happen to think that the true you is a beautiful thing to behold."

"You aren't so bad yourself."

"It touches me that you've revealed all of this to me," she says. "I can't help but thinking there's a reason for it. It can't be that we're going to have a little fun and then we'll just go our separate ways. I don't want to scare you, but it just feels like something special is happening."

"Yeah….I know. It just feels right somehow, even how we kinda just decided to start sleeping together. It just felt like the right thing to do."

"I know. It seemed strange in some way. Like you were saying, it seemed like it should have been more romantic. But maybe it didn't need to be that way. Maybe it was just destined to happen, so….we let it."

"Yeah….I know what you mean. It just seems natural to be

together."

"I just realized something," she says.

"And what's that?"

"I caught the fucking bouquet at your wedding."

"That is kinda funny, isn't it?"

"That's doesn't mean I want to get married."

"I know."

"It just seems like some sort of twisted sign or something."

"Yeah, maybe."

It does seem natural to be with Lisa. And I can't say the same is true of April. We have a good time, boy, do we have a good time. But there really is something missing there. There is a distinct emptiness to whatever it is that April and I have.

Laid out there like that, the choice seems obvious. But maybe it isn't so obvious. Do I really want to go right into another relationship? And to add to that, do I want to be in a relationship with someone who has obligations? Brett is almost grown now, but do I want someone who has a kid? Or should I opt for the April route? She has a kid, too. But what she promises is something much less restrictive. But is that life what I really want? Or am I much more traditional than I would want to admit? I'm really not sure which path I will choose. There is indeed much to consider.

Chapter 74

Saturday August 23rd, 2003

"Well, I guess this is it," I say. "The last time we'll have lunch in this old diner."

"Yep, all my loose ends are tied up," says Jim. "Mexico is my new home, starting Monday."

"It's kind of amazing how fast this all occurred."

"The question then becomes, will we replace this diner with some old cantina in Mexico?"

"I really don't know, Jim. In some ways I want to, but in others I don't."

"Damn, I was really hoping you'd come now that Statesville's about wrapped up."

"I know, and the last day for most of the guys at the plant is Friday."

"So….what are you waiting for?" he asks. "You have to do something."

"Well, the thing is….I'm kinda seeing Lisa."

"Hmmmm….no wonder you've been content doing the Statesville gig all this time."

"Yeah, it's definitely made it more bearable, to say the least."

"I'll bet," he says. "When did this start?"

"Like the second week up there."

"Damn, that was fast."

"Well, I think we'd kind of admired one another from afar for years now. But the way's clear now…. for the both of us. It just happened."

"Well, I guess that about decides it then, doesn't it?"

"Well, I don't know. I do have another option."

"Yeah, what's that?"

"April's willing to come to Mexico with me."

"Shit."

"And, she still doesn't want to get serious or anything like that," I say. "She says we can be free to fuck other people. We would kinda just keep our thing like it's been…..casual."

"So what in the fuck are you waiting for? I know what I'd choose. Shit, that's a fucking dream come true, a hot woman that'll let you play the fucking field."

"Yeah, I know."

"And let me tell you, that you're going to have plenty of hot latina ass to choose from," he says. "Those girls are just throwing themselves at me."

"Yeah...but that's you. You're smooth. You've got game, man. I don't have that ability."

"Well, for one, you must have something. You've got your choice between two hot women. Secondly, you don't need any sort of game. Some of these other Americans who are down there helping with the startup are getting all the pussy they want and believe me, you look better than them and you'd just appeal to those women more than they do. They're just all over us because we're Americans."

"What do they expect?" I ask. "Do they think you're going to marry them and take them away from their life down there?"

"I don't know, and I don't care. I just know that I'm having the fucking time of my life. And if you come, I will absolutely guarantee that you will, too."

"Guarantee?"

"Yes, I guarantee a healthy dose of pussy if you choose to come down."

"I never have been able to really sow my wild oats, the way they say you should."

"You'll sow plenty down there, believe me," he says. "And you do need to do that. I did sow my wild oats when I was younger, but I'm having a ball down there, anyway."

"You make it sound so enticing."

"And the money, too. Don't forget the money we're gonna rack up."

"I know....it's a great opportunity," I say. "There are many reasons to go. But there are other reasons to just take the Statesville job."

"And the main one being this budding relationship with Lisa?"

"Yeah, I guess she is the main reason."

"Why in the hell do you want to go straight from a marriage right into another relationship?"

"I don't know, Jim. I kind of like having someone to come home to. I need that, I guess."

"But you will have someone to come home to, and her name's April," he says. "But with her, if you find someone else to go home with then you go home with her. Believe me, you'll be far from lonely."

"But it is possible to be lonely even when you're not alone."

"Not for me."

"Well, maybe I'm different," I say. "I like having someone I can rely on. I can't say that about April. She could be gone as soon as we get down there."

"But that may be a good thing. You could be gone as soon as you get down there. You may find you a hot Mexican chick and decide to set up house with her."

"I know what the possibilities are."

"Is Lisa the only reason you resist paradise?"

"No, there are other reasons."

"Like what?"

"Jim, this isn't really what I want to keep doing with my life. I want another career. I've got to do something else at some point."

"Okay, but one way or another you have to make a living until then. Statesville is temporary. Why can 't you just look at Mexico as temporary?"

"I'm worried I may get permanently distracted down there."

"Well, that's most definitely a possibility," he says. "A pretty sweet possibility, if you ask me."

"Sounds good.....it really does. But that would be the easy route to take. I've got work to do."

"What kind of work? We've got work to do down there."

"I'm writing a book."

"A book? About what?"

"Well, it's semi-autobiographical," I say. "There are characters based on some of the people at the plant. I'm intent that one way or the other I'm not going to work in factories the rest of my life."

"Okay, but why can't you write your book down there?"

"I just think that I'll get too easily distracted with all the women you say will be throwing themselves at me."

"Or...you may just end up with more material for your book....or the next one."

"Yeah....it would be an adventure."

"Yeah, get out there and live a little," he says. "That's what good writers do."

"You do have a good point. Many of the great writers lived quite interesting lives."

"Exactly."

"It's something to think about."

"I think I know what that means."

"No, I am really thinking about it."

"You know, the plant closing was probably the best thing that could have happened to either of us."

"Yeah, sometimes you just need something to give you that little push to get you going," I say. "Something to push you in a new direction. Something to just shake you awake."

"Yeah, we're both out of the rut now, my friend."

"That we are…..that we are."

That is a good point. Good writers have to live. Good writers have to experience things. This is such a great opportunity for that. Who would have thought that the plant closing would have presented such a great opportunity as this? And who would have thought that I could have just fallen into another relationship so quickly? I have thought about asking Lisa to come to Mexico with me. Brett is sixteen. He could stay with his father for a couple of years. I feel as if she would do that for me.

But wouldn't bringing her along kind of screw up the whole idea of doing this? Isn't the whole idea of the Mexico thing that I could live a little? April will let me fuck who I want to fuck. She would let me experience anything I wanted. But Lisa sure won't.

The choice is more than a choice between two women. The choice is between two entirely different ways of life. The choice is between something that is very similar to what I've had and something that is totally new and unknown to me. Both have their positives and both have their negatives. One is very comfortable and familiar. The other is very exciting and fresh.

Chapter 75

Sunday August 24th, 2003

"Does Lisa know you're still fucking me?" asks April, as we lay in bed after having done just that.

"Well….I suspect she does," I say. "But it isn't like it's totally serious yet."

"So…what is it then?"

"I don't know. It just is what it is."

"So, she approves of this?"

"No, I wouldn't say that. I think she just doesn't want to scare me off or something. That's not the right way to put it. She just knows how restrictive my marriage was and doesn't want to start off like that."

"Start off? That's makes it sound like you think it will turn into something serious."

"I really don't know," I say. "I just mean the start of whatever it is."

"So, she's gonna let you keep fucking me?"

"Well, we're getting really close to decision time. I'm not going to have the option of fucking the both of you."

"I've told you what I'm willing to do," she says. "It's up to you now."

"I know."

"Do you know what you're gonna do. I can take it. If you choose Statesville and Lisa, then that's fine."

"And you're definitely going to Mexico, if I choose to go?"

"Yes. Haven't I made that clear?"

"I guess you have," I say. "I guess I'm just surprised that you're willing to follow me down there."

"Why? Don't we have a good thing going?"

"Yeah, it is. But it's just that I don't think of you as a girlfriend."

"Well, that may be accurate," she says. "Or maybe you just have a different idea as to the meaning of the term."

"In other words, you're a girl and you're a friend."

"Exactly….I'm a friend you fuck."

"Okay, then maybe you are my girlfriend."

"Why is it so hard for you to just do this?" she asks. "Why do you have to keep looking for excuses to not do it?"

"I really want to."

"Then just fucking do it."

"It sounds like I'm your ticket down there or something."

"So? What's wrong with that?" she asks. "I'll definitely earn my keep. I think you know that."

"Yeah, I'm sure you will. But it's not like that's a one way street or something."

"Listen, I'm not planning on getting down there and running away with the first Mexican guy I meet. And I'm not planning on fucking a whole pile of men. We can have what we have here. I've only fucked a couple of guys since we've been seeing each other. And you're my only regular guy. And down there you will be my only regular guy."

"Really?"

"Yes, really."

"So, we just keep doing what we've been doing and if we happen to run across a hot piece of ass along the way we both have the freedom to indulge?"

"Exactly. And you know that Lisa will not let you have that privilege for long."

"Yeah, most women wouldn't"

"And I'll take it a step further," she says. "We've talked about this before…..but I'd be willing to try the swap thing."

"What? Me fuck some other woman while you fuck the man?"

"Yeah."

"You know how to sweeten the pot."

"I've already got a sweet honey pot, but you know that already."

"Yes, that you do."

"And just think about all the hot latina models you could get down there?"

"That's one thing I haven't mentioned to Lisa yet," I say. "I haven't told her about wanting to do nude photography. I get the feeling that would be hard for her…..me taking pictures of naked women."

"But you have a real eye for the artistic side of it. The stuff you've done of me isn't like what you see in Playboy or Hustler, it's really artistic."

"You make a good model."

"Why do you want to tie yourself down again? You're already keeping shit from her because you're afraid she won't approve. Don't get into another relationship where you can't be all you want to be. You're free now. Keep it that way."

"And I know that you don't care about that shit."

"No, I don't," she says. "You can not only take pictures of as many women as you want, you can fuck them all, too, if you so desire."

"You just feel that way because what we have is so laid back."

"No, I'd feel that way anyway. And why do you think this relationship is anything short of what it should be. You act like this isn't really a relationship."

"It is different though."

"So? Maybe I just define relationships differently than many women."

"I just want to understand what it is."

"Why do you even worry about it? I like what we have. Why do you insist on trying to define it?"

"Habit....I guess."

"Bad habit."

"Perhaps."

"When are you going to let me know something?" she asks.

"Soon."

"Okay.....but that seems kinda open ended."

"I know."

"Don't procrastinate on this like you tend to do when it comes to difficult decisions."

"I can't wait but so long," I say. "Jim has some pull down there, but he won't be able to guarantee a spot forever."

"I know what you're going to do. You're going to just keep going to Statesville. It's the easy route."

"It is the easy route. There's no doubt about that. But don't assume I'll do that."

"Okay, I hope I'm wrong."

"I must say that you and Jim make a very compelling case for Mexico."

Chapter 76

Friday August 29ᵗʰ, 2003

"So this is it, huh?" I ask. "The last day in the plant for most of us."

"Drop by any time you like," says David.

"How long do you think you guys will stay with the plant, Butch?" I ask.

"Well, with these two numbskulls they left me with, it may take a while to get this place secured," responds Butch.

"What the hell does that mean?" asks Jerry. "I'm a hard worker, ask anyone."

"Except for me," I say.

"Well, I'll stand up for you," says Lisa. "You were an excellent choice to stay with the plant..... after it's shut down, that is."

"Such friends I've made here," says Jerry.

"Shit, don't think that we aren't going to be doing anything," says Butch. "There's a lot that has to be done here."

"It's kind of eerie walking through here now with everyone gone," I say. "All the machines quiet. Weird."

"We have a lot of memories in this place," adds Lisa.

"So, they gonna move all of the machinery out of here?" I ask.

"Yeah, they're putting everything in a warehouse in Mayfair," says Butch. "Easier to sell it off with it being in a central location. You got all the spare parts crated up and ready to ship that are going to Statesville?"

"Yeah, we got all that we think they'll need in their short run," I say.

"That they'll need in their short run?" asks David. "Don't you mean what you'll need in your short run?"

"Well, I don't know," I say.

"He's not sure which one he wants yet," says Lisa.

"Statesville or Mexico?" asks David.

"Me or April."

"Oh....shit."

"That isn't the choice at all," I say.

"Isn't it?" she replies.

"Can we talk about this later?"

"Fine."

"A lover's tiff?" asks Jerry, with a big grin painted on his face.

"Jerry, just shut the fuck up," I say.

"How are things going in Statesville," asks David. "I know that things came right down to the wire as far as getting it running to meet the deadline for shutting down completely here."

"Everything's up and running," says Lisa.

"Yeah, I know that there was some hope that Statesville wouldn't get going and that would prolong things here," I say. "But that was never going to happen."

"Yeah, if you two wouldn't have done such a good job, this place could have run a while longer," jokes Jerry.

"I doubt it," I say. "They were intent on it happening when they said it would."

"I wish we could have been here on the last day of production," says Lisa. "Just to say goodbye to everyone, at least the ones who were still here."

"That was weird, leaving on Monday with the plant still running, then show up today and it's totally shutdown," I say.

"Yeah, we've had shutdowns throughout the years, but this is a different sort of silence," says Jerry.

"Well, it was inevitable," says Butch. "We actually hung on longer than many of our competitors."

"You know, you sure have lightened up boss," I say. "I don't remember ever shooting the shit with you like this."

"Why the fuck shouldn't I?" responds Butch. "You might as well say I'm the goddamned plant manager now."

"With only two employees," I say.

"How about I fire your ass," says Butch.

"Actually, you can't," I point out. "Lisa and I work for Gene. Too bad, motherfuckaaaa......"

"Yeah....you goddamn asshole.....get off of my partners fucking back," says Lisa, smiling.

"Bet that feels really good," says Butch, smiling. "But don't you two fuckers get any ideas. Your asses still belong to me."

"Don't worry, boss," says David. "I'll save whatever I have to say for my last day."

"Shit......maybe I won't," says Jerry.

"Try me son.....try me," says Butch.

"I'm gonna be unemployed eventually anyway," says Jerry, smiling.

"Fuck, let's go to the diner and get some lunch," says Butch. "The fucking company's paying, whether they want to or not."

"I just wish more of the guys would have hung on the whole week," I say. "I was hoping to say goodbye."

"I know," says Lisa.

"Let's just go to the diner," says Butch. "I think you'll find what you're looking for."

"Will I?" I ask "Will I find what I'm looking for?"

"I'm just talking about the idiots you worked with," says Butch. "I can't help you with any deep philosophical questions."

"I know, boss," I say. "I'll have to figure that out on my own."

Chapter 77

August 2006

Here Jim and I are in a little cantina somewhere in central Mexico. It's a very similar situation from where we were just three years ago.

"Damn, I cannot fucking believe that they're giving up on this plant this fucking soon," I say.

"Well, we always knew that they were chasing their tail," says Jim.

"Yeah, it's apparent now that the company itself won't exist much longer."

"No, it clearly won't."

"Okay, so, what's next?"

"You aren't going to take off back up to the states?" asks Jim.

"No, we're staying."

"April isn't done with this little adventure?"

"No, she's willing to stick it out."

"I'm still amazed that you chose to come down here with April rather than going to Statesville with Lisa."

"Yeah, I wasn't sure till the end what I was gonna do."

"What was the deciding factor?"

"Freedom."

"Freedom?"

"Yeah, it's as simple as that. This choice offered me the most freedom. I needed that. I needed a drastic change. Lisa would have been too much like what I already had."

"In other words, you wanted the freedom to fuck who you wanted to fuck."

"No, Jim, it's really more than that. Lisa is far from a prude, but she's nowhere as liberated as April. Not just sex. This is about a whole way of looking at things."

"April is most definitely something."

"I know some people back home think I've just gone completely off the fucking rails, but this is just how it had to be."

"And if they knew how much of this local latina pussy you've sampled they would think you were a downright heathen."

"Yeah, I'm sure they would."

"Why did you even bother bringing April down here if you were going to play the field like you have?"

"I don't know, Jim. I guess that was some sort of concession to wanting some sort of security. I guess I just wanted someone to come home to if I choose to come home."

"I can see that. And she definitely isn't the type to get in your way when it comes to other pieces of ass."

"No, most definitely not."

"Have you heard anything from Lisa since they closed the plant in Statesville?" asks Jim.

"Yeah, she got a job at some plant in Oxford that's making solar panels. She's making more money than at Raymond."

"I'm glad she landed on her feet."

"Well, she is a good electrician."

"So, is she over you?" asks Jim.

"Oh…fuck yeah. We had only been seeing each other for a few months when I left."

"But she did take it hard."

"Yeah, I guess she just thought we were meant to be or something. But I think she realizes now that I'm just not the one for her."

"Why is that?"

"I'm just too much at loose ends. I just can't be tied down like that."

"You're not tied down with April? It has been four years."

"No, it's just not the same. We both want the same thing. Or….I should say that we both want to avoid the same thing."

"And what, pray tell, is that?" asks Jim.

"I guess you could say that we want to keep our distance. I never thought I'd actually find a woman who wouldn't want to be but so attached. She just has the same philosophy as I do when it comes to relationships. We don't want to be everything to each other. We aren't soulmates and we have no desire to be."

"And not to mention her being kinda freaky."

"Well, yeah, that helps as well."

"Yeah, I'll bet it does."

"You know…..we've even watched each other fuck other people," I say. "Do you know how hot that is….to watch her fuck some other guy?"

"And she likes to watch too?"

"Until she joins in."

"Damn, you're doing shit that I haven't even done."

"Well, April has set me loose…..I guess."

"Pardon me, but how did you go from being this somewhat ultra-religious person to being basically a swinger?"

"I never really was that ultra-religious person. That's the problem. I was really just pretending to be that. I was pretending to be so many things. For the first time in my life I'm being true to who I really am……or at least much closer than I've ever been before."

"Well, what an evolution. That's all I can say."

"Yeah, I know that it seems dramatic."

"So….are you just a heathen now?" asks Jim, with a laugh.

"Jim…..I've just had it with conventional religion. There's just something that doesn't ring true there. I wasn't the only one pretending."

"Well, I'm glad you see that."

"I say all of that…..but I still believe the bible. Well……I guess I believe in what the bible is trying to point us toward."

"Ok….."

"Yeah…..I'm not quite sure what that means myself."

"I have to admit though, that some of our discussions at the plant were interesting sometimes…..at least entertaining."

"I just had to be free of all that church shit."

"And free of conventional morality….I take it?"

"Well…..I guess. I don't know. I just believe I have to be free if I have any hope of finding meaning to all of this."

"Who the fuck needs meaning?"

"Well, I do, I guess."

"I figure we'll find out when we're supposed to. That is, if we're ever supposed to."

"I do agree with the idea that we don't need to try so hard to figure it out. That's what I'm doing. I'm stepping away from all that shit."

"You don't think you're going to hell for all this fucking you're doing down here?"

"I'm not saying it's right. Actually, I don't really know what's right or wrong anymore. That's the whole point to me."

"No, the whole point should be is why does there have to be a right and wrong?"

"But there are certain things that by any measure are just plain wrong," I say.

"I know. But those are a given. I'm talking about all these moral stances that Christians take all the time, homosexuality, pre-marital sex, fucking a whole lot of people. Those things don't hurt anyone else. Why should they be wrong?"

"I know."

"I just don't get why God would create us like we are then say we can't do all these things that seem so natural to us."

"Well, there is theology to explain that."

"Yeah, I know."

"The bottom line is that you shouldn't have to try so hard to find God. Religion is all about putting all this effort in to make yourself conform to some standard that supposedly makes you acceptable to God. That just doesn't make sense. And as far as Christianity goes, that whole concept is contradicted in its own theology."

"Well…..at any rate, you seem to be in a better place now."

"Absolutely, I'm more liberated than I've ever been."

"Yeah, I thought you were supposed to be so goddamned dysfunctional with women, yet here you are fucking up a storm."

"The only thing I can say is that I feel free to let the real me show now, for the first time in my life. I always said that shyness was about hiding something about the real me. Well, I don't have anything to hide anymore. Plus, I guess it doesn't hurt that these Mexican chicks seem to have a real hard on for us gringos."

"Yeah, it's not all that hard, is it?"

"No, it really isn't," I say. "But back in the day, before April and all that shit, it wouldn't have mattered. I still wouldn't have been able to close the deal, unless of course the girl in question was to just strip down and bend over in front of me."

"Yeah, well, some of them almost do that, don't they?"

"Yeah, true."

"They think we're going to take them away from all this or something."

"I know, I feel bad about taking advantage of that…..sometimes."

"Yeah, I know, but not often."

"Well, Jim, I guess we'll find out how the women are as we work our way through Central America now."

"Yeah, I've got a lead on what could be our first stop. American Textiles is opening a plant in Belize, I believe. They of course want some technical support to get the place up and running and to get the natives trained."

"Ok, I'm in."

"Yeah, you'll be in alright, all up in that Belizian pussy."

"Damn, you're making me feel like a goddamn heathen now."

"No, like you said, we have to be free."

"And I never thought I would, never would have thought it in a million years."

"Never would have thought what, lover?" asks April, as she joins us.

"I was just saying I never would have thought I would ever be this free," I say.

"That you are," she says. "It is amazing how shy little Don is big swinging dick Donnie now."

"You gotta love her," I say.

"I was just telling Don that Belize may be the next stop," says Jim.

"Cool, sounds good."

"I've gotta go now, Marisol is waiting back at my place," says Jim.

"Alright, man, talk to you later," I say.

"Belize, huh?"

"Have you ever wanted to fuck Jim?" I ask.

"Where the hell is this coming from?"

"Well, I know what the women always said, that he looks like some soap opera star or something. I just figured you'd want a piece of that too."

"Well, sure, I'd fuck him. But I'm not going to because he's your friend."

"But you think he's hot."

"Sure, but don't you think Marisol's hot?"

"Well, yeah."

"But you wouldn't fuck her because of Jim."

"Okay, I get your point."

"Do you?" she asks. "You still have some adjusting you need to do when it comes to our relationship. You still don't quite trust what we have going on here."

"I know."

"Have you written Karen yet?"

"No, I guess I need to."

"Yes, you most definitely owe her that."

"You are one hell of a woman, you know that?"

"Yeah, actually, I do."

"And you're so modest too."

"Fuck modesty."

"Fuck everything," I say. "Fuck it all."

"What's that mean?"

"No, it's just my new philosophy. Fuck it. Stop trying to hard to make things fit. Stop trying to make sense out of everything. Stop trying so hard to conform to some fucking standard."

"Ok."

"Fuck it....and let it just come to you when the time is right."

"Well, I'd like to believe I already live that way."

"That you do. That you do. And thank God for taking me along for the ride."

"My pleasure."

"For the first time in my life I feel like I'm actually gaining the upper hand on the shyness. I guess that's what's behind what I've been doing down here."

"You mean all the girls?"

"Yeah, it just feels so fucking good."

"Yeah, I'll bet it does."

"You know what I mean."

"Yeah, I do Don."

"I just look back now and am amazed how one stupid fucking thing could so thoroughly fuck my life up."

"But it isn't fucked up now."

"No, it most definitely is not," I say. "It's not fucked up at all."

Dear Karen,

I'm sorry for the almost total lack of communication for the three years since I left. I just didn't know what to say. I know that you're getting the money I send every month. I trust everything is well with you.

I'm writing because I know that I owe you some sort of explanation. I did things that hurt you and I'm truly sorry. But I need you to know why these things happened.

The simple truth is that our marriage was cursed from day one. This is because I was pretending to be someone I wasn't. This wasn't intentional. And this didn't just have to do with you. This all relates back to the shyness. I was living in a shell when I met you. The real and true Don just wasn't there. You basically married a shell of a man. I wasn't whole. I thought, at the time, that perhaps you could make me whole. But that just isn't how it works.

My biggest regret is that I went through with the wedding at all. I knew it wasn't right from the beginning. But I was so convinced that it was ordained by God or something that I tried to make it fit. I tried to make it all make sense. I was so screwed up and desperate for a woman in my life that I didn't want to let go of you. I thought you were my only chance. This was at least true up to a point.

This brings me to Gina. I know you knew about her from the beginning. I just couldn't bear to admit it until everything else fell apart. I just didn't want to spoil the whole thing of my being a virgin sent to you by God. I just thought that you wouldn't look at me the same if you knew I had a drunken one night stand with some stranger. So, I went through the charade of pretending it didn't happen for all those many years.

Then, of course, there's April. I know that you are bound to know that she's down here with me. I know that her sister has probably told you. And I also know that you most likely think that I've just totally turned my back on God by coming down here with her. But that isn't true.

I do still seek God. I do still seek to know the truth. I just have a different way of going about it now. I needed to be free. I needed to come out of my shell. I needed to find the true me. And I am well on my way to accomplishing all of that. I guess the best way to describe what I have now is an imperfect faith. I'm not worried about making myself conform to any standard. I'm not perfect and that's just fine.

The point I always tried to make is that God wants honesty above all else. In many, many, ways I was far from honest with you, others, and most of all with myself. I was never true to what was inside of me. Religion, to me, is about covering over the true you. That just doesn't make sense to me. And it just isn't healthy. If who I really am isn't good enough for God, then I'll just have to trust that he'll give me the power and wisdom to change what needs to be changed. But I refuse to make myself change based on the pressure and guilt that religion imposes on us. It just isn't the right way.

I sincerely wish the best for you. You deserve a good godly man who believes what you believe. I will always love you. I care for you as a person. But I wasn't ever in love with you. I don't think I'm capable of that actually. And I really don't want to be.

Anyway, before I ramble on too much, I'll just end it here. There is more I could say, but what's the real point. The bottom line is that one word defined me for so long. That word is shy. I made so many mistakes because of that one little condition. I missed so many opportunities. My life is so profoundly different than what I would have liked it to have been, all because of being shy. It seems like such a small thing. But it caused so much damage, so much hurt. I'm truly sorry that you got caught up in the middle of it. I really never meant to hurt you.

God Bless you Karen, and I hope you have a wonderful life.

Love,

Don

www.ingramcontent.com/pod-product-compliance
Lightning Source LLC
Chambersburg PA
CBHW071337020726
47502CB00001B/131